WINTERBER(

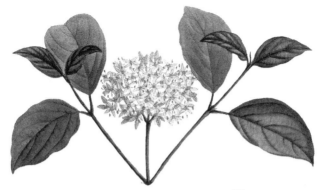

JAROSLAV RUDIŠ

WINTERBERG'S LAST JOURNEY

Translated from the German by **Kris Best**

JANTAR PUBLISHING
London 2024
www.JantarPublishing.com

JANTAR PUBLISHING 2024
First published in London, Great Britain by
Jantar Publishing Ltd
www.jantarpublishing.com

WINTERBERG'S LAST JOURNEY
JAROSLAV RUDIŠ

Original title:
WINTERBERGS LETZTE REISE, by Jaroslav Rudiš
© 2019 by Luchterhand Literturverlag
a division of Penguin Random House Verlagsgruppe GmbH, München, Germany.

Translation & Introduction copyright © Kris Best 2024
Cover and book design by Davor Pukljak, Frontispis.hr
based on a photograph by © Mary Crnković Pilaš

A CIP record of this book is available from the British Library

ISBN
978-1-914990-24-3 (paperback)
978-1-914990-25-0 (hardback)

Printed and bound on paper sourced from sustainable forests by
Imprint Digital, Exeter, England

This translation was made possible by a grant from the German Translators' Fund
as part of the 'NEUSTART KULTUR' programme with financing from
the German Federal Commissioner for Culture and Media.

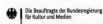

CONTENTS

Introduction by Kris Best   7

WINTERBERG'S LAST JOURNEY

- From Königgrätz to Sadowa   13
- The Crossing   41
- From Berlin to Reichenberg   69
- The Feuerhalle   103
- From Reichenberg to Königgrätz   125
- The Englishman   139
- From Königgrätz to Jitschin   157
- From Jitschin to Budweis   167
- From Budweis to Winterberg   179
- From Winterberg to Pilsen   187
- From Pilsen to Linz   191
- From Linz to Vienna   199
- The Imperial Crypt   205
- Love   213
- The Arsenal   223
- The Daughter   243
- The Noose   263
- The Central Cemetery   277
- From Vienna to Brünn   305
- St. Anne's   311
- From Brünn to Budapest   339
- From Budapest to Zagreb   375
- From Zagreb to Sarajevo   381

- The Shark   393
- From Zagreb to Berlin   407
- From Berlin to Peenemünde   419
- The Storm   427
- Berlin   433

Index of Place Names   437

INTRODUCTION

Jaroslav Rudiš and I first met in the train. We'd originally planned to meet in Berlin, the city both of us call home, but the man is so often on the road – or more accurately: on the rails – that the train became the most convenient place for us to speak. It turned out to be a serendipitous choice. Like the titular Winterberg, Rudiš is most at home on the railway. Along with Central Europe and the tangled, often tragic history of the European continent, it comprises one of the most consistent themes in his writing from his earliest works to the present day. Unlike Winterberg, however, Rudiš prefers to let others do the rambling – and he listens.

Many of the digressions and anecdotes that add to the extraordinary depth (and humour) of the world in *Winterberg's Last Journey* began as conversations on the train. From that first train journey together, it became clear to me that Rudiš simply attracts stories in the same way that others might attract fame or misfortune. Complete strangers of all backgrounds feel almost unnaturally compelled to open up in his presence – as if they can sense, correctly, that this man will value their stories, file them away and one day weave them into a larger work of art. I'm not immune to this aura myself; it almost feels harder *not* to tell your stories to Jaroslav Rudiš. He absorbs it all in earnest, like a priest taking confession.

Despite being so often on the rails, Rudiš' writing is deeply rooted in a sense of 'homeland', which for him comprises the entirety of Central Europe. Born in 1972, he grew up in communist Czechoslovakia, coming of age just as the Iron Curtain fell. His hometown of Lomnice nad Popelkou in northern Bohemia was part of the infamous Sudetenland, a region with a mixed German/Czech population before World War II which belonged to Austria-Hungary before World War I. Much of his literary work can be understood to exist at these cultural crossroads, focusing on elements that bind Central Europe beyond its linguistic differences: the railway above all; the beer, the pubs, the food; the complex interactions of history, borders and identity. Like Jaroslav Rudiš himself, his works are Central European at their core.

The interaction of German and Czech culture that defines the history of his home region has been a prominent theme in Rudiš' writing since the publication of his first Czech-language novel, *The Sky Under Berlin*, in 2002. The following years saw the development of one of his best-known works in partnership with illustrator Jaromír 99: the graphic novel series *Alois Nebel*, later adapted into an award-winning animated film. Out of his six Czech-language novels, two more (*Grand Hotel* and *National Street*) would also receive film adaptations in his home country. Rudiš has also written numerous original stage and radio plays as well as three bilingual rock albums with his *Kafka Band*, further solidifying his reputation as one of the most prominent and versatile figures in the Czech cultural scene over the last twenty years.

Winterberg's Last Journey, published in 2019, is Rudiš' first novel to be originally written in the German language, representing both a break in and continuity with his previous body of work. Linguistically, it marks a clear turn in his oeuvre, as Rudiš would go on to write four more books and a graphic novel in his adopted language. Thematically, however, it continues where his Czech-language books left off, featuring many of the same elements that characterise his earlier work: the railway, the intersection of cultures, the blend of tragedy and comedy. But it probes even deeper into the darker themes that have always been present in his work as well, like the interaction of history with the present and the legacy of war, expulsion and dictatorship. This is not a coincidence; in discussing his work, Rudiš states that writing in German gives him distance and perspective to engage with subject matter that feels too raw in his native language. *Winterberg*, he claims, is a book that he could have *only* written in German – that if he had tried to write it in Czech, it would have turned into a different book entirely.

In portraying the character of Winterberg, a 99-year-old Sudetenland German with a brain addled by age and history, Rudiš relies heavily on rambling and repetition that often takes on a near-melodic quality. A number of themes and phrases appear over and over again: laying railway tracks across the Alps; the various sorts of corpses burned in his father's Feuerhalle; *'the beautiful landscape of battlefields, cemeteries and ruins'*; the Battle of Königgrätz. There are moments when Winterberg's rambling pushes our patience. The reader is subjected to this onslaught of history in the same way that Kraus is subjected to this onslaught of history. We feel what Kraus feels: Winterberg's stories are intriguing, but exhausting. Sometimes, they're too much; sometimes, we tune them out. Yet his words creep into our thoughts and take hold there, forcing us to admit, like Kraus, that the elderly Winterberg often has a point.

The use of place names will stand out to readers as a unique feature of the text and reflects the story's setting among the shifting borders and overlapping cultures of Central European history. Winterberg, a German Bohemian born at the fall of the Austro-Hungarian Empire, refers to cities and landmarks around Central Europe by their historical German names, which are often so old or so obscure that even modern German readers will not recognise them. Kraus, a Czech Bohemian born in postwar Czechoslovakia, usually refers to these locations by their modern names. The use of historical vs. modern names follows the original German text. Sometimes the connection is easy to identify (Brünn/Brno), other times less so (Reichenberg/Liberec); an index has been included at the back of this book for readers to look up the modern equivalents.

Winterberg's Last Journey was clearly a labour of love for Rudiš, with an astonishing level of attention to historical and locational detail for those who delve deeper into its world. The 1913 Baedeker is real, as are all the passages quoted by Winterberg; there really is a Feuerhalle on the Monstranzberg in Liberec/Reichenberg, it really was the first crematorium in Austria-Hungary and Wagner's *Parsifal* really was played at its opening ceremony; the streets and hotels and restaurants and the landmarks that Winterberg remembers from his youth all actually existed in the 1920s and '30s, and many still exist today. *Winterberg* is accurate enough to be a guidebook itself, as I learned while personally following the journey of Winterberg and Kraus across Central Europe during the long process of its translation. Like Rudiš, I was keen to portray the world of *Winterberg* with all the care and precision it deserved. For me, too, it was a labour of love.

Kris Best
Berlin, January 2024

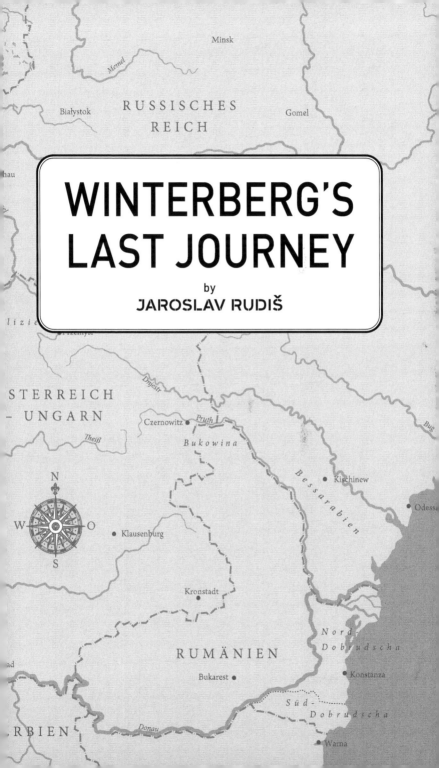

WINTERBERG'S LAST JOURNEY

by

JAROSLAV RUDIŠ

FROM KÖNIGGRÄTZ TO SADOWA

'The Battle of Königgrätz runs through my heart,' said Winterberg, looking out the foggy window of the train. He squeezed his breast so tightly, it seemed that he wanted to crush not only the thick wool of his old, grey coat, but his ninety-nine-year-old heart as well.

'The Battle of Königgrätz is the beginning of my end,' he continued, staring out of his horn-rimmed glasses at the snowy Bohemian landscape as it passed us by.

The small train moved slowly, swaying like a lonely ship without a captain on the high seas. The young conductor gazed at her phone and swayed along with it. As did we.

'The Battle of Königgrätz is the beginning of all my calamities, the beginning of all our calamities, if you were born under the sign of the Battle of Königgrätz, you were lost forever. That's why I'm lost, that's why this country is lost, and that's why you, dear Herr Kraus, are lost, whether you like it or not, yes, yes, there's no escape, it's not as easy as laying railway tracks across the Alps. The Battle of Königgrätz is like a trap, one that we set ourselves, which we lured ourselves into and into which we willingly fall, the Battle of Königgrätz is an abyss into which we all plummet, the Battle of Königgrätz grasps at our necks, it's closing around my throat, it's like a cord, like a noose, always getting tighter, yes, yes, like the rope with which we all hang ourselves in the end, whether we like it or not, yes, yes, and noose corpses aren't a pretty sight, as my father always said,' rambled Winterberg, still looking out of the window.

'Look at that, Herr Kraus, the wild boar on the edge of the forest, aren't they beautiful? I'd just love to paint them. I used to love to paint, especially peaceful winter landscapes like this, but even the boar are lost, yes, yes, the Battle of Königgrätz is an ever-sprawling *Cornus sanguinea.*'

Winterberg rambled on while I looked out at the animals on the edge of the forest.

'Half a million soldiers back then, today half a million ghosts, you have to be able to imagine it, I imagine it, yes, yes, I see through history, yes, yes, I'm not historically blind, I don't care what you think, dear Herr Kraus, whether you can or even want to imagine it. The battle is here, and so are we.'

'Those were deer.'

'What?'

'Over there by the woods. Those weren't wild boar.'

'Exactly, wild boar, that's what I said.'

'But they were deer.'

'Yes, yes, deer and boar and stags and foxes and people and houses and fields and forests and winter landscapes and picture-perfect panoramas, everything is lost, tragic, tragic. My grandfather was a hunter, and he said that killing animals was nothing good, but if you must kill an animal, then do it quickly, the Battle of Königgrätz knows no mercy, the Battle of Königgrätz is our deepest abyss, the Battle of Königgrätz is our downfall, and it has been for the last hundred and sixty years. Why can't you see through history, Herr Kraus? You should really read something about history, then you would understand, then you would understand me, like the Englishman and my Lenka understood me, then you would know and understand what I mean by *Cornus sanguinea*. You wouldn't just stare at me like a fool…'

'Those were deer.'

Winterberg coughed lightly.

'Deer?'

'Yes, deer. The animals from before. A whole herd of deer.'

He continued to cough. I handed him a bottle of water. He didn't want to drink.

'What kind of deer?'

'Doesn't matter.'

He fixed me with a serious look. Then he glanced over at the conductor. Then he looked back out of the window at the snowy fields. And then continued to ramble on.

'The Battle of Königgrätz doesn't just run through my heart, it also runs through my head, and through my brain, and through my lungs and liver and stomach, it's part of my body and my soul. Two of my ancestors lost their lives, dear Herr Kraus, one on the side of the Prussians, and the other on the side of the Austrians, Julius Ewald and Karl Strohbach, yes, yes, I can seek out either side, but in the end I'm laying with both of them in the grave, I don't know if you can imagine that, I want to understand it, I want to finally understand everything in my life, you understand, dear Herr Kraus, that's why we're here now, in order to understand it, you understand, dear Herr Kraus, here at Königgrätz was where the entire tragedy began,' rambled Winterberg, still looking out of the window. 'Shouldn't we be in Sadowa? This must be Sadowa. We've got to get off this damned cold train.'

'No, that's not Sadová. That's… agh, it doesn't matter.'

Winterberg wasn't listening to me.

Winterberg never listens to me.

'The Battle of Königgrätz tears me in two,' he rambled on, while the conductor sat down on the bench across from us and briefly closed her eyes. 'The Battle of Königgrätz robs me of sleep. It was because of the Battle of Königgrätz that I lost my first wife, and because of the Battle of Königgrätz that my second wife went mad, yes, yes, she grew up in Berlin in the Stresemannstraße, which used to be called the Königgrätzer Straße, that can't just be a coincidence, dear Herr Kraus. We met in a dance hall in the Skalitzer Straße, yes, yes, that's right, you're correct, dear Herr Kraus, the whole affair isn't a happy coincidence of history, it's a tragic accident of history, a misunderstanding that one can never make right, yes, yes, it's all because of the Battle of Königgrätz that I suffer from history and from historical fits, yes, yes, dear Herr Kraus, I know what you're going to say, the Battle of Königgrätz isn't as easily overcome as the Alps by the railway, there are too many fault zones, if you know what I mean by that, dear Herr Kraus.'

I wanted to say that I had no idea what he meant by 'fault zones', but I knew that there was no point. His head is one big fault zone. I nodded as I always nodded when I listened to him and thought what I always thought when I listened to him. Winterberg coughed again and I handed him the water bottle. He didn't want to drink.

'There was also some quite heroic combat near Skalitz in 1866, we have to go there, too, it's all in my Baedeker. And also to Trautenau and to Jitschin, the city of Wallenstein, which he chose to be the capital of his empire, yes, yes, we have to go there, there was also fighting around Jitschin, many Saxons and Austrians drowned in the pond there, and many Prussians later in the beer, when they stormed the Jitschin brewery.'

I wanted to say that I was once in Jičín back in my childhood, with my parents, but it was impossible; Winterberg could not be stopped.

'A good friend of mine in Berlin lived in the Gitschiner Straße, my best friend in Berlin, he was also a tram driver, before the war he played football in Oberschöneweide. Of course you don't know, because you don't see through history, but for a long time the stadium was called Sadowa, yes, yes, after Sadowa here in Bohemia, where we're getting off the train, yes, yes, precisely, named after the glorious Prussian victory and the glorious Austrian defeat. But the victory became a rather notorious defeat for the Prussians later on, like all victories throughout history, yes, yes; how often I allowed myself to be tortured by an unrelenting football game there, football had really never interested me, yes, yes, it was only because of Sadowa, only because of Königgrätz, that I went. No one else cares, but I know it, everything is connected to Königgrätz, yes, yes, our entire calamity began with Königgrätz, and I know what you're going to say, dear Herr Kraus, mad, it's all mad. You're right, it is mad,' Winterberg continued, without looking at me once the entire time.

He looked out of the window at a sleepy field.

At country houses.

At an old church.

At two children with a dog on a country road.

'It's beautiful here, so beautiful, truly *"the beautiful landscape of battle-fields, cemeteries and ruins"*, as the Englishman always said.'

'Him again.'

'Yes, yes.'

'But who was he?'

'The Englishman could see through history, unlike you. Why don't you read any history books, dear Herr Kraus? You could have long known all of this, with *Cornus sanguinea* and Königgrätz and Sarajevo and the railway. It's all because of the Battle of Königgrätz that my third wife was deathly ill. It's all because of the Battle of Königgrätz that I had to care for her for thirty years. It's all because of the Battle of Königgrätz that you had to care for me. Why can't you see through history? That factory there, isn't that the Sadowa sugar factory, dear Herr Kraus, where the Austrian infantry so bravely made their stand? yes, yes, the famous Bohemian-Moravian-Austrian sugar industry, I didn't know for a long time that sugar cubes come from Datschitz in Moravia, did you know that, dear Herr Kraus? now where was I, yes, yes, the Austrians wouldn't melt like sugar, they turned the sugar factory into an Austrian fortress, and on the wall they wrote in tall words: "Behind us is Vienna", I read about it all. But it was in vain. Within three hours they were all dead.'

'No, we're not in Sadová yet, and that isn't a sugar factory, it's an electrical substation,' I said, but Winterberg wasn't listening, and he was trembling as he often did during his historical fits.

'That must be the Bistritz river, which was fiercely contested. And that over there, that must be the famous Svíb Forest! A paradise of *Cornus sanguinea*, yes, yes, we must go there, to the Road of the Dead that winds through the forest, we've got to go there. We may even find the two graves right there, the graves of my Prussian great-grandfather from Tangermünde and my Austrian great-grandfather from Ottensheim near Linz, one grew up on the Elbe, the other on the Danube, both killed on the same day, here, at Sadowa, at Königgrätz, on the third of July, 1866, the German war in the Bohemian Paradise, madness, madness, I know, you're right, dear Herr Kraus, it makes no sense at all, and yet it does make a sort of sense, *Cornus sanguinea*, the Road of the Dead. We've got to go there.'

I nodded as I always nodded and thought what I always thought. I couldn't stand Winterberg for much longer.

'I know, I know; quiet down now, everything's all right, yeah? We're not at war.'

I cracked open a beer. The foam dripped to the floor.

'You shouldn't drink so much, or else you'll get foggy again, just like yesterday and the day before, beer corpses aren't a pretty sight, as my father always said, and he had to know, he saw many beer corpses and drank beer himself, tragic, tragic, it isn't good that you drink so much, it's not healthy, it's not proper, you won't get to be ninety-nine like that, you won't get to be as old as the Republic of Czechoslovakia, as old as the *Feuerhalle*, yes, yes, you won't get to be as old as me like that.'

'I don't care, I don't want to be that old. I don't want to live in pain.'

'I'm not in pain. I still feel young, I'm not transparent.'

'Transparent?'

'Transparent. To the women, I mean.'

'I don't understand.'

'It doesn't matter. You should drink less.'

'But I want to drink. I like beer. And you should drink more, too. You haven't had anything to drink yet today.'

'I did have something to drink.'

'You didn't.'

'You have no place telling me whether I drank or didn't drink, yes, yes, I know when I drink and when I don't drink, yes, yes, perhaps I drink too little, but you, dear Herr Kraus, drink too much.'

'Someone has to do it. That's how we achieve balance, as my father used to say. Some drink and others don't.'

The train drove on, and I thought about how I hadn't really wanted to start drinking again so soon. During a 'crossing', I never drink. Only after it's over.

I drink to forget.

To free myself.

To be able to start anew with the next crossing.

But this time it was different. It was the first crossing that had been interrupted. And so, I had to drink.

Otherwise, I would be long gone, and Winterberg, too. Without the beer, I would have done away with him already, and then myself soon after, because who would be able to stand this ridiculous journey without beer? No one. Just me.

The train ran along a small river, and perhaps it really was the Bystřička, because at that moment the conductor suddenly announced: 'Sadová.'

Winterberg sprang to his feet.

Two abandoned and slightly crooked railway tracks. An abandoned station building. And an abandoned dog pissing into the wind.

Otherwise: nothing.

We were the only ones who exited the train. I helped Winterberg out of the carriage, which he did not appreciate. The train drove off, and I lit up a cigarette.

'You shouldn't smoke so much, dear Herr Kraus,' said Winterberg, and coughed again.

He took in a deep breath of the cold winter air.

'Beautiful, it's so beautiful here. Something very beautiful is hanging in the air, yes, yes, we had excellent luck with the weather, dear Herr Kraus. The battle may have taken place at the height of summer, hopefully you know that, but the weather back then was just like it is now in November, after a couple of hot days came a day like an early winter, yes, yes, a day like today. A shift in the weather, as they say, with much mist and rain, yes, yes, and the fog of war on top of that, yes, yes, that's how it has to be with a shift in the weather, wonderful, wonderful, we have excellent luck with this bad November weather, dear Herr Kraus. I love bad weather, because you can usually be alone wherever you want to be. I don't need any tourists around, no, no, certainly not, tourists are historically blind, like you, it's difficult to discuss history with you, too.'

'Don't we want to get going?'

'What?'

'Or do you have something more to say?'

Winterberg was silent for a moment and glanced at the abandoned station building. The empty, broken windows. The bricked-up door. The damp grey walls. I lit my next cigarette, took a few steps, and looked over at a couple of teenage boys sitting in a car parked on the main road. They were watching us, smoking, and snickering.

'Beautiful, it's beautiful here by Königgrätz, much more beautiful than I imagined it. Look, it's starting to snow. My last wife didn't like bad weather, she always wanted to spend holidays at the beach, tragic, tragic, a misunderstanding right from the beginning, you can't even imagine, dear Herr Kraus, what luck we've had with the bad weather. My Lenka loved bad weather and solitude, yes, yes, if you were born in Reichenberg, you had to love bad weather and solitude, always nothing but rain and mist and snow, often from October to April just snow and wind and solitude, it's because of the mountains, they surround the city like a great wall, yes, yes, and that's how it is in the whole country, if you were born in Bohemia, you have to love the bad weather and the solitude, bad weather makes many people melancholy, the bad Bohemian weather drove many of our fellow countrymen to madness, it didn't matter whether they spoke German or Czech, yes, yes, but Lenka loved the bad weather, she loved when it was snowing, like it is right now, yes, yes, my Lenka, the first woman in the moon.'

Winterberg calmed down and looked up at the sky. It was true, the first delicate snowflakes were already drifting down towards us. I was cold. I thought, tomorrow we'll both be lying in the hospital with hypothermia. I would finally have my peace over a tea with rum, Winterberg would be transported by helicopter back to Berlin, and there he could ramble on about whatever he liked. And I would finally drown myself in beer and schnapps like I do after all my crossings, and forget everything.

I thought, maybe I'll stay here.

In the country that I left.

That I had to leave.

That left me.

'We were lucky with the bad weather, wonderful, wonderful, of course the train station wasn't here back then, they didn't lay tracks in this part of Bohemia until later, but let's not allow ourselves to be disturbed or distracted by it. Over there, look, on the main street, that must be the inn! A simple inn near the battlefield, as it says in my Baedeker, yes, yes, it's all just as it was back then, just as it was in 1913, when my book was written, just as it was in 1866. We'll go there first, every soldier needs a bit of reinforcement before the battle, even a soldier from the Army of Last Hope, yes, yes, a soldier like you, dear Herr Kraus, since a bit of hope is all a geriatric nurse like you can offer, you're completely right. Change the diapers of the dying, that's all you can do. Nothing more.'

For once, Winterberg was right.

. . .

And so, it wasn't long before we were standing in front of the inn on a busy thoroughfare.

Winterberg was looking at the first set of graves from the Battle of Königgrätz. He read the names of the dead, the names of the ghosts, as he called them. The names of the July corpses, as he called them. He read them loudly and at the same time solemnly and slowly, as if he wanted to wake the ghosts and then soothe them and send them back to sleep. He read them out loud while it snowed, as little clouds of mist formed around his mouth.

A name.

A little cloud of mist.

He read the German and Czech and Croatian and Polish and Hungarian names out loud; don't know him, don't know him, he always added, as if he would know the others, as if the other fallen soldiers were friends of his, as if they'd just had a beer together.

As he then finally turned around and moved to cross the street towards the inn, he was nearly run over by a Polish lorry.

I pulled him to the side.

The inn *U Kanonýra Jabůrka*, the 'Cannoneer Jabůrek', wasn't full. We ordered goulash soup and two beers, one normal and one non-alcoholic.

Winterberg opened up his small red book.

His history book.

His Bible.

His travel guide from 1913.

The Baedeker for Austria-Hungary.

The Baedeker for his life.

His book, as deep a red as the blood spilt by the Prussians and Saxons and Austrians at Königgrätz, as he said. *Cornus sanguinea*. His book, which was supposed to accompany the two of us to the end of the world. To the end of our trip, in which I was an involuntary participant. To Sarajevo.

Winterberg took out his magnifying glass and flipped through his book until he found the correct spot, and read it out loud and fast, as if he were being carried off by a storm that was pulling him in the direction of the past, of history.

As always.

'In the hilly areas northwest of Königgrätz between the Bistritz and the Elbe…'

But suddenly he stopped and looked up and started to think out loud.

As always.

'When we talk about the Monarchy, we often refer to it as the "Danube Monarchy", but in doing so, we forget about the Elbe, dear Herr Kraus, which is simply unacceptable, I don't like such simplification, yes, yes, history is never easy, history is complicated, and for the Bohemians, the Elbe was always more important than the Danube. Yes, yes, in fact, instead of calling it the Danube Monarchy, we should call it the Danube-Elbe Monarchy. We also can't forget the Moldau, a fateful river, as my father always said, so perhaps it would be better to call it the Elbe-Moldau-Danube Monarchy, but then the Croats and the Slovenes will pipe up and ask where their Sava is, yes, yes, also a fateful river, then perhaps the Elbe-Moldau-Danube-Sava Monarchy, yes, yes, that would be proper, but then the Bosnians would certainly also come and say, where is our Bosna?, yes, yes, also a fateful river, so then I suppose the Elbe-Moldau-Danube-Sava-Bosna Monarchy? No, no, I fear no one could keep track of that, it's too complicated, why is it always so complicated, then perhaps we should stick with the Danube Monarchy after all, even if it's a brazen simplification. Where was I again? You keep interrupting me, Herr Kraus.'

'Me?'

'Yes, who else? I can't concentrate like this, I'm constantly being interrupted by you, by others, by thoughts, by history, now where was I, here, here… northwest of Königgrätz… on the third of July, 1866, the Battle of Königgrätz was fought, the Austrian Army, with a total strength of 178,000 Austrians and 20,800 Saxons, yes, yes, the poor Saxons, why are the Saxons always forgotten by history, 770 artillery units under quartermaster Benedek, tragic, tragic, he should have stayed in Italy. So… the army… had taken up a very strong defensive position stretching along the shallow valley of the Bistritz, down in a crescent formation from Račice, Hořiněves and Benátek in the north southwards through Sadowa towards Probluz and Přím, yes, yes, the Saxon brigade, of course, of course, the Saxons are so often forgotten by history, tragic, tragic… now where was I again… yes, yes… the formation.'

His rough voice began to blend with the country music playing from the radio. But it didn't bother him.

'The right flank of the Prussians, the Elbe army under Herwarth von Bittenfeld, stood by Smidar; the First Army, under Prince Friedrich

Karl, by Hořitz; the Second Army, under the Crown Prince, by König-inhof; we came through there on the train, yes, yes, the stretch between Reichenberg and Königgrätz, why it was so damn cold in the express train, I don't understand, but where was I… yes, yes, and Gradlitz, twenty-two kilometres away, the Prussians with 220,984 men strong, yes, yes, and at eight in the morning the battle began, yes, yes, that's right, a battle must begin at the latest by eight, like instruction in schools, the Prussians pressed towards Sadowa and Benátek, held their ground under heavy casualties, but weren't in a position to push forward under the enemy's artillery, so the battle came to a standstill by midday. At about two o'clock the Second Army intervened… the objective of their advance: the two widely visible linden trees on the Tummelplatz near Hořiněves, yes, yes, did we see the linden trees? We did travel right by Hořiněves, I mean, we saw the linden trees, we're not blind after all, and Chlum, the key Austrian position, was stormed by the First Guards Division around three in the afternoon, and with that the battle was settled, did we see the lindens, dear Herr Kraus, or did we miss them?'

'I don't know.'

'It makes me a bit melancholy that we don't know, then maybe on the return trip, but it'll already be dark, or tomorrow, we must see the lindens after all, yes, yes, the losses of the Austrians, including pris-oners of war, totalled 1,313 officers and 41,499 men, and of the Saxons, 55 officers and 1,446 men, the poor Saxons, people always forget the Saxons when they talk about the Battle of Königgrätz, when they talk about history, they always forget the Saxons, both the living Saxons and the dead, why are the Saxons so often forgotten, dear Herr Kraus? My book hasn't forgotten the Saxons and I haven't either, yes, yes, the Prussians lost 360 officers and 8,812 men, many monuments remind us of these fallen soldiers, yes, yes, *"the beautiful landscape of battlefields, cemeteries and ruins"*, as the Englishman always said.'

His voice blended in with the next country song on the radio, which had something to do with Christmas, a train ride, and an abandoned church. The song didn't bother Winterberg. He continued to read and talk to himself.

'Visiting the battlefield requires ten or eleven hours via carriage, yes, yes, with a lunch break in Sadowa, yes, yes, the visit is of particular interest for military personnel, precisely, precisely, that's all correct, provisions are recommended, do we have provisions, Herr Kraus?'

He looked briefly up at me.

I told him that I only had two beers and a pack of cigarettes, otherwise nothing, but it's not as if we would die, we could certainly still pick something up from the store, and in any case, every village had an inn; after all, we weren't in Saxony or Brandenburg, we were in Bohemia.

'Precisely, precisely, please see to that. And please ask, dear Herr Kraus, whether they have a coachman.'

'A coachman?'

'Yes, a coachman, don't give me that ignorant look, it says so in my book. Ask for a coachman or similar, that's what it says.'

. . .

The innkeeper didn't know of any coachmen, nor any taxi drivers. She only knew Josefa.

'She comes to the inn around twelve for lunch.'

She said, perhaps she can drive us to the battlefield; she lives out there.

As I returned to our table, Winterberg was lying asleep with his head on top of the open book, as he so often did after a historical fit.

'Is he dead?' asked the innkeeper.

'He's just fallen asleep. He's always like that. Cork pulled. Air out. Eyes closed. Good night.'

'Is that what he says?'

'No, that's what I say.'

She laughed.

'He's very old, your father.'

'He's not my father.'

'I thought he was your father.'

'He's not.'

'But you resemble each other.'

'What? No, we don't.'

'Yes, you do.'

'Absolutely not. You think we resemble each other?'

'Yes. The way he acts. The way he sits there.'

'It can't be true, we're not similar at all.'

'You just seem very alike.'

I looked over at Winterberg. Finally, some peace. I ordered another beer and a tea with rum. I ate my soup. I ate his soup. And I ordered another beer. And Winterberg continued to sleep on top of his book, on the pages detailing the Battle of Königgrätz.

. . .

One hour later, we were sitting in Josefa's carriage, which was really neither a carriage nor a car, but rather an old tractor of the Zetor brand from Brno. Josefa was about forty and worked on a farm. A hundred pigs, fifty cows, two horses and a dog. Josefa spoke a bit of German, since she had worked at a large farm near Krems in Lower Austria after finishing school, but she hadn't liked it there, since the owner wanted to sleep with her.

Winterberg yawned. He was awake again. He looked out at the hilly landscape.

'Look at that, dear Herr Kraus, it was right here that the imperial army assembled and set its sights on the Prussians, yes, yes, this is where the battle began, in fact it was just after seven in the morning, in the mist and the rain, not at eight, as it says in my Baedeker, that's not what any historian had written.'

He yawned again.

'It's already the afternoon, but we shouldn't let ourselves be bothered by that. I can already hear them, the initial volleys, the first screams, I can already see the offensive of the First Prussian Army. Do you hear it too?'

I didn't hear anything, but I nodded as I always nodded, and thought what I always thought.

'Wonderful, wonderful, that you hear it too.'

The tractor drove along the edge of the narrow street, and Josefa told us about how her husband had left her years before.

'But it's all fine.'

Then she turned the tractor and slowly drove up the mountain. The tractor groaned and shuddered, and Josefa told us about how her mother had died the year before.

'But it's all fine.'

It was snowing, and Josefa told us about how her son had fallen in with the wrong crowd and was now using drugs.

'But it's all fine.'

'But you must still be a happy woman, though,' Winterberg said to Josefa. 'Because you live in Chlum, in the epicentre, yes, yes, in the eye of the hurricane of the Battle of Königgrätz. I know people who dream of living in Chlum.'

'Really?'

'Yes, yes, many people dream of it…'

'Are you serious?'

'Yes, yes, people like me, who see through history. You must be a happy woman.'

'I don't know. It doesn't matter to me.'

She told us about pigs and cows. About corn and potatoes. About rye and wheat. About droughts and fires and floods. She told us what her grandfather had told her about the war, which his grandfather had also told him. She told us about how those living in the village had to bury the bodies. The bodies of the men and also of the horses. She told us about how the earth was unable to stomach all of the dead. She told us about how the earth shifted over the years. How the earth sank into itself. How the earth opened up. How the farmers and woodsmen stumbled over the bones. How they fell into deep graves from the battle that had turned into wells of water.

'But this water was no mineral water, the water stunk and was green and yellow and oily, because the earth was unable to stomach the dead, the earth wanted to break free of them and be rid of them, maybe even bring them back, as my grandfather said, but I don't know how it was…'

'Yes, yes, it was exactly so. Yes, yes, too hard, too heavy was this Prussian-Austrian-Saxon meal for the meadows and fields and forests and people of Königgrätz, yes, yes, too difficult for this beautiful Bohemian landscape, yes, yes, truly, the *"beautiful landscape of battlefields, cemeteries and ruins"*, as the Englishman always said to me,' said Winterberg, looking out over the fields at a monument in the distance.

'The earth keeps spewing the dead back up, even today,' said Josefa. 'Three years ago, someone found an open grave on the edge of the Svíb Forest. It was almost empty. The dead were gone. It's said that the dead are still stumbling through the forest.'

'Look at that, Herr Kraus, I can't stomach heavy food either, it all comes from this battle,' said Winterberg.

'You have to drink schnapps. A Becherovka always helps, as my father said. Or a Sliwowitz; I like to drink one after a pork roast,' said Josefa. 'But on the other hand, in the fields over the graves, we always have a great harvest, and that's still true today. It's just the ghosts – they can be difficult.'

'Listen to that, Herr Kraus: ghosts.'

'Yes, the ghosts. But you get used to it. Around here everyone's seen a ghost, in the forest or in the fields.'

'You too?'

'Me too.'

'The ghosts – that's just a fairy-tale,' I said.

'Yes, it's true. But they live here with us. Where else should they go? The ghosts just won't go away, as my grandfather always said. And so, we have to live with them.'

'Yes, yes, precisely, *"the beautiful landscape of battlefields, cemeteries and ruins"*.'

'I don't understand any English.'

'It's beautiful here. I would love to live here,' said Winterberg, who was looking out of the window at a cemetery.

'Those are just the Prussians. My uncle owns the land around the cemetery. The best fertiliser for men is other men, as he always said over a beer. You must visit our village pub, it's directly over the battlefield. A drunk farmer once bludgeoned another drunk farmer over the head with an axe there.'

'Axe corpses aren't a pretty sight, as my father used to say.'

'The one farmer was dead at the scene, and the other went mad. He bludgeoned him because he was jealous of the better wheat that grew on the other man's field.'

The tractor wailed, and Josefa steered around a pothole.

'That's how it is here these days. Oh, you should come in summer. Nowhere in the world is more beautiful than here, when everything is fragrant and in bloom. And in the Svíb Forest you'll find the best mushrooms around, which make us the envy of all our neighbours, and it's all due to the graves, the dead, the battle.'

'And the ghosts?' I asked.

'Oh, everyone around here knows how to deal with them.'

'You must really be a very happy woman,' said Winterberg to Josefa. 'I also call the dead "ghosts". They're among us, I know, I know.'

Josefa laughed. It continued to snow.

'I don't know if I'm happy… but yes, perhaps you're right… maybe I am truly happy. I couldn't live anywhere else.'

Winterberg said that the farmers are perhaps the last victims of the Battle of Königgrätz in 1866, the last fruit of the *Cornus sanguinea*, the last ghosts.

'Of course, I mean that without consideration for myself or for you, dear Herr Kraus. Because we're the next in line, whether you like it or not, that's how it is, yes, yes, but I don't feel sorry for the dead and for the ghosts, I only feel sorry for the survivors, yes, yes, I only feel sorry for those who carry their grief forward.'

'The last victim was old Málek from Mlékojedy,' said Josefa. 'Two years ago he found an old artillery grenade in the Svíb Forest and tried to use it to clear his blocked chimney.'

'A Prussian or an Austrian grenade?'

'I don't know.'

'Or maybe a Saxon grenade?'

'I don't know.'

'Too bad. But I know this for certain, grenade corpses aren't a pretty sight, as my father always said, and he had to know, he saw far more bodies than all of us put together.'

'It doesn't matter what kind of grenade it was.'

'I suspect it was an Austrian grenade, yes, yes, they were built far better, a Prussian grenade would have already come apart in the earth.'

'The body was in bad shape, anyway. They never found his right hand; the grenade devoured it whole.'

'The Prussians were afraid of the Austrian artillery, yes, yes, and yet they still won the battle.'

'To this day, no one wants to buy his house. They all fear the dead.'

Josefa pointed out a small village house with a low red roof and an old apple tree in the front garden. Frozen and forgotten apples hung from the leafless branches.

'Well, perhaps we can buy the house, dear Herr Kraus, when no one wants to have it?'

'Sure, maybe.'

'I'm not afraid.'

A flurry of snow blew over the street.

And then we were already in Chlum and turned onto an even narrower street.

It began to snow even harder. As we climbed off, the whole landscape lay still in front of us. The entire battlefield of Königgrätz was buried under a fine layer of snow, with all its bodies and ghosts and sorrow. Winterberg walked over to a signpost and looked out into the distance through the billowing snow. It was impossible to see anything.

It was impossible to hear anything.

'Nice view,' I said. 'It was worth it.'

'Yes,' said Josefa, who laughed, and turned towards me. 'Do you have a wife?'

'No.'

'Sorry to ask so bluntly, but that's how I am, I just ask.'

'It's fine.'

'Do you have kids?'

'No.'

'And the little pear over there?'

'Pear?'

'He does look like a thick little pear. What has he got going on?'

'*Cornus sanguinea*.'

'What does that mean?'

'War.'

'War?'

'War.'

'All the Germans know war.'

'Not just the Germans. Maybe all of us.'

'Sure, all the men. Not the women, although, who knows… you should really see it here in summer, in July, during the anniversary of the war, when all the men come here and play-act the war like small children. A few women play along with them. And then they all leave. No one comes in the winter, in the winter we have our peace, and the dead, too. In the winter only nuts like him come this way.'

We laughed.

We smoked.

We said goodbye.

'Maybe I'll see you later at the inn,' I said.

'Yeah, maybe.'

It was snowing, and I watched her tractor leave until it gradually disappeared into the snow. I wanted to go right back to the inn. I was cold. I wanted tea with rum. I wanted beer. I didn't want war. Or Winterberg. Or the dead. Or any of this nonsense. I looked out into the snowstorm and wished that the snow would swallow Winterberg whole and allow him to simply disappear.

There was nothing to be seen, but then Winterberg noticed something.

. . .

'There, look at that, Herr Kraus, there!'

An illuminated tower loomed over the snow and fog. A sandstone pillar with the statue of a woman who held up a small wreath in her hands. As if she was giving her blessing. As if she wanted to lay her wreath over the entire country itself.

'Austria, goddess of love, goddess of freedom, goddess of the dead, goddess of *Cornus sanguinea*, yes, yes, the Queen of Königgrätz, isn't it wonderful, dear Herr Kraus, that we're here right now, here in *"the beautiful landscape of battlefields, cemeteries and ruins"*, as the Englishman said when I met him in Berlin, yes, yes, the Englishman saw through history, *"the beautiful landscape of battlefields, cemeteries and ruins"*.'

Winterberg, who had appeared exhausted during the ride here, was once again beaming. He marched forward through the snow and the wind towards the monument, and the ice that had formed on the path crunched beneath his boots.

'To the heroes of the Battery of the Dead.'

He read out loud the words that stood on the pillar of the monument.

'They died a hero's death at this place following tenacious combat in the Battle of the Third of July, 1866… don't know him… don't know him… don't know him… August van der Groeben, I know him.' Then he looked up, long and aghast, at Austria, who looked back down at him, exactly as long and as aghast.

At him.

At us.

At the snowy battlefield of Königgrätz.

At the frozen flowers that lay on her pedestal.

'*Cornus sanguinea.* Look at that, dear Herr Kraus, someone from Budapest was here, he was also searching for his dead, for his corpses, for his ghosts, yes, yes, the Hungarians are loyal, they don't forget their dead. Yes, yes, we'll go there as well, my Lenka was also in Budapest, she sent me a postcard, yes, yes, she was in Brünn and Vienna and in Budapest and in Zagreb and in Sarajevo after she had to leave Reichenberg, yes, yes, she sent me postcards from all these places, yes, yes, we were supposed to meet in Sarajevo and then continue on together to Greece and then take a ship to Palestine, that was our plan, dear Herr Kraus, yes, but now Lenka is dead, my Lenka, she was just as beautiful as the Austria of this monument, yes, yes, the only woman I truly wanted to marry, Lenka Morgenstern, the first woman in the moon, tragic, tragic, it still makes me so melancholy. Since we're on our way to Sarajevo, we certainly have to stop at the Budapest healing baths, that should warm us up nicely. In Budapest we'll also experience a shift in the weather, yes, yes, you can already look forward to that.'

Winterberg quivered in excitement and pulled me through the snow into the forest.

'Herr Kraus, I know it's cold, but we have to keep going, like the Austrians, like the Prussians, like the Saxons, yes, yes, we have to see it, the formation of the Battery of the Dead, who sacrificed themselves here, who turned this hill into a heroic fortress of fire, and then into a furnace, and finally into a fiery tomb, just like my father turned the Monstranz-berg in Reichenberg into a fortress of fire and into a furnace and into a fiery tomb, yes, yes, tragic, tragic, isn't it wonderful that we're here.'

He pulled me deeper and deeper into the forest.

'Look, dear Herr Kraus, there's another monument. And another over there! Look at that, here, yes, yes, and here and here, these depressions in the ground, these were the positions of the imperial artillery... the Battery of the Dead didn't die right away, the Battery of the Dead fired towards the Svíb Forest and towards Sadowa, it fired in the direction of the First Prussian Army, it fired and fired and fired, and it hit its target, yes, yes, the Austrians were good gunners, that had been clear since at least the Battle of Solferino, if you even know what Solferino means, although the Austrians lost the Battle of Solferino so magnificently, as with many other battles, like Königgrätz, but despite all that, the imperial artillery was superior to all other artillery units, yes, yes, it's tragic, tragic, dear Herr Kraus.'

It was snowing. The snowfall was no longer light, but heavy and wet. Winterberg dragged me further and further through the silent winter forest.

'Unfortunately they didn't know that they had the Second Prussian Army right at their back, no, no, no one knew that, yes, yes, the infamous fog of war, they should have read Clausewitz, the Englishman had read Clausewitz, yes, yes, the fog of war, they all sacrificed themselves as they covered the retreat of the Austrian army back to Königgrätz with their flamethrowers, only a single Austrian officer survived the battle, only a single cannon was recovered by the enemy from this fiery tomb. And so time goes by, everything comes to an end, everything passes by, oh, how time goes by.'

We stood at the edge of the forest under a ramshackle hunters' perch. It had stopped snowing. We looked down over the shallow valley. In the distance, I could see a herd of deer. A small green car was driving down a country road. I saw three grey stables, perhaps from the farm where Josefa worked.

Winterberg also looked down at the hills and forests and fields.

'Do you see, dear Herr Kraus, how the Battle of Königgrätz runs through this landscape? It runs not just through this country, yes, yes, but through all of Europe, after this battle it was all different from before, all of it, there, there, do you see them, the two trees in the distance, those must be the two trees of Hořiněves, do you see them?'

I looked in the direction that he pointed, but I couldn't see anything through the mist.

'We have to go there too, you should finally read something about history, then you would understand all of it, dear Herr Kraus, yes, yes, look at the scars, go ahead and touch them, Herr Kraus, it's all mad, it's all still here, the poor Saxons, the poor Austrians, the poor Prussians, *Cornus sanguinea.*'

Winterberg reached into the frozen earth, into dark-brown Bohemian clay that clung to his fingers, which he then wiped off on his grey coat.

'Everything that we see, everything that we are now, is this battle, which runs through my heart like a wound that can't be healed, yes, yes, it makes me a bit melancholy.'

Winterberg closed his eyes and spread his arms, as if he wanted to embrace the entire landscape. As if he wanted to be one with the landscape. As if he wished for nothing more than to be swallowed up by the landscape. As if this would finally bring him peace.

I looked at him, shook my head, lit another cigarette, and noticed another couple of deer, suddenly quite close to us, and one of the deer stared for a long time back at me. And then it disappeared with the other deer into the forest.

'You shouldn't smoke so much, dear Herr Kraus. There, it must be there, that must be the Svíb Forest, the Road of the Dead, the main street through these woods, the main street of the Battle of Königgrätz, *Cornus sanguinea.*'

He pointed towards a snowy forested area on the other side of the valley.

. . .

It was quiet in the forest. Only a single chainsaw was groaning somewhere in the distance. The snow under our feet was mixed with downed branches and green leaves. We walked along a series of tall, thin trees and found ourselves suddenly standing before a simple cross formed out of black metal. Three metres away loomed another cross. And then another. And then Winterberg spotted a bush.

'*Cornus sanguinea*, I knew it!'

He tore off a couple of frozen branches and showed them to me.

'*Cornus sanguinea*, blood-red dogwood, or in Czech, *Svída krvavá*; *krev* as in blood, you must know that, it grows all around here, yes, yes, the blood, we must come back in the summer or in autumn, when the leaves turn so wonderfully blood-red, yes, yes, as red as her lips, as red as her earrings with the Bohemian garnets, Lenka loved this colour, yes, yes, the colour of the leaves drew in the soldiers in like a trap, all the Saxons and Prussians and Austrians, who all lie here on top of one another and whom the earth can't stomach, yes, yes, precisely, precisely, as Josefa told us, this forest is named after *Cornus sanguinea*, this too is no happy coincidence of history, but a tragic accident of history. The leaves are blood red, like the earth beneath us, yes, yes, a live exposition of its corpses, there's no escape.'

'I don't understand you.'

'Yes, yes, you haven't understood me this whole time because you don't see through history, that's how it is, tragic, tragic, it makes me melancholy.'

We continued further, and the snow and ice and branches crunched under our feet.

The entire time, I had the feeling that someone was with us. Someone was looking at us. Someone was following us. Perhaps it was the dead. The ghosts of Königgrätz, which the earth underneath us couldn't stomach.

I heard a chainsaw.

I looked around.

I didn't see anyone.

'We should go.'

'Where? Why?'

'Back. It'll be dark soon.'

'No, no, we've just arrived. We'll stay here forever.'

'You're crazy.'

I saw something in the bushes. It was moving. Perhaps an animal. A wild boar or a deer. No, it appeared to be larger.

Like a man.

Like a soldier.

Like a ghost.

'Someone's there,' I said, indicating towards the forest.

But Winterberg wasn't listening.

'Yes, yes.'

'Someone's there!'

But Winterberg didn't care. He was looking over a grave.

'We're here.'

I shouted into the forest. 'Hey! Hey!'

I grabbed a branch, broke it in half, and threw it in the direction of the shadow in the bushes.

Something moved and ran away. What it was, I couldn't see.

Winterberg didn't see it either.

'Let's stay here. Isn't it beautiful?'

'No, let's go.'

'Lenka, Lenka, where are you? Are you here?'

'You're crazy, seriously. I'm leaving now.'

I looked over at the bushes and saw nothing. I was cold. I wanted to leave.

And then Winterberg began to dance. With a bouquet of *Cornus sanguinea* in his hand, he danced from tree to tree.

'Lenka, Lenka, I know you're here.'

Winterberg danced through the forest. From cross to cross. From grave to grave. From monument to monument. The historical fits, this storm in his soul, had always driven him forward; this storm which was no longer a storm, but a hurricane. The Svíb Forest was accompanying him with music that only he could hear.

'Lenka, Lenka!'

'Lenka isn't here, Lenka is dead!'

But he wasn't listening.

'Don't know him… don't know him… don't know him… yes, yes, I don't know him… don't know him… we have to find them.'

'Lenka? Lenka is dead, Lenka isn't here.'

'We have to find them, my ancestors, when we find them, we're that much closer to the murderer, the murderer we're looking for…'

'Which murderer is that again?'

'Lenka's murderer, of course.'

'But that happened somewhere in Sarajevo, or wherever else.'

'This is where the story begins, don't you understand? Why can't you just understand? Don't know him… don't know him… we have to find them.'

'Herr Winterberg, wait… wait!'

I grabbed his coat.

He looked at me. He was sweating and shaking.

Still in the grip of the historical fit.

'This is absolutely crazy.'

'Yes, yes, mad, it's all mad, that's how it is.'

'We should go.'

'It's all mad, mad.'

'We're leaving. Now.'

'Yes, yes, it's all mad. You're right.'

But he still didn't want to go. He continued to dance from grave to grave. I wanted to stop him again, but he refused to be held back, he refused to calm down.

'Lenka, Lenka, Karl, Julius…'

And then Winterberg suddenly stopped by a tree. He was breathing heavily and looked over at me and started to scream: 'You have no idea about history, you have no idea what it's like for me, you have no idea what happened to Lenka, you have no idea why we're here, you have no idea what happened here in the rain and the mist on the third of July, 1866.'

'You know what? Then just stay here. I'm leaving. You can stay here until you croak, for all I care. I'm done with you. I don't need your money. You belong in a mental ward, you know that? A mental ward! You're sick. You're mad. Stay here with your dead. I'm going, otherwise I'll go mad too. Kiss my ass, you old fool!'

He slapped me hard across the face. I didn't expect it at all. And then he slapped me a second time. I tasted blood in my mouth.

'You can't leave, you can't do that. You're responsible for me, it's not my fault that I'm alive. I wanted to die, I wanted to finally have my peace, yes, yes, I didn't ask for you to save me. You brought me back to life, woke me up, otherwise I would be long dead and everything would be wonderful, it's your fault, not mine, it's you, and you, and you, and you, you fool! Who asked you to intervene? I didn't want to go on living.'

I looked at him.

He looked at me.

He sweat and shook and sweat and breathed heavily.

And I, too, was exhausted. I had the feeling again that someone was embracing me hard enough to squeeze the life out of me. My heart raced and burned.

We stood under the tree next to one another and leaned against the cold tree trunk and looked out into the winter forest, which was already growing dark.

It was an old beech tree.

We said nothing more.

We looked down at a tree that had fallen during the last storm, which lay before us.

Over the snowy forest trail.

Over a simple cross marking a grave.

I lit another cigarette. I knew that Winterberg was right. It was my fault. When his daughter brought me to him and paid me for the crossing, for me to accompany him up to the end, he was already lying in his deathbed.

One sentence, one single sentence, had changed everything. A single word.

'It's a bit interesting. Your name is Winterberg, and I came from Winterberg, from Vimperk in Bohemia, which used to be called Winterberg.'

That's what I said to him that night.

I didn't know that he was listening.

He just lay there and slept.

But he had heard me.

He had opened his eyes.

And after that, everything changed.

And so we ended up here.

On the battlefield of Königgrätz.

In this snowy forest.

'So do it, "revenge for Sadowa", as the French called it. So just kill me,' cried Winterberg. 'Revenge for Sadowa. Have the guts to do it, you coward, just kill me!'

I looked at him.

He looked at me.

The forest around us was quiet, cold, and dark.

And someone else was watching us. A ghost. A dead soldier in uniform with a firearm in hand.

'What the devil are you doing here?' he asked, approaching us.

It was an elderly forester, and he was holding a chainsaw in one hand.

Winterberg said nothing; he was breathing heavily, sweating and shaking.

As did I.

'We're looking for Karl Strohbach and Julius Ewald,' I said.

* * *

We walked down the wide, straight path, which divided the forest like an unending scar.

'This is the Road of the Dead,' explained the forester. 'On our left, corpses; on our right, corpses; under us, corpses.'

I had to help Winterberg. The storm in his soul, the historical fit, had settled. He was exhausted and small and fragile like the frozen branches of *Cornus sanguinea* that he held in his hand.

We left the forest.

In the middle of the field stood a sandstone monument.

'Karl Strohbach, Julius Ewald,' said the forester, and indicated towards the names chiselled into the stone.

'I know every tree here, every grave and every one of the dead. My father taught me everything. And his father before him. We've always been foresters in these woods.'

The sky was dark grey. It was snowing again, and Winterberg looked at the obelisk. Then he laid down his bouquet.

Cornus sanguinea.

* * *

38

We sat in the tavern. Winterberg, Josefa and I. The radio was playing country music, and the television, football. Winterberg slept with his head over the open pages of his red book. And I ordered another beer.

One for me.

One for Josefa.

We drank our beers, and I looked Josefa in the eyes. In her deep, beautiful grey eyes.

'What's wrong?'

'Nothing.'

'What are you staring at?'

'You have beautiful eyes.'

'You think so? I don't. I like blue eyes. Your eyes are beautiful.'

I looked into her eyes, and she looked into my eyes.

And I saw in her eyes another set of eyes that were just as deep, beautiful, and grey.

Carla's eyes.

'What's wrong?' Josefa asked again.

'Nothing.'

THE CROSSING

His first word was *Feuerhalle* – 'Fire-hall'.

When children learn to talk, their first word is often 'mama' or 'papa' or 'food' or 'shit' or – for all I care – even 'prick'; but no child's first word has ever been 'Feuerhalle'.

And yet Winterberg said:

'Feuerhalle.'

I know that Winterberg isn't a child. Winterberg is moving in rather the opposite direction at the moment. He's moving in the same direction that we all do; some slower, some faster, but all of us are heading towards the same place.

Whether we like it or not.

Whether we fight it or not.

Whether we're healthy or not.

That place where we're all going, where we *must* go; there, in the fog at the end of the road, at the end of the journey – at the end of the 'crossing', as we, the Soldiers of Last Hope, call it. There, we all meet our beginnings. For just a moment, we see our own reflection in the mirror.

We see what we are.

We see what we were.

Maybe the mirror shatters, in that moment when we see ourselves.

Maybe there's nothing behind it. Maybe a dark wall. Maybe a springboard into a great emptiness. Into a hole. Into eternity. Into mortality.

Maybe God is waiting there.

Maybe the Devil.

Maybe a pub with freshly tapped beer, where all those who came before sit and wait for the rest of us. When we step through the door, they raise their beer glasses and say: hey, it sure took you a while!

And then they drink to our arrival.

To our reunion.

To our death.

But maybe, on the other side, there's simply nothing. And when I say nothing, I mean really, truly, nothing. Perhaps in the end we're just lost. We evaporate like the morning fog. Maybe it's better that way. Maybe that means that it's finally over.

But maybe there really is a mirror there, and we're able to take the time to examine our own reflection. I like to tell the story about the mirror, about the meeting with our own selves. It's not a rebirth, or anything like that. Just a meeting. A brief exchange of knowing glances. That's what I believe. I don't want to meet any others when I die. I just want to meet myself; understand myself.

What I am.

What I was.

I like to tell the story about the mirror when my fellow sailors are lying in their beds. Day to day and night to night. I tell them that story in winter and in spring and in summer and in autumn and then again in the winter – if they've made it with me to the next winter. Storytelling remains the last and only hope for my sailors.

What I mean is that many of those whom I have taken with me on the crossing, whom I accompanied up to their deaths – cooked for them, fed them, gave them medication, washed them, combed their hair; many whose mouths and eyes and arses I wiped, many whose teeth and ears and noses I cleaned, many whom I fought and calmed, many to whom I read aloud from books and newspapers, and then later cooked for, fed, and medicated, and then wiped their mouths and eyes and arses again, shaved them again, changed their diapers, held their hands; many of them were and are and will be nothing other than small, lost, homeless children, who have been tossed out of this time and this world, who are simply waiting on the side of the road until someone comes to pick them up.

Small, lost children, who need to be looked after.

Small, lost children, who cry and scream and bite and spit and mock and scratch and sleep and dream and cry again.

Small, lost children making the crossing.

Like Winterberg.

But then he said: 'Feuerhalle.'

And I said: 'Feuerhalle?'

And he said: 'Feuerhalle.'

And everything changed.

It surprised me a bit, and I think it would have surprised anyone.

I didn't know the word. I was hearing it for the first time. I wasn't sure what it meant. I didn't know how often I would come to hear that word.

There was a lot that I didn't know.

About Winterberg. About Lenka Morgenstern. About his daughter Silke. About Reichenberg and about the Feuerhalle. About the many corpses, and about love. About the war. About history and about the railway. About Königgrätz and about Sarajevo.

About me.

. . .

'My father suffered a severe stroke.'

We sat at a large kitchen table and drank coffee.

'It's his third stroke in such a short time.'

The kitchen was the only room in the apartment where one could neither see the trains nor hear them.

'The doctor said that the first one alone was quite serious.'

The kitchen was probably the only room where one could sleep undisturbed.

'The doctor said that the second was even worse.'

But there was no bed here. The large window opened up towards an inner courtyard; I saw rubbish bins and a small cluster of trees.

'The doctor said that it's a miracle my father survived.'

A spruce and two birches and a linden tree.

'But he still managed to get a bit better.'

Underneath the linden tree was a bench on which two construction workers in undershirts were sitting and smoking and sweating and arguing amongst themselves.

'But then he collapsed here in the kitchen and was brought to the hospital. He suffered his third stroke shortly afterwards.'

The sky was blue, the air humid and warm.

On days like this, I often feel a bit faint. Agnieszka said that I should go to the doctor, that my blood pressure was far too high.

But I don't like to go to the doctor.

'Here in the kitchen was also where he found my mother after her stroke. He took care of her for all those years; it's really incredible when I think about it.'

Agnieszka said that I should get more exercise and do more sports.

But I don't like sports.

'I have to work. And so I called you, Herr Kraus.'

'Yes.'

'I hope we can work something out.'

Agnieszka said that I shouldn't drink so much.

But I always had to drink when I returned from the crossing. And sometimes even during the crossing as well, when the sea was too rough and the waves too high.

'You probably know better than I do what needs to be done.'

'Yes.'

'Good.'

She looked at me.

Silke Winterberg.

Late 30s or early 40s and very thin, perhaps too thin, torturously thin, as Agnieszka would say. With thin lips and short, light hair.

She said that she had her own apartment not far from her father's. She said she was often busy. She said that if something happened, I should call her immediately. She said that if she didn't answer, she was probably in a meeting and would call right back.

'Here are the keys. There's a safety latch and an older lock, but you don't need to lock the older one.'

'Okay.'

'I'll show you the room where you'll sleep.'

We stood up. The two workers in the courtyard continued to fight over which of them had arrived late. I took my suitcase and followed her. The apartment was large, much larger than I'd thought. Some of the rooms appeared to be unused. In the long corridor hung historical maps and photos.

'I wanted my parents to move into a smaller apartment, but my father refused. He said he would miss the trains, he can't sleep without the trains; well, anyway, I'm happy not to hear any trains going by in my apartment. I hope you can get used to them. My apartment is much quieter. But I'm so often out.'

We continued.

'I like trains, that's not a problem.'

'Really? My father would be happy to hear that. He loves trains. And history.'

'I don't know much about that, unfortunately.'

'Me neither. But he does.'

'Did he study history?'

'No.'

'What did he do?'

'He was a tram driver.'

'A tram driver? I've never looked after a tram driver before.'

'He says he was the last tram driver in West Berlin.'

'I see. And was he?'

'I don't know, but that's what he says. He was the last tram driver, then the trams in the West were scrapped. It's true, I saw something about it on TV. They didn't scrap them in the East.'

'And your mother?'

'She was a teacher.'

'History?'

'Maths and physics.'

'I don't know much about that, either.'

'I do, a bit.'

She looked at me questioningly.

'I know that you were in prison.'

'Yes.'

'At eighteen… for four years. That couldn't have been easy.'

'No, it wasn't easy.'

'I don't know what for. I only know that you were there.'

'It's a long story, and an old one.'

'But you came very strongly recommended.'

'Ah.'

'Frau Sikorska said that you were one of the best.'

'I don't know about that.'

'Yes, yes, that's what she said.'

'Well, if that's what Frau Sikorska said.'

'She also says that you drink.'

'Well, drinking… everyone drinks. It's not a crime, after all.'

'She said that you had a problem with alcohol. A small problem.'

'I drink, yes, I drink a bit, but only ever afterwards.'

'Afterwards? What do you mean afterwards?'

'Only afterwards, that's it. Well… mostly.'

'Mostly… uh-huh.'

'Sometimes it's hard. You can try it for yourself.'

'I hope that I can rely on you.'

'Yes, of course.'

'Good. This is the room.'

She opened the door and showed me my room, which used to be her childhood bedroom, as she told me. In the moment when she mentioned it, she blushed slightly, as though it were uncomfortable and embarrassing for her to mention it. But perhaps it was also just the heat and humidity of that day.

She gave me the keys and then went briefly to her father, who was laying in bed and gazing out of the window into the distance, where he saw things that no one else could see. She gave him a kiss on the forehead.

'Herr Kraus will look after you now. He knows what he's doing. Bye, Papa, I'll be back in three days, I have to hurry off to Basel today.'

'With the train?' I asked.

'No, I'm flying.'

'Then have a good trip. And look after yourself.'

'What do you mean by that?'

'Oh, well, I mean, you never know. I mean, with flying.'

She gave me a severe look.

'Sorry.'

She held out her hand to me.

Her hand was thin and her fingers long and delicate.

Like her neck.

Like her arms.

She smiled at me.

She looked at the large watch on her wrist.

She left.

I stood in the kitchen and drank coffee. I looked at the calendar on the wall.

It was the twenty-first of August.

There were always celebrations on this day back home in Vimperk, although there was nothing to celebrate. My father would come home from the barracks, go into the garage, and open a bottle of vodka, although he never drank vodka on any other occasion; he would turn up the music on the radio and begin to complain about the Soviets, who invaded our country on August 21, 1968. He drank Russian vodka against the Soviets, as if his vodka drinking could drive the Red Army back out of the country; as if his vodka drinking could bring my little sister back from the grave.

He didn't drink to the Soviets; he drank against the Soviets. But more than anything, he drank to the health and well-being of my little sister, who was run over by the Soviets on a summer evening.

That was his resistance.

That was his war.

Afterwards he would fight with my mother, who was afraid that one of the neighbours would report my father. Our apartment block was full of soldiers and communists like my father, after all. And so my mother only ever spoke to my father in German, which her German mother, my grandmother, had taught her. My mother thought that if she spoke German, no one would understand her – just my father. But at the same time, she had to know that speaking German would also draw attention.

They fought in German and Czech. They embraced each other in German and Czech. They wailed at the table in German and Czech in front of the photos of my little sister. And then they made love in German and Czech. That, too, I heard from my bedroom, while looking over at the small bed where my little sister used to sleep.

After the vodka, my father always became violently ill, because although he could drink our beer just fine, he could never manage vodka. He would go to bed early. During the night he would vomit again, and on the next day, he would have to march back to the barracks and think about how in three days he could be standing with his tanks on the Rhine.

I don't know if Silke Winterberg knew what had happened in Czechoslovakia on August 21, 1968. I didn't know if she knew what continued to happen to me on every anniversary of August 21, 1968.

I had to recall that it wasn't just the Soviets, but the Poles as well, who invaded Czechoslovakia on August 21, 1968.

And the Hungarians.

And the Bulgarians.

And the East Germans were on the verge of joining them, as my father always said.

* * *

When I saw Winterberg for the first time as he lay in his bed, I thought to myself that our crossing would not take long.

Maybe three weeks, like Marianne in Munich, who called me Josef, because that was her husband's name.

Maybe six weeks, like Jutta in Schwerin, whose son put a bullet in his head during our crossing due to his debts, and I couldn't let Jutta know about it.

Maybe ten weeks, like Annemarie in Potsdam, who only spoke French with me, even though she had spent her entire adult life in Germany. But I already knew that this was often how it went during the crossing – that one starts to forget everything at the end, except for their mother tongue.

Maybe thirteen weeks, like Johann from Baden-Baden, who asked me to wet his lips with beer, and not just any beer, but beer from the small brewery in Görlitz where he grew up; and he would always be able to tell if I wet his lips with any other. And so we had to get the beer specially delivered from Görlitz, since no supermarket in Baden-Baden carried beer from Görlitz on the Neisse, because no supermarket manager in Baden-Baden had any idea that somewhere in Germany was a city called Görlitz or a river called the Neisse.

Johann was my kind of guy. Because when it comes to beer, I don't tolerate any tricks.

When it comes to beer, I get serious.

When it comes to beer, I stick to my guns.

When it comes to beer, I'm a Czech.

Still.

I looked at Winterberg, the last tram driver in West Berlin. I looked at Winterberg, who loved trains and history, as explained to me by his daughter, who could have just as easily been his granddaughter, great-granddaughter, or even his great-great-granddaughter. I looked at Winterberg and heard the trains rushing by through the window.

I looked at Winterberg and I knew that it would not take long. I know the colour of death. It isn't black. It's grey and white and blue. I know the pallid faces. I know the eyes that keep sinking deeper. The eyes that start to fade.

I looked at Winterberg and heard the trains. The S-Bahn and the regional trains and the intercity trains and the express trains.

I looked at Winterberg and saw the triangle of death. I know it well. That triangle between the mouth, nose, and cheeks, that Bermuda Triangle of human life into which we all plummet, in which we all become lost, where we disappear for eternity.

I know that look: the one that no longer gazes out into some far-away distance, but only into one's own depths.

I know the short, shallow breaths of a body that is no longer pushing onwards, no longer moving forward at all, but only stumbling and lurching and floundering and jerking.

I know the sighing and the rustling and the crying and the screaming. I know it all.

As I looked at Winterberg's grey face, his small, deep green eyes surrounded by dark circles, his pale, thin, dry lips, I knew that I would only stay for a few weeks, and then I would move on.

But then he said:

'Feuerhalle.'

. . .

It was Agnieszka from Poznań who recommended me for the job, just as I often recommend her for other jobs. It was Agnieszka from Poznań who called me and asked: are you free at the moment, they're looking for someone; the woman will pay well, I recommended you.

'Free' means, for us, that we're back in our home port.

That we had just managed it.

We'd been drinking.

We were hungover.

We sobered up.

We had pulled ourselves back together.

We were ready to go again, and the ship could set sail for the next crossing.

It was Agnieszka who didn't drink, but who knew that I did. It was Agnieszka who recommended me for this job. It was Agnieszka whom I often slept with. It was Agnieszka who knew and understood why I drank. Why I always had to drink after the crossing.

After the first beer in my home port, I began to forget the crossing. I always wanted to forget. I had to. I know someone who hanged themselves after the tenth crossing. I didn't want to hang myself. At least, not because of the crossings. After each crossing, I wanted to stop and do something else, but I never did. And so I had to drown myself in beer after each crossing. Not in schnapps. Just in beer. In a sea of beer.

But this time, everything was different.

It was Winterberg's fault.

It was Agnieszka from Poznań, whose home port was still Poznań because that's where her family lived, who recommended me for this job in the apartment near Savignyplatz in Berlin.

It was Agnieszka from Poznań, whose father back in Poznań was currently having his arse wiped and his hands held by Olga from Lviv, Ukraine, in his communist-era block apartment, because he, too, was in need of care, while Agnieszka was busy in Germany wiping German arses and holding German hands to pay Olga from Lviv for the arse-wiping and hand-holding of her own father. That's how the chain of arse-wiping in Europe works these days.

Who wipes the arses in Ukraine, Agnieszka doesn't know.

It was Agnieszka from Poznań who recommended me to Winterberg's daughter. We're always getting recommended by someone these days.

From house to house.

From door to door.

From bed to bed.

For the crossing, we never have to worry about finding a job; there's always someone there who needs us, who can't do it, who doesn't want to do it. We aren't many. And we're growing in demand.

And so I move from state to state.

From city to city.

From house to house.

It's only after the crossing that I stay briefly in the place where I actually live – in the neighbourhood of Wedding, Berlin, where I have a ship of my own. And I mean an actual ship, one that I sketch and work on and save up for, on which I'll one day disappear out on the high seas.

When I looked at Winterberg, I was certain that our crossing would not last long. But then came the first night, and I said 'Winterberg', and Winterberg opened his eyes and looked at me.

· · ·

After Winterberg awoke the next day, and after I had bathed, changed and fed him, I showed him my Bible. The grey German tome, the big, thick Duden dictionary from 1938, which I stole from the library and have carried with me ever since. I began to play my game with him.

The trains could be heard rolling by through the window, and every time a train passed, the house shivered and groaned.

I showed Winterberg the images in the book and waited to see what happened. But as I suspected, nothing did. Winterberg stared mutely at the pictures and said nothing.

But I continued to flip through the book.

Page by page.

Image by image.

Person I.

Silence.

Person II.

Silence.

Person III.

Silence.

Person IV.

Silence.

Person V.

Silence.

Nurse. Doctor. Dentist. Paramedic. Hospital.

Silence.

Men's clothing. Women's clothing. Children's clothing. Underclothes. Uniforms.

Silence.

Hair and beard.

Silence.

Jewellery.

Silence.

House. Kitchen. Dining room. Study. Living room. Music room. Bedroom. Bathroom. Child's bedroom.

Silence.

I enjoyed the game with my book. You quickly learned how things stood. Winterberg was awake. I watched his eyes. They were looking at the pictures. I made note of that.

Courtyard. Garden.

Silence.

Vegetables. Fruit I. Fruit II. Garden plants.

Silence.

Plant reproduction. Weeds. Garden pests and agrarian pests.

Silence.

Window boxes and house plants.

Silence.

Farm.

Silence.

Farmwork I. Farmwork II. Farmwork III.

Silence.

Farm machines.

Silence.

Crops.

Silence.

Livestock I. Livestock II.

Silence.

Animal feed.

Silence.

I skipped a few pages.

Church I.

Silence.

Church II.

Silence.

Church III.

Silence.

Church IV.

Silence.

Funeral.

I wanted to turn the page. But suddenly his lips moved. They trembled, and Winterberg moved his eyes back and forth, as if he saw everything and wanted to say something to me with his green eyes that his mouth was unable to speak. I saw how he looked at the image, a picture of a cemetery. With a chapel. And with another building.

And then he said:

'Feuerhalle.'

'What?'

'Feuerhalle.'

'That's a crematorium.'

'A Feuerhalle.'

He looked at the picture with curiosity and fascination. The illustration showed someone digging a grave, someone being buried, a woman, a man, a child – it wasn't clear. It showed a priest standing at the graveside and looking down into the grave at the coffin.

And I realised that Winterberg was trying to search for something deep in his mind, a rope that he wanted to pull to the surface. A rope on which something very heavy was hanging. And that heavy thing was the second word.

'Grave.'

'Grave?'

Winterberg nodded.

'What kind of grave?'

'Grave.'

'Hm. It's a nice grave. Where is it?'

Silence.

I turned the page and showed him the next image.

Church V.

Silence.

Transportation. Ship transportation. Automobile transportation. Air transportation.

Silence.

Railway.

And then he said the third word.

'Locomotive.'

'You see? You haven't forgotten everything, something's still there. That's right, it's a steam locomotive. And this here?'

Silence.

'What's this here?'

Silence.

'It's where all the trains are housed.'

'A train station.'

'That's right. A train station. Wonderful, that's four words! Locomotive, train station, grave, Feuerhalle. You're so clever! We'll manage it yet.'

I smiled at him, but he began to scream. He grabbed the bed sheets. He wanted to get up. Get away. But he didn't have the strength. He was exhausted. And he gave me a tired look.

I thought he would fall asleep. But he began to speak.

'My father had …'

'A locomotive?'

'No…'

'A grave?'

'No… a Feuerhalle.'

'Where?'

'In Reichenberg.'

'In Liberec?'

'Yes.'

'Wonderful, so we have a locomotive, a train station, a grave, a crematorium – I mean, a Feuerhalle, I know… and yes and no and Reichenberg. I'm excited to hear what comes next.'

'The Feuerhalle is in Reichenberg.'

'Ah, I see… And the train station, too?'

He nodded and I gave him some water.

'And the grave, too?'

'No.'

Winterberg wanted to say something else. But in that moment he fell asleep.

Cork pulled.

Air out.

Eyes closed.

Good night.

. . .

The next day, we continued our lessons.

And the day after that, too.

After one week, Winterberg could speak in simple sentences.

After three weeks, he could read the Duden by himself with a magnifying glass.

And shortly after that, he began to read his favourite book. The Baedeker for Austria-Hungary from 1913. The last one before the war and the collapse, as he said.

I taught him how to eat.

I taught him how to drink.

I did physiotherapy with him.

I helped him get up.

I helped him take the first steps.

In his room and in the apartment.

In the street and in the park.

With the walker and without the walker.

With the cane and without the cane.

He showed me the abandoned tram station where he used to work.

And we laid flowers there.

He showed me the Heerstraße Cemetery, where his three late wives were buried near the wall and where he would also lay buried when he died, because the Heerstraße Cemetery is surrounded on two sides by train tracks, and he couldn't imagine falling asleep without the sound of the trains.

And we laid flowers there.

He showed me the military cemetery on Columbiadamm, where the monument for the dead from the Battle of Königgrätz in 1866 stood.

And we laid flowers there.

He showed me the Union Berlin football stadium, which used to be called Sadowa.

And we laid flowers there.

He showed me the Stresemannstraße, which used to be called the Königgrätzer Straße.

And we laid flowers there.

He showed me the Skalitzerstraße.

And we laid flowers there.

He showed me the Gitschiner Straße.

And we laid flowers there.

He showed me the bench at the Zoologischer Garten train station, where he always loved to eat and watch the trains.

And we laid flowers there.

We watched the women.

He read to me from his Baedeker.

He told me about the history.

The historical coincidences.

The historical accidents.

He told me about the historical fits that he suffered from.

It was summer.

And then late summer.

And then Indian summer.

And then the autumn.

And Winterberg was beaming and talking and couldn't be stopped.

He was back.

He came back.

No one could believe it.

Least of all me.

But it was true.

Winterberg was the first sailor that had survived my crossing.

Winterberg was the first one who made it back with me.

. . .

I laid my book down on the heavy wooden table. I stood up, made myself a cup of coffee, walked out to the balcony, and lit a cigarette. The strong wind tossed the branches of the trees, which rustled and groaned. The first storm this autumn.

I went over to Winterberg's room. He slept while I looked around his bedroom. On the wall beside his bed hung several old maps in frames. I had first thought that they might be old sea charts, that perhaps someone in Winterberg's family had been a captain, like the father and grandfather of Carla, whom I had looked after in Bremen. And whom I had loved. And who continued to visit me in my dreams, where she pulled me in and held me so tightly that it always woke me up. Carla was gone. But I would wake up sweating, and felt pressure in my chest, and my heart burned and raced.

They weren't sea charts. On the wall hung battle maps. The Battle of Austerlitz, 1805. The Battle of Leipzig, 1813. The Battle of Solferino, 1859. The Battle of Königgrätz, 1866. The Battle of Metz, 1870. Military maps of Austria-Hungary. Next to these hung old city maps. Berlin. Leipzig. Prague. Reichenberg. Graz. Vienna. Brünn. Budapest. Preßburg. Agram. Laibach. Sarajevo. And a large railway map of Central Europe from 1913. And a railway map for the Kingdom of Austria-Hungary, also from 1913.

I found Bremen.

And thought about Carla.

I found Poznań.

And thought about Agnieszka.

I found Pilsen.

And thought about beer.

I found Vimperk.

And thought about my father and mother, and about my little sister, and also about Winterberg.

I found Karlsbad and thought about my flight.

Outside, another train was rolling by. It was a long, white Polish intercity train, and the house trembled in its wake.

Winterberg slept and I looked again at the map with the Battle of Königgrätz.

And suddenly Winterberg said:

'The Battle of Königgrätz runs through my heart.'

I turned around. He was no longer asleep.

Winterberg was staring at me.

'Hradec Králové?'

'I have to go there. I have to go to Königgrätz. And to Reichenberg. And to Sarajevo.'

'You should go back to bed, Herr Winterberg. Everything will be all right. Go back to bed.'

'Nothing will be all right. I have to go to Sadowa, near Königgrätz. And then further. I have to find them both.'

'What?'

'I have to find my ancestors, they're lying buried there. It's the beginning of my story, the beginning of my disaster. And I have to find her, too.'

'Who?'

'My first wife.'

'We already found her, though. In the Heerstraße Cemetery.'

'Not her… I mean the first woman in the moon.'

'Lovely. She's waiting there. Tonight will be a full moon; I heard it on the radio.'

'I have to make this trip.'

'Sure.'

'Our honeymoon trip, yes, yes, our funeral trip. I see her. Lenka Morgenstern, the first woman in the moon.'

'Your first wife's name was Henriette, your second Ute, and your third Johanna. We were already there at the cemetery.'

I thought that perhaps Winterberg was lost once again. Perhaps our crossing would soon continue onwards after all.

'But I see Lenka, she's still there, she's waiting for me. She wants me to go. Us to go.'

'You should get more sleep. Relax.'

'You have no place telling me whether I should sleep or not sleep. I don't want to sleep,' he said, before immediately falling asleep.

I also went to bed. In my room, which was the childhood bedroom of Winterberg's daughter, Silke, who was always travelling and stopped by once a week to see how things were going.

The first woman in the moon, sure, of course, I thought to myself.

One train after the other drove past the house, the walls trembled, and I thought about Lenka Morgenstern, and then about Silke Winterberg, and then I dreamed of Carla de Luca.

She came to me. She lay next to me in bed and held me the way that I had always held her, since she could no longer hold me back then, as her arms were already too weak. Just like her legs. Just like the rest of her body. But now, she held me. She pulled me close to her.

'Sleep well,' she said. 'Sleep well, my love.'

She held me so tightly that I couldn't breathe.

'Promise me that you'll never leave, promise me that.'

I woke up. I couldn't breathe. My heart was racing.

It was as if my chest was filled with fire. I opened the window. The storm continued to rage. I heard the wind. I heard the trains. The walls shuddered and I thought that I would die.

* * *

The next day, Winterberg showed me his secret room.

It was actually two rooms, connected by a massive model railway.

'Ho, of course, the royal gauge,' said Winterberg. He pressed a button.

The lights and signals came on and the trains began to move.

The freight trains.

The passenger trains.

The fast trains.

And also the military trains with soldiers and little tanks and medical carriages.

The trains drove on and Winterberg directed the traffic.

'The northern railway, the southern railway, the western railway, the eastern railway, yes, like in my book.' Winterberg pointed out the parts of his model railway.

'In which book?'

'In my Baedeker. I built them according to my book. But unfortunately I didn't finish it, as you can see, yes, yes, that makes me a bit melancholy... this model railway should be my farewell tour, my honeymoon trip, I didn't build it for myself, I built it for Lenka, Lenka Morgenstern.'

'I don't understand.'

'It's complicated, indeed.'

'You built it for Lenka?'

'Yes, yes, that's right... but only a third is complete, the rest is not, after thirty years, no, no, I wouldn't manage it, no, no, I would need at least another hundred years, tragic, tragic, in the centre of my layout is Vienna, of course, the railway heart of Central Europe, as you can see, dear Herr Kraus, the railway heart of the Monarchy, and there's Reichenberg with the Jeschken and the Feuerhalle, there's Königgrätz, I still need to work a bit more on the battlefield, yes, yes, I ordered the soldiers long ago, not half a million of course, hopefully a hundred pieces will be enough, yes, yes, about forty Prussians, forty Austrians, and twenty Saxons, yes, yes, whenever I look at the battlefield, it pains me, whenever I look at it, I feel derailed, I feel like I've been cut down to my core, yes, yes, it all comes back, the whole history, the vivisection of a living torso, yes, yes... there are the ruins of Trosky Castle, yes, yes, no one in Germany knows Trosky, but the Englishman, he knew Trosky, yes, yes, he loved the castle ruins, yes, yes, *"the beautiful landscape of battlefields, cemeteries and ruins"*, as he always said of Bohemia and of Central Europe, yes, yes, I also have to build a cemetery, without a cemetery, my model won't be complete, but when, when...'

The signals changed colours and the trains drove on and Winterberg began to tremble. A historical fit.

'Yes, yes, the Englishman understood me and I understood him, yes, yes, the Englishman was also historically sick just like I'm historically sick, the Englishman suffered from history and from historical fits just like I suffer from history and from historical fits, yes, yes, *"the beautiful landscape of battlefields, cemeteries and ruins"*, he was right, that's how it is, battlefields and cemeteries and ruins, all so beautiful, all so dreadful ... there's the Bohemian Forest with Winterberg, that's where you're from after all, do you see it? There's Pilsen and the brewery, there's Budweis and the other brewery, there's the old horse-drawn train to Linz, the first railway in Austria, yes, yes, laying tracks through the Bohemian Forest was just as difficult as laying tracks through the Alps, yes, yes, of course there are no horses pulling the trains these days, no one needs horses these days, not even the military, not like at Königgrätz; my daughter always wanted to have a horse, I fear she's still upset to this day that I didn't buy her a horse, that's why she's a bit melancholy to this day ... now where was I, you mustn't interrupt me, dear Herr Kraus ...'

'But I didn't say anything.'

'No, no, you're talking the whole time ...'

'Me? I'm just looking at the trains. You're talking the whole time.'

'Precisely, precisely ... now where was I ... yes, yes, my daughter is very lonely, perhaps I should still buy her that horse, or a husband ... yes, yes, now I remember ...'

Winterberg showed me Bad Ischl. And Salzburg. And Brno. And Kraków. And Lviv. And Košice. And Budapest. And Zagreb. And Ljubljana. And Trieste.

And then he showed me Sarajevo.

'Yes, yes, precisely, Sarajevo is the end of my line, the Bosnian narrow-gauge railway ... the small black carriage there, you see, there, that's the car with the Archduke, in a moment he'll be shot, and his wife too, yes, yes, in a moment the whole world will fall apart ...'

The signals changed colours and the trains drove on and Winterberg trembled even more.

'No, no, I didn't want to get lost in the details during the construction, and yet I kept going into ever greater detail, as you can see, dear Herr Kraus, history is unfortunately so complicated and so detailed that you can quickly lose your mind, yes, yes, you can become mentally deranged, and yet the maddest ones are those who claim to have understood history, who try to explain it to us, yes, yes, they are truly mad and sick and dangerous, because history can't be understood, history isn't a craft that can be learned, yes, yes, I know a thing or two about that, I was the last tram driver in West Berlin, three wives and three lines, I had a lot of time to read books about history, Clausewitz and *The Construction of the Alpine Railways* and my Baedeker, for example… yes, I know, dear Herr Kraus, I know what you're going to say, too many stories and too much history, yes, yes, there's no escape, history can't be overcome as easily as the Alps by the railway, or as easily as the Bohemian Forest, history defends itself, it attacks us, yes, yes, in history you can only lose yourself, yes, yes, but perhaps you really do have to lose yourself in history in order to truly understand it, you have to become mad in order to not be mad.'

'I really don't understand you.'

'That's not important. Not everyone can see through history.'

The trains drove through the tunnels and over the bridges and through the smaller and larger train stations and Winterberg was no longer trembling. He clung to the back of his chair and stared straight ahead looking depressed and exhausted.

'I can't do it.'

'Do what?'

'Understand it.'

'What?'

'History… but I can't give up. I've got to try to understand.'

'I really don't understand you.'

'You have to help me, dear Herr Kraus.'

'Help you how?'

'You have to come with me.'

'Where?'

'To Königgrätz, to Reichenberg, to Brünn, to Vienna, to Budapest, to Zagreb, to Sarajevo. That's where Lenka's trail went cold.'

Someone was suddenly standing in the doorway. It was Silke.

'Papa, you're playing.'

'Playing, we're not playing, what we're doing is learning history.'

'Sure, sure, how are you doing today?'

'Good… Are you upset that I didn't buy you that horse?'

'Papa…'

'I can buy it for you, if you want… or a husband.'

'Papa, please.'

'Why don't you have a husband? Herr Kraus is surely asking himself the same thing, aren't you, Herr Kraus?'

'Well… I… no…'

'Papa!'

'I always wanted to be a grandfather.'

'Papa!'

'Or a wife, you could also have a wife…'

'What?'

'Do you think I'd have something against it? I'm progressive, I'm nearly a hundred… we were already quite progressive eighty years ago in Reichenberg, let alone in Berlin… just not during the war, at that time it was different, at that time it wasn't progressive, although…'

'Papa, please…'

'I wouldn't have anything against it… right, Herr Kraus? Would you have something against it if your daughter were together with another woman?'

'Well… I… no…'

'You see, Silke? Herr Kraus is progressive, too…'

'Papa, leave it alone, please… I mean, that's…'

'I know, I know… You have to work, I know…'

'I spoke with your doctor.'

'And?'

'You're healthy.'

'What?'

'Yes, perfectly healthy.'

'No.'

'Yes.'

I looked at Winterberg.

'She's right, I also think you're genuinely healthy. I think I should be leaving.'

Winterberg pressed the button and the lights turned off and the trains stopped in their tracks.

He looked at us.

'That won't do. I'm not healthy.'

Silke looked at him.

'Papa, you're old, you mustn't put too much strain on yourself, but you're more than healthy for your age. The doctor said he's never seen anything like it.'

'Me neither. I have nothing more to do here, really.'

'No, I'm not healthy.'

'Yes, papa, you're healthy.'

'I'm not! You have no place telling me whether I'm healthy or not.'

'But papa!'

'The doctor has no idea how I'm doing! You have no idea how I'm doing. I'm sick! You might not be able to see it, but I'm sick, yes, yes, I am… Herr Kraus, you must stay here, that simply won't do, yes, yes, you must stay here.'

'But I can't…'

'I need you, Herr Kraus.'

'But…'

'He's right, papa, it won't work, I'm sure Herr Kraus has his own family to look after.'

'He doesn't! He stays here!'

'Or other people who need his help.'

'He has to stay here! Herr Kraus, please…'

He was sweating and trembling and his whole face was turning red.

'I'll come visit you, Herr Winterberg, I promise.'

'Yes, you see? He'll come visit you,' said Silke. 'Of course, you'll still receive your pay up to the end of the month, Herr Kraus.'

'So, I'll go pack my things then. A beautiful model railway, Herr Winterberg, incredibly beautiful.'

I went into my room and packed my things. It wasn't a lot. Then I smoked a cigarette on the balcony and listened in on an argument. I didn't know what it was about. I only heard individual words and sentences. I went back into the room and sat on the bed. Outside the trains rode by, the walls shook, and Winterberg yelled and his daughter cried.

And then it was quiet.

I took my bags and went to the kitchen and opened the door. They were sitting across from one another at the table.

'Herr Kraus, please stay here with my father. I'll keep paying you. Please stay.'

* * *

I lay in my room, which used to be the childhood bedroom of Silke Winterberg. She was already back on the road. To Cologne. Or to Paris. Or to Warsaw.

I lay in my bed, which used to be her bed, and heard the trains and saw the white lights dancing on the wall.

From left to right.

And from right to left.

And again from left to right.

The walls shook and I couldn't fall asleep and thought about Carla and then about Silke and then about Carla again.

I can't remember what my first word was as a child. But my first German word, that one I can remember exactly. It wasn't 'Feuerhalle' or 'locomotive' or 'grave'; it was 'Hitler'.

As kids, we always played war. The good guys were the Russians. The bad guys were the Germans. The baddest of them all was always Hitler. The kids knew that I had a German grandmother. And that my mother fought with my father in German.

Maybe that's why when we played war, I always had to play the German. Hitler.

Maybe that's why I always had to die.

Maybe that's why Hanzi took me along on the trip.

Although I had already heard a bit of German at home, I only properly learned the language with my stolen Duden.

Hanzi was already dead by that time.

So was my mother.

And my father in any case.

Just Carla – she was still alive.

* * *

On one evening, Winterberg said:

'I have to get that bastard.'

We were watching a football game together.

'Who?'

'That arsehole.'

'What?'

'The arsehole that did it to her.'

'Okay. To whom?'

'Lenka. And I'll do it, too.'

'Do you want some more tea?'

But Winterberg didn't want any tea.

'He can't be allowed to get away. I know where he's hiding.'

'Or juice?'

But Winterberg didn't want any juice.

'In Sarajevo.'

'In Sarajevo, of course.'

'Or at Königgrätz … or maybe in Vienna or in Brünn or in Budapest, just somewhere in my book, yes, yes, in my Baedeker. But I suspect that it happened in Sarajevo.'

'Sure. Should I turn off the television?'

But Winterberg didn't want me to turn off the television.

'We have to go everywhere.'

'We will. Maybe a banana?'

But he didn't want a banana.

'I really mean it.'

'And when do you suppose it happened, with Lenka?'

'I don't know. During the war. We have to find her murderer, yes, yes, I'll pay you well, dear Herr Kraus.'

'For what?'

'If you come.'

'It's not possible.'

'Yes, it is.'

'But that was so long ago. He's surely already dead.'

'No, no, he's not.'

'How do you know?'

'I just know it.'

'I see.'

'I have to make this journey. Now or never, yes, yes, please, come with me.'

Winterberg looked at me.

'Do you have a driver's licence, Herr Kraus?'

'Yes. But I don't have a car.'

'I don't either. But my daughter does.'

'I won't do it.'

'No?'

'No.'

'Really, no? Please.'

'No, I'm sorry.'

. . .

I woke Winterberg at six in the morning.

I asked him again if he really wanted to do it.

He pointed to the envelope on the desk.

'You'll get the second half in Sarajevo.'

'And afterwards, once we get there, what will you do then?'

'That's none of your business.'

'You don't want to leave a letter saying where we're going?'

'No.'

'They'll look for us.'

'I know. But they won't find us, don't worry.'

'And your daughter?'

'This journey is none of her business. It's no one's business, yes, yes, it only concerns me and Lenka. And now you, dear Herr Kraus.'

We drove off in the car and Winterberg beamed.

He wanted us to set the car on fire. Blow it up. Push it into the Spree.

'We can't leave any trail behind, dear Herr Kraus.'

'We could also just drive the car to Sarajevo.'

'No. Never. I hate cars. And they would find us immediately. The car is just a decoy to make them believe that we're travelling by car.'

'So where should I drive us?'

'I don't know.'

'I don't know either. I only know when our train leaves. So into the Spree, or what?'

'Just drive.'

'Just drive, just drive… but where?'

We drove the car multiple times around the block and then parked the small vehicle just two streets down from his house. I called us a taxi.

As the taxi arrived, Winterberg took my phone and stamped it into the ground, collected the pieces, and threw everything into a rubbish bin. I saw an older woman with a dog who looked at us and shook her head.

We drove off and Winterberg looked out of the window and said:

'And so time goes by, everything comes to an end, everything passes by, oh, how time goes by.'

FROM BERLIN TO REICHENBERG

Although Berlin Central Station was much closer, Winterberg wanted to go to the train station in Spandau, because he didn't like the new main station. In the taxi, he counted off all the train stations in Berlin that no longer existed.

He told me about Görlitzer Bahnhof and Potsdamer Bahnhof. About Schlesischer Bahnhof and about Lehrter Bahnhof.

He also told me about Anhalter Bahnhof, where the trains from Prague arrived.

He told me that before the war, you could drink a Pilsner Urquell in the hotel across from the station.

'Compared to the new Central Station, every one of these stations, dear Herr Kraus, even the smallest among them, was a *proper* train station. The new Central Station is a trap, yes, yes, a sparrow's nest, an autopsy theatre, a mouse-hole of glass and steel. An architectural König-grätz. A train station with almost no tracks, almost no junction switches, almost no railwaymen, yes, yes, a train station without railwaymen is no train station. A train station without railwaymen is a cemetery.'

A short time later we were standing with our tickets on the platform in Spandau and waiting for the train from Hamburg, which would continue onwards to Leipzig. Winterberg looked around warily. The Spandau train station, too, had long since ceased to be an 'Old World' train station.

The train arrived, and we boarded with our baggage.

And as our train stopped at Berlin Central Station – in that damp cellar, as Winterberg called it – he closed his eyes and asked me to wake him after we had passed by Südkreuz station.

And so I did.

We sat in the dining carriage. I was craving a beer and wanted to get properly smashed, here and now, as if I already knew that first morning that this whole journey would be a trap. As if I already knew that it couldn't end well.

I ordered an alcohol-free beer, Winterberg ordered coffee and cake, and the countryside vanished into the morning fog.

'Yes, yes, the way the fog embraces the landscape, it always makes me think of war and schnitzel.'

'War?'

'Yes, the fog of war.'

'What?'

'Surely you understand that much…'

'And what does schnitzel have to do with fog?'

'Yes, yes, much more than you'd think… it always makes me think of my mother, how she would crumb the schnitzel. She always said that the breadcrumb coat isn't a coat of armour, the breadcrumbs have to be as light and soft as a light fog over the countryside, yes, yes, like a light dress, that's how a good breadcrumb coat has to be, the breadcrumb coat is often underappreciated, but my mother never underappreciated it, my mother fried the best schnitzel, just like my grandmother. The two of them waged a schnitzel war for years, yes, yes, the schnitzels were both equally good, yes, yes, the only wars that make sense are culinary wars, they always end well, I know a thing or two about that, the old Bohemian cuisine, I'm so looking forward to finally having a good schnitzel, you just can't get one in Berlin… the Prussians have no appreciation for fine culinary skill, the Prussians would always lose the culinary war against Bohemia and Austria, surely Reichenberg still has wonderful schnitzel, made from real veal, of course, although the meat isn't the decisive bit, it's all about the right breading, yes, yes, dear Herr Kraus, my mother always made the breadcrumbs from scratch, she would never buy it pre-made, yes, yes, it's wonderful that we'll be in Bohemia soon.'

The train travelled quickly and quietly through the misty winter landscape, and Winterberg asked me whether I was bothered that our journey began so quickly and quietly. A quiet train ride, he said, is not a proper train ride.

And shortly afterwards he said the same to the conductor, as well.

He complained that the train travelled too quickly and too quietly. He said it was no wonder that someone was always getting caught unaware on the tracks, that people out there often failed to hear the train coming, that a little Königgrätz was always playing out on the rails.

'Yes, yes, precisely, just like at Königgrätz... railway corpses aren't a pretty sight, as my father always said, and he had to know, he saw a lot of corpses.'

The conductor stared at him in bewilderment, nodded, checked our tickets, smiled at Winterberg and continued on his way.

And Winterberg said:

'He didn't understand, tragic, tragic, he doesn't see through history at all. He doesn't know a thing about Königgrätz.'

Winterberg looked out of the window at the fog, sipped at his coffee, and failed to touch his cake. He looked out of the window and said:

'Königgrätz. We know how and where it ended, but we will never know how and where it began. Do you understand, dear Herr Kraus? When it comes to romance and crises, yes, yes, and especially to wars, we always know when it's over, but we never know when things first started to crack.'

And then Winterberg read from his book, his red Baedeker for Austria-Hungary from 1913.

'The 29th edition with complete regional and city maps, yes, yes, the edition with Galicia and Croatia and Bosnia and Herzegovina, of course. The other editions don't matter, those are all lesser editions, only this last edition matters.'

He read his book and he read it out loud, as if he wanted to read it to me, or his Lenka, or to both of us.

'Yes, yes, there is no passport requirement within Austria-Hungary, but a passport or identity card is always welcome, yes, yes, money transfers or registered letters can be also received in Austria-Hungary upon presentation of a German-issued postal identity card, take note of that, dear Herr Kraus, yes, yes, and now the customs inspections... tobacco and cigars can be imported in an amount up to three kilograms against payment of the customs tax, yes, yes, and now onto the language, knowledge of the German language is widespread enough in the Slavic and Italian regions of Austria to spare the traveller from discomfort; railway and customs employees, gendarmes, and police constables as well as attendants in hotels and train station restaurants throughout the country almost all speak German. In Hungary, however, outside the capital, garrison towns, well-trafficked tourist destinations and the few German-speaking areas, understanding of the German language is only to be expected on major train lines, Danube steamships and in the better inns, that's good to know, perhaps we'll have to learn some Hungarian, dear Herr Kraus.'

I looked out of the window and longed for a beer and a cigarette. Winterberg read aloud from his book and the other passengers in the dining carriage kept looking around in his direction. Winterberg rambled and read so loudly that he dominated the entire carriage.

It didn't matter to him in the least whether I was listening to him. Whether anyone else was listening to him. Whether he was disturbing anyone else or not. He dominated the room as surely and naturally as an actor dominated the stage.

'Yes, yes, dear Herr Kraus, the travel costs in Vienna, Budapest and in major resort areas are about a third higher than in major German cities, take note of that, expect to pay a significant amount in tips, be prepared with a generous supply of two and ten heller coins, yes, yes, we should always remember the tip, nothing is more embarrassing than forgetting the tip, dear Herr Kraus.'

Winterberg spoke to me, but never looked up in my direction from his Baedeker. As would become his custom later on. He continued to read from his Baedeker, and perhaps I already knew in that moment that he was not travelling with me, although he was speaking with me, but was only travelling with himself. And with Lenka. Lenka Morgenstern. And with his ghosts.

'With respect to the variety of the landscape and the wealth of culturally- and historically-notable cities, the Austrian half of the empire is by far the more significant, yes, yes, obviously, that's common knowledge, the following destinations are particularly worthwhile, how exciting.'

He read on and on, and somehow I knew that he had already read through it often enough that he knew it all by heart. And yet he continued to act as if he was reading it all now for the first time.

He read about Lower Austria and Upper Austria.

About Salzburg and the Salzkammergut.

About Vienna and its surroundings.

About the Semmering Railway and the Southern Railway.

And then he told me about the many tunnels and gorges and bridges. About the historical breakthrough.

And about Carl Ritter von Ghega.

'Yes, yes, without Carl Ritter von Ghega it would have all turned out differently, yes, yes, precisely, the Semmering Railway, even today some go mad during the journey and have to be taken directly from the train station to the mental asylum in Graz, yes, yes, it's mad, I know what you're going to say, dear Herr Kraus, it's all mad, completely deranged... you're right, some tunnels are so long and some bridges so high that even today one can easily lose their grip on reality, yes, yes, I know, completely deranged... now where was I, yes, here...'

He read about the Danube between Passau and Vienna. About Gmunden and Traunsee. About Bad Ischl.

'Exactly, we'll go there as well, Schafberg, Salzburg and its surroundings, we'll see if we can manage it, yes, yes, Liechtenstein, we'll probably have to leave that out, it's rather uninteresting from a railway perspective, and from a historical perspective, too, at least for me...'

He read about Golling and Zell am See.

About Tyrol and Innsbruck.

About Lake Achen and Kufstein and the Zillertal.

'Yes, yes, the Zillertal Railway... an incredibly beautiful narrow-gauge railway using the Bosnian rail gauge of 760 millimetres, I suppose we'll have to go there as well...'

He read about the Kitzbühler Horn and the Hohe Salve.

About the Arlberg Railway.

'Yes, yes, Julius Lott's famous Arlberg tunnel, also a masterpiece, yes, yes, Lott died so young of consumption, yes, yes, all the tunnels in his lungs were clogged and then suddenly collapsed; if you suffer from consumption, dear Herr Kraus, there's often no escape... consumption corpses aren't a pretty sight.'

He read about Bozen and Meran, about South Tyrol, about the 'Balcony of the Monarchy', as he called it.

About the Brenner Railway.

'Yes, yes, that's right, exactly as it says here... the Brenner Railway with picturesque views from the train... I suppose we have to go there, too.'

He read about Lake Garda and the Great Dolomites Road.

About Bohemia and Moravia.

About Eger and Karlsbad and Marienbad.

About Olmütz and Brünn and Reichenberg.

'You see, dear Herr Kraus, even back then Reichenberg was an important city, even though the Reichenberg Feuerhalle, the centre-piece of the city, wasn't opened until 1918, and so naturally it isn't mentioned in this book...'

He read about Ostrau and Kraków and Lemberg and Galicia.

About Preßburg and Budapest and Hungary.

About Klausenburg and Hermannstadt and Siebenbürgen.

About Sarajevo and Mostar and Bosnia and Herzegovina.

'Wonderful, wonderful, dear Herr Kraus, I'm already looking forward to the Bosnian narrow-gauge railway, which was partially built out into a cogwheel railway, as it says here, we'll see whether it still exists... yes, yes, listen to this... the former Turkish provinces of Bosnia and Herzegovina are worth visiting not just for their landscapes, but also because they offer a glimpse into the oriental world and have recently become popular with tourists... that's why we're headed there, but one thing at a time. Oh, I'm so excited; what a country, don't you think? So big, so beautiful and all lost... and yet perhaps not. Is that Leipzig already?'

But it was only Wittenberg. I was already exhausted from his constant chatter. But Winterberg wasn't tired. Quite the contrary.

The train raced across the flat, monotonous countryside and he continued to read out loud from his Baedeker and lose himself in the history.

Carried away by his curiosity.

Carried away by his insanity.

Carried away by his historical fit.

When we finally alighted in Leipzig, Winterberg remained standing on the platform. His glasses had fogged over. He wiped them off and then looked up.

Towards the great wide arches of glass and steel.

Towards the ceiling.

Towards the sky.

Winterberg told me about how he had admired this train station for as long as he could remember. He told me about the most beautiful terminus station in Germany. The most beautiful terminus station in Europe. The most beautiful terminus station in the world. He told me about how Leipzig had lost its terminus station to a tunnel under the city. He told me that he didn't want to see the tunnel. He told me that it made him melancholy.

'Yes, yes, many railheads have been lost to history, and many heads as well, our headless panic won't end well, tragic, tragic, but perhaps that's just how it is; but we, Herr Kraus, the two of us, won't let ourselves get lost. We won't allow ourselves to be destroyed through human stupidity, dear Herr Kraus… we will persevere, just as Ghega did when he built the railway through the Alps.'

We stood on the platform and the next train arrived, a delayed high-speed train from Frankfurt. The outgoing passengers streamed past us, making a wide detour around the two of us, since we were standing in their way with our luggage.

Winterberg rambled on about the train station and gesticulated wildly around him, pointing with his hands and fingers and feet in every direction, as if conducting a grand orchestra. He rambled on, and clouds drifted from his mouth in the cold air as if from a steam locomotive.

'Yes, yes, there on the left was the Prussian platform, yes, yes, and the Saxon platform on the right, yes, yes, and still further to the right was the military platform, yes, yes, a platform only for military personnel, not a common sight at a passenger station, in fact it's quite a rare sight indeed, I can't recall if I've seen it at any other train station… and between them, as you can see, is the concourse, which links and completes the Saxon and the Prussian and even the military platforms to this day.'

The high-speed train from Frankfurt had by now continued on its way to Dresden. I'd thought to myself that we could have taken that train, since we were also headed to Dresden. But Winterberg didn't want to take any more high-speed trains. He found the train too fast, and he no longer felt any urgency.

'The train station was a reconciliation project, dear Herr Kraus. After the Battle of Königgrätz in 1866 and after the Prussian conquest of Saxony, yes, yes, after the historical violation of Saxony by Prussia, it was intended to finally bring together and reconcile and link the Prussians and Saxons for good, just like the concourse here in the train station still links the Saxon and Prussian and military platforms to this day, as you can see. That was precisely how the architect, Rudolf Bitzan, envisioned it, dear Herr Kraus…'

Winterberg looked at me as if I actually did want to say something, but I didn't want to say anything. I was just cold and craving a beer or a grog or both. I lit a cigarette.

'Yes, yes, I know what you're going to say… a passenger station with a military platform, that isn't a good omen, that can't end well, and you're right, it didn't end well. I swear that the military platform wasn't Rudolf Bitzan's idea, that's how my father explained it to me, he knew Bitzan quite well from Reichenberg, yes, yes, the construction of the Feuerhalle in Reichenberg made them good friends, yes, yes… now where was I?'

Winterberg began to tremble.

'Don't we want to get going?'

'No, we don't.'

'But we should get going.'

'Yes, yes, precisely, perhaps the military platform was what caused the dispute over the true creative father behind the Leipzig main train station, because Rudolf Bitzan knew where the trains from the military platform would be heading, yes, yes, surely he knew. My father said that Rudolf Bitzan was a genius. The main station was opened during the First World War, in December 1915, and if you ask me, it wasn't a particularly grand celebration for a city as big as Leipzig, for such a stunningly beautiful train station; but in 1915, the people and even the railwaymen and even the architects had much bigger things to worry about, yes, yes, that's right, the money and the fame was being used for cannons and cannon fodder and coffins, tragic, tragic, the two other architects were happy to adorn themselves with that fame, Lossow and Kühne drove Rudolf Bitzan out of Leipzig, away from his own masterpiece, they scratched out his name, scratched out his personhood, obliterated him. His name is nowhere to be found today, not a single word about this trace of Bohemia in the Leipzig main train station, even though it was Rudolf Bitzan who designed most of the Leipzig main train station, if not the whole thing, as my father always said. Bitzan was driven out and scratched out and obliterated and then devoted himself to smaller projects, although they were no less important, like the Feuerhalle in Reichenberg, which was the first crematorium in Austria and is exactly as old as I am, dear Herr Kraus. Exactly as old as me and exactly as old as the Republic of Czechoslovakia. Bitzan found comfort in the Feuerhalle, my father said, the Feuerhalle gave his life purpose again, yes, yes, the fortress of fire, as he called his design, the fiery tomb into which we'll be descending when we reach Reichenberg… oh, it'll be lovely, dear Herr Kraus.'

'Yeah, it'll be lovely.'

Winterberg was breathing heavily and trembling. It was cold, but he didn't want to leave. He didn't care if anyone was listening to him, if I was listening to him. He simply rambled on because he had to ramble on. A historical fit.

'Yes, yes, and so there was a direct connection that ran from the train station in Leipzig to the Feuerhalle in Reichenberg, yes, yes, that's why I simply had to come to Leipzig. Our historical journey starts here, yes, yes, dear Herr Kraus… the Saxons fought on the side of Austria in 1866 against the Prussians, yes, yes, the Saxons were still heroes then, they didn't want to submit to the Prussians, and so they heroically fought on the side of Austria and then were heroically defeated… my father loved the Saxons. He always said that the Saxons were a modern people, the Saxons built the first long-distance railway lines with the first proper railway tunnels in Germany, the Saxons built the first Pilsner brewery outside Bohemia, the Saxons organised the first European Congress for Cremation in 1876, yes, yes, my father truly loved the Saxons.'

Winterberg looked over briefly at another platform where the next high-speed train was just arriving.

'Yes, yes, the train station in Leipzig was supposed to reconcile the Saxons and the Prussians… but you surely must have seen the point switches as we arrived, yes, yes, the switches link us together, the switches also split us apart, sadly, sadly… it takes just one switch in the wrong position for the entire thing to turn into a Feuerhalle all over again, just like the rail accident here at the main station in Leipzig back in 1960, yes, yes, railway corpses aren't a pretty sight, yes, yes, the cursed 'Switch of Death', Switch 262, a site of misfortune like the fiery tomb at Königgrätz, every railwayman in Leipzig knows the Death Switch 262, yes, yes, everyone who knows trains knows the Switch of Death… I know what you're going to say, dear Herr Kraus, I know… the train stations aren't to blame, nor are the switches nor the trains nor the Feuerhalles. And certainly not Rudolf Bitzan, the architect of the main train station in Leipzig and the Feuerhalle in Reichenberg… I don't know who's to blame, who keeps pulling the wrong switches of history, I truly don't know.'

The next train arrived, the passengers alighted and walked right past us. I hoped that they would take us with them and carry us away from the platform.

Into the station hall.

Into the tram.

Back home.

I thought: they could take us with them into their own lives. But then suddenly they were gone, and we were standing alone again on the platform. Winterberg trembled and looked at me and I could see his breath in the cold.

'I know what you're thinking, dear Herr Kraus. You think I'm mad.'

'No, you're not.'

'No, no, they all think that.'

'I'm just cold. We should go.'

'Me too… but you're right. I really am mad. I'm ill. I suffer from history, I suffer from historical fits, yes, yes, but better history than hysteria, don't you think?'

I laughed a bit. And he laughed too.

'Do you think they're already looking for us?'

'Maybe. But probably not. Your daughter isn't coming back for a few days.'

'She'll call, there's no one at home and you don't have your phone anymore.'

'Well…'

'I think they're already looking for us. But there's no need to be afraid, dear Herr Kraus. Where we're going, no one will find us.'

Winterberg looked out towards the end of the platform. Off in the distance, the tracks began to blend into the mist. To disappear.

'We should continue on. We have to reach Reichenberg before the end of the day. The fortress of fire. Are you excited? You don't have to be excited.'

'I'm excited.'

'Wonderful.'

A short time later, we were standing with bratwurst in hand across from the train station in front of a tall pillar of brownish-red sandstone. The railway monument for the Leipzig-Dresden line.

'The only other thing that interests me in Leipzig is this monument.'

On the way back to the train station, Winterberg was nearly run over by an old Czechoslovakian tram. I pulled him to the side at the last minute.

'Thank you, Herr Kraus… tram corpses aren't a pretty sight.'

And then we drifted onwards through the flat, soggy countryside. We drifted through Saxony. Past abandoned houses. Past factory halls. Past small villages. Past small train stations on the way to Dresden.

I was tired, but somehow Winterberg was not. He appeared to perk up with each kilometre of our journey.

He wiped off his glasses, re-opened his Baedeker, and read aloud to himself with the aid of his magnifying glass.

'The eateries have the same facilities across the entire Monarchy and the cuisine is almost universally of good quality, especially in the larger cities; soup, beef, and pastries, the typical middle-class lunch fare, for the most part sublime, yes, yes, wine and beer fresh out of the casket can be found everywhere at a moderate price, even in the most genteel of restaurants.'

I yawned.

'Aside from the main dining room, many restaurants offer a more modest street-facing guest room or public bar with lower prices. Service is provided by the food porter and the drinks waiter, also called the *piccolo*; female wait staff are only encountered in the German alpine regions, yes, yes, that's interesting but true, dear Herr Kraus, women never drew beer in Reichenberg. I wonder how it is today? Payment is collected by the designated head waiter… menus are often full of dialect expressions.'

He read about garnished beef and gulyás. About pork tenderloin and caraway. About sailor roasts and lung roasts and hussar roasts, about steamed cabbage and beef sirloin.

'Make note of that, dear Herr Kraus. Can you cook?'

'Yes, very well.'

'And what do you cook?'

'Eggs.'

'That has nothing to do with cooking…'

'Sure it does. I can cook them. Soft, hard, scrambled. It's not that easy. And you?'

'Me?'

'Yes. Can you cook?'

'No.'

'Not even an egg?'

'No. I had great luck with my wives and I've always been grateful to them. My daughter can't cook at all unfortunately, yes, yes, maybe that's why she's alone… now where was I, yes, yes, here…'

He read about Hungarian partridge and salted veal.

'I can always eat veal. I don't think I've ever eaten partridge, even though my grandfather was a hunter.'

He read about carfiol.

'No, I can't eat cauliflower, it always gives me terrible gas.'

He read about apples of paradise.

'I can't eat tomatoes either, they're too sour for me.'

He read about kren.

'I can eat horseradish, but it can't be too spicy, kren is best served with a bit of cream or apples.'

He read about aspic.

'I can eat jellied meat, but only if it doesn't have too much vinegar, that would be too sour for my stomach, yes, yes, but a good jelly is an under-appreciated treasure of Bohemian cuisine, as my father always said…'

He read about häuptlsalat.

'Yes, yes, it's butterhead lettuce, I can always eat that.'

He read about risi e bisi.

'Yes, yes, rice with peas, my mother often made that when I was a child.'

He read about beuschel.

'Yes, yes, veal lung in a sour cream sauce, my father loved that, the best beuschel was in the pub across from the hospital, my father called it 'The Putrid Foot', yes, yes, the stink in that pub was often truly nauseating, it sometimes made me ill, but the beuschel was always good, it never made me ill… the owner always saw ghosts in the pub, and they later found out that her pub was built on top of a former cemetery, yes, yes, it's no wonder they saw ghosts… people always believed in ghosts in Reichenberg, and I'm telling you, dear Herr Kraus, I believe in ghosts too, there's little in this life that can surprise me… now where was I… perhaps we should have beuschel tonight, perhaps the pub is still there, unfortunately it's not mentioned in my Baedeker…'

He read about young venison.

'Ragout or viscera of venison or poultry, I don't particularly like that, but if that's what it's going to be…'

He read about kaiserfleisch.

'Yes, yes, smoked pork belly, I like that.'

He read about tafelspitz.

'We had that only rarely. Beef was always expensive.'

He read about frankfurters.

'A pair of small smoked sausages… I always get confused with that one, we always called them wieners… a single sausage is called an *Einspänner*, but a single sausage, no one eats them like that, or at most only when they're sick, as my father always said.'

He read about the popular pastries. About crepes and pancakes and strudel with stewed fruit and kaiserschmarrn and Bohemian dalken and plum jelly and powidl and fleckerln.

'Where are the fruit dumplings? My father loved fruit dumplings, just like the Archduke Franz Ferdinand loved them… where are the dumplings more generally? The dumplings are often forgotten, just like the Saxons, but what would our Central Europe be without the dumplings and the Saxons? No, no, one can't forget the dumplings and the Saxons.'

He read about beer.

'Beer is consumed in half-litre glasses or in pints or in three decilitre glasses as a small serving, a *seidel*, yes, yes, you only drink a small beer if you're sick or pregnant, as my father always said… for beers from Munich, there's also the one litre stone mug. The beer is served cold almost everywhere, right from the source, yes, yes, warm beer is worse than the plague, dysentery, and the Spanish Flu all together, as they say in Reichenberg.'

He read about wine.

'The house wine is provided in open bottles or in glasses… in Vienna, the better wines from the surrounding areas are white Weidlinger, Gumpoldskirchner, Nussberger, Setzer, Mailberger, and red Vöslauer, make note of that, dear Herr Kraus… even the Lower Austrian wines from Manhartsberg have a good reputation, that's good to know, but I don't drink wine, I find it too sour and it makes me ill… in Tyrol, yes, yes, it's mostly red wine, the best ones are called *Spezial*… Bohemian wine, yes, yes, Melniker, Czernotzeker, but I would still recommend drinking the beer in Bohemia, it won't make you ill…'

He read about the coffeehouses.

'Coffeehouses can be found everywhere in cities and resort towns, one would be well-advised to take their first breakfast here between eight and ten in the morning, yes, yes, that's exactly what we'll do, a *kipfel* is a croissant, yes, yes, the best croissants in Reichenberg were baked by my uncle at the Tuchplatz, unfortunately he and my father weren't exactly friends, because my uncle, as a die-hard Catholic like my mother, was no friend of fire burial, quite the opposite from my father, who was a die-hard Protestant, as a child I only went in secret to see my uncle in his bakery… he always said to me that Nepomuk wasn't drowned in the Moldau so that men could go about burning other men, but that the wrath of God will come sooner rather than later… only over his dead body would he allow his dead body to be inciner-ated in the Feuerhalle, yes, yes, just like my mother. My father and my uncle had no love for each other, and yet the dead body of my uncle was indeed incinerated in the Feuerhalle, because my aunt was not a die-hard Catholic and cremation was also much cheaper, as my father always said, yes, yes… now where was I, dear Herr Kraus…. ah, yes, here, the busiest hours are in the afternoon and in the late evening. A large selection of newspapers, especially the Viennese papers, are availa-ble everywhere, as well as a smaller number of *reichsdeutsche* papers, yes,

yes, I know, dear Herr Kraus, what you're going to say, *reichsdeutsch* isn't a particularly nice word, it stands in my book as proof that the whole story can't end well unfortunately, that's how it is, tragic, tragic, there's no escape, but that's how it was back then… after finishing one's coffee, one will usually be presented with two glasses of water and may remain for a longer time to while away the time reading newspapers at one's leisure, precisely, precisely, in the coffeehouse *Zur Post* you could sit for hours and read newspapers, you could even read *Die Einäscherung*, the Journal of the Friends of Fire Burial and the Hygienic Movement in Reichenberg, before going out later in the evening to the theatre or to the cinema, or even later to the nightclub under the coffeehouse to dance with the girls and get into fights over the girls, yes, yes, that's how it was back then in Reichenberg, but people got into fights over politics above all, yes, yes, the interior was also designed by Rudolf Bitzan, but I heard that after the war, it was all destroyed and burned, that would surely make Bitzan very melancholy, it would surely give him a heart attack, it's a good thing that he'd already died and been cremated before the war, yes, yes, heart attack corpses aren't a pretty sight.'

And then finally he was quiet again. Winterberg looked briefly out over the distant countryside, over the dark trees and over the river.

A bit pensive.

A bit lost.

A bit of both.

A freight train passed in the opposite direction. And Winterberg again returned to his book. And I thought, no, no, please, no. Please just a bit more peace and quiet. But he read and rambled and rambled and read and brought it all into disarray.

'Now where was I… yes, yes, here, Herr Kraus, here, the coffee is usually excellent, after lunch typically comes a small cup of black coffee, or the very small *Nußschwarzer*, or a small cup of coffee with milk, a *Kapuziner*, or the even smaller *Nußkapuziner*… breakfast and afternoon coffee is usually served in larger cups or in glasses with cream, yes, yes, they call it a *Melange*, the cream is called *Obers*, ordering a portion of coffee – that is, a large coffee – is not as common, in that case one receives the coffee and milk separately, but pays the price of two glasses for one and a half… yes, yes, it's worth it of course, for a single person, a tip of between six and ten hellers should be given to the *Zahlmarqueur*, the "pay-waiter", no one would understand that word in Reichenberg, perhaps they would in Prague, certainly in Vienna, but in Reichenberg no one knows to this day what a "pay-waiter" does, and the serving waiter should receive at least four hellers, please make note of that, dear Herr Kraus, I can't keep track of it all myself…'

He read about confectioneries and sugar bakers and bonbons and tortes.

About Linzertorte and Sachertorte and Pischingertorte.

About ice cream.

About red currants.

He read about marillen.

'Marillen are apricots, yes, yes, any idiot knows that marillen are apricots. Are we in Dresden yet?'

'That's just Riesa, that must be the Elbe.'

The train travelled across a bridge over the wide, grey river, which snaked its way through the landscape in long, large arcs.

'Yes, yes, the Elbe, a fateful river, the railway of the Middle Ages, as the Englishman called it, and he was right, the Elbe linked Bohemia with the North Sea exactly as closely and as permanently as a train line, yes, yes, the Englishman… we still have a while to go before Dresden, I can read a bit more.'

'Who is the Englishman?'

'The Englishman is the Englishman.'

'You don't need to tell me. But I'd be interested to know.'

'Oh, this here could interest you far more, dear Herr Kraus, the sale of tobacco, cigars and cigarettes in Austria-Hungary is a state monopoly and is possible only in the so-called tobacco *Trafiken* and in train stations, popular brands are Virginia for 11 hellers, caution, very strong, Britannica for 16 hellers, Trabuco 18 hellers, Regalita 20 hellers, and in larger cities there are special shops for Cuban cigars, yes, yes, I'd like to try a Cuban cigar, have you ever smoked a Cuban cigar, Herr Kraus?'

'No.'

'You shouldn't smoke so much anyway, I never smoked.'

'Someone has to do it, otherwise humanity would be too healthy. I'm making sure we balance things out.'

'Look at this, this is also interesting, the postal systems in Austria, Hungary, and Bosnia-Herzegovina still have their own stamps...'

'You're not listening at all.'

'... which are only valid in the country of issuance, here you can already sense that everything is falling apart, yes, yes, here you can already sense the whole catastrophe...'

'You don't care what I'm saying.'

'... postage for letters up to 20 grams within Austria-Hungary and Germany costs 10 hellers, up to 250 grams 20 hellers, for international post up to 20 grams 25 hellers, fee for registered mail 25 hellers, the postcards – precisely, precisely, that interests me, I always liked to write postcards and to receive them too, I always asked Silke to send me postcards, she travels so much after all, but she prefers to call me, How are you doing, Papa? Good. And you? Good. Great. Great. Bye. Bye... yes, yes, tragic, tragic, no one writes postcards anymore these days, yes, yes, maybe that's our problem... and yes, the correspondence cards, if they still exist, 10 hellers, yes, yes...'

'But me, I always have to listen to you.'

He looked at me.

'Did you say something?'

'No.'

'Good. Now where was I, yes, here... stamps and postcards can also be purchased in the tobacco *Trafiken*, for post to Hungary it's recommended to add the Hungarian place name next to the German name in the address, yes, yes, good to know.'

I dozed off.

And when I awoke, we were nearing Dresden.

Winterberg hadn't noticed that I was asleep. He looked out of the window and continued to talk to himself.

'Yes, yes, Rudolf Bitzan also designed new train stations for Darmstadt and Karlsruhe, but unfortunately they were never built, yes, yes, they didn't appreciate Bitzan in Darmstadt and Karlsruhe. Have you seen the train stations in Darmstadt and Karlsruhe, dear Herr Kraus? Tragic, tragic, my father saw the plans for Darmstadt and Karlsruhe and also for the Feuerhalle in Freital, he knew how much Rudolf Bitzan suffered when they scratched out his name in Leipzig, when they scratched out his whole existence. The construction of the Feuer-halle in Reichenberg was his consolation, his salvation, my father said. Bitzan was also a Feuerhalle person like my father and a train person like me, like you, dear Herr Kraus. Yes, yes, I know what you're going to say, stations, trains and Feuerhalles, tragic, tragic, and you're right, I too know where the whole journey is headed, I know it all, it's all mad, there is no escape, perhaps that's why I have to make this journey.'

And then Winterberg looked back at his book.

'Austria-Hungary and Serbia are on Central European Time, Romania is on East European Time, which is an hour ahead of Central Europe, make note of that, dear Herr Kraus. I'm excited to see what time we'll have in Reichenberg and Sarajevo. My watch is always on time, my father gave me this watch on my eighteenth birthday. The Feuerhalle also turned eighteen that day.'

* * *

In the restaurant of the Dresden train station, we drank coffee and ate soup and Winterberg read aloud from his book and looked at his rail map and said that we could attack Bohemia via Pirna and Aussig and then take the train from Lobositz to Reichenberg in order to attack the city from the south. Or we could even take the train all the way to Prague and then to Turnau in Bohemian Paradise in order to attack Reichenberg from there, but he decided on the 'classical variant', as he called it, attacking Reichenberg, Bohemia and Austria just like the Swedes did in the Thirty Years' War, just like the Prussians did in 1741 and 1744 and 1745 and 1757 and 1778 and 1866.

'And just like the Wehrmacht did in 1938.'

'Yes, that too.'

'But we're not soldiers though, we're tourists, visitors. We aren't attacking anything.'

'Tourists are the soldiers of today, no, the tourists are even worse, they attack and destroy everything.'

And then he began to talk again about Rudolf Bitzan. He talked about the architect of the Feuerhalle in Reichenberg. About his father's best friend. He talked about how Rudolf Bitzan was born near

Reichenberg. How he went to school in Reichenberg. How he later lived in Dresden.

'Yes, yes, dear Herr Kraus, everything is tied together with the railway, all these stories and all this history too, whether we like it or not, yes, yes, but Bitzan wasn't happy here in Dresden, as my father always said, he missed the mountains, the Iser Mountains, yes, yes, and also the beer and the fruit dumplings, which he loved as much as the Archduke did… yes, yes, he said that a Bohemian always suffers homesickness regardless of whether they speak Czech or German, yes, yes, I suffered from homesickness too, yes, yes, it makes me very melancholy that I couldn't visit my Bohemia, my Reichenberg, for so long… Bitzan always said that a Bohemian is doomed to that particular brand of melancholy, and that's why they always try to be funny, that's where this dreadful Bohemian humour comes from, it doesn't matter whether they speak German or Czech, there's nothing I hate more than this dreadful Bohemian humour, yes, yes, wherever a Bohemian turns up, it's expected that they be in good humour, that they engage above all in a self-deprecating humour; no, no, a Bohemian isn't funny, a Bohemian is melancholy, a Bohemian thinks an awful lot about death, yes, yes, also about death on their own terms, because a Bohemian is rejected everywhere, because we're so melancholy and have this dreadful Bohemian humour which is nothing more than sorrow, yes, yes, this humour that no one but a Bohemian understands, not even in Saxony, as Rudolf Bitzan said, not even there, as one might otherwise expect… maybe in Moravia and in Austria, in Vienna, where a lot of Bohemians live, would people understand the Bohemian humour, this Bohemian melancholy… but as a Bohemian you're constantly rejected, as a Bohemian you never feel at home, and so every Bohemian suffers from homesickness and toys with the idea of hanging themselves or shooting themselves or throwing themselves in front of a train, yes, yes, and they fight it with this dreadful Bohemian humour, yes, yes, tragic, tragic, I know, many people love Bohemian humour, many love it, but I can't stand it at all. You only feel at home in Saxony if you're a Saxon, as Bitzan always said to my father, but that was so long ago, long before Dresden was also turned into Feuerhalle, a fiery tomb; maybe these days a Bohemian can feel at home in Dresden after all, and be happy…'

Winterberg told me about how after finishing the Feuerhalle in Reichenberg, Bitzan immediately designed the next Feuerhalle for Freital in Saxony. He told me that the Feuerhalle in Freital was unfortunately never built. He told me that it made him very melancholy. He told me that in spite of that, Bitzan turned into a true specialist in Feuerhalle construction.

'Yes, yes, like how Ritter von Ghega became a specialist in the tunnels and bridges of the Semmering Railway, or how Benedek was a specialist in Austrian artillery, which unfortunately didn't help him much at Königgrätz, but that's how life is, yes, yes… Rudolf Bitzan suffered so much homesickness that he allowed himself to be cremated in his own Feuerhalle in Reichenberg, yes, yes, just like my father allowed himself to be cremated in his own Feuerhalle in Reichenberg. But despite that, Bitzan is lying buried somewhere here in Dresden, his wife requested it… perhaps we should go look for his grave, what do you think, dear Herr Kraus?'

I wanted to say something.

But Winterberg didn't let me say it.

'No, no, I know, you're right, we must move on. We have to mount the attack on Bohemia together, we have to make it to Reichenberg.'

And so we continued our journey.

And in the train, Winterberg finally fell asleep.

We travelled through Radeberg. Through Wilthen. Through Ebersbach. Towards Zittau.

The sky was heavy and grey. The trees barren and black. The leaves yellow, grey and red.

The countryside frozen over. The large and empty station buildings abandoned and derelict.

And I considered whether I should alight somewhere and leave him alone in the train. Someone would surely take care of him.

We had to change trains in Zittau and stood briefly in front of the station. I lit a cigarette and looked at the empty buses in the station square.

My heart was racing and I was sweating; it felt as if someone were standing behind me and holding me in their arms so tightly that I could no longer breathe, and it made me think of Carla and our embrace. I felt a bit faint and hoped that the train to Reichenberg wouldn't come, that it would derail, that the entire train system would break down and we would stay here and not be able to travel further.

To Bohemia.

To the Czech Republic.

Because the entire time I've lived in Germany, I've been terrified of this trip. Of this return. Because the entire time in Czechoslovakia, they threatened us with death. And I thought, who knows, perhaps I'll be a dead man the moment I'm back.

'Yes, yes, Zittau, what a shame we have so little time, dear Herr Kraus… unfortunately, Zittau is exactly as underappreciated in history today as all of Saxony is underappreciated in history, yes, yes, we're practically already in Bohemia here, the city crest still carries the Bohemian lion to this day, yes, yes, it was also Bohemian for nearly three hundred years, but who remembers that these days. Once Bohemian, always Bohemian, as my father and Rudolf Bitzan always said, yes, yes, that's how it is, the umbilical cord remains, it can't be so easily cut.'

I continued to stare at the empty buses and lit another cigarette.

'Are you not feeling well, dear Herr Kraus? You're red in the face and shaking, you shouldn't smoke so much. Lung cancer corpses aren't a pretty sight, as my father always said.'

. . .

The train left the station and Winterberg looked out of the window and pointed to a couple of old green train carriages on the other side of the platform.

'Yes, yes, look, Herr Kraus, the narrow-gauge train to Oybin in the Saxon rail gauge of 750 mm, once we're in Bosnia, if not sooner, I'll tell you a bit about the Bosnian rail gauge of 760 mm, yes, yes, the Bosnian rail gauge can be deadly, the Archduke would have had something to say about that if he weren't already dead, yes, yes. I'll have more to tell you about the narrow-gauge rail war that continues in Europe to this day; look, over there, a train used to run from Zittau directly to Friedland as well, yes, yes, this must have been where the tracks branched off, yes, yes, precisely.'

I wasn't feeling well. My heart was racing and I was sweating. I would have preferred to disembark and travel right back in the other direction. What business did I have in Bohemia? I'd had to leave the country, and since then, I've spent the entire time terrified that I might one day have to go back.

Winterberg briefly glanced at me and said:

'I know what you're going to say, dear Herr Kraus, the tracks lead to Friedland in Bohemia and to Wallenstein, to his palace. If Wallenstein had lived a hundred and fifty years ago, he most certainly would have been a railway entrepreneur, yes, yes, a railway pioneer, because Wallenstein always knew how to make money, yes, yes, if Wallenstein had lived a hundred and fifty years ago, Friedland would have been an important railway hub, and Jitschin too, yes, yes, the train to Friedland was also a narrow-gauge track in the Saxon gauge of 750 mm, the only Saxon gauge in Austria, yes, yes, but this connection hasn't existed for a long time, the tracks were dug up by an excavator. They probably landed in a Polish strip mine somewhere.'

The train travelled over a long, high bridge.

And Winterberg looked out of the window and said:

'The Neisse river, yes, yes, also a fateful river, always so calm, so inconspicuous, but even the Neisse can quickly turn restless and malicious, just like every living thing, as my father always said... quite high, this bridge, don't you think?... I've no idea why so many people are attracted to high bridges. Bridge-jumper corpses aren't a pretty sight, as my father always said.'

The sun slowly began to set. The sky was overcast and the dark grey clouds lay above us like long, gentle waves. In the carriage were only the two of us and four exhausted retirees with hiking poles and backpacks who fell asleep as soon as the train pulled out of the station.

I yawned and Winterberg said:

'Look at that, Herr Kraus, that's the Jeschken.'

He pointed to a tall mountain in the distance.

'Yes, yes, whenever I saw the Jeschken, I knew I was back home, yes, yes, in a moment we'll be in Austria, in Bohemia, in the Czech Republic, yes, yes. But the most beautiful mountain is the Monstranzberg.'

The train sounded its horn and Winterberg opened up his book again and read from it out loud. One of the retirees briefly awoke and glanced at him. Then he fell back asleep.

'The trains have facilities similar to those in Germany, but the travelling speed and comfort of German *D-Züge* are only achieved in Austria by the international luxury trains, yes, yes, no wonder, this here is clearly no luxury train, it's not even a *D-Zug*, it's a regional train.'

At the end of the bridge the train braked suddenly and then carefully travelled forward at a snail's pace.

'Yes, yes, now we're travelling briefly through Poland, of course Poland wasn't here back then, that's how it is, nothing in Europe has been shunted around as much as the borders, that's how it was, that's how it is, that's how it's going to be, yes, yes, sometimes I think borders only exist to be moved… the express trains are often standing room only, the state railways operate through-trains and multiple sleeper carriages and dining carriages on most major lines, yes, yes, we absolutely must try it, dear Herr Kraus, a goulash or wiener schnitzel with a view of the Alps from the dining carriage, wonderful, wonderful… so-called 'Canadian observation carriages' are also used in the Alps, caution, non-smoking sections are usually in short supply, yes, yes, even back then travellers were terrorised by smokers, caution, train platforms may only be accessed with a valid ticket, yes, yes, but rightly so, it helps avoid train accidents and human accidents, yes, yes, railway corpses aren't a pretty sight.'

The train continued to creep forward very slowly and swayed on the old tracks like an aged tooth that couldn't hold on much longer to the jawbone of the rail bed.

'Yes, yes, I'm telling you, the tracks were laid down by the old Reichsbahn and no one has looked after them since then, the entire stretch from Zittau to Reichenberg was operated by the Reichsbahn, that was an anomaly here, yes, yes, the Saxons built this stretch, the Saxons were much more interested in the connection to Reichenberg and Austria via Zittau than the Austrians were in the connection to Saxony, yes, yes, the Saxons were much more cosmopolitan than the Austrians back then, but who remembers these days, the Saxons are often forgotten by history, but this stretch was operated by the Saxons, and then later it was taken over by the Deutsche Reichsbahn, yes, yes, also an anomaly, but who's interested in such anomalies these days, only very few people see through history these days, yes, yes, only the historically ill, who still knows these days that Bohemia and Austria were attacked from this direction again and again by the Prussians, yes, yes, and before that by the Swedes, yes, yes, this is where it begins, *"the beautiful landscape of battlefields, cemeteries and ruins"*, as the Englishman always said, yes, yes, I know what you're going to say, dear Herr Kraus, too much history and too many stories, the country and the countryside can't stomach it, and you're right, tragic, tragic… but the country and the countryside have to stomach it, people come and go, but the country and the countryside always remain… now where was I, you can't keep interrupting me… yes, yes, I remember, even later on in Czechoslovakia, the trains between Zittau and Reichenberg were operated by the Reichsbahn, now that was a true anomaly.'

The train swayed from side to side and the four retirees slept and swayed along with it. As did we.

'Train tickets and ticket books can also be purchased from the tourist authority in larger cities, make note of that, dear Herr Kraus, supplementary tickets can also be purchased in the train for an additional charge of 40 hellers, seat reservations on certain express trains are available for two or three crowns, perhaps we don't need those, you can always find a spot on the train, yes, yes, checking luggage is expensive, take what you can with you into the carriage, yes, yes, that's exactly what we're doing, baggage porters should receive between 30 and 60 hellers, make note of that, dear Herr Kraus, maybe we'll be tired and won't be able to carry the bags ourselves, luggage can be stored at the train station for up to four weeks at a fee of 10 to 12 hellers per day, the train station restaurants in larger stations are generally quite good, yes, I'm glad to hear that, I loved to sit in the station restaurant in Reichenberg and eavesdrop on the railway workers, yes, yes, they always stank so wonderfully of coal and lubricant and soot, yes, yes, when stopping by only briefly, be sure to pay the waiter immediately after receiving your order, please make note of that, dear Herr Kraus, I can't keep track of everything.'

The train finally sped up a bit. And then immediately had to brake.

The sun was setting even further and we were in the Czech Republic.

In Austria, as Winterberg called it.

In Bohemia.

Winterberg was excited and I felt ill. My heart was racing and my head was roaring. I wanted to get out and spring into the train across the platform and travel right back in the opposite direction. I looked for the border guards. For the police. But I didn't see any men in uniform. No dogs. I had to think of Agnieszka, who told me, one day you'll go back, one day you'll do it. And how I laughed at her and told her that I would never go back, there's nothing more for me in that country.

And now I'm here.

We were in Hrádek nad Nisou.

In Grottau, as Winterberg called it.

The retirees noticed nothing and continued to sleep.

'Finally in Bohemia, dear Herr Kraus, finally back home.'

Winterberg was excited. But his joy didn't last long. The train was suddenly filled with families, workers, and screaming schoolchildren. Two boys with large caps threw their backpacks onto the seats across from us and began to play music from their phone. They were grinning and reeked of cigarettes and beer, and Winterberg eyed them warily.

'Timetables for the trains, steamships, and postal service in Austria-Hungary can be found in the Austrian rail guide published eight times a year, yes, yes, we absolutely must get ourselves a rail guide.'

The music was loud.

'Prices for the Austrian state railways for trips between 1 and 400 kilometres are 3.5 hellers per person and per kilometre in third class, 5.5 in second, and 9 in first, make note of that, dear Herr Kraus, for trips longer than 50 kilometres, the ticket price is calculated per zone of 10 kilometres each, please make note of that, prices for express trains include an extra fee per kilometre over the usual passenger train prices, make note of that, no return tickets, yes, yes, dear Herr Kraus, you see? There are no return tickets, there is no return, there is no escape. We have to go on.'

He looked gloomily at the boys. The music got even louder.

'In the year 1913 we would have only needed one rail guide, today we need a rail guide for the Czech Republic and one for Austria and one for Slovakia and one for Hungary and one for Slovenia and one for Croatia and one for Bosnia. And if we decide to travel to Lemberg, we'll also need to buy a Polish and a Ukrainian rail guide, yes, yes, the problem with the rail guides these days can't be as easily overcome as the Alps by the railway. It's a good thing you've come along, dear Herr Kraus, you can carry everything, a rail guide is heavy, you can bash in someone's skull with a rail guide, yes, yes, that happened once in Reichenberg in the station restaurant, a foreman was bludgeoned to death by a switch operator with the rail guide for the Czechoslovakian State Railway because the foreman made fun of his much-too-tight uniform, which the switch operator couldn't properly button up because he was terribly ill from all the beer, yes, yes, like many Bohemians… rail guide corpses aren't a pretty sight, yes, yes, we'll have to get a rail guide right away.'

The boys laughed and played another song and Winterberg looked at them with anger and gloom and gloom and anger, and I noticed that he wanted to say something to them, but he didn't say anything, he just sighed and stared even more gloomily out of the window. The train raced quickly through a deep valley, through a gorge, which briefly swallowed the train. We saw only the forest high above us and the river deep below us.

The boys turned up the volume even louder.

Winterberg paged nervously through his Baedeker, looking for something. Then he turned several pages back. And then a couple ahead. And then another couple pages back. And then he read aloud.

'Reichenberg, yes, yes, station restaurant, hotel *Goldener Löwe*, the 'Golden Lion', Gutenbergstraße 3, 100 rooms, yes, that's where we'll stay, prices between three and ten crowns, breakfast one crown, make note of that, dear Herr Kraus, lunch between three and five crowns, yes, yes, that's where we're going, my parents had their wedding reception at the 'Golden Lion'; *Schienhof* and *Zentral-Hotel* and *Eiche* and *Café Post*, yes, yes, that's where Lenka and I celebrated our engagement, secretly, of course, because that's how it had to be back then, beer halls, finally something for you, too, dear Herr Kraus, the *Ratskeller* restaurant under City Hall, wine too, yes, yes, the Ratskeller was my father's second home after the Feuerhalle, yes, yes, and after our apartment in the Wallensteinstraße, the restaurant *Urstoffhalle* at Altstädter Platz 6, the self-serve *Automatenrestaurant* in Hotel *Schienhof*, entrance on the north side, yes, yes.'

The train travelled on and the boys looked over at Winterberg and one of them turned up the music even louder. And Winterberg read even louder still and with greater determination.

'Electric trams from the train station via Altstädter Platz to the city park, 3.3 kilometres, 20 minutes, 12 hellers, from Röchlitz to Rosenthal, to Heimatstal at the base of the Jeschken, post office and telegraph station at Altstädter Platz, the Stadttheater is closed in the summer, isn't it wonderful that we're travelling in winter, dear Herr Kraus, yes, yes, my Lenka loved going to the Stadttheater, especially to the operas, yes, yes, she also lived in the Mozartstraße, yes, yes, she played the piano beautifully, she was very musically gifted, unfortunately I was not so gifted, yes, yes, and so I became a tram driver, before the war in Reichenberg, after the war in West Berlin.'

Winterberg was no longer just loud, he was practically screaming. But the boys turned up the music even louder and grinned at him.

'Reichenberg sits between 340 and 413 metres above sea level on the Neisse, an industrial city with cloth factories and spinning mills established by Johannes Liebieg, yes, yes, Reichenberg owes all its wealth to Liebieg, Reichenberg should be called *Liebiegstadt*, 'Liebieg City', as my father often said, 70,000 German inhabitants, yes, yes, I know, and a few thousand Czechs as well.'

Winterberg was screaming to himself. And his voice was becoming increasingly hoarse. I handed him the wattle bottle, but he didn't want to drink. He continued to read even louder from his Baedeker.

And the boys with the large caps also turned up their music louder.

'From the train station down the Bahnhofstraße, then across the Tuchplatz and to the right, yes, yes, that's where my grandmother lived in the Breite Straße, almost directly at Tuchplatz, then down the Wiener Straße, and the Museum of the Organisation 'Friends of Nature' is on the left side in number 18 on the second floor, yes, yes, on the first floor was the office of the Organisation 'Friends of Fire Burial', the Friends of Nature and the Friends of Fire Burial didn't particularly like each other, as my father always said, tthere was a lot of mutual face-slapping, continue onwards to Altstädter Platz, where the City Hall was built by Neumann in 1888–93 in the German Renaissance style, beautiful views, behind the City Hall is the Stadttheater built by Fellner and Helmer in 1883, yes, yes, the musical theatre in particular was of a very high standard in Reichenberg, yes, yes, I mean the musical theatre, I mean the proper beautiful old music!'

The boys wanted to turn up their music, but the volume couldn't go any higher.

Only Winterberg could get even louder. He was screaming and sweating and trembling and screaming. His voice was getting hoarser and gruffer.

'The Schützenstraße begins past City Hall – either continue straight ahead for twenty minutes along the Kaiser-Joseph-Straße to the city park, or take a right down the Gebirgsstraße to the Harzdorf Reservoir, yes, yes, in the summers we always went swimming there, in the winters always ice-skating, yes, yes, in the Kaiser-Joseph-Straße on the left is the North Bohemia Museum of Industry, built in 1898 based on designs by Ohmann & Grisebach, Museum Director Dr. Schwedeler-Meyer, my father knew him very well, he was also cremated in the Feuerhalle, yes, yes, Dr. Schwedeler-Meyer's corpse was indeed a pretty sight, as my father always said, in the vestibule modern decorative arts, in the gallery around the atrium exquisite Bohemian glasswork, comprehensive collection of ironwork and book-binding and ceramics and pewter, yes, yes, the Liebieg Collection...'

The train travelled on and Winterberg was screaming and rambling and was no longer looking at his book, but rather at the two boys who were staring back at him and grinning, and it became clear to me once again that he had long since learned his Baedeker by heart.

'Not far is the Kaiser Joseph Park with a bronze statue of the father of modern gymnastics, Jahn von Gerhart, erected in 1902, a bronze bust of Kaiser Joseph by Brenek from 1882, and the restaurant *Volksgarten*, yes, yes, unfortunately the beer there was often sour, yes, yes, poor sanitary standards, tragic, tragic, they didn't properly clean out the piping, as my father said, and you've always got to properly clean out the piping, whether it's in a restaurant or in the Feuerhalle. Electric trams, see page 348, animal enclosures nearby, just a twenty minute walk from the public park is the lookout point at Hohenhabsburg, yes, yes, scenic views, return to the Altstädter Platz and continue west over the Bismarckplatz and Wallensteinstraße to the Church of the Holy Cross, built in 1696, we lived in the Wallensteinstraße, dear Herr Kraus, my father admired Wallenstein, my mother hated Wallenstein, my father saw through history, my mother didn't, Wallenstein's corpse wasn't a pretty sight, as my father always said, Wallenstein was the wealthiest and most powerful man of his time, and yet he still lay naked in his casket in Eger like a beaten dog, it was a very plain casket, my father said, frankly just a wooden box cobbled together out of a few coarse planks, the Kaiser would have preferred to have Wallenstein's corpse burned, my father said, but back then Austria didn't have any Feuerhalles yet, yes, yes, dear Herr Kraus, we often fear the dead more than the living, I was baptised in the Church of the Holy Cross and so was my brother, he was a child of the war in 1914, born that summer, died that winter, I didn't know him, my brother's corpse wasn't a pretty sight, my father said, my brother's corpse was beautiful, said my mother, my parents fought terribly over my brother's corpse, yes, yes, they nearly divorced, it wasn't until I came along that they reconciled, the replacement child, me, born in 1918, a child of Czechoslovakia, me, a child of the Feuerhalle in Reichenberg, yes, yes, we should go on foot to Jeschken, elevation 1010 meters, inn, lookout tower, scenic views over Bohemia, yes, yes, *"the beautiful landscape of battlefields, cemeteries and ruins"*, winter sports, sled runs! Sled runs!! Sled runs!!!'

The music had long since ceased to play. The boys had run out of battery. They listened to Winterberg in stunned silence. Winterberg didn't notice and continued to ramble.

He talked on and on to himself. He screamed.

And then he stopped.

It was quiet.

The other passengers in the train stared dumbfounded at Winterberg and Winterberg looked around in surprise, as if he didn't know where he was. Or what was happening.

The train came to a stop at the platform. We were in Reichenberg. The other passengers left the train and we remained sitting in the carriage. Winterberg was sweating and trembling and sweating.

A historical fit.

I had to help him out of the train. All the other passengers were quickly swallowed by the underpass. We remained on the platform, and Winterberg sat down on a bench and drank water and struggled to catch his breath. I lit a cigarette. Winterberg began to cough. I stamped the cigarette out.

It was already dark, as it tends to be in November. I looked out at the black silhouette of the surrounding mountains and saw the light from the hotel tower on the Jeschken. In the darkness, it looked as though the hotel wasn't sitting on top of a mountain but hovering in the air like a little star. The only star in the sky.

Then a light snow began to flutter down.

And Winterberg began to quietly ramble.

'Do you hear that silence? It was just like this back then, yes, yes, on the day when the Czechs had to leave the city, when they handed the city and the station over to the Germans.'

Winterberg talked about the emptiness and the silence that hung over the Reichenberg train station at the beginning of October 1938. He talked about the train station without trains. Without steam locomotives. Without train carriages. Without railwaymen. Without people. 'I still see that emptiness, I still hear that silence, I still have that emptiness before my eyes, yes, yes, that silence before the war, which began in Reichenberg with the smashing of my father's skull in the Ratskeller, yes, yes, that's how it goes in life. My father's corpse wasn't a pretty sight.'

I lit the next cigarette and sat next to Winterberg and he began to talk.

He talked about the trains to Gablonz and Tannwald. About the trains to Turnau and Königgrätz and Prague and Vienna. About the trains to Zittau and Friedland and Görlitz and Berlin. About the cogwheel railway from Tannwald to Grünthal. About the one true mountain train in Bohemia. He explained that laying tracks through the mountains of the Riesengebirge was no less arduous than laying tracks through the Alps. He talked about the trains to Böhmisch Leipa and Bodenbach and Eger.

'It's a wonderful stretch of railway… have you ever been to Eger, dear Herr Kraus?'

'No.'

'A great mistake, dear Herr Kraus! And not only because of Wallenstein, who found his death in Eger, yes, yes, Wallenstein was also our countryman, perhaps we should travel to Friedland and Jitschin and

Prague and Pilsen because of Wallenstein, following in Wallenstein's footsteps, yes, yes, it's worth travelling to Eger for Wallenstein alone... my father admired Wallenstein because he didn't put up with any nonsense, just like my father didn't put up with any nonsense when he built his Feuerhalle despite the resistance from Vienna, yes, yes, my father was the Wallenstein of the Feuerhalle era.'

He flipped quickly through his book.

'Eger, Eger... here... yes... industrial city with 28,000 German inhabitants, all the cities were industrial back then, they don't need to emphasise it over and over again, it's self-evident, I would be rather interested and surprised to see something about a "non-industrial city"... but where was I...'

'In Eger.'

'Yes, yes, sitting atop a hill on the right bank of the Eger river, first documented in 1061... the main city of the Egerland region... train station, station restaurant, the *Bahnhofstraße* leading from the station to the city centre – every city had a Bahnhofstraße back then, the Bahnhof-straße was often the most important and most modern street in the city, the best address, where everyone wanted to live, no one was bothered by the trains and steam locomotives and the loud rail operations, unfor-tunately that's not usually the case now, the Bahnhofstraßen don't have a particularly good reputation these days... now where was I again...'

'In Eger.'

'Yes, yes, precisely... Eger, right, thank you, too many stories...'

Winterberg looked back in his book and read out loud.

'The Bahnhofstraße leads to the medieval market square with a bronze statue of Joseph II by Wilfert, erected in 1887, and a fountain of Roland... yes, yes... the Schiller House, where the famous poet kept a flat in 1791 while doing research for his Wallenstein Trilogy... we're getting closer... yes, yes, of course, the death of Wallenstein is mentioned too... here... yes, yes... look, dear Herr Kraus... the *Stadthaus*, the former living quarters of Mayor Pachelbel, where Wallen-stein was murdered on February 25, 1634, by the Irishman Deveroux, which made Wallenstein a February corpse, as my father always said... yes, yes, you can never trust an Irishman, as the Englishman always said, although he did love to drink Irish beer... inside on the left is the city museum, open in the summer from 7am onwards, but what it's like in the winter, they don't say, perhaps it's closed in winter, that's possible, who would travel to Eger in the winter, better to go to Karlsbad or Marienbad, they're not far at all… yes, yes, entry tickets for 60 hellers, the exhibition catalogue, 20 hellers, I would buy that as a souvenir, left of the anteroom is the Wallenstein room, the "Death Room of the Friedländer", quite beautifully written, don't you think? On the right wall, the polearm he was supposedly speared with, a portrait of Wallenstein, a portrayal of his murder from the year 1736, yes, yes, Wallenstein's corpse was surely a quite a mess… next to the exit is a portrait of Wallenstein as a six-year-old child, yes, yes… wonderful, wonderful, perhaps we should travel to Eger, perhaps we could stay overnight in the Wallenstein room, perhaps that's allowed, these days anything is possible… and when we have enough of Wallenstein, we can go have a look at Eger Castle… uninhabited since 1634 and in ruins since 1734. Scenic views.'

He slammed the book shut.

'Now where was I… yes, yes, Wallenstein and Eger and the train station… I would be interested in the Eger train station more than anything, yes, yes, the great locomotive flight to Eger, does that ring a bell for you, dear Herr Kraus? No, no, I'm not surprised, the locomotive flight to Eger doesn't ring a bell for anyone these days, the murder of Wallenstein has overshadowed everything else, yes, yes, and yet I would be more interested to see the train station, because the locomotive flight to Eger was the greatest act of heroism in the history of the Saxon railway, yes, yes, and it all comes back to the year 1866, when Saxony fought against Prussia… yes, yes, the locomotive flight to Eger could be described as an act of Saxon resistance, as a part of the Saxon partisan war against the Prussians, yes, yes, that's right, Herr Kraus, just like Clausewitz, nearly the whole of Saxony was already occupied by the Prussians and the war was nearly decided, the Prussians had their eyes on the Saxon locomotives, which they wanted to use in the war against Austria, but they found no trains, they were all gone, they were all evacuated to Eger in Bohemia, yes, yes, never before and never again was the train station in Eger so full of locomotives, train traffic was paralysed for weeks as a result, what a shame that the Saxons are so often forgotten by history, because the Saxon train operators were the true heroes of the war of 1866, the Saxons shouldn't be forgotten by history if just for the Eger locomotive flight alone, but the Saxons lost the war of 1866 against Prussia just as much as the Austrians did, just as much as we all did, dear Herr Kraus, because that's how it always is, we all lose in the end, yes, yes, the Reichenberg train station, so many lines, so many tracks, so many switches, much more than in the Berlin main station, yes, yes, so many stories, so much history, the train station was the last place in the city that Lenka saw when she had to flee, the train station was the last place that I saw when I had to go off to war, so many routes, so many possibilities, you can't be surprised when it drives one mad.'

I nodded like I always nodded, and got a bit lost in his stories as I so often got lost in his stories. I lit another cigarette.

'Were you ever here? In Liberec? I mean, since the war?'

'Yes. Once.'

'And how was it?'

'Not good.'

We sat in silence and a shunting locomotive drove by with two empty carriages.

'And you, Herr Kraus? How is it for you?'

'Also not good.'

Winterberg looked at the station clock and then looked at his own watch.

'The clock is on time, yes, yes, the time is correct here. That's interesting. The clock in Dresden was behind.'

We went down the stairs to the underpass.

And there, in the long, cold, yellow tunnel, Winterberg suddenly stopped. As if he wasn't sure himself whether it had been a good idea to go on this trip. To attack Austria and Bohemia and Reichenberg.

And then he said: 'This tunnel is where I saw Lenka for the last time. I brought her to the train, but she didn't want me to come up to the platform, yes, yes, she was afraid that if I did, she wouldn't get on the train.'

We were entirely alone, and every word that Winterberg said echoed back and forth across the long tunnel.

'This is where we said goodbye, yes, yes, and then we never saw each other again.'

THE FEUERHALLE

There were no rail workers in uniform sitting in the station pub that evening. And it didn't reek of coal and soot or even of lubricant, but rather of beer and fryer oil. Each table was occupied by a man sitting alone. The one was young, the other old, and every one of them was staring at his own table.

At his beer glass.

At his phone.

At his newspaper.

Or simply out into space, where a film was playing that only he could see. No one moved. No one spoke. Not even the waitress. She drew one beer after the other while a small golden cross swung above her breasts.

One hand motion. One beer. One life.

Every man to whom the waitress brought a beer looked briefly after her as she walked away. She wore a tight black dress that was the same black as her stockings and her long, dyed hair.

We were the only ones who were sitting at a table together. I ordered a beer, and Winterberg a cola.

And the waitress said: 'Okay.'

And remained standing at the table, looking at me questioningly.

'And? Something to eat, perhaps?'

'No.'

'All right.'

And so we sat there for some time in which we, too, didn't speak. I drank my beer, my first beer in Bohemia after all these years. The foam tasted smooth and creamy, and the beer mild and hoppy.

Although I was very thirsty and above all very eager, I drank the beer slowly, and with each sip, I remembered all the beers that I drank in Bohemia before I had to leave.

I remembered all the friends with whom I'd drank and had to leave behind.

I remembered all the pubs where it was always too loud, because everyone had a story they were eager to get out.

Their memory.

Their opinion.

Their wisdom.

Their own truth.

In the pub it was always so loud that everything was drowned out by the noise. Perhaps that's why none of us ever came home smarter and wiser and had to try again the next night.

I thought about the *Korea* pub in Vimperk. In Winterberg. *Korea* wasn't the name of the pub, but that's what we called it, and no one knew why. It was never as quiet there as it was now in the station pub in Liberec. In Reichenberg. Here all the wisdom had already been shared, all the stories already told. It looked as if something had happened in the country, as if something really had changed in the many years that I'd been gone.

Winterberg opened his book and began to read aloud. Everyone looked over at him and listened, although he was reading in German and they surely wouldn't be able to fully understand him.

'The horse-drawn cabs, yes, yes, especially the ones drawn by two horses, the fiacres, are fast, but not cheap... one can protect himself from price-gouging by agreeing on a specific price in advance, and in the non-German parts of the Monarchy, by reassuring oneself as to whether the coachman can communicate in German, yes, yes, between 20 and 40 hellers for shorter rides, please make note of that, dear Herr Kraus.'

Winterberg continued to read aloud to himself, the men listened, and the waitress drew one beer after another and the golden cross on her breast swung back and forth like a little ship on the high seas.

'For longer trips the price is accordingly higher. In the warmer seasons, steamship cruises, especially on alpine lakes and on the Adriatic Sea, offer a particular allure.'

'You don't need to read it; you already know everything in that book.'

'Says who?'

'Me.'

'You haven't read the book; you have no idea.'

'I saw you earlier in the train, with the boys. You know the whole thing by heart.'

'But I want to read it.'

'But why? You know all of it already. I don't understand.'

'One can never know everything.'

'But you do know it.'

'Leave me be.'

'Yeah, fine, but it's just a bit strange. You're reading aloud from a book that you've long since memorised.'

'Just leave me be!'

Winterberg glared at me. And then continued to read aloud from his book. And I ordered another beer.

'Now where was I … you can't interrupt me while I'm reading, otherwise it's all lost … it's none of your business why I read it, I don't know everything, no one can know everything, only fools believe that they can know everything, you should know that it's impossible to know everything…'

Winterberg read again from his book and I looked at the waitress. She drew the next beer with a single motion.

'Yes, yes, here… on the Adriatic Sea, a particular allure, precisely, precisely.'

A life in a single motion.

'Yes, yes, and if one has the time, on the Elbe between Leitmeritz, Aussig and Dresden…'

All so easy.

'…as well as on the Danube between Passau and Vienna and between Vienna and Pest, although between Belgrade and Orşova the rail connection is preferable.'

All so complicated.

And then Winterberg fell asleep. As suddenly as only he can.

Cork pulled.

Air out.

Eyes closed.

Good night.

He began to snore, and everyone stared at him. The men, the waitress, and myself as well. Winterberg lay with his head on his thick, red book and in front of him stood a cola that he hadn't touched.

I finished my beer, paid, and asked the waitress whether the hotel called *Goldener Löwe* still existed.

She nodded, and I ordered us a taxi.

. . .

I brought Winterberg to his room, went to my room, showered, got into bed, and stared at the ceiling. I couldn't fall asleep. I thought about Hanzi. I thought about our first and last trip together. I also thought about Carla. And then about Silke Winterberg. Perhaps she really was looking for us already. Perhaps I'd be arrested soon.

I got dressed again and went out in front of the hotel to smoke. The parking lot was empty, like the hotel. The city slept peacefully in its dark bed.

I walked through Liberec.

I walked through the empty streets.

I slipped on the wet cobblestones.

I walked on and lit another cigarette.

I walked and walked and looked at the shops, which looked exactly like the shops in Germany.

I walked on and stopped in front of the buildings to read the name plates on the doors.

The Czech names, which felt so foreign to me.

The German names, which felt so familiar to me.

Everything felt so new and so strange and yet so old and familiar.

I walked on through the city, which used to be more German than Czech, and thought back over all the years that I'd been gone.

I walked on and I didn't know where I was going.

I saw a ginger cat sitting on a rubbish bin, a cat on the prowl, watching me. As I came closer and moved to stroke it, the cat ran away.

I walked on and it snowed and despite the snow, the city was becoming darker and emptier and quieter.

I walked on and the buildings above my head in the narrow alley looked like castles and castle ruins that couldn't be reached.

I walked on and in another alley I saw two drunken men peeing against the wall. One of them shouted something after me, I didn't understand him, I turned around only briefly and saw his blackened teeth.

I walked on and found an empty pram with old newspapers that someone had forgotten. I took an old newspaper and under the streetlight I read a bit about the country that I had to leave, and to which I had now returned for the first time.

I walked on and everything was quiet, and I felt unwell. I was sweating and my heart was racing, and it made me think of Agnieszka, who always told me that I should go see a doctor about my heart.

I walked on and the air stunk of brown coal, and it made me think about how it had always stunk of brown coal in Vimperk and how I had somehow forgotten the stench.

I walked on and saw a police car driving slowly through the snowdrifts.

I walked on through the empty, cold, dead city and found a bar where I ordered another beer. The music was playing and a young woman was consoling another young woman who was crying. They were speaking Czech, and the language sounded so familiar and yet so foreign to me at the same time.

I walked on and came to the main square, which was covered in a fresh blanket of snow.

I stopped in front of the towering City Hall, turned around and saw the footprints that I had left in the snow across the square.

They disappeared into the distance.

. . .

The next day, we spent the entire morning on the tram.

The temperature had dropped even further and a light snow was falling again, but it was warm inside the tram. We rode up and down through the city on the number 3 tram, and Winterberg read loudly from his Baedeker and rambled and showed me the city and rambled again and read aloud from his Baedeker.

He showed me the small, inconspicuous house where his father was born.

'In the major cities as well as in the larger spa towns and summer resorts, the top-ranked inns are generally very good, yes, yes, the room prices, especially in the modern luxury hotels, are relatively high.'

He showed me where he went to primary school.

'In order to avoid unpleasant surprises, one should inquire after a room immediately and heed the notices posted in the rooms... look at that, dear Herr Kraus, the Jeschken has disappeared behind the clouds again, yes, yes, if you see the mountain, the rain is coming, and if you don't see it, it's already raining; if it's not raining, it's snowing, and if it's not snowing and you can't see anything, it's often not due to the night, but rather the fog, as my father always said, and that's how it is here to this day, and that's not just true for Reichenberg, but for the entire country, for all of Bohemia, for this whole shallow valley that binds us all together, whether we like it or not, whether we hate each other or love each other, whether we speak Czech or German, yes, yes, dear Herr Kraus, and the most tragic ones, the ones who were most lost, were always those who spoke both languages, like my father, like my Lenka, like you, dear Herr Kraus, because they were aware of the full tragedy... the people who stood in-between were hated the most, and from all sides, there's no escape, yes, yes, my father spoke fluent Czech and I also spoke a bit of Czech, I can still understand a bit of it, yes, yes, but unfortunately too little.'

He showed me where he went to vocational school to become a tram driver.

'My father thought his Feuerhalle would bring together all Bohemians, regardless of whether they spoke Czech or German, he even wrote an article about it in *Die Einäscherung*. Unfortunately, he was wrong.'

He showed me where he'd gotten drunk for the first time and continued to read from his Baedeker.

'In second-class accommodations, the room prices are about one-third lower, and accommodations in the countryside can be quite inexpensive, yes, yes, but outside the German alpine regions, the cleanliness sometimes leaves much to be desired... yes, yes, dear Herr Kraus, that's how it is, it was always very clean at our house, and at the Feuerhalle too, but in the Ratskeller tavern, it always stunk of beer and tobacco and sauerkraut.'

He showed me the park where he'd gotten into his first fight.

'Tips are common at the larger inns in the following amounts: for chambermaids, 40 hellers a day; for stays of three to five days, one crown; for eight days, between one and a half and two crowns; please make note of that.'

He showed me where a horrible tram accident occurred, with many tram corpses, as he called them.

'For room service waiters, one crown per week, for the day porter and night porter one to two crowns each for eight days, hired help for the cleaning of clothes and boots, yes, yes, we'll certainly need that, I had to clean my father's shoes for him every week, yes, yes, he said the shoes needed to shine like the tiles of his Feuerhalle… as well as for the transport of luggage, 50 hellers per day… make note of that, dear Herr Kraus.'

He showed me where the tram line used to run to Rochlitz.

He showed me where the tram line used to run to Rosenthal.

He didn't want to get out and go by foot.

He showed me where Lenka lived.

He showed me where he first met Lenka in a coffeehouse. He just wanted to keep moving.

He showed me the empty lot along the city highway where the Urania cinema once stood, and where they had often gone together.

'Here, look, this is where we saw that film.'

'Which film?'

'*The Woman in the Moon* by Fritz Lang with the beautiful Gerda Maurus playing the lead, yes, yes, Lenka fell in love with her, she wanted to be just like Gerda Maurus in the film, so strong and free… Lenka was already afraid to go to the cinema back then, Henlein's goons were raising hell everywhere, but we went anyway, they used to also show old films at the Urania, even the silent films, which only the older generation and people like us went to see. We saw *Woman in the Moon* here twice… Henlein's goons didn't raise hell in this cinema, they weren't interested in the old films, and yes, the owner, a certain Herr Polatchek, was also a Jew, like Lenka… he fled from Henlein's goons later on, he managed to get away, he had to flee, just like Fritz Lang had to flee, and Lenka, too… yes, yes, he opened a cinema later in Buenos Aires and called it Urania Reichenberg, yes, yes, he only showed German films and did well there, a lot of people lived in Buenos Aires who spoke German and suffered from homesickness, who were happy that someone was showing old German films, films like *Woman in the Moon*… but all the same, Herr Polatchek shot himself later in the foyer of the Urania Reichenberg in Buenos Aires, because he couldn't bear that so many of Henlein's goons came in, they had also fled to Argentina after the war, just as so many Jews fled to Argentina before the war from Hitler's goons, yes, yes, tragic, tragic, bullet-to-the-head corpses aren't a pretty sight, as my father always said… now where was I… yes, I know, across the street was the Hotel *Zentral*, that was also a popular place to go.'

He showed me the building where Lenka's father had his business, before Henlein's goons punched in the windows.

He showed me where the synagogue once stood.

He showed me the house where the man who torched the synagogue along with other men had lived.

'After that, I knew that Lenka had to leave, she was only half Jewish, but we both knew that half was all it took for Lenka to burn like the synagogue. Lenka had relatives in Vienna and Brünn, but then she had to leave those places too, that was apparent, she wanted to go on further, via Budapest, Sarajevo and Greece to Palestine… the last postcard I received from her was from Sarajevo, that's why we need to go there, dear Herr Kraus… I fear that something happened to her in Sarajevo, perhaps we'll find the murderer there… yes, yes, everything is connected to everything else, yes, yes, Königgrätz and Sarajevo and the First World War and Second, yes, yes, why don't you see through history? If you could see through history, you would understand, dear Herr Kraus, how everything is connected; tragic, tragic, it makes me a bit melancholy that you don't see through history, but that's how life is.'

And then we finally alighted from the tram and walked to a tenement building in the Wallensteinstraße where Winterberg used to live. He showed me the window in the third floor. I wanted to ring the doorbell, I thought it would be nice if we could see the apartment, but in the moment that I pressed the button, Winterberg fled. An elderly woman opened the window. I didn't know what to say; I greeted her and then stood in silence and looked around for Winterberg. She assumed that I wanted to sell her something and pulled the window closed.

I ran after Winterberg.

He was angry with me.

'It's over, it's over, you can't do something like that.'

'I'm sorry.'

'I didn't want that.'

'I thought… the woman was actually quite nice.'

'Who asked you to do that?'

And then we fell into silence and walked to the main square. And then down Pražská Street. And suddenly Winterberg saw something in the window of an antique bookstore and disappeared into the shop.

It was snowing again, and I lit a cigarette and watched the people who spoke the language that still seemed so foreign to me, although I understood everything. I had to think again about whether it had been a good idea to return to this country. Again, I felt the fear that I would be arrested. I would be beaten. I would be hanged. I would still be punished today for what happened back then with Hanzi.

Winterberg returned and handed me a book.

Chronological Notes on the History of Winterberg and its Surroundings 1195–1926, written by Josef Puhani, the Forester of Schwarzenberg.

'Incredible… do you know this book?'

'No.'

'You must read it right away, dear Herr Kraus.'

I looked at the book.

'Take it as a Christmas gift. It's not so far off.'

'Sure.'

'Do you like it?'

'Yes.'

'I'm happy that you like it.'

'Yes.'

And I stuffed the book into my backpack and knew that I wouldn't read it.

I don't want to read it.

I can't read it.

I hate this country.

I hate this city.

I hate Winterberg.

I hate Vimperk.

We continued walking and I lit another cigarette.

And then we were standing still, and Winterberg pointed through a gap between the houses.

'There, do you see it? There! That's the mountain of fire, yes, yes, there it is, the world-renowned Feuerhalle of my father and Rudolf Bitzan. That's where we'll go next.'

'So you didn't want to visit your old house… but the crematorium, yes?'

'It's "Feuerhalle". Not crematorium.'

* * *

The Feuerhalle loomed high into the heavens.

We stood in the square before it and Winterberg said:

'My father was a post employee, he was drafted right in the summer of 1914 and already returned to Reichenberg as a wounded veteran that autumn with a bullet in his shoulder blade that the surgeons couldn't remove.'

The Feuerhalle held up the dark, heavy clouds.

'And so his right arm, his whole right half, was nearly frozen, he couldn't properly move it… yes, yes, dear Herr Kraus, as a wounded veteran and a stranded veteran you can only hang yourself or become an undertaker, according to my father, who was a medic in the war and saw plenty of corpses, bullet-to-the-head corpses and gunshot-to-the-gut corpses and gunshot-to-the-throat corpses and hand grenade corpses and artillery shell corpses.'

Everything was still. We could see the city below us. The mountains. The Jeschken.

'Yes, yes, Rudolf Bitzan might have designed a couple of churches, but his Feuerhalle is meant to have nothing in common with a church, no, no, dear Herr Kraus, he imagined the construction rather more like a bird with outstretched wings, like an eagle taking off into the sky and disappearing with the dead, as he told my father… it should all be very simple and clear, because the whole of human life is in fact clear and simple; it's just us who keep turning it into some great problem.'

Winterberg rambled and I thought about my ship. And about my crossing. About our crossing into another world that had been interrupted.

We looked at the two large knights. Two guardians of the dead with eagles' wings made out of sandstone that looked sternly down at us from their towering positions on either side of the entrance, and I lit myself a cigarette. And Winterberg said that I shouldn't smoke and should instead take a closer look at the faces of the guardians of the dead.

'But they're the same.'

'They're not.'

Winterberg told me that the knight on the right carried the face of his father, and the knight on the left carried the face of Rudolf Bitzan.

'I'm probably the last person who knows that… but now you know it too, dear Herr Kraus, that makes me happy… yes, yes, I should really tell my daughter too, but she wouldn't believe me, unfortunately she doesn't see through history at all.'

Winterberg looked at the shields that both knights carried, which hid their legs from view.

'They're the same.'

'Yes, they're the same.'

He looked at the four animals in a circle on the knights' shields.

The eagle.

The snake.

The lion.

The owl.

Strength and freedom.

Rebirth.

Courage.

Wisdom. And the long sleep, as he called it.

And then he looked all the way up at the large words over the entrance. They were in Czech, but he read them aloud in German.

'"*Reines, urgöttliches, herrliches Feuer, nimm in die Arme den erdmüden Leib* – O pure, primal, glorious fire, take this world-weary body into your arms"... yes, yes, my father chose that, he loved poetry, he also dabbled a bit himself... the line comes from Anton August Naaff, a poet from Komotau, my father knew a bit of his work, my father was the absolute exception, because almost no one else knew Naaff, no one had read him and today it's certainly no different. But here Naaff has been immortalised for eternity, this here is his greatest literary achievement... I hope that the Czech translation is good, dear Herr Kraus... I only understand *ohni*... "fire"...'

Then we climbed the steep stairs and I briefly had to help him.

The heavy wooden door was unlocked.

The lights were on and we could hear music.

I didn't want to go in, but Winterberg didn't wait, he pulled open the tall, heavy door and walked right inside.

Music was playing and there weren't many funeral guests sitting in the hall. They looked down at the ground, they looked up at the high ceiling, they looked over to the tall, thin windows, they looked at the wreaths and flowers, they looked at the black coffin on the catafalque. The dead man was named Josef Müller. I thought we would be disturbing them, but no one noticed us come in.

Only one man in a blue suit with a black tie, who was very old and yet still much younger than Winterberg, turned around and looked at us as if contemplating whether he knew us, and asking himself whether perhaps we knew him, too.

We sat down in the last row. The music played and Winterberg once again started to ramble. As always, I wanted to stop him, but he couldn't be stopped.

A historical fit.

Winterberg told me about how the orchestra of the Reichenberg Stadttheater played the prelude to Richard Wagner's *Parsifal* at the opening of the Feuerhalle.

He told me that his father told him that it was a magnificent performance. He told me that his father told him that it brought tears to his eyes. He told me that his father loved music and could also play a bit as well.

'Right there on the left, next to the catafalque, is where they played; that has to be it.'

He told me that it was the dearest wish of the architect Rudolf Bitzan to have *Parsifal* played at the opening of the Feuerhalle. He told me his father would have preferred the *Vltava* by Bedřich Smetana. He told me his father believed that the *Vltava* connected the Bohemian Germans and the Bohemian Czechs. He told me that only music possessed that kind of power.

'Yes, yes, the Moldau binds and reconciles us, yes, yes, that's the magical power of the river, the magical power of music … it binds and reconciles us, just like beer and dumplings and roast pork with sauerkraut and the Battle of Königgrätz bind us, yes, yes, just like Wallenstein binds us, just like the fire of this Feuerhalle binds and reconciles us, as my father always said, all of it binds us together, whether we like it or not … but my father was also fond of *Parsifal*, and above all fond of Rudolf Bitzan, who became his good friend.'

Winterberg looked towards the front, as if the orchestra of the Reichenberg Stadttheater was still playing *Parsifal* there.

A different man in a suit and tie, who was very old and yet still much younger than Winterberg, turned and hissed at us to be quiet. But Winterberg didn't take notice or didn't want to take notice.

'The architect Bitzan named his design for the Feuerhalle the "Fortress of Fire". In fact, my father told me he didn't actually win the competition for its construction, he came in third place, but the Feuerhalle committee chaired by my father liked his design best.'

Winterberg told me how Bitzan and his father had thought about building the Feuerhalle on top of the Jeschken. He told me that the Feuerhalle was supposed to stand right next to the *Berghotel*. He told me it would have been the mountain's crowning achievement. He told me it would have been the crowning achievement of Reichenberg.

'But the transportation of the corpses would have been too burdensome.'

He told me how the Feuerhalle committee then decided on the Monstranzberg Hill. He told me that it wasn't the main square, nor the City Hall, but the Monstranzberg and the Feuerhalle that formed the heart of the city of Reichenberg.

The old man in the black suit with the blue tie turned around and shushed us again. The slow, sombre music played on and Winterberg continued to ramble.

'Yes, yes, dear Herr Kraus, soon I'll be one hundred years old… I'll be exactly as old as this Feuerhalle, exactly as old as the Republic of Czechoslovakia, yes, yes, soon we'll all be celebrating our birthday together, the Feuerhalle, the Republic, and I. We'll celebrate both the birth and the downfall, the establishment of the Republic and the demise of the Monarchy, my birth and the opening of the Feuerhalle in Reichenberg, yes, yes, perhaps there'll be a party here in the Feuerhalle as well, perhaps we should come here next year and celebrate my birthday here together, there's still a bit of time left to go, one more year, and then that's it, then we'll be one hundred years old, me, Czechoslovakia, and our Feuerhalle, it'll be a lovely party, I think we'll have to come.'

The old man in the black suit with the blue tie turned around and shushed us. And the other old man in the blue suit with the black tie also turned around and looked at us as if contemplating whether he really did know us and whether we might know him, too.

'We really should be quiet,' I said.

'We're not bothering the dead man.'

Winterberg briefly stopped talking, the music played, it was an old Czech song that the dead man evidently loved. The widow sobbed and Winterberg started to ramble again.

He told me that his father had the good fortune to be permitted to incinerate the first corpse as the first-ever Feuerhalle Master in Bohemian, no, in Austrian history, atop the Mountain of Fire, in his Fortress of Fire, on the 31st of October, 1918. He told me it was just three days after the overthrow and collapse of Austria and the establishment of Czechoslovakia. He told me the Feuerhalle had already been completed for more than a year, but in old Austria, the burning of corpses hadn't been allowed. He told me they had only cremated two dogs and a horse, because they wanted to make sure that the Feuerhalle was working perfectly. He told me that everything did work perfectly. He told me how it made his father terribly melancholy that the Feuerhalle stood empty for a year and that the ovens were cold. He told me that October 31, 1918, was the greatest day of his life. He told me the first corpse was the corpse of his father Eugen, Winterberg's grandfather, whose father, Winterberg's great-grandfather, fell at the Battle of Königgrätz. He told me his father kept a chronicle of the Feuerhalle.

He had to know everything about each corpse. Their birthplace and birthdate and birth year. Their age at death. Their confession. Their civil status and occupation and place of residence. Their cause of death. The name of the attending physician and the coroner and the medical examiner. The day and the year and the hour of death. The day and the hour of cremation. The day on which the 'ash remains', as he said, were handed over to the relatives.

He told me how reading the chronicles of the Feuerhalle always soothed his father, just as reading the Baedeker always soothed him. He told me his grandfather had actually died at the end of September, making him a September corpse, as his father would have said.

He told me that his father had kept his corpse the entire time in the cold store, because he had a feeling that the old empire was about to collapse. He told me that in the chronicles of the Feuerhalle, each death and corpse and urn carried a number.

He told me his grandfather will always remain Number 1.

The first corpse to be cremated in Reichenberg.

In Czechoslovakia

In Austria.

He told me his grandfather was cremated at ten in the morning on October 31, 1918.

The cause of death was a kidney infection.

He told me the second corpse was cremated that same afternoon at four o'clock.

The cause of death was arterial calcification.

He told me the first suicide was cremated one week later.

The cause of death was a severe gunshot injury.

He told me that his father said the Feuerhalle reconciles everyone with their fate, whether they like it or not.

The music played and the one old man glared at us.

Winterberg told me that his father wrote an article over the first cremation for the readers of *Die Einäscherung*.

'Yes, yes, *Die Einäscherung* was a very popular journal in Reichenberg, because in Reichenberg there were many Friends of Fire Burial and of the Hygienic Movement.'

Winterberg told me that his father wrote about the importance of the downfall of the Monarchy and the establishment of Czechoslovakia on October 28, 1918, for the Feuerhalle.

'You can't buy *Die Einäscherung* any more these days, tragic, tragic, *Die Einäscherung* was a very good publication, perhaps it would have more readers these days, since more people opt for cremation now compared to then, these days it's progressive, these days the Feuerhalles are successful businesses, and at the beginning of this success story stands my father and his Feuerhalle.'

The music played and the widow cried and the one old man glared at us again and shushed.

'My father loved Czechoslovakia, which is something you certainly can't say about all the Germans in Reichenberg, no, no, many of the Reichenberg Germans hated Czechoslovakia, yes, yes, they hated this new freedom, and so it shouldn't surprise anyone that they went on to crush Czechoslovakia and greeted Hitler with the Nazi salute on the main square in front of City Hall, including my mother, yes, yes, Hitler met with no resistance in Reichenberg, everyone loved Hitler and Henlein, and not just my mother... I did too.'

He told me that his father was a staunch Czechoslovak Republican. He told me that his mother was a staunch anti-Czechoslovak anti-Republican. He told me that his father didn't like Austria, because Austria had allowed him and Rudolf Bitzan to build a Feuerhalle and yet forbade them to cremate anyone. He told me that his mother loved Austria. He told me that his mother longed for the old times and for the Kaiser and for the beautiful blue uniforms of the Imperial Royal Army and for the many wonderful trips to Vienna or Salzburg. He told me that his mother had actually never been to Vienna or Salzburg.

'My mother wasn't interested in the Feuerhalle, no, no, my mother didn't want to be cremated, I believe she was ashamed of my father, to her he was a heretic, just like Jan Hus, who was cremated atop an execution pyre in Konstanz in 1415, yes, yes, my father was a die-hard Protestant and my mother was a die-hard Catholic, and when they fought with the window open towards the Wallensteinstraße, it really looked like the next Bohemian Defenestration, yes, yes, as far as defenestrations are concerned, we Bohemians are world champions, regardless of whether we speak German or Czech, yes, yes, and when anyone around the world gets it in their head to plan a defenestration, an overthrow, a collapse, they ought to come to Bohemia first and ask how it works, and above all, how it worked out afterwards, yes, precisely, precisely, I know what you'd like to say, dear Herr Kraus, the many Bohemian defenestrations and overthrows and collapses and defenestration corpses and overthrow corpses… I always thought it'd be either my father flying out of the window or else my mother, no, no, defenestration corpses aren't a pretty sight… I thought I'd then be either fatherless or motherless, and I wondered which would be better… yes, yes, in our flat in the Wallensteinstraße it often looked like the next Thirty Years' War between the Protestants and the Catholics, it looked like the next Battle of White Mountain near Prague, it looked like the next Battle of Lützen, where the Swedish King Gustav Adolf fell in combat after he lost his unit in the fog and was ambushed and shot by imperial soldiers, yes, yes, there we have it again, the fog of war, just as it occurred later at Königgrätz and at Austerlitz, the fog isn't to be underestimated, not in war, not in human existence, not with the railway, not in love, yes, yes, everyone ought to read Clausewitz… now where was I again…'

'We should be a bit quieter.'

Winterberg trembled and continued to ramble.

'Yes, yes, I know… but it all turned out differently, even my anti-Czechoslovak mother had to cry when my father became victim to his Czechoslovak sympathies, when on March 15, 1939, in the Reichenberg Ratskeller, a day labourer from a cement factory and brain-dead Heinlein lad and Hitler lad, yes, yes, that's right, a Henlein goon and a Hitler goon, took a beer mug and shattered my father's skull, because my father opined that there was nothing to celebrate about that day, certainly not the Wehrmacht's invasion of Prague, yes, yes, and so my father became a March corpse, as he would say.'

He rambled and trembled and cleaned his glasses and trembled and rambled. And the one old man shushed. And the other old man looked at us as if he knew us, and we knew him.

He told me that on that evening, his father was sitting all alone in the Ratskeller. He told me it wasn't the first time his father sat at the table alone. He told me that no one had wanted to share a table and have a beer with his father for some time. He told me that Rudolf Bitzan was already dead by then. He told me that he, too, has been cremated by his father. He told me about the side-eyes and rude remarks. He told me how his father didn't much like the beer in the Reichenberg Ratskeller anymore. He told me that he still went there every evening. He told me his father hoped that he could still chat with his drinking mates. He told me no one wanted to chat with his father anymore. He told me how his mother told his father that it was all his own fault.

'Yes, yes, she told him, it's your own fault, you're ashamed to be German, no one is ashamed to be German these days, how daft can you be... and so my father sat all alone in the Ratskeller and drank beer and read this very Baedeker, yes, yes, he read all the old stories that he used to mock, that he used to describe as fairy-tales, he read and dreamed about an old, lost world, which may not have had any Feuerhalles, but which also had no Hitler and no Henlein... and I'm certain that he was reading it aloud, yes, yes, and this image makes me very melancholy, dear Herr Kraus... my father, who so deeply loved other people and never drank beer alone, because no one in Bohemia can be permitted to drink beer alone, and if someone is damned to drink their beer alone, that's the greatest punishment one could imagine... yes, yes, he was suddenly abandoned by every-one in the Ratskeller, just as Wallenstein was abandoned by everyone in Eger.'

He told me how his mother became a widow. He told me how his father was cremated in his own Feuerhalle. He told me not many mourners came to his cremation.

'Tragic, tragic, my father ought to have earned a big, beautiful crema-tion, no one in Reichenberg was as excited about the new Republic and the opening of the Feuerhalle as my father. Least of all my mother, who wasn't cremated in the Feuerhalle, because she suffered an accident in the bathtub during a spa treatment in the summer of 1941 in Karlsbad and lies buried over there...'

The one old man looked around at us and shushed.

Winterberg told me his father's corpse was unfortunately not a pretty sight. He told me that unfortunately he doesn't know if his mother's corpse was a pretty sight. He told me he hadn't seen his mother's corpse. He was already off at the war.

'Yes, yes, my mother hated Czechoslovakia, my father loved Czechoslovakia. My father lost his father to the flames of the Reichenberg Feuerhalle and on the same day gained me at the Reichenberg Hospital, and the orchestra of the Reichenberg Stadttheater accompanied the first cremation in this new country and my birth with the prelude to Richard Wagner's *Parsifal*... the memories of this day always made my father a bit joyful and at the same time a bit melancholy, sometimes more melancholy and sometimes more joyful, sometimes he thought more about his father, sometimes more about me, but he always remembered this first cremation. Yes, yes, the first cremation in Reichenberg runs through my heart just like the Battle of Königgrätz... it makes me more melancholy than joyful.'

The last piece of music began to play, a beautiful, tranquil piece of classical music, and Winterberg turned to me in amazement, and then looked around in amazement, as if he were searching for someone.

'No... no... that's it.'

'What.'

'Wagner's *Parsifal*. The prelude.'

I didn't recognise the music.

'It doesn't surprise me that you don't know it, but that's what it is. Just as it was back then. Nothing has changed in Reichenberg. Oh, how I love this music, and how I hate it... when I die, please don't play Wagner, but rather Smetana... this music haunts me, why has it been haunting me, dear Herr Kraus?'

He told me about the coffins with the corpses that were sent by train to Reichenberg from Vienna and Graz and Linz and Villach and Salzburg and Brünn and Prague and Pilsen and Königgrätz. He told me that the friends of fire burial and hygiene were everywhere, and that they wanted to be cremated in Reichenberg. He told me that in the Reichenberg Feuerhalle, the Monarchy continued to exist despite the collapse. He told me about zinc coffins and oak coffins and beech coffins and spruce coffins. He told me how he had often played in the

Feuerhalle as a small boy and knew every corner. He told me that he wasn't afraid because no one needed to be afraid. He told me that it wasn't the flames in the oven, in the core, as he called it, that embraced a human corpse and burned it to ash. It was the hot air, a sweltering storm, a scorching tornado, as his father said. He told me that the flowers burn first, then the coffin, then the clothes, and then the corpse.

'Yes, yes, and after an hour and a half, everyone fits in a three-litre urn.'

'Can you please just stop?'

But Winterberg wasn't listening to me or didn't want to listen to me and continued to ramble.

'Yes, yes, that's how it is, everything in life can be overcome like the Alps by the railway, except for death.'

'We're disturbing them here.'

'Yes, yes, that's how it is… and then the soul can drift off.'

The eulogist then stood up and told us to stand up as well. And the widow stood up, and so did the other funeral guests, and so did Winterberg and I. The music played and the coffin with Josef Müller disappeared slowly and gently into the depths of the Feuerhalle and everyone cried and Winterberg and I cried as well.

And then Winterberg went to make his way to the widow in order to console her.

The old man in the black suit with the blue tie intercepted him and glared at him. And the other old man in the blue suit with the black tie also approached us and said:

'Karl. Karl. Já to věděl. I knew it. You came!'

'Yes.'

The man embraced Winterberg.

But the other man said:

'Co seš to za nevychovaného idiota, co neumí držet chvíli hubu?'

He was glaring angrily at Winterberg.

'But this is Karl! Leave him be; this is Josef's older brother! Jeho brácha… Karl! You're looking well.'

'Yes.'

And then Winterberg squeezed the widow's hand and said:

'My sincerest condolences. I loved him dearly. And missed him so.'

The widow cried.

'It's Karl. Karl from Dortmund, his brother…'

The widow, a small, fragile woman, embraced Winterberg.

'We've missed you so much. You got our letter after all… it's so wonderful that you're here… and is this your son?'

And Winterberg looked at me and said:

'Yes, this is my son.'

. . .

They invited us to join the funeral party at the Ratskeller tavern.

There was beer and schnapps and goulash and beer and schnapps. Winterberg told his stories, and everyone was thrilled that Karl, the older brother of Josef Müller, was still alive. Winterberg told his stories and I often had to translate, as not all of them understood German.

Winterberg rambled on and someone expressed surprise that Karl could barely speak Czech anymore. Winterberg said he'd learn it again. He took out his magnifying glass and opened up his Baedeker.

'The most important words for travellers are, for example, *hostinec* – inn, *restaurace* – restaurant, *pokoj* – room, *postel* – bed, *svíčka* – candle, *oheň* – fire, *jídelna* – dining room, *vidlička* – fork, *nůž* – knife, *sklenice* – glass, *láhev* – bottle, *voda* – water, *víno* – wine, *pivo* – beer, yes, yes, that's very important, *pivo*, as we can see…'

Winterberg read out loud and everyone at the table laughed and raised their glasses and imitated Winterberg as he read.

He learned Czech and they learned German and the widow said, yes, yes, just as my Josef said, it was always a riot with you.

'*Káva* – coffee, *chléb* – bread, *maso* – meat, precisely, precisely, and so on with everything one needs to survive… yes, yes, *železnice* – railway, that's very important, *nádraží* – train station, that's vital, yes, yes, *vchod* – entrance, *východ* – exit… the Czech word for "Feuerhalle" isn't here, unfortunately… and here's even a full sentence: *průvodce, doveďte mne do X – Führer*, driver, take me to X… *Führer… Führer…* I don't know… we probably shouldn't say that anymore, don't you think… moving on… *nosič* – porter, yes, yes, that's a lovely word… *pomalu* – slow, *rychle* – fast, *dobrý* – good, *špatný* – bad, *příliš drahý* – too expensive…

but the most important word is surely still *pivo*. But take care; beer corpses aren't a pretty sight.'

Everyone laughed and repeated what Winterberg was saying.

'*Pivo, pivo, pivo, pivo* … beer, beer, beer, beer…'

But Winterberg suddenly became silent and stared over at a large table in the corner. Four young Czechs were sitting at the table and drinking beer and laughing.

'What's wrong?' I asked.

'That's where it happened.'

'Where what happened?'

'That must be the table.'

'What table?'

'That's where they shattered my father's skull. Yes, yes, my father's corpse was truly not a pretty sight.'

FROM REICHENBERG TO KÖNIGGRÄTZ

The next day, we were standing back at the train station. I smoked a cigarette and was warned by the conductor that smoking was not allowed on the platform. Winterberg studied an old diesel locomotive. Behind it was a row of several train wagons filled with coal. And then we boarded the train and waited for it to leave the station. Winterberg looked at the coal train and said:

'The history of modern warfare is tied to the history of the railway and also to the history of Feuerhalles, yes, yes, the coal was transported via rail to Reichenberg and then by car up to the fortress of fire, my father actually wanted Moravian coal, from Ostrau, he thought the coal from Ostrau was much better than the coal from Kladen, but Ostrau was far away, farther than Kladen, and so it would have been too expensive… the first stoker at the Feuerhalle was called Ponocný, an expert, according to my father; he had previously worked as a stoker on a steam locomotive, I suspect on a 434.0, built in Floridsdorf in Vienna, yes, yes, they could often be seen in Reichenberg pulling the heavy freight trains. Ponocný said that for him not much changed, the firebox of a locomotive was always hungry, just like the hearth of the Feuerhalle, which he also called a "firebox", yes, yes, and he called the two furnaces in the fiery tomb, Furnace No. 1 and Furnace No. 2, the "cores"… he liked his new job in the Feuerhalle, because he often caught cold from the drafts in the locomotive, and there was no danger of that in the fiery tomb.'

He told me that the 434.0 was a wonderful and powerful locomotive. He told me it was developed for the heavy freight trains of the Arlberg Railway and the Brenner Railway and the Semmering Railway. He told me that even on the lines between Turnau and Reichenberg and Reichenberg and Böhmisch Leipa, which of course can't be compared with the Alps, the railwaymen held the sheer power of the 434.0's firebox in great esteem. He told me that in the First World War, a freight train without a 434.0 at the front was nearly unthinkable.

At the front of a train carrying infantry.

At the front of a train carrying artillery.

At the front of a train carrying the dead and wounded.

'Yes, yes, in the First World War, too, the locomotives of the 434.0 series from Floridsdorf in Vienna really showed what they could do.'

The train was not full, and soon began to move.

We rolled past the maintenance depot, and Winterberg said that the stoker Ponocný had often brought him here when he visited his old colleagues. He told me that the other stokers mocked him, that they called him 'corpse-burner' and refused to shake his hand because they believed it would cause their early death.

We rolled past tracks with freight wagons. Past the tall signal box. Past a small hill.

But then the train braked and came to a stop.

Winterberg looked over at the hill. A diesel locomotive pushed freight wagons loaded with wood towards the slope and then braked, allowing two of the wagons to detach and roll down the hill.

'A hump yard. Or a *"Rollberg"*, as we called it.'

Winterberg watched as the next wagon rolled down the hill.

He told me the 'Rollberg' had already been here back in his time. He told me he often came to the train station as a child with his father. He told me his father was pleased with his passion for locomotives and for the railway. He told me they often watched the shunting together. He told me how it always fascinated him to see how one train forms into new trains. How they disintegrate over the hump yard. How they perish. How the new trains were reborn below the hump.

And then he said nothing more and simply watched how the train continued to come apart.

'We're nothing more than these wagons, dear Herr Kraus. We don't know what's happening to us, either… the only question is: who is driving the locomotive that pushes us over the hump and lets us fall, yes, yes…'

Then our train finally began to move again and the conductor apologised for the delay. The brakes protested slightly.

We were in Rychnov u Jablonce. A small family got off and a small family got on.

And Winterberg looked in his Baedeker and said:

'Reichenau bei Gablonz… precisely… branch line to Gablonz, yes, yes, by "branch line" they probably mean the tram line, it doesn't seem to exist anymore, yes, yes, I only see a bus, you see buses everywhere, buses are spreading like the plague, bus transport is the death of rail transport… if you ask me, I would ban buses, and cars too. And the worst of all is rail replacement service with buses, just the thought makes me physically ill, yes, yes, it really is that bad, dear Herr Kraus, I would prefer to walk.'

We were in Hodkovice nad Mohelkou.

And Winterberg said:

'Liebenau. They already spoke German here… in Reichenberg it was a bit mixed, but here they spoke almost exclusively German.'

We were in Synchrov. And Winterberg said:

'Synchrov, here they spoke more Czech, coming right up here is a long tunnel, yes, yes, my fateful tunnel, without this tunnel I wouldn't be here, yes, yes, somewhere up there must be the castle and the park of the Prince of Rohan, I was often there too, yes, yes, all tunnels have secrets, yes, yes, this tunnel was built by the Italians, my father said, and my mother said I was conceived in this tunnel… the train was stuck here for some time, the locomotive didn't have much steam, they had a long wait, my mother said, until the water in the boiler could be cooked up to steam, and in the meantime, they cooked me up too, my mother told me about it once when she was a bit drunk, yes, yes, my mother didn't usually drink much, yes, yes, it was probably after a family get-together, I can't remember anymore, but I know that without steam, even the strongest and best steam locomotive can't go anywhere, the stoker has to always keep an eye on the steam manometer, otherwise it can all happen quickly, the train gets stuck halfway down the line without steam, yes, yes, in a tunnel… above all, the mountain lines were always a challenge for the stokers, always a gruelling test, they often needed to send a second locomotive down the line to help the crippled train, in Reichenberg there was always a locomotive in the depot primed and ready to go in order to help other locomotives stranded on the line, yes, yes, trains can almost always be helped, but men, unfortunately not… where was I again?'

'The tunnel,' I said, and our train had already long left the tunnel.

'Yes, yes, precisely, I know, without steam you can't make any children either, making love seems quite similar to a train running through the mountains, yes, yes, all the groaning and sighing, as I said, this long tunnel is my fateful tunnel… where were you cooked up, dear Herr Kraus, if I may ask? No, no, you don't need to tell me… the tunnels should keep their secrets, we'll surely learn a bit more about the construction of tunnels, about the laying of tracks over and under the mountains, especially the Alps, yes, yes, perhaps when we're in Austria.'

We were in Turnov.

And Winterberg looked out of the window and then in his Baedeker and said:

'Turnau, they only spoke Czech here, but of course everyone understood German as well, yes, yes, that's how it was back then, people understood each other… train station restaurant, *Grand Hotel* inn on the market square, train station hotel, a small hilltop city on the Iser… Iser is an old Celtic name, dear Kraus, just like the Moldau or the Eger, yes, yes, the Celts settled in this Bohemian valley long before the Germans and the Slavs, but who remembers that these days, Turnau was violated so many times by history, yes, yes, by the Hussites and by the Prussians and for the last time perhaps by the Wehrmacht, of course I don't know what happened here in 1968, but as you can see, the city seems to have more or less recovered well from the blows of history, yes, yes, lovely, lovely, only the tower of St. Mary's Church still hasn't been completed, you see there, on the other side, behind the trees, dear Herr Kraus, my father said that people would place bets on when the tower of St. Mary's Church would finally be completed… now where was I?'

'In Turnov.'

'Yes, yes, Turnau, precisely, a significant garnet industry… my mother loved the red Bohemian garnets that were as dark red as human blood, yes, yes, like *Cornus sanguinea*, my father gave her several earrings with garnets and also a stunning necklace, yes, yes, for our engagement I also gave Lenka a necklace with blood-red Bohemian garnets, she took the necklace with her on the journey from Reichenberg to Palestine, yes, yes, on her last journey, when I think about the blood-red necklace on her long, thin, pale neck, it immediately makes me think about *"the beautiful landscape of battlefields, cemeteries and ruins"*, as the Englishman always said, yes, yes, that makes me a bit melancholy, the entire tragedy and beauty reflected in this blood-red necklace, there's no escape … now where was I again just now …'

'In Turnov.'

'Yes, yes, precisely, in Turnau, thank you … does it happen that often to you, too, dear Herr Kraus, that you so often forget where you were? Yes, yes, I know what you're going to say, too many stories, too much history, there's no escape, one can only lose themselves, yes, yes, you're right, dear Herr Kraus, perhaps one even has to lose themselves and hope to find an exit, to come out of this fog alive again and with a clear head. But I often fear that you can't find the exit, you can only lose your mind, the trains roll on, the Feuerhalles roll on, and history, too, rolls on, now where did I leave off again …'

'In Turnov.'

'Where?'

'In Turnov.'

'Yes, yes, precisely, Turnau, you can't keep interrupting me so often, dear Herr Kraus … here … a worthwhile hike on foot from Turnau to Trosky, yes, yes, through the woods to the poorly constructed Waldstein ruins with a panoramic view, the ancestral castle of the Friedländer built on and in the rocky hillside, as far as I know, Wallenstein didn't take much care of the castle; of Jitschin yes, of Friedland too, but not of Waldstein; it was already a ruin during his time, yes, yes, Wallenstein also had other things to worry about at the time … where was I …'

'Turnov.'

'Yes, yes, that's right, Turnau, thank you, continue along a good forest path, a lovely view on the left towards Groß-Skal, the palace of the Baron von Aehrenthal, across from the good hotel-restaurant *Stekl*, precisely, I was there, I actually wanted to marry Lenka there, it's truly beautiful, perhaps we should go there next time, from here one may undertake the journey in three hours, yes, yes, there and back, at the behest of the *Führer*, the guide, that's really what it says here, but of course we'll manage it without a guide, dear Herr Kraus, yes, yes, a visit to the worthwhile Trosky ruins, located on and between two tall, rugged melaphyre rocks, Panna… what does Panna mean again? I've forgotten.'

'Virgin.'

'Exactly, the Virgin… and Baba. Along with a tavern. What does Baba mean?'

'A very old, not particularly beautiful woman.'

'Exactly, a virgin and an old, not particularly beautiful woman, they go very well together, the life of a woman portrayed in a castle ruin, that's art, dear Herr Kraus, they should bring the whole ruin to Berlin and put it on exhibition, my second wife loved exhibitions, yes, yes, she was an exhibition woman… my first wife was more of a theatre woman and my third more of a cinema woman… yes, yes, from Groß-Skal up through the mousehole passage and keep to the right, hiking trails lead off to the worthwhile "rock city" with manifold stone formations, but we're already travelling onwards… the train line from here offers a series of splendid forest and sandstone landscapes, yes, yes, a very romantic land-scape, it soothes me, it makes me less melancholy, I would recommend a train journey like this to anyone, far fewer people would hang them-selves if they would take a similar train journey through the beautiful countryside, through history, just like we're doing…'

We were in Malá Skála and Winterberg said:

'Kleinskal, yes, yes, not to be confused with Groß-Skal, that could perhaps throw someone… on the right bank of the Iser, a pantheon with a memorial for the wars of liberation in the Napoleonic era, yes, yes, war everywhere, even in this romantic valley, there's no escape… there, look, somewhere around there, a classmate of mine drowned himself in the Iser, Lanky Max… I don't remember his actual name, we called him Lanky Max, tragic, tragic, a bit weak in the head, but a talented football player, he always wanted to play for Rapid Reichen-berg, yes, yes, they only managed to fish Max out of a flood guard on the Iser well past Turnau several weeks later, my father said that unfor-tunately Max's corpse wasn't a pretty sight, my father didn't like water corpses, because they reminded him too much of the 'water corpse' sausages that he loved to eat in the Ratskeller, you know the ones I mean – those Bohemian sausages marinated in vinegar for weeks at a time… oh, another tunnel, just like it says in my book, you see… and now we're travelling through the Lischnei tunnel, just like it says in my Baedeker, all just as it was in 1913, it's not a fairy-tale, like my father often said about the book, everything is still there…'

We were in Železný Brod and Winterberg said:

'Eisenbrod, train station restaurant, branch line to Tannwald-Schumburg, on the right the large *Neu-Hamburg* factory, yes, yes, the Hamburgers are also everywhere, my neighbour in Berlin was from Hamburg, he didn't see through history at all, he didn't even know where Reichenberg is, he didn't even know where the name of the Reichenberger Straße in Kreuzberg came from, tragic, tragic, and he never said hello, I always had to greet him first so that he would greet me… now where was I again…'

'In Hamburg.'

'Yes, yes, but what links Eisenbrod with Hamburg, that I don't know, unfortunately… perhaps the water of the Iser, yes, yes, and then the Elbe… but what I know for certain is that my mother got all the glasses in her kitchen from Eisenbrod. And in the Reichenberg Ratskeller, too, they only drank beer out of beer mugs from Eisenbrod, they were very popular among innkeepers because they were so heavy and firm and indestructible, yes, yes, and it was true, the beer mugs were indestructible, unlike the human skull, unfortunately, and so my father died instantly when it happened to him in the Ratskeller… we should sit on the right side of the train, according to my Baedeker, come, Herr Kraus, we have to sit on the right.'

Winterberg stood up and moved over to the right side, and I did as well. The valley was narrow and the forest thick and dark and the trees dusted with snow and the train a bit fuller. And suddenly the valley was even narrower and the Iser even wilder. The rapids crashed over the stones and logs that lay in the river, and the rocks were so sharp that one could slit their wrists, as Winterberg said.

We saw stone and rock.

We saw the river and the forest.

We saw snow and ice.

'Yes, yes, precisely, the train enters the romantic Iser valley, four tunnels, isn't it lovely, I've already ridden this train a number of times of course, back then, with Lenka as well, wonderful, wonderful, the tunnels and the wild Iser.'

We were in Semily and many of the passengers left the train.

And Winterberg said:

'Semil, no station restaurant, tragic, tragic, but look, there are some men standing at the kiosk and drinking beer, how much beer does one need to drink to get a belly like that, yes, yes, beer corpses aren't a pretty sight, as my father always said… not far is the Isertal industrial park, yes, yes, the city has no military importance, but my father loved it here, because the first electric Feuerhalle in Central Europe was built in Semil in 1937, yes, yes, no coal, no soot, just electricity, all much cleaner, much more hygienic, the electric Feuerhalle in Semil was a real first, as my father always said, just like our Feuerhalle in Reichenberg was the first Feuerhalle in Austria… Semil was always known for its woodworking industry, the best wooden toys came from here and so did the best wooden coffins, yes, yes, they built coffins from the planks and toys from the scraps, yes, yes, the toys and the coffins, those were the major exports from Semil, as my father always said, before the First World War they delivered wooden toys and wooden coffins as far as Vienna with the railway, and so my father always ordered the wooden coffins for his Feuerhalle here, a full freight wagon of coffins each month, often two, sometimes even three, seldom four… it always depended on the weather and the season… most of the coffins were in the standard sizes, of course, but there were always a few children's coffins too, and some larger and particularly sturdy coffins for the heavier corpses, yes, yes, precisely, for the beer corpses, yes, yes, my father had to think about them too, those coffins were of course a bit more expensive, but you have to take that into account when you're a beer lover… yes, yes… now where was I…'

'Semily.'

'Yes, precisely, my father was often here, he always inspected and selected the coffins before ordering them, and then he'd always go out for goulash. My mother found out later that it wasn't just for the coffins that he was so often in Semil, he had something going with the secretary from the coffin factory, yes, yes, whether they still produce such lovely children's toys here, such lovely coffins, which burned so well… yes, yes, it's exactly as it says in my Baedeker, look at that, dear Herr

Kraus, it's good that we're sitting on the right-hand side, the train enters the Woleschka valley, multiple viaducts, I'm looking forward to it.'

We travelled over a short, high bridge. On our left, a set of tracks and another train; on our right, a set of tracks and another train; all three trains were heading in the same direction.

We were in Stará Paka. A railworker sat down next to us and read the newspaper.

And Winterberg said:

'Alt-Paka, station restaurant, looks like it's closed, unfortunately... look at that, dear Herr Kraus, how red the soil is here, my father said the soil here was bleeding, this is where the Bohemian garnets were born, but personally I think the soil in Königgrätz bleeds a lot more than this. We could take the train to the Riesengebirge here, to Trautenau or Hohenelbe, I went hiking there with Lenka once, or via Chlumetz to Prague, or via Lomnitz an der Popelka and Sobotka to Jungbunzlau, yes, yes, Rudolf Bitzan built a house in Lomnitz too, not a Feuerhalle though, but a residential building for the workers of a textile factory, my father and I visited Bitzan at the construction in Lomnitz once, yes, yes, I was quite small back then, I can't remember Lomnitz an der Popelka at all, just the train ride through the many tunnels, just Bitzan's house, just the brewery, yes, yes, Wallenstein had the beer from Lomnitz an der Popelka delivered to him on the battlefield, yes, yes, to Lützen or to Stralsund, while he laid siege to the city... yes, yes, Wallenstein only wanted to drink the good beer from Lomnitz, who knows whether he was able to drink that beer from Lomnitz in Eger, I suspect not, perhaps that's why he was so weak, so alone, so abandoned... whether the Wallenstein brewery is still there, whether Bitzan's house is still there, who knows, who knows... perhaps we could go to Lomnitz too, yes, yes, I know what you're going to say, there are so many possibilities, so many lines, so many stories, and only one lifetime, how can you possibly do it all, yes, yes, you're right, dear Herr Kraus, you can't possibly do it all, that makes me a bit melancholy, yes, yes... the train continues through a wooded area, as it says in my book... the train reaches its highest elevation here at the Borowitz Plateau, 520 metres... petrified forest near the village of Stupná, lovely, lovely, you don't see that very often, a petrified forest, what a shame that history can't be petrified, that it continues to rip us limb from limb, it makes me a bit melancholy. Yes, yes, exactly, just as it says in my Baedeker, the train reaches the green, meadow valley of the Elbe, with the ridge of the Glatzer Mountains and the Riesengebirge visible in the distance to the east and the north.'

We were in Dvůr Králové and the railworker folded up his newspaper and left the train.

'Königinhof. *Deutsches Haus* inn… yes, yes, perhaps next time, a city with 15,000 Czech inhabitants, why do they recommend the *Deutsches Haus* then, I don't know about that, were you ever here, dear Herr Kraus? I've never been here, yes, yes, how exciting, listen to this… the name is well-known thanks to the Königinhof Manuscript discovered by Václav Hanka in 1817, yes, yes, have you ever heard of it, Herr Kraus? Fragments of old Czech folk songs, yes, yes, but it was a forgery, it's kept at the National Museum in Prague, perhaps we should go take a look at this nationalist hoax, yes, yes, it happens over and over again, it never ends, when the one wants to be greater and more important than the other, then…'

And then Winterberg finally conked out.

Cork pulled.

Air out.

Eyes closed.

Good night.

And in the train it was suddenly so quiet that I fell asleep too.

I dreamed about Carla. I dreamed about us. About our trip which never took place. I embraced her. And she embraced me. So tightly that I could no longer breathe.

My heart raced.

My heart burned.

My heart hurt.

I was sweating again and felt afraid and woke up.

The train stumbled over the switch points. We were in Jaroměř. And Winterberg also awoke.

'Now where was I? Yes, yes, Jaroměř.'

And I thought, I'll grab him now by his coat. I'll drag him to the door and toss him out and he'll stay here forever. He can prattle on here for as long as he likes.

'Station restaurant, precisely, precisely, it's still here, Hotel *Veselý*, who knows if it's still around … somewhere around here is Josephstadt, a military fortress until 1888, just like Theresienstadt, yes, yes, Josephstadt is easy to defend, you can flood the whole landscape with the Elbe, yes, yes, what a shame that no one thought to flood it in 1866, Josephstadt has a good rail connection through Jaroměř, we really should see it, yes, yes, perhaps we can manage that too, perhaps we can manage to visit both cities, the sister fortresses of Josephstadt and Theresienstadt, as the Englishman always said …'

'Herr Winterberg?'

'… two sister fortresses and two sister cities, the Englishman knew Bohemia quite well …'

'Herr Winterberg …'

'Hermanitz must not be that far either, the small village where Wallenstein was born …'

'Herr Winterberg … hello?'

'The Englishman was there, yes, yes, not every village and not every city had the fortune to survive Wallenstein and the Thirty Years' War, but Hermanitz survived all of it, yes, yes, perhaps we'll go there too.'

'Herr Winterberg, can you hear me?'

'Yes, of course, I'm not deaf. What is it?'

'Nothing. Can you please just say nothing for a bit? Is that possible?'

'I'm not saying anything.'

'You're jabbering on the whole time.'

'Me?'

'Yes.'

'That's not true.'

'It is.'

'I'm not the one doing the talking.'

'So who is, then?'

'You.'

'Me?'

'Yes, yes, you're chatting away the whole time.'

'What?'

'Yes, you. You're constantly asking me questions and then I have to answer.'

'No, you're rambling on the entire time. I don't need to ask you anything.'

'Me?'

'Yes.'

'Really?'

'Yes. You don't notice?'

'I do... yes, all right... that might be true, perhaps I am rambling... yes, yes, perhaps I'm rambling a bit, but I can't help it. I have to tell it. I thought it interested you.'

'Yeah, but... it's just...'

'You don't find it interesting?'

'I do, but...'

'Well, there you have it. It can't be too much if it's interesting.'

But then it actually happened. Winterberg went silent. He looked gloomily out of the window, didn't say a word, and his book sat open on the little table.

'I don't have to say anything if it's not wanted.'

'You can. Of course you can... just not so much.'

'But it's complicated, don't you understand? You can't just tell the one story if you want to understand the history, if you want to understand us.'

'I'm also just tired, the beer yesterday...'

'Yes, yes, that's what I thought... my father would eat a hefty broth when it was him... well, it is how it is, not everyone can see through history... people today would rather get emotionally invested in a polar bear at the zoo than in history, yes, yes, that makes me a bit melancholy.'

'Uh-huh.'

I stood up and went to the toilet. I lit a cigarette in the narrow cabin and looked down through the hole in the toilet bowl at the rails and sleepers and ballast racing by underneath the train.

By the time I returned, we were almost arriving in Hradec Kralové.

And Winterberg opened his book and read aloud.

'Königgrätz... industrial city... fortified until 1893... on the western side of the Ringplatz, the Gothic cathedral, founded in 1312, with a beautiful tabernacle from 1492, that doesn't interest me in the slightest, honestly... I'm only interested in the Battle of Königgrätz. Exactly, look at that, dear Herr Kraus, here, the branch line to Sadowa, that interests me too, yes, yes, that's where we'll go… I'm telling you, without the battle of 1866, no one would know Königgrätz today, yes, yes, the city of Königgrätz should forever thank the Saxons and the Prussians and the Austrians for the catastrophe of Königgrätz.'

'The city of Königgrätz should be thankful for the catastrophe of Königgrätz?'

'Yes, of course, that's how it goes.'

'And whom should they thank? The dead?'

'Why don't you see through history, dear Herr Kraus? It's so simple. Without Königgrätz, then perhaps Königgrätz wouldn't exist at all, just like Austerlitz wouldn't exist without Austerlitz, or Lützen without Lützen… no one would know this place. Yes, yes, that's history for you, no Königgrätz without Königgrätz, no Eger without Wallenstein, no Sarajevo without Franz Ferdinand, and of course, no Pilsen without Pilsner beer, no Budweis without Budweiser beer, and no Reichenberg without the Feuerhalle, yes, yes, that's how it is, I'd love to travel right out to the battlefields, but's already getting dark, what a shame, what a shame, but it'll be that much nicer tomorrow.'

Winterberg closed his book and looked out of the window while the brakes of the train screeched to a halt.

We had arrived.

THE ENGLISHMAN

The hotel where we stayed in Hradec Králové wasn't the *Grand Hotel* in the Georgsgasse that was recommended in the Baedeker. Nor was it the *Merkur* or the Hotel *Schwarzes Ross*. Our hotel wasn't listed in our thick red guidebook.

It was too new for that.

And yet already quite old.

The hotel was a socialist housing block directly across from the main train station. Winterberg was exhausted and shaken after our trip to the battlefields, after his worst and largest historical fit so far, and didn't want to look for a different one. He had a warm bath and went to bed.

I sat in the hotel bar. It was just after eleven. I looked at my half-empty beer glass and over at two men who were having a conversation about winter tyres and snow chains and the snowstorm somewhere up in the Krkonoše mountains last winter that had nearly buried them. They were speaking Czech, and the language, my native language, already sounded a bit less foreign to me than it had in Liberec, and yet somehow still strange. I wanted to order another beer in Czech and it came out in German.

Music was playing. Slow, light rock. I was tired too, but I couldn't get to sleep because my head was roaring. I knew that I had to just keep drinking. I had to numb myself with beer.

It was all too much for me.

Too much Königgrätz.

Too much forest.

Too much snow.

Too much frost.

Too much *Cornus sanguinea*.

Too much blood-red dogwood.

Too much *svída krvavá*.

Too much war.

Too many corpses.

Too many ghosts.

Too many graves.

Too many soldiers.

Too much Benedek.

Too many Saxons.

Too many Prussians.

Too many Austrians.

Too many trains.

Too much Baedeker.

Too much Reichenberg.

Too much Feuerhalle.

Too much history.

Too many stories.

Too much Winterberg.

And yet I knew that Winterberg was right.

There was no escape.

From his history.

From my history.

I ordered another beer, the men were still talking about the snow-storm in the Krkonoše that cut a village off from the world for three days, and I saw a night bus stop in front of the train station.

I drank beer and thought about Josefa, who had held my hand in the tavern on the battlefield, who had brought us back to Hradec Králové, who had wanted to stay for the night.

I thought about how disappointed she was when she asked if I didn't like her.

I thought about how I said that yes, I do, very much so, you're a very lovely woman, but I just can't.

I thought about how she asked me if there was someone else.

I thought about how I looked at her and didn't answer.

Josefa then got back onto her tractor, the tractor from the Zetor brand. She started up the motor, the exhaust shook and let out a cloud of smoke, and Josefa slowly drove back home and didn't look back. But I watched the tractor drive off until it disappeared at the next intersection.

I drank my beer and thought about all my sailors from all those crossings who were no longer alive.

I thought about my father, who was no longer alive.

I thought about my mother, who was no longer alive.

I thought about my little sister, who was no longer alive.

I thought about Carla, who was no longer alive.

I thought about Agnieszka, who was in fact alive, but if her husband ever found out what occasionally transpired between us, she wouldn't be alive for much longer, and neither would I.

And then I thought about Hanzi, who was also no longer alive.

Hanzi was from Hradec Králové. He was the one who had organised everything back then. He was the one who brought me along. He was the one who fired the gun. I'm still certain that he didn't mean to do it. But he did it. He aimed at his throat and pulled the trigger. I thought about the shot and suddenly I heard the pop. I thought about the blood and suddenly saw it flowing through my beer glass.

I ordered a shot of schnapps.

And then another one.

I knew it wasn't a good idea.

I knew it wouldn't help.

I knew that I had already lost again. I wouldn't be able to stop drinking once I had already started back up. I knew myself too well for that.

Then I paid for my drinks, took my key and left.

Everything was a bit blurry.

The stairs.

The elevator.

The hallway.

My room.

Everything was reeling and wobbling and I was reeling and wobbling too. I collapsed on the bed and immediately fell asleep and was awoken a few hours later. I heard someone moaning. And screaming. And crying.

It wasn't Hanzi, who had just been in my dreams.

Hanzi was dead.

He hanged himself later in prison.

It was Winterberg.

* * *

Winterberg stood on the balcony that was shared between his room and mine.

I pulled on my jacket, walked out of my room, and lit up a cigarette. Winterberg coughed. I saw a small man in a winter coat and winter hat and winter gloves standing on the balcony, a small, old man with a slight hunch, a bit crooked, as if he were seeking his stories not in the present and in the past and in his red book, but on the ground, on the street, in the snow and rain, under his feet. Or at that moment, on the balcony.

The night was cold and clear and so was the air. Winterberg stood on the balcony gripping the railing and looking over at the train station. He sobbed and moaned and cried and coughed and rambled and coughed again and cried and rambled to himself.

He was speaking with someone only he could see.

'Yes, yes, that's how it was, I know… I'm sorry… I know… no, no, it's my fault, not yours, it's my fault… no, no, please, Lenka, don't say that… I know what I did… it wasn't right… Lenka, Lenka, I beg you, take the train to Brünn, yes, yes, you might have to continue to Vienna, and then onwards… yes, yes… do you have everything, yes… it'll be all right, don't be afraid… no, Lenka, maybe Vienna isn't a good idea, no, no… go to Budapest instead and then onwards from there, yes, yes, or as you say, go…'

He coughed and his hoarse voice filled the empty night over the city. He took off his glasses, wiped his eyes and didn't notice that I was there. That I saw him. He coughed and cried and continued to speak with Lenka, whom only he could see. I lit another cigarette.

'Yes, yes, Lenka… I'll come to you, I'll come after you… wait for me, yes… write to me as soon as you arrive… write to me how you're doing… tell me what hotel you're staying in… you have money, yes… yes, that should be enough… yes, that should surely be enough until I get there… no, I won't forget you, no…'

The sky was clear. Clearer than it had been in a long time. As clear as the sky can only be in the height of summer or in the depth of winter. But the stars were nowhere to be seen. Everything was flooded out by the warm light of the train station. By the lights of the city.

'No, no… don't cry, you can't cry, Lenka… come, give me a kiss… let me hold you… the train is leaving in a moment, you have to get on board, come, I'll help you… no, I won't forget you… come…'

A heavy freight train with a blue-white electric locomotive drove into the station. The brakes screeched and the wagons groaned like animals that had just been shot by a hunter.

'Yes, yes, I'll come after you, don't be afraid, Lenka… write and tell me where you are… Brünn or Vienna, yes, yes, then Budapest… and Zagreb… and then Sarajevo and Belgrade and Skopje and Thessaloniki and then onwards with the ship… yes, to Haifa… I'll follow you… write to me from each city… why haven't you written to me, Lenka, write to me… Lenka… why haven't you written… wait for me, Lenka… I'll come after you… it won't be long… I'll follow you… wait for me, Lenka… the necklace, do you still have it… the Bohemian garnets… beautiful… beautiful…'

The next freight train left in a different direction. The old diesel locomotive sighed and rattled and struggled with the heavy load. Another diesel locomotive pushed the train from behind.

'I'm glad to hear that, Lenka… the necklace looks good on you, the Bohemian garnets, no, it's not blood, don't be afraid… yes, that dress is beautiful too… you're not too cold, are you… it's cold… I'll come after you soon, Lenka… no, I won't forget you… don't forget me either, all right… take care of yourself… get in, the train is leaving soon… have a safe trip and I'll see you soon, write to me immediately, yes… oh, Lenka, why aren't you writing, what's wrong… we'll meet in Brünn… or in Vienna… or in Budapest… or in Zagreb… or in Sarajevo… or in Haifa… write to me… why haven't you written, Lenka…'

The freight train was long and heavy. It left the station only at a crawl, inch by inch. It looked as if it didn't want to leave the station at all, as if it just wanted to brake, as if it wanted to go back, as if it didn't dare to depart on its lonely journey through the night. On its journey into uncertainty. Into infinitude. Into finitude.

Winterberg stopped talking to Lenka and began to cry.

He also looked over at the train and I lit a new cigarette. And I had to cough. It was only at that moment that Winterberg noticed my presence, but he didn't immediately turn to look at me. He only briefly jerked his head. He coughed and wiped his eyes and didn't speak and I smoked and the cargo train finally managed to get on its way and disappeared under the bridge and the night was cold and still.

'Are you all right?'

But Winterberg didn't respond.

'It's cold. You'll freeze out here.'

But he didn't respond.

'We should go to bed.'

But he didn't respond.

He wiped his eyes again, coughed and looked over at the station.

And then he started to talk.

He told me about how he was interested a different sort of Feuerhalle than his father, in the Feuerhalles of steam locomotives, because the furnace of an express locomotive or a freight locomotive was in no way lesser than the furnace of a Feuerhalle.

He told me about how he wanted to be a locomotive driver, but his eyes weren't sharp enough to be a locomotive driver for the Czechoslovakian State Railways. His eyes were just good enough to be a tram driver on the tram lines of the City of Reichenberg.

He told me about how, as a soldier in the war, he felt haunted by history.

He told me about how Wallenstein haunted him in his dreams.

And Gustav Adolf.

And Jan Žižka with his Hussites.

And Napoleon.

And Benedek.

He coughed and told me about how he wanted to get away.

Away from Reichenberg.

Away from his family, which was cursed, because it had come together in the shadow of the Battle of Königgrätz.

Then he coughed again and looked at me.

'I believe I caught a bit of a cold yesterday in the Svíb Forest, dear Herr Kraus. I'll have to drink a warm beer tomorrow, that's what my mother always made for me when I caught cold, yes, yes, the warm beer always helped me.'

He coughed and I smoked and made sure that the smoke didn't drift in his direction. I was still quite drunk, and as I looked down from the balcony, I suddenly felt nauseous and had to grip the railing to steady myself, just like Winterberg gripped the railing to steady himself.

The next freight train arrived at the station. It too was endlessly long and the wagons were loaded with wood.

And Winterberg coughed and resumed telling me about how he wanted to get away.

Away from the graves.

Away from the Feuerhalle.

Away from the hall of flames.

Away from the fortress of fire.

Away from the fiery tomb.

Away from the cremation.

Away from the coffins.

Away from the dead.

Away from the Friends of Fire Burial and the Friends of Hygiene.

Away from the Ratskeller.

Away from Reichenberg.

'And then it happened and I succeeded, dear Herr Kraus… the war started and it freed me and it laid a thick new layer over *"the beautiful landscape of battlefields, cemeteries and ruins"*, yes, yes, madness, madness, I know, you're right, dear Herr Kraus… the war truly drove me away, much, much farther than I thought, much, much farther than I could have imagined, much, much farther than I wanted, far, far, far away. And the same war also drove Lenka away, this war whose stench hung in the air for so long, this war which had already begun here in Königgrätz in 1866, and yet everyone thought the war wouldn't come, and it came so much faster than we imagined, yes, yes… I wanted to go after Lenka, but suddenly it was no longer possible, I thought we would find each other, but suddenly it was all over, and all that remained were letters and hope and love… yes, yes, the entire time I thought about Lenka, about the first woman in the moon… and then the war was over, I never returned to Reichenberg, and neither did Lenka. But I was alive, and Lenka wasn't, no, no, I don't know what happened to her, no, no, I don't know where it happened, but I know that it happened, yes, yes, I know she didn't return, and I want to find her murderer, I have to find him and I have to continue, I have to keep going, to Vienna and Brünn and Budapest and then to Sarajevo… what a drop this is, dear Herr Kraus, one really must hold on tight.'

Winterberg coughed and leaned against the railing. He stood up on his toes and looked down at the drop bellow us.

At the empty parking spots.

At the train station.

At the sleeping city.

I still felt sick.

'We're so high up… it's good that neither of us suffer from a fear of heights, it's good that we only suffer from history, from the Battle of Königgrätz, where everything began, yes, yes, it's good that we only suffer from the fog of war, perhaps one really can solve everything as easily as laying tracks through the Alps, yes, yes, have you read the book *The Construction of the Alpine Railways*, it's an important book if you're serious about history and about the railway, if you want to see through history, you must read it… where was I… yes, yes, fear of heights… even as a child I was drawn to heights, yes, yes, when we went hiking with my father in the Iser mountains and climbed up onto the cliffs… I never had a fear of heights, no, no, I just always wanted to throw myself into the void… yes, yes, I know what you're going to say, dear Herr Kraus, I can't keep my thoughts in line, I'm always getting lost in thought, lost in the stories and in the history, yes, yes, and yet the cycle will soon be complete, believe me, it's good that we're here, that you visited the battlefields with me, it's good that we found both graves, yes, yes, the beginning of my misfortune… Lenka, poor Lenka, she's already waiting for me, she's calling me to her, yes, yes, and afterwards I won't be getting lost any longer…'

A shunting locomotive whistled several times and the whistle echoed through the night. Winterberg coughed and looked over at the train station.

'After the war I also wanted to get away, yes, yes, away from the graves, away from the war, away from history, away from the memories… I was in Holland and it took some time before I could go home, but it wasn't possible, I didn't have a home anymore. Peter, who was with me over there, brought me to Berlin, and so I became a tram driver, yes, yes, and then the last tram driver in West Berlin… I married immediately in order to forget Lenka, to forget everything, I wanted to have children with my wife right away, in order to forget, but it didn't work, a small issue with the plumbing, as the doctor said, but he didn't know whose pipes were clogged, then I married my second wife, but it still didn't work, another issue with the plumbing, as the doctor said, the problem was with me, my pipes were clogged, it only worked then with my third wife, there the plumbing worked, yes, yes, my wives helped me to forget and I loved them for that, but the whole time I knew that there was only one woman I loved, my woman in the moon… I was looking for the moon in the sky tonight, dear Herr Kraus, but I couldn't find it. Have you seen the moon tonight, dear Herr Kraus?'

Winterberg coughed and looked up at the sky and searched for the moon, but although the night was so clear, he wasn't able to find it.

The whole sky was flooded by the light from the city.

I was dizzy after all the beer and schnapps, after all the stories, in which it was not Winterberg but me who was the one getting lost.

I lit another cigarette.

'You shouldn't smoke so much, dear Herr Kraus… you won't get to be as old as me that way, as old as Czechoslovakia, as old as the Feuer-halle in Reichenberg, no, no, I never smoked, not even during the war, when everyone smoked. Now where was I again… yes, yes, I remember, I wanted to get away from the war, away from the graves, I've never told anyone what I saw in the war, how I had to dig graves in the war, yes, yes, in sand and in clay, in the woods and in the fields, during the war I was damned to deal with the graves. Even though during the war I was still a tram driver and then an S-Bahn driver and a locomotive driver, I also had to dig the graves, yes, yes, and in the meantime I drew winter landscapes and above all Lenka, I wanted to forget everything, I wanted to forget her… but look at where I am now, dear Herr Kraus, where we are now, in Königgrätz, yes, yes, *"the beautiful landscape of battlefields, cemeteries and ruins"*, as the Englishman always said… there's no escape and I didn't forget anything, yes, yes, there's nothing to do but hang yourself on a tree in the Svíb Forest. You hope that you can forget, that you can escape history, that you can flee, that you can hide somewhere, that you can leave everything behind as time goes by, but it doesn't work… you drag the entire history along with you like a rope, whether you want to or not, like a rope with which you hang yourself in the end, whether you want to or not, yes, yes, dear Herr Kraus, that's how it is in life, there's no running away. And so we all perish, piece by piece and step by step, we all become a part of *"the beautiful landscape of battlefields, cemeteries and ruins"*, as the Englishman always said, yes, yes… it really is quite high up here, don't you think?'

Winterberg stood once again on his toes and looked at the drop beneath us and the next freight train arrived and the brakes screeched and groaned and the shunters stamped out their cigarettes and returned to work and the shunting locomotive whistled loudly several times in a row.

'Lenka wouldn't be able to handle this balcony, because Lenka suffered from a fear of heights, yes, yes, perhaps that's why she loved the film *Woman in the Moon*, because the heroine had no fear of heights, yes, yes, the heroine, the astronomy student Friede Velten, played by Gerda Maurus, was a strong and brave woman, Lenka liked that a lot, she wanted to be exactly like her… the Englishman wasn't afraid of heights either, he was a navigator in the Royal Air Force and visited all the places in Germany and Bohemia and all of Central Europe where he had navigated his Lancaster, yes, yes, he wanted to see all the cities and get to know them… it must have been over fifty years ago now when we met by sheer chance in Berlin, in the *Heidelberger Krug* pub in Kreuzberg, it must have been over fifty years ago now that the Englishman told me there about *"the beautiful landscape of battlefields, cemeteries and ruins"* over a beer… the Englishman spoke good German, he learned German after the war because he wanted to understand the Germans, he wanted to grasp the Germans, he had read a lot about history and could see through history very well, he wanted to understand why the Germans did it, yes, yes, the Germans, and also the Austrians and the Italians and the Slovaks and the Croats and many others, but above all the Germans, he wanted to know, yes, yes, why the Germans turned all of Europe into one big, burning Feuerhalle… yes, yes, he wanted to know everything about *"the beautiful landscape of battlefields, cemeteries and ruins"*, as he called it, he wrote that sentence for me on a beer coaster in the *Heidelberger Krug* so I wouldn't forget it, this English sentence which isn't really a proper sentence, but to me it's one of the most beautiful sentences that I've ever heard, dear Herr Kraus, because this sentence, these few words, say everything, the whole truth about us and about our history and about Bohemia and about Europe, about our entire tragedy, yes, yes, about love, about *"the beautiful landscape of battlefields, cemeteries and ruins".*

Winterberg coughed, stood up on his toes and leaned again over the railing and looked at the drop beneath us, and I prepared to hold him back in case he leaned out any further.

'This sentence which isn't a sentence is our homeland, yes, yes, our home… we can hide ourselves in this sentence, because in this sentence no one would find us. In this sentence we're safe, yes, yes, that's how it is, at least for a moment… *"the beautiful landscape of battlefields, cemeteries and ruins",* so true, so beautiful and so tragic, maybe no one can understand it, just myself and the Englishman… it always makes me a bit melancholy when I hear that sentence, yes, yes, we really are standing terribly high up here, dear Herr Kraus.'

Winterberg coughed and stood up again on his toes and leaned over the railing and the next freight train slowly left the station.

'The Englishman was in Berlin and Bremen and Hamburg and Duisburg and Munich and Nuremberg and Dortmund and Linz and Aussig and Brüx and Pilsen and Peenemünde on Usedom, yes, yes, the Englishman travelled everywhere the bombs from his plane had fallen, he turned all those cities into Feuerhalles, just like the Germans turned many English and French and Polish and Russian cities into Feuerhalles before him, yes, yes, his trip was a journey of reconciliation with his history, with our history, just like our trip is a journey of reconciliation, dear Herr Kraus, and a honeymoon trip with Lenka and a parting trip as well… the Englishman was also here in Königgrätz, because the Englishman could see through history and knew what I know and what you hopefully now also know, dear Herr Kraus, it all starts with Königgrätz, our entire misfortune, the Englishman had read a lot about this battle, he knew as much about it as I did, for an entire week we met every evening in the *Heidelberger Krug* just to talk about the Battle of Königgrätz, about this battle that runs through my heart, that rips me apart, this vivisection of a living torso, my gaping wound, which bleeds and hurts and can't be healed, because you can't heal the wounds of a corpse, yes, yes… the Englishman was very moved by this, he said it was the same for him, and so the Englishman understood me like no one had ever understood me before, yes, yes, not even Lenka understood me like the Englishman did, I have to admit that, although in my time with Lenka I didn't know much about Königgrätz yet, my father did tell me stories about it, and about the two family graves in the Svíb Forest, but I didn't see through history back then, I wasn't interested in it yet, I was more interested in Lenka, in her lips and breasts and legs, my interest in history only came later, during the war, it hit me suddenly and I felt where all of it was leading me, I felt the cold wind of the Svíb Forest, the damp graves of Königgrätz, yes, yes, I know what you're going to say, dear Herr Kraus, it's all mad, yes, yes, and you're right, it is mad... oh, it's really very high, I fear that I am a bit afraid of heights, dear Herr Kraus, I don't know why the void draws me in...'

Winterberg coughed and I smoked and Winterberg looked down at the drop.

'One time in the Iser mountains I nearly fell from a cliff, the pull from the void below was that strong, it's good that we have this railing here... my father rescued me back then, he didn't let me fall. When he saw how the void was drawing me in, he grabbed me and pulled me back, and my mother was afraid that we would both fall over the edge... from the cliffs we had a beautiful view over Friedland, yes, yes, that's right, the city of Wallenstein, yes, yes, perhaps our whole misfortune actually begins with him, back in the Thirty Years' War, yes, yes... I never would have thought that I could converse with an Englishman about Wallenstein and Gustav Adolf and Radetzky and Benedek and Clausewitz, yes, yes, about the whole history, about the whole misfortune, about Lützen and Austerlitz and Königgrätz, I always thought that the English have no idea about history, but my Englishman was an exception, my Englishman fell in love with the beautiful Bohemian landscape around Königgrätz during his trip, *"the beautiful landscape of battlefields, cemeteries and ruins"*, as he always said. He travelled in a car, I hate cars, as you know, I hate cars and buses like the plague, but the Englishman understood my passion for the railway and history, like I understood his passion for cars and planes and history... the Englishman said that he can't travel by train because he destroyed so many train stations and carriages and locomotives with his bomber, he killed so many travellers and railwaymen with his bombs, yes, yes, and bomb corpses aren't a pretty sight... and so the Englishman drove by car to Königgrätz, his car was brand-new back then, it was a

Volvo, he said, and as he approached the Svíb Forest, his car got stuck on that country road, yes, there, where we found the graves, right there, his car got stuck in that sludge. He couldn't go forwards and couldn't go backwards and the distance reading showed 1866 kilometres, yes, yes, that's what happened to him, exactly like that, why should I lie about it now and make up something like that, dear Herr Kraus, that's what happened, his car got stuck in the mud and so did his mileometer and he got stuck in history, the battle of 1866 caught him like it caught me too, like it caught us, there's no escape, dear Herr Kraus, yes, yes, the Englishman understood me and I understood him too, he told me how the gates of the fiery tomb of the Svíb Forest then opened up before him and he saw what we saw. And when he told me that he had been to Königgrätz, I knew even more that I had to go as well... if we should make it back to Berlin, we'll go together to the *Heidelberger Krug* in Kreuzberg and I'll show you the table where I sat with the Englishman, like I showed you the table in the Ratskeller where my father's skull was shattered, yes, yes, I'll show you the table in the *Heidelberger Krug* where we talked for an entire week about history, about *"the beautiful landscape of battlefields, cemeteries and ruins, yes, yes"*... what makes me a bit melancholy is that in the end it'll all be forgotten, all these stories, our entire knowledge, in the end we'll all be abandoned, just like Wallenstein was abandoned in Eger and Benedek after Königgrätz, we die all alone and our stories die with us, because there's no one around today who's interested in our stories, no one who sees through history or wants to see through history, you can't be surprised then at what's happening these days, no, no... you must really know everything about death, dear Herr Kraus, you being a nurse for the elderly, a nurse for the dead, a Soldier of Last Hope... we're always surprised by death, just like Wallenstein was surprised by death that night in Eger, we'll all be abandoned, like Wallenstein was abandoned, we'll all be abandoned by those who loved us and and those whom we loved, yes, yes, but I'll never forget that week of my life... I don't know if you understand it, Herr Kraus, maybe it can't really be understood, *"the beautiful landscape of battlefields, cemeteries and ruins"*. It was so beautiful.'

'I do understand it, I understand English. I learned a bit of the language.'

'Well, well.'

'Did you love him?'

He looked at me in surprise.

'What?'

'The Englishman… are you still mourning him?'

'Where did you get that idea?'

'I just thought… you talk about him so much, almost more than Lenka. Or just as much.'

Winterberg coughed and wanted to say something. He opened his mouth, but he said nothing.

He said nothing and coughed and cried a bit more and stared out into the night and then over at the train station.

He looked over at the empty platforms. At two shunters with red helmets on their heads who stood in front of a small building smoking while they waited for the next train.

'I've always admired the railway shunters, perhaps because I so often feel derailed, pulled this way and that, uncoupled and hanged up and then brought away, yes, yes, like a freight wagon… yes, yes, always outside, all day and all night, that's what it comes down to, in the cold and in the heat, always outside. It's a very dangerous job, it only takes one small misstep, just a minor mistake and they're crushed between two wagons and shunted to death, yes, yes, shunting corpses aren't a pretty sight, as my father always said, as a shunter there are only two possibilities, either you're crushed to death between two bumpers, yes, yes, stamped between the two bumpers, or you're cut in two by the wheels of the train, yes, yes, as my father always said, yes, yes, being a shunter is a good job, but a dangerous one. I always wanted to be a locomotive driver instead, but my eyes, my eyes…'

'Is he still alive?'

'Who?'

'The Englishman.'

'I don't know.'

'Where did you learn English?'

'In school. And you?'

'In prison.'

'In prison?'

'In prison.'

'In Bohemia?'

'In Germany… I thought you knew. Your daughter knows.'

'Yes, my daughter knows everything, of course… she knows everything better than everyone else, and yet she's alone and has to do yoga and take pills in order to feel a bit of happiness… what a shame that I didn't buy her that horse.'

'I learned German first, and then a bit of English.'

'And why were you in prison?'

I didn't say anything and lit another cigarette.

'You don't need to tell me.'

'It doesn't matter. It wasn't my fault. I didn't shoot anyone.'

'Someone got shot?'

'Yeah.'

'Who did the shooting?'

'Hanzi.'

'But why?'

I didn't say anything and smoked and saw before my eyes how it all went down at the time. I wanted to tell Winterberg. But I couldn't.

'It was an accident, but no one believed him. It wasn't part of the plan.'

'And what was the plan?'

'Getting out of here. Out of this shithole.'

Winterberg was silent. The shunting locomotive came back and whistled and the two shunters climbed aboard and the locomotive left with them.

'Were you ever married, Herr Kraus?'

'No.'

'But there's a woman you were in love with?'

'Yes.'

'What was her name?'

'Carla.'

'A Czech?'

'No.'

'A German?'

'No, an Italian, but from Bremen.'

'Then maybe you'll be able to understand… I loved Lenka, truly, more than anything… but with him, the Englishman, how should I say it… something like that had never happened to me. Never before. Never since.'

'So we're not just following Lenka, but the Englishman too.'

'Yes. They're both along for the journey.'

'Nice that we're not alone.'

'I really did love Lenka, Herr Kraus.'

'I know.'

'With the Englishman, it was… well… different. Has it ever happened to you?'

'No. But maybe that's exactly what counts, these moments.'

'Yes, perhaps… everything else is only death, yes, yes… everything else is just a grave. All of Europe is one deep, wet grave, and yet not as deep as one might think. The dead want to return. They're here. I see them…'

'So what was his name?'

'George.'

'And where was he from?'

'Birmingham.'

'Have you ever been there?'

'No.'

'Maybe he's still alive?'

'I wouldn't think so.'

'You should go to bed now. It's cold. Tomorrow we'll continue on.'

'Who brought us to the hotel?'

'Who else? Josefa. You were asleep.'

'But she was drinking.'

'We were all drinking.'

'I didn't drink.'

'You did, you drank a lot. Two grogs and two beers. And you fell asleep immediately afterwards.'

'Josefa fancied you a bit.'

'I know.'

FROM KÖNIGGRÄTZ TO JITSCHIN

The next day, we rode the small, rickety railcar to Jičín. Winterberg had caught cold, and I was hungover. We were so tired that we slept the entire way, although the trip was turbulent and the carriage swayed from side to side, and I thought the whole time about the ocean. About my crossings. About my tired, lifeless sailors, the ones I brought to the opposite shore, who stood there before the great mirror and observed themselves. Who were already dead. Or not. Who knows about any of that.

It made me think about my own crossing, about my trip around the world. I thought about my own ship, the one I'd finally build with the money from Winterberg.

After that, I'll take off.

After that, everything will be different.

After that, everything will be great.

After that, no one will look for me.

After that, I'll be lost.

Our train approached Sadová again. I saw the deer on the edge of the forest again, an entire herd, and shortly afterwards, I also saw the two large, bare trees on the horizon. I thought, those must be the two linden trees near Hořiněves, I wanted to wake Winterberg and show it to him, but he refused to get up and slept with his head propped on his chest.

The train stopped in Sadová. No one got on or off this time. We drove on. I felt ill, a hundred drills were humming in my head, and it made me think of my father, who always said that the hangover is the only certainty there is in Bohemia. The only certainty that no one can take from us. The entire country can be occupied. The entire country can be free again. We ought to fight. We ought to celebrate. But we're always hungover and so we don't do anything at all. Because we're hungover, and the only thing we can do is drink the next beer.

At the railway crossing in front of the inn, a tractor of the brand Zetor from Brno was waiting behind the barrier, and I swear, I saw the driver at the wheel and the driver was Josefa, who was probably just heading to the inn for lunch. I turned towards Josefa and I'm certain that she saw me too. Winterberg noticed nothing, he coughed and slept and lurched from side to side, just like the little carriage lurched over the rails.

We travelled through Hořice.

We travelled through Ostroměř.

We travelled through the villages that were always called something different and yet always looked the same.

A little church.

An inn.

A pond.

And plenty of small houses.

And when the train stopped and the doors opened, it always stunk of brown coal. It stunk exactly as it had stunk in my childhood. Back in Vimperk. In Winterberg.

And then we were in Jičín.

I bought us tea with rum and a sausage and drank a beer and immediately felt a bit better.

Winterberg didn't want to look around the city.

He didn't want to visit Wallstein's palace.

He didn't want to visit the monastery that Wallenburg founded in order to be buried there.

The monastery that is now a prison.

Winterberg was tired and ill and just wanted to travel on, and it seemed to me that he didn't care where we were going.

So we drifted onwards.

We travelled to Turnov and from the train window we saw Trosky and Baba and Panna and shortly afterwards the ruins of Waldstein Castle as well. Winterberg coughed and shivered from the cold and ran a fever and said nothing. He didn't look at his book. He didn't look out of the window.

He only wanted to travel on.

In Turnov, we changed trains and rode to Mladá Boleslav via Mnichovo Hradiště, where Wallenstein was buried, as I knew from Winterberg. But he didn't want to get out of the train.

He wanted to travel on.

In Mladá Boleslav, we changed trains and rode past the old castle in the direction of Libuň. Always the same villages and towns. Always the old, rickety rails. Always the same stench of brown coal when the doors opened. Always the same people, who always stared at us. A bit curious because we were speaking German. A bit irate because we were speaking German. And a bit indifferent because we were speaking German.

And it made me think about my grandfather, who always said that the bad Germans were in the West, and the good Germans were in the GDR, but even with those ones, you had to watch your back.

It briefly snowed and then turned to rain again and we travelled on through the region called 'Bohemian Paradise'.

In Libuň, I briefly stepped out onto the platform and lit a cigarette. Winterberg sat in the train and slept, I saw his head leaning against the window. And then I once again saw Trosky and Panna and Baba in the distance.

A young woman and an old woman.

Both dead.

Both petrified.

It made me think about all the women I'd accompanied on the crossing. Whom I'd consoled. Whom I'd fought with. Because none of the dying want to die.

Everyone fights with death, and every one of the women had thought that I was death.

But I was not, and am not, death.

Everyone fights and thrashes and bites and curses and cries and spits, but the battle doesn't last long.

I looked at Panna and Baba and at Winterberg, sleeping behind the window, and thought about all the women whose hands I'd held.

About the old women.

And about the young women.

And then I had to think about the youngest woman I'd brought to the other shore.

About Carla.

Carla de Luca.

Winterberg slept and I smoked and looked out at the castle ruins of Trosky and thought about Carla, who was also long dead and petrified like Baba and Panna.

And yet I remember to this day the sound of her voice.

I remember to this day how she smelled.

I remember to this day how she moaned when we made love.

Carla, my little Italian from Bremen.

I smoked and Winterberg slept with his head leaning against the window and the red sun set over Bohemian Paradise, and it looked as though the white, snowy landscape was bleeding. The Bohemian garnets.

And then the conductor asked me if I was coming or not.

From Libuň, we rode up the hillside and then right back down again towards Lomnice nad Popelkou and Stará Paka.

It was snowing and cold and Winterberg coughed and shivered from his fever and I worried about him.

But he wanted to travel on.

From Stará Paka, we rode to Ostroměř.

But he still wanted to travel on.

From Ostroměř, we rode back to Jičín.

And here we alighted and couldn't travel on. We had to look around the city after all, since the last trains still running from Jičín that evening were heading towards Sadová and Hradec Králové, and we didn't want to go back. We'd both had enough of the Battle of Königgrätz.

We looked for the hotel *Hamburg*, which was recommended in the Baedeker, with 20 rooms let for between 2.40 and 4 crowns at the time, and a woman told us that *Hamburg* was now called *Paris* and showed us the way. It wasn't far.

Winterburg coughed and ran a fever, but he didn't want to see a doctor. He took a warm bath and drank a warm beer and sweat under the blankets. Then he fell asleep.

On the next day, he wanted to get right back on the train, but as he tried to get out of bed, he fell right back down. We stayed another night in the hotel *Hamburg*, which was now called *Paris*, and then another, and then another.

Winterberg wasn't doing well. He didn't want anything to eat, he only wanted to drink warm beer like his mother would give him. But

I always forced him to have a bit of chicken soup, too, like my mother would give me.

Every evening, I would go out on my own. I walked around the city, constantly slipping on the shiny, wet cobblestones, and walked past the many pubs. I wanted a beer, but I couldn't manage to drink. Then I sat every night in the cellar bar of the *Grand Hotel Praha*, which was also called *Grand Hotel Praha* before, as someone told me, and would probably always be called *Grand Hotel Praha*, because Prague clearly didn't offend anyone in Jičín; Prague wasn't Hamburg.

I sat there at a small, simple wooden table, and drank alcohol-free beer, and the small, stocky waiter, who looked like a blood sausage, asked me if I was sick or pregnant or both, since I didn't want to drink a proper beer, and I said, yeah, I'm a little bit pregnant.

He laughed and I laughed, too.

He said he understood me; he was also a little bit pregnant, he also couldn't drink. He hadn't had any beer in twenty years, otherwise he would have drowned in beer long ago, just like his father and his grand-father. Just like the whole country.

'Well, that's just how it is, some inherit a heap of cash, some inherit a house, and I inherited a love of beer. So I can't drink any more.'

I drank the next alcohol-free beer and ordered a pale 'water corpse' sausage, which was properly soaked-through and deliciously sour, and it made me think of all the water corpses that Winterberg had told me about, and every night, I watched the same four men who sat under an old painting and drank beer and argued about football and politics and history and then reconciled and drank beer and left to piss and then drank the next beer and argued again about football and politics and history and then reconciled again.

I saw that the picture hanging over them on the wall, a yellowed painting with the hilly local landscape and a wooden bridge and a horse-drawn carriage with a white canvas, hung a bit more crooked every night, as if the picture were threatening the men, as if it would one day crash down on them, swallow them, absorb them into the painting.

Every night, I drank the alcohol-free beer in the *Grand Hotel Praha* and sat just metres away from the *Hotel Paris*, where Winterberg was sleeping, and I hoped that he would feel better tomorrow. I drank the alcohol-free beer and the bartender told me that *Paris* hadn't just been called *Hamburg*, but also *Stalingrad* and *Astra*.

I drank the next alcohol-free beer and tortured myself by looking at the men under the picture, who were drinking proper beer, because they weren't pregnant like me.

I knew exactly how creamy the foam tasted.

I knew exactly how smooth the beer tasted.

But I held out.

And I knew I wouldn't hold out for long.

Tomorrow I'll get pissed.

Tomorrow, or the day after tomorrow at the latest.

I settled my tab again and went out through an old stone gate at the hotel *Hamburg* towards the main square. On the wall behind the gate I read in the posted obituaries about who in the city had recently died. It made me think of my mother, who always said that they were the only news that interested her, the only news that she knew to be true, because no one lied about that.

And then I was completely alone on the wide Wallenstein Square. In the middle of the square stood a Christmas tree twinkling in the night, and I thought, it really will be Christmas soon. A light snow was falling and I stood in the square and looked at the city palace, which Wallenstein had constructed as the centre of his empire, as its core, as Winterberg had told me.

The square was dark and empty. I saw a couple of parked cars. And the palace stood there too, quiet and empty and dark.

And then it happened.

Suddenly, in the palace, all the lights sprung on. Wallenstein's palace shone in the darkness of the night and I turned around and didn't know what it meant and whether anyone else saw it. The palace shone like a large head over the dark square, like a head without a torso, like a massive, lonely, chopped-off head, and it made me think of Wallenstein, who had been re-buried three times, as Winterberg had told me.

I looked at the glowing palace and thought about Wallenstein, about whom I knew almost nothing, because until now I'd known so little about history. I stood alone on Wallenstein Square in the Wallenstein

City of Jičín in front of Wallenstein's palace and thought about Wallenstein's loneliness.

About his death in Eger.

About his murder.

I looked in the windows of the palace. No one was there. It was snowing and I walked back to the hotel, and as I turned once again at the door to look back, I still saw Wallenstein's palace glowing in the night.

The soft yellow light reflected off the cobblestones and was slowly being buried by the snow. And then suddenly the lights went out, and the palace was dark as before.

* * *

Winterberg wasn't doing well. He was feverish and coughing and didn't know where he was. He was feverish and spoke to me and to Lenka and to the Englishman and to Benedek and to Wallenstein and to Ghega and then to me again. He mistook me for Lenka and for the Englishman, he spoke German and English and also a bit of Czech, and then he mistook me not just for Lenka and the Englishman, but also for his daughter Silke, who was probably already looking for us. Surely she'd already called Agnieszka. Surely she'd already alarmed the police.

Winterberg was feverish and also mistook me for his three wives, who couldn't be looking for us, because they were buried next to each other in the Heerstraße Cemetery. But suddenly they weren't dead. They were here. With us in the small room in the Hotel *Paris* in Jičín.

Winterberg was feverish and cried and wanted to apologise to them for everything. But then he immediately shouted that they were nagging him, that they were horrible cooks, that they didn't want sex, that they didn't understand him, only Lenka and the Englishman and I, too, understood him. And then he immediately apologised again and cried.

Winterberg was feverish and was briefly in Reichenberg and then in Berlin and then somewhere in Holland and then on the Baltic Sea and then back in Reichenberg and then in Königgrätz and then sitting in the train, drifting onwards.

Winterberg was feverish and I gave him warm beer with paracetamol and chicken soup.

Winterberg was feverish and lay in bed and was exhausted and quoted from his Baedeker and rode the train in his fever dreams onwards and onwards.

From Jičín to Prague.

From Prague to Budweis.

From Budweis to Linz.

From Linz to Bad Ischl.

Winterberg was feverish and spoke with Lenka and with the Englishman and with me. He saw Lenka sitting at his bedside and cried and wanted to hug her and hugged me. 'You can't go, Lenka... you can't go...'

Winterberg was feverish and sat again in the train and told me about changing trains in Attnang-Puchheim to Gmunden and Bad Ischl.

'The railway crosses the Ager river... on the right, Puchheim Palace, then the Aurach... it travels through the pleasant Aurach valley to Gmunden, elevation 481 metres, electric tram... pleasant city at the outlet of the river Traun on the Traunsee, popular climatic spa and summer resort... worth visiting the Salzkammergut Museum at Franz-Joseph-Platz, yes, yes... don't cry, Lenka, that's just the wind from the train, it's not salt, it's the Salzkammergut... shaded esplanade at the lakeside, the wooded Grünberg on the left, then the near-vertical rise of Traunstein mountain... do you see it, Lenka?... where's the Englishman, where's Herr Kraus? Herr Kraus, don't leave me here... many of the better inns are closed in the winter... everything's closed in winter, there's no escape... I have to go, Lenka, Lenka, we have to go, dear Herr Kraus, we have to go... *"the beautiful landscape of battlefields, cemeteries and ruins"*, everything is closed... where's the Englishman... we have to go... no... Silke, you have no idea, leave me alone, you don't see through history at all, I know, you're still angry that I didn't buy you that horse... why don't you have a husband... or a wife... why don't you have children... yes, yes, I know, you think you know everything... no, Lenka, stay here... yes, yes, we have to go, dear Herr Kraus... where's the Englishman, we've all got to go... everything will be closed... an acquaintance of mine fell to his death from Traunstein, that was in winter, too, just after the war… yes, yes, it wasn't an accident, he was my comrade-in-arms in the war, another stranded veteran like me, he couldn't do it, he saw the bombed corpses and the burned corpses, which he had to sprinkle with lime like flakes of snow… we have to go… yes, yes, bombed corpses aren't a pretty sight, and neither are burned corpses… we have to go… otherwise they'll catch us… yes, yes, Silke, of course I love you, too… we have to be quick, otherwise they'll catch us… we have to find the murderer… there's no escape… we have to overcome it, no, no, we have to try, just like von Ghega tried… there's Benedek, but he should be long dead by now, what's he doing here, dear Herr Kraus… where's Lenka… where's the Englishman… where are you, dear Herr Kraus, don't leave me here… take me with you… don't leave me here…'

Then he fell asleep and I called for a doctor the next day. The young doctor wanted to take Winterberg right to the hospital, but Winterberg didn't want to go. She prescribed him an antibiotic and gave me her number and I mixed the antibiotic with warm beer and chicken soup.

Winterberg was feverish and coughing and sweating and I thought he wouldn't make it. I thought, we're heading back, we're back on my ship and now I have to accompany him to the other shore. I thought, we're back on the crossing and I'll be returning home alone.

'From Gmunden to Ebensee, it's preferable to take the steamship over the Traunsee… the train passes behind the palace of the Duke von Württemberg and approaches the Traunsee, sit on the left… we have to sit on the left, yes, yes, Lenka, why are you sitting on the right, you have to sit on the left, otherwise you won't see anything, Silke, you too, why do I always have to explain everything to you, we all have to sit on the left… where's the Englishman, he wanted to come to Bad Ischl to see the Kaiservilla too… where are you, dear Herr Kraus… we have to go, otherwise they'll catch us… the landscape becomes even more magnificent; behind Traunstein is the Hochkogel, then the beautiful Erlakogel, picturesque views, we have to go… Traunkirchen am Trauensee… otherwise they'll catch us… only onwards, onwards… otherwise history will catch us… otherwise it'll catch up with us and finish us off… Traunkirchen, a village with a stunning location atop a headland… two short tunnels, then the 1428-metre-long Sonnstein Tunnel… sit on the left… why is no one sitting on the left… why is it just me… why doesn't anyone understand me… why does no one see through history… Ebensee… *Zum Auerhahn* inn, handsome locale with a brewery… splendid location… onwards through the Traun valley… like a painting… yes, yes, my Baedeker is right, it's as beautiful as a painting, like your breasts, Lenka, like your legs, like your neck, like your necklace with the Bohemian garnets… no, no, it's not blood… yes, yes, come here, hold me… where are you, Herr Kraus… where is the Englishman… Silke… over the Traun river to Bad Ischl… yes, yes… where are you… why is no one sitting on the left, why is it just me… we have to go…'

Winterberg fell asleep again. I had to call his daughter. I looked in his bag; he had to have her number written down somewhere. I didn't find any notebook. I didn't find any number. I didn't find anything. And yet I did find something.

A rope. And a pistol. I looked at both. The rope was sturdy and the pistol loaded.

I packed the pistol and the rope back in his bag and went over to Winterberg. He was feverish and it was snowing outside. A fierce snowstorm was raging in the streets of Jičín. I listened to the wind groaning and sat on his bed and opened up a beer.

And then another one.

And then another one.

'Where is everyone, they're waiting for us… the Kaiser is there… the Kaiservilla is too large… yes, yes, the villa is too large, the garden is too large, it's all too large… it's all too damp, all too frail, all too old… yes, yes, just like the whole of Austria… it's all so beautiful, but all too damp, all too frail, all too old… it's all so large that you can't hold it together, *"the beautiful landscape of battlefields, cemeteries and ruins"* … yes, yes, that's the only way out… the only possibility… yes, yes, just like the Englishman said… where's the Englishman… where's Lenka… Silke, where are you… Herr Kraus… sit on the left, we have to sit on the left, otherwise we won't see anything… why isn't anyone sitting on the left, why is everyone sitting on the right… Herr Kraus, where are you… we have to go… do you see this table, this is where the Kaiser wrote *To My People*, his war manifesto, on July 28, 1914 … *It was my dearest wish to devote the remaining years that God may grant me to works of peace and to protect my people from the heavy sacrifices and burdens of war... Providence has decided otherwise...* Where are you, Herr Kraus... *The machinations of a hateful opponent force me, after long years of peace, to take up the sword to protect the honour of my monarchy, to safeguard its reputation and its authority...* yes, yes, the Kaiser and his sword, he's already quite old, he can't hold a sword anymore... *I have verified and considered everything...* Silke, why are you angry at me... *It is with a clear conscience that I tread the path that it is my duty to follow...* no, Lenka, I won't forget you... *I trust in my people, who have always gathered round my throne in harmony and loyalty in times of hardship and have always been prepared to make the ultimate sacrifice for the honour, greatness and strength of the Fatherland...* I'll come after you, Lenka... *I trust in the devotion and enthusiasm of Austria-Hungary's brave armed forces...* don't be afraid, Lenka... *And I trust in the Almighty, that He will grant me victory in the fight...* yes, yes, "the beautiful landscape of battlefields, cemeteries and ruins"... yes, yes, the fog of war... where's the Englishman... from Königgrätz to Sarajevo, from Sarajevo to Bad Ischl, from Bad Ischl to the front lines... there's no escape... sit on the left, sit on the left... look there on the wall, the Kaiser was also a hunter, just like the Archduke, so many trophies, but every hunter will one day become the hunted, as my grandfather always said, and he had to know, because he was a hunter... there's no escape... war corpses aren't a pretty sight... the endless corridors... the snow in the garden... the trees are lying in the garden, felled by the recent storm... a birch and a spruce and a beech... look at that, Herr Kraus, two deer with locked antlers found dead in the mountains... casualties of love... like all of us... where is everyone... Silke?! Lenka?! Where is the Englishman... we have to go, otherwise they'll catch us... Herr Kraus, where are you... Herr Kraus, please don't leave me here... Herr Kraus... where are you?'

'Here.'

'Where are you, Herr Kraus...'

'Here. I'm here.'

I held his hand and he opened his eyes.

'Where am I?'

'Here.'

'Where?'

'At Wallenstein's.'

FROM JITSCHIN TO BUDWEIS

The next morning, Winterberg was doing better. I suggested that we stay for a couple more days, but he wanted to travel onwards immediately. We ended up staying one more night and Winterberg slept, and when he wasn't sleeping, he stared out of the window at the snowy rooftops.

'Yes, yes, if history were a railway network, Jitschin would be a main station… Wallenstein, the war of 1866, even Bismarck was here, yes, yes, it's all mad, there's no escape… when you're aware of all that occurred in such a small, beautiful place, then you know that it can't end well, you can only shoot yourself or hang yourself or drown yourself in beer… it's good that so few people can see through history, otherwise they'd all be dead, yes, yes, they'd all go and hang themselves if they knew all that happened here.'

And I had to think about the pistol and the rope in his bag. I wanted to ask him why he had packed them, but I didn't.

A short time later, we were standing at the train station and leaving for Nymburk. Winterberg cleaned his glasses and looked eagerly out of the window again and was excited about everything he saw, or rather, what he could have been seeing, since there wasn't all that much to see on this particular day.

Everything lay under a thick fog.

He took his magnifying glass and read aloud from his Baedeker and an elderly woman listened to him in fascination, even though she didn't understand him.

We travelled from Jičín to Nymburk.

From Nymburk to Kolín.

And from Kolín to Prague.

I thought that Winterberg would want to see Prague, like everyone, but he didn't.

'We'll see Prague in Vienna.'

He told me that he had already been to Prague once, before the war, with his father. He told me that the only thing which really interested him in Prague, as a train person, was the main station, the railway heart of Bohemia. And it remains so to this day.

And so he sat for a long while on a bench on the platform and watched the trains and told me about how in the hotel *Zum Blauen Stern* in Prague on August 23, 1866, the Treaty of Prague was concluded, which ended the war, the unfortunate war for Austria, as it said in his Baedeker, which one could also read to mean that it was a fortunate war for Prussia.

'Yes, yes, and the Prussians believed it, too. But they were terribly mistaken; a war can only ever be unfortunate.'

He watched the trains and told me about all the Prague Defenestrations and all the Prague Defenestration corpses, which may not have been a pretty sight, but had still made history.

He told me about the number eight, which was bound with so many collapses and overthrows in Bohemia and beyond.

He told me about the overthrow and collapse in 848, when the Franks came. About the overthrow and collapse in 908, as the Hungarians came. About the overthrow and collapse in 1278, as King Ottokar II fell in the Battle at Dürnkrut. About the overthrow and collapse in 1378, as Emperor Charles IV died. About the overthrow and collapse in 1468, as the Hungarians came again. About the overthrow and collapse in 1608, as the Hungarians came with the Austrians. About the overthrow and collapse in 1618, as Slavata and Martinice were thrown from the window of Prague Castle. About the overthrow and collapse in 1648, as the Swedes came to Prague. About the overthrow and collapse in 1758, as the Prussians came. About the overthrow and collapse in 1778, as the Prussians came again. About the overthrow and collapse in 1848, as Austria foundered and Czechoslovakia was born. About the overthrow and collapse in 1938, as the Wehrmacht and the SS came. About the overthrow and collapse in 1948, as the Communists came. About the overthrow and collapse in 1968, as the Soviets came.

He told me about anger.

About resistance.

About death.

About despair.

Winterberg told me that the years 1866 and 1989 were the two exceptions to this series of eights in Bohemian history. But he was certain that the next revolution and the next disruption would return with the number eight at the end.

In the station restaurant, we ate goulash and schnitzel and drank beer.

And then we drifted on.

We sat in a train heading south.

To Budweis.

There was still nothing to see. The wide, shallow Central Bohemian valley had become a great pot which was cooking fog that day instead of dumplings and sauce. But Winterberg didn't let it bother him.

He read about Austria-Hungary. About the most centrally located country in Europe, as it said in his Baedeker. He read about the country that no longer existed, except in his book. And in his head.

'Austria-Hungary consists of a range of diverse landscapes with different climates and ethnic groups, yes, yes, you see, it was all complicated from the start, too many climates and too many ethnic groups, dear Herr Kraus, too many problems, they can't be overcome as easily as the Alps by the railway, which of course wasn't easy at all, as we'll soon see… including large parts of the Alps in the southwest, extending deep into the Sarmatian flatlands to the northeast, containing an autonomous chain of the German uplands, the Bohemian massif, in the northwest… was that Beneschau?'

'What?'

'Beneschau.'

'I don't know.'

'That must have been Beneschau. Right around here is Konopischt, the castle of the Archduke Franz Ferdinand, the castle of the Crown Prince, yes, yes, I know what you're going to say, dear Herr Kraus, the Archduke should have stayed in Konopischt and not gone down to Sarajevo… I visited the castle when I was in Prague with my second wife. My wife felt sick from all the hunting trophies on the wall, yes, yes, you have to imagine it, dear Herr Kraus, hundreds, no, thousands, no, tens of thousands, no, hundreds of thousands of hunting trophies, yes, yes, Konopischt is a castle of death, dear Herr Kraus, my wife was physically ill, my wife couldn't manage to look at it, yes, yes, she had to leave the tour and was sick again in the park while she waited for me outside the castle… my wife had never before seen so much death and so much pain as in the wonderful castle of Konopischt, in the castle of death, yes, yes, that's what she said to me, and I tried to console her and explain to her that the Archduke always found his peace in the hunt, that the hunt was a passion for the Archduke, just as history and the railway are for me, I tried to explain to her that the Archduke lived for the hunt just as I lived for the railway and for history… yes, yes, the Archduke loved the hunt, until he became the victim of a hunt himself on a beautiful day in June in Sarajevo, when he and his wife were turned into June corpses, as my father would say… but my wife wasn't so easily soothed, she just kept crying and couldn't be calmed. The poor animals, the poor animals! she cried, it's good that the archduke was hunted down too, it's good that they did away with him! He deserved it… My wife loved animals, she didn't eat meat either, she accused me of bringing her to Konopischt on purpose to torment her, but that wasn't it at all, dear Herr Kraus, even back then I was just interested in the history, yes, yes, even back then I suffered from history, yes, yes, from the historical fits, just like my wife suffered from hysterical fits…'

Winterberg gave a short cough and looked out into the thick fog.

'We visited Konopischt with a tour group, all the tour groups from the West visited Prague and Konopischt Castle and Karlstein Castle and the brewery in Pilsen, and so did we, and then we travelled onwards to Reichenberg, because many in the tour group had been born in Reichenberg, like me… my wife cried and that made me very melancholy and also angry, yes, yes, I'll admit that, I was also angry, everyone was staring at us, everyone was talking about us, everyone was accusing us of spoiling the holiday-making spirit of our tour group… yes, yes, my wife was also violently ill several times on the bus, yes, yes, for days she couldn't get the dead animals, the hunting trophies of Franz Ferdinand, out of her mind… I can understand my wife now, it's all mad, she actually saw through history very well, because she knew that every hunter eventually becomes the hunted, eventually becomes fair game, like the Archduke in Sarajevo, yes, yes, it all comes full circle, that's how it always goes with history, yes, yes…'

Winterberg rambled and coughed a bit and continued to ramble, and I nodded like I always nodded, and the countryside lay drowned in mist and my eyelids were so heavy that I soon fell asleep.

And as I awoke, we were somewhere not far from Tábor.

There was still nothing to see. Just silhouettes of houses and forests and ponds. Small stations and cars sitting at the railway crossing. It was no longer fog outside, but a thick milk that someone had poured out over the country. And we were lost in this milk and trying to swim.

Winterberg was still reading aloud from his Baedeker and dominated the entire carriage, just as he always dominated any space, and I knew that he was feeling better.

'The merging of such disparate regions with entirely different economic fundamentals appears surprising at first glance, but is in fact well-grounded in the positional relationships of the individual parts, yes, yes, I don't know about that, perhaps that's exactly what started this whole catastrophe, dear Herr Kraus… they revolve around Vienna as their natural centre point, yes, yes, perhaps that was also the problem, too much Vienna all around, just one heart for such a large body, for such a large country… from which the state's growth has emanated and which has achieved international notoriety thanks to its favourable location at the intersection of the Danube and Baltic trading routes… the central valleys and passes of the northeastern Alps and the west Carpathians all point toward this place, where the Alpine foothills and the marshy lowlands meet the Hungarian plains… I'm already looking forward to Hungary, dear Herr Kraus, especially to Hungarian fish soup with lots of paprika… and Bohemia, encircled on three sides by forested mountains, is easiest to reach from this side, the eastern Alps and the Bohemian and Hungarian lands make up the central landscapes of the Austro-Hungarian Monarchy.'

The train stopped.

We were in Tábor.

And Winterberg exclaimed:

'Tábor, the old Hussite fortress! Yes, yes, all of Europe once trembled before the Hussites…'

He tried to open the window, but it was a newer train and it didn't open. He looked out of the window. The train station was the only thing visible.

'František Křižík built Austria's first electric railway in Tábor, there, there, do you see it?'

He pointed to a small train.

'That's it, yes, yes, the train to Bechin, built back in 1903, yes, yes, Křižík was also a railway pioneer, yes, yes, just like Gerstner or Carl Ritter von Ghega… they always believed in the power of electricity in Bohemia, Bohemia was always a land of progress, yes, yes, the first electric train was built in the Hussite fortress of Tábor and the first electric Feuerhalle in Semil, that region was also plundered by the Hussites, by the way, and later came under the possession of Wallenstein, yes, yes, in Bohemia, everything is connected to everything else… the Bohemians can look back upon their electric history with pride.'

The train left the station and Winterberg sat down and said nothing for a moment and looked out at the fog. And then he opened his book again.

'Austria-Hungary is justifiably referred to as the "Danube State", yes, yes, we already touched on that, yes, yes, the Elbe-Moldau-Danube-Sava-Bosna Monarchy, perhaps that would be only right after all, right and fair to all… the country stretches from the 42nd to 51st parallel and a longitude of 9° 31' to 26° east of Greenwich, and covers 676,062 square kilometres with a population of 51.4 million, make note of that, of which 300,005 square kilometres and 28.6 million people belong to Austria, please make note of that, dear Herr Kraus, and 324,857 square kilometres and 20.9 million to Hungary, no one can remember it all, while the region of Bosnia and Herzegovina, which is shared by both halves of the Monarchy, covers 51,200 square kilometres and has a population of 1.9 million, I can't remember any more of it, it's too much, but how do you think it looks today, dear Herr Kraus? The map of the distribution of nationalities is highly mixed, yes, yes, and perhaps that was the problem, too… a wide central area, which reaches from the Alpine foothills and the northern and northeastern Alps to the Hungarian plains through to Transylvania, houses three different ethnicities, Germans, Magyars, and Romanians, who are tasked with separating the northern Slavs from the southern Slavs, yes, yes, isn't that nicely written, the Slavs aren't solely responsible for the downfall and collapse…'

Winterberg coughed a bit and I passed him the bottle of water.

He read about Czechs and Slovaks and Poles and Ruthenians.

About Slovenes and Croats and Serbs and Bulgarians.

About Italians and Ladins.

About the Germans in Bohemia and in the Alps and in the Alpine foothills and in northern Moravia and in northern Silesia.

About the German linguistic enclaves in Hungary. In the Sudetenland. In Galicia. And in Bukovina.

He read about the Saxons in Transylvania.

'Yes, yes, prior to the 8th century, Germans had only settled in Upper Austria and in a few Alpine valleys… the occupation of the remaining linguistic regions took place through colonisation efforts in the 9th to the 11th centuries, of course I already knew all of that, but perhaps you didn't know it, dear Herr Kraus…'

He coughed a bit.

He read about the agricultural colonies in Hungary and in the vast forested regions.

About the mining towns and the cities.

He read about the more recent colonisation waves.

'10 million Germans live in Austria, where they form the relative but by far not the absolute majority, yes, yes, that's how it was… the Magyars live in the Hungarian plains and in some basins of Transylvania…'

And then suddenly Winterberg fell asleep.

Cork pulled.

Air out.

Eyes closed.

Goodnight.

The train stopped somewhere.

And then continued on its way.

And Winterberg slept and everything was quiet. So wonderfully quiet. And I fell asleep, too.

I dreamed of Carla. I dreamed that we were travelling somewhere with the train. Somewhere on the seaside. And then I was sweating and my heart raced and burned.

Winterberg woke up again. He coughed, cleaned his glasses, and picked up his book.

'Now where was I... yes, yes... they learned sedentism and agriculture from the Slavs and took over political organisation from the Germans, whose colonists had laid the foundation for clearing the more forested tracts of land and for developing the mining industry... the Germans had a similarly beneficial effect for the northern Slavs... in whose lands they had founded numerous cities and mines. These are inhabited by 6 million Czechs in central Bohemia, central and southern Moravia, and small parts of Silesia, and their linguistic neighbours, 2.5 million Slovaks, in the whole of the western Carpathians up to the edge of the Hungarian plains and eastwards to the Hegyalja foothills... the Poles live in eastern Silesia and western Galicia, but also form the cultural elite in the cities of eastern Galicia, whose population, the Ruthenians, are a Russian tribe... the Ruthenians also inhabit the Hungarian side of the Wooden Carpathians and northern Bukovina, interesting, interesting...'

I was already awake too, but I closed my eyes again. The train rattled on towards České Budějovice and Winterberg once again couldn't be stopped. And I thought, why can't he just shut his trap. What kind of sickness is that, anyway. Historical fits. Is it contagious?

'Overall, the ethnic borders have by and large remained the same for the last 700 years, yes, yes, and now to religion... in terms of religion, there are fewer differences... in Austria, 90.9 % adhere to the Catholic faith... then the Protestants... mostly present in the cities and in northern Bohemia... yes, yes, there were many in Reichenberg, without the Protestants there would be no Feuerhalle, as my father always said... Galicia and the Bukovina have a large population of Israelites, the dominant Magyar nation in Hungary is Catholic or Calvinist... the Romanians, Bulgarians and Serbs are Greek Orthodox... the Ruthenians are Greek Catholic... in Bosnia there are Roman Catholics, Greek Orthodox, and 32.3% adhere to the Muhammadan faith, yes, yes, you see, Herr Kraus, and yet it all still worked... but caution, dear Herr Kraus, it's not possible differentiate further by territory, as the Turkish laws concerning the holding of estates have privileged Islam... as mentioned, German culture, with its penetration into the east, has had a significant influence on the Slavs and the Magyars, which can be seen in the architecture and in household and business customs, this influence is clear to see as far as Carniola and Hungary, and also in and around Krakow, yes, yes, I wouldn't overdo it with the German influence there… but Krakow, I've never been there, have you ever been to Krakow, dear Herr Kraus?'

I said nothing and pretended to be asleep. But Winterberg wouldn't let me sleep.

'Hello… Herr Kraus… I know you're not sleeping…'

'I'm sleeping.'

'Then don't.'

I opened my eyes and yawned.

'What is it?'

'Have you ever been to Krakow?'

'No.'

'Me neither. Perhaps we'll go there, too.'

. . .

And then we were in České Budějovice.

In Budweis.

We alighted from the train and Winterberg remained standing on the platform. He opened his book and studied the old city map. I lit a cigarette.

'*Grandhotel Beneš*… should be good. The *Silberne Glocke* on the Ringplatz, good, the *Kaiser von Österreich*, also good… a hotel called *Kaiser von Österreich* couldn't possibly have been bad then… a city of 45,000 inhabitants, more than half of whom are Czech, pencil factory, tobacco factory, lumber trade… Radetzkystraße… Radetzkyplatz…'

'Let's go, it's cold.'

'Yes, yes, the Bohemians can be proud of the field marshal Radetzky whether they spoke Czech or German, what a shame that Benedek was no Radetzky, they said that it wasn't the Kaiser but Radetzky who held the empire together, but Radetzky would have been 100 years old in 1866, as old as I nearly am now… yes, yes, I'm not sure whether you can hold an empire together at 100 years old, you're no longer watertight, you often have to be in a state to hold other things entirely…'

'Herr Winterberg…'

'Yes, yes, but who remembers the field marshall Radetzky in Bohemia today, tragic, tragic, unfortunately human forgetfulness and historical idiocy aren't as easily overcome as the Alps by the railway.'

'I'm leaving now.'

'Yes, yes, his statue in Prague was torn down with the old Monarchy, just after I was born, and yet he was a proud Bohemian, just like I am, yes, yes, just like you are, dear Herr Kraus… we should really visit his grave in the crypt on the Heldenberg near Wetzdorf, they brought him there from Milan, where he died.'

'Can we finally go? It's cold. You'll get sick again.'

'Down the Schmerlingstraße to the entrance of the historical centre. The short Wiener Gasse leads straight to the Ringplatz.'

'Can we go? Hello?'

'In the park, a bronze statue of the highly-lauded industrialist Adalbert Lanna von Pönninger, city museum and German club house on the left.'

'So, I'm going now.'

I grabbed my luggage and walked towards the underpass.

'The brewery, Herr Kraus, the world-famous Budweiser brewery is missing from my Baedeker… it can't be true, it has to be a mistake, no, no, that can't be. Wait for me.'

We went to the hotel *Silberne Glocke*, 'Silver Bell', on the main square, which was now just called *The Bell*.

We went for a beer and a 'water corpse' sausage.

And I also ordered the brawn, because I like brawn. Winterberg tried it. But it was too sour for him, and he feared that it would make him sick.

'Yes, yes… my stomach has seen too much and experienced too much… did you ever go back to Winterberg, I mean, after the fall of communism?'

'No.'

'I've never been there, but my father was there once… they built beautiful coffins in Winterberg, too. They were cheaper than the coffins from Semil, but it was just too far away. At the tavern in Winterberg they all laughed about his name, yes, yes, it's not often that a Winterberg comes to Winterberg, yes, yes, a Winterberg from Reichenberg.'

I said nothing and ordered another Budweiser.

'Good beer.'

'Yeah.'

'Do they still make coffins in Winterberg?'

'I don't know.'

'I don't know where coffins are produced these days.'

'Maybe in China. Or in India…'

'But do they burn as well as the coffins from Semil?'

'Good question.'

'Why did you never come back?'

'There's no one there for me anymore. I'm not interested.'

'Perhaps you should go while we're in the area.'

'I don't think so.'

We paid and went to bed.

. . .

I dreamed about Vimperk that night.

About Winterberg.

I dreamed about my little sister. About my father. About my mother. And then again about my little sister.

It wasn't pleasant.

I woke up.

And went right back to sleep.

I dreamed about Carla.

I embraced her, and she embraced me.

She held me so tight that it hurt my chest.

So tight that I couldn't breathe.

So tight that it burned in my chest.

So tight that my heart was burning.

I woke up and my heart was racing as if it wanted to leave my body.

And I thought about Agnieszka, who said that I should see the doctor about it.

I was covered in sweat.

I had to shower.

And then I stood at the window, smoking and looking down at the empty market square of České Budějovice, and couldn't remember the last time I was here.

Perhaps that time when I met Hanzi.

Yes, that was it. It must have been there, in the pub on the corner. He came from somewhere in the Bohemian Forest and continued on to Hradec Králové the next day. We stayed the night with friends. Hanzi certainly didn't know anything about the Battle of Königgrätz in 1866 either. But he knew a lot about banned music. And about banned books, too. The name of the pub where we drank together escapes me. But what we discussed there, I've never forgotten.

I looked down at the square. It was still empty. Nothing was moving. Nothing at all.

At rest.

Cardiac arrest.

That's how it is when you die. When you arrive at the other side of the crossing.

That's what death looks like.

Not dying.

Death.

It was snowing. I grabbed another beer from the minibar and sat on the bed. And then I saw two flies. Two winter flies awoken by the warmth from their winter sleep. They flew back and forth, flew into the walls and into the window and into each other. They were confused and tired and drowsy and half-dead, and yet they were alive.

FROM BUDWEIS TO WINTERBERG

It was snowing as we returned to the train station. I went to buy our tickets to Linz, but Winterberg said that he wanted to go to Winterberg.

'No. I'm not going there.'

'Why not?'

'Because.'

'Herr Kraus… I'm begging you… My name is Winterberg and I've never been to Winterberg. I want to see the city.'

'It's like every other city. A castle… a market square… a cemetery… the barracks… nothing special.'

'You see! A castle. We're going.'

'No. We're not.'

'Yes, we are. I want to go to Winterberg and that's the end of it.'

'But we need to go in the other direction. You want to go to Bad Ischl… and the Alpine railways… and to Vienna and Budapest and Sarajevo…'

'I don't want to go to Bad Ischl, we were already in Bad Ischl.'

'What? When?'

'I don't know anymore… but I know we were already there…'

'You only dreamed about Bad Ischl when you were ill.'

'I've already been there, I don't need to go… but I haven't been to Winterberg yet. And then we'll take the train onwards to Pilsen, as long as we're already here, to compare the beer.'

'No.'

'Yes.'

'I'm saying no! NO! Do you understand? Or don't you? No! No! No! I. Won't. Go.'

Winterberg looked at me. And a few passers-by as well.

'German dolts,' said someone in Czech.

'What's all this about?' said Winterberg.

'I just don't want to go… I'll wait here for you.'

'No, you're coming with me… and you'll show me the city, yes, yes, I'm paying you for it. You have to come… and it'll do you good as well, believe me.'

And so we went.

It was snowing and Winterberg was beaming and reading about Pilsen and I felt ill and had to go smoke in the toilet and the conductor scolded me and I didn't feel better.

'Pilsen… *Zum Kaiser von Österreich* hotel, here too, just like nearly everywhere else, yes, yes, Smetana promenade, that would be nice, especially with some musical accompaniment from Smetana… or *Pilsener Hof* in the Zeughausgasse, both have good reviews, see, Herr Kraus… beer is served at the inns… for example in *Salzmann*, Prager Straße 8, perhaps it's still there, perhaps we'll go to *Salzmann* tonight… three hours are enough for a quick overview of the city, yes, yes, three hours should be enough for us, too.'

Winterberg wanted to take the longer and prettier mountain route to Winterberg through the Bohemian Forest, but the woman at the ticket counter said that the rail service in the mountains was disrupted and that they weren't using trains but buses. Rail replacement service. Winterberg didn't want that. So we travelled to Winterberg via Strakonice.

'The street signs are in Czech, that shouldn't be a problem as long as you're around… promenade is *"sady"* in Czech, yes, yes, nothing else is translated here, perhaps all you need to know in Pilsen is that promenade is *"sady"* and beer is *"pivo"*, yes, yes, now where was I again… yes, yes, Pilsen, industrial, yes, yes, once again this horrible word, and a famous beer city, that's not horrible at all, of course, that's lovely, 82,000 residents, including 9,000 Germans, lies at the convergence of the Mies and Radbuza rivers… I'm already looking forward to it.'

We changed trains in Strakonice and continued in the direction of Vimperk. The valleys became narrower and the hills taller and the curves sharper and the rickety little railcar squeaked and looked exactly as it did back then, when I took this train for the last time. We called the carriage the 'greenhouse' in the summer because it would often make you sweat like sitting in a greenhouse. And 'Siberia' in the winter because you'd often freeze here like sitting in Siberia. My father called the carriage 'swine', because in the curves it always squealed something awful, like a swine being slaughtered, he said.

It was snowing as we were travelling, and I felt as if an invisible rope, an invisible noose, were closing around my neck, and I couldn't breathe and my heart was racing and I felt ill.

'Wallenstein's conspiracy played out partly in Pilsen, you see, dear Herr Kraus, the Friedländer again, yes, yes, Wallenstein runs through our history like a spectre… straight ahead from the train station, then to the right below the viaduct, continue down the Bahnhofstraße, *Nádražní třída* in Czech, the Podiebradstraße, yes, yes, named after the Bohemian King Georg von Podiebrad an der Elbe, yes, yes, after that great European, what a shame no one knows him anymore, we really should have gone to see the castle in Podiebrad, we were so close, dear Herr Kraus.'

The tracks rose slowly into the Bohemian Forest and everything was covered in snow.

When I took this train for the last time, there was no snow. It was summer. June. I was travelling to Karlovy Vary, because Hanzi said that we would meet there at the colonnade, and there I would learn more details about our trip.

'Yes, yes, then left over the square *U Zvonu* and down the Zeughausgasse to the Ringplatz, or *Velké náměstí* in Czech, yes, yes, you see, with my Baedeker you can also learn Czech, yes, yes, in the centre, the Cathedral of St. Bartholomew, completed in the 15th century, with a 102 metre high tower, no, no, Lenka wouldn't like that, that would be much too high, you remember, dear Herr Kraus, her fear of heights… but perhaps we could do it, we aren't afraid of heights after all, yes, yes, 102 metres, that's really quite high, don't you think? Looking down from the top, the call of the void has surely taken a few already, yes, yes, the void has that kind of power, you often can't do anything to fight it… my father didn't like the jumpers either, tower-jumping-corpses aren't a pretty sight, as he always said, now where did I leave off again… yes, I know… here… a madonna statue on the main altar… did you ever read that book about Winterberg that I gave you in Reichenberg?'

'No.'

'Yes, yes… all in good time, could I perhaps have it this evening?'

I nodded.

And Winterberg read on.

'…on the north side, the city hall, built in 1558, lovely, lovely…'

I had never been to Karlovy Vary before. My parents thought I was going to school, to the lyceum, as usual. I was in my final year. My parents were very proud that I'd been accepted to the lyceum. My mother wanted me to become a doctor or a lawyer. My father, on the other hand, wanted me to go into the military, to study in Moscow, since his father and my grandfather had came to Bohemia from Moscow, from the Soviet Union. They were both born somewhere in today's western Ukraine. The Bohemian colonists who remained there until the war. My grandfather was later a colonel in the Czechoslovak Army and one of the liberators of the country. He was a communist, just like my father was a communist. He drank just like my father drank. He died of his diseased liver just like my father died of his diseased liver. Liver cancer corpses aren't a pretty sight, as Winterberg would say.

But Winterberg didn't know what I was thinking about. He continued to read aloud from his Baedeker.

'The West Bohemian Museum of Applied Arts… entrance by registration in the office, Director Josef Skorpil, yes, yes, I also knew a Skorpil in Reichenberg, he played first violin in the orchestra of the Reichenberg Stadttheater, a good acquaintance of my father's, he loved fine dining and became diabetic already as a young man, tragic, tragic, by the way, Skorpil's corpse was quite a pretty sight, my father said, an exception, because diabetic corpses otherwise aren't a pretty sight.'

My parents thought I was going to school, but I went to the train station and took the train to Strakonice and then to Plžen and then to Cheb and to Karlovy Vary.

Winterberg rambled on and read aloud from his book and lost himself in his history and his stories and I wasn't listening to him. I wanted to say to him, yes, actually, I was in Cheb, I was in Eger, at the train station in fact, I forgot that I'd been in Eger. You asked me in Reichenberg if I'd been to Eger, and I have been there, I caught the train to Karlovy Vary there. In 1866, it was all about the locomotive flight and about the German War. In 1986 it was also about a flight and about the

Cold War. My Cold War. My flight. I wanted to tell him, but he was in the grip of another historical fit and couldn't be stopped. And anyway, it doesn't concern anyone. It's just my own history.

'In the first floor, the historical museum … on the right, firearms, over 300 items, yes, yes, that interests me, certificates, old Pilsner prints, records, pictures of the city, that interests me too, in the second floor, applied arts museum, glass, ceramics, embroidery, that doesn't interest me …'

I said nothing and thought about my war and looked out of the window at the snow-covered forest and the white meadows and the increasingly taller hills and the small villages that were so familiar and yet also so alien to me, and I noticed how ill I felt, how I trembled and sweat and how my heart raced and how the rope around my neck was getting ever tighter.

I didn't want to go back to Vimperk.

To Winterberg.

I couldn't.

'But now this here interests me, and I'm certain it will interest you, too, dear Herr Kraus … listen to this … north of the train station, the Civic Brewery, founded in 1842, entry during the week, mornings from 9 to 11am and afternoons between 2 and 4 pm, with stone cellars, yes, yes, you need good, soft water and deep stone cellars, and then good hops as well, probably from Saaz in western Bohemia, I'm quite certain, yes, yes, but above all you need a good brewmaster, that's not so easy, the first Pilsner beer was brewed by a brewmaster from Bavaria, yes, yes, on the 5th of October, 1842, a fateful day, as my father always said, yes, yes, Pilsner Urquell is a fateful beer, yes, yes, a healing water, a holy water, that always reconciles the Bohemians, whether they speak Czech or German, yes, yes, beer reconciles us all, just like the fire of the Feuerhalle, everyone is equal there, too, just like in a tavern, as my father always said … the beer in Reichenberg was unfortunately never as good as in Budweis or Pilsen, the brewmasters weren't proper experts, as my father always said, the Reichenberg brewmasters were sadly proper idiots … not far to the east, the First Pilsen Joint-Stock Brewery, yes, yes, that's right, competition is always good and important, my father would have had nothing against a second Feuerhalle in Reichenberg, but it was never built… oh, I'm looking so forward to Pilsen, tonight we'll have a beer together, dear Herr Kraus.'

When I arrived in Karlovy Vary back then, I went to the colonnade. And there I met Hanzi and the others. Hanzi said it was time and asked if I was ready. It was all happening tomorrow. I was ready. I didn't know what was going to happen, how we were going to do it. But I wanted to get away.

I hated it.

The school.

The city.

My father's barracks.

I wanted to get out.

I wanted to live a little.

And yet I was also thinking that I could come back any time. To visit my parents.

It wasn't clear to me that it wouldn't be possible.

I was young.

I was stupid.

'To the west of the city, the world-famous Škoda factory, machines, locomotives, steel, artillery, yes, yes, locomotives and artillery… here we have it again, the railway and the war, yes, yes, it wasn't just tanks, many of the parts for the missiles in Peenemünde were produced here, yes, yes, and also in Prague and in Königgrätz… right up to the end of the war, they didn't just brew beer in Pilsen, they also built tank destroyers for the SS, yes, yes, the "light agitators", that's what they called them, yes, yes, the Englander also bombed the Škoda factory with his Lancaster, yes, yes, he turned parts of Pilsen into a Feuerhalle, just as the Germans turned many other cities into Feuerhalles, yes, yes, I know what you're going to say, dear Herr Kraus, *"the beautiful landscape of battlefields, cemeteries and ruins"* …'

I didn't know that I would never see my father and my mother again.

'But now for something about Winterberg, certainly we must be nearly there… your lovely city… and in a way, mine too.'

It was snowing and Winterberg flipped through his book.

'Here… I've found it… from Strakonitz to Wallern… five hours by train, no, no, we're not travelling that far, we're only going to

Winterberg… although, we really should do it, yes, yes, it's the highest railway line in the Bohemian Forest, after all, yes, yes, it's really a must-see for train people like us, it's a real mountain line, the highest point is the station in Kubohötten at 995 metres, yes, yes, it's more than 100 metres higher than the apex of the Semmering Railway, one can hardly imagine it… no, no, laying tracks across the Bohemian Forest certainly can't have been easy either…'

The train squealed in the forest high over the river.

'So, Winterberg… 696 metres, the *Habsburg* inn, twelve rooms, 2 to 4 crowns, good, perhaps it's still there, perhaps the *Habsburg* inn is still good, dear Herr Kraus, is the *Habsburg* inn still called *Habsburg*, probably not, I imagine… so, Winterberg… a small city 20 minutes southwest of the train station with 5,200 German residents on the Wolinka, that's the little river there… towered over by a castle of the prince of Schwarzenberg… which Schwarzenberg was it, dear Herr Kraus, there are so many Schwarzenbergs… notable timber industry, large crystal glass factory, oh, I'm looking forward to it… and you needn't be afraid, dear Herr Kraus, I'll look after you, we'll manage it.'

The train squealed and I saw the building where we had lived. A small communist-era apartment block where my father received an apartment from the army with a balcony and a view of the communist apartment block next door. I saw the hospital where my mother had worked as a nurse. I saw the roofs of the elementary school and the lyceum. I saw the curve where my little sister had been run over by the Soviets. I saw the tower on the market square. I saw the old barn where we'd secretly smoke in the back. I saw the castle of the prince of Schwarzenberg, which really did tower over everything, as Winterberg had said.

The train squealed and it made me think of the night when a few drunken soldiers from my father's tank company looked at the two bears in the castle trench and two of the soldiers had bet that they could bring down the bears in hand-to-hand combat. The two bears were much better than the soldiers in hand-to-hand combat, and so it was the bears who brought down the soldiers, driven by all the hate they harboured against humans and all of humanity, as the bears had been tormented for years by humans in the castle trenches.

The train squealed and Winterberg stopped rambling and looked out of the window.

On the horizon, we could see the highest peak of the Bohemian Forest.

Šumava.

Right behind it was Bavaria.

Bavorsko.

The train whistled and I saw the entry signal from the train station. Two yellow lights stacked on top of each other. I didn't know what the signal meant. But I knew we were here.

In Vimperk.

In Winterberg.

End of the line.

The train stopped and the doors opened and the cold air drifted in and stunk of brown coal.

The train station lay buried in snow. The passengers left the train. And Winterberg, too, stood up, packed his bags, and went to the door.

But I remained seated.

Winterberg looked at me.

But I remained seated.

'We have to get off.'

But I remained seated.

'Are you feeling unwell, dear Herr Kraus?'

I said nothing. I remained seated and stared at the floor and couldn't move. I was petrified. Like Panna and Baba, like the two petrified towers of the castle ruins of Trosky in Bohemian Paradise. I had also become a castle ruin, a fortress of stone and fear, and no one could do anything to help me.

Not Winterberg.

And certainly not the conductor, not under any circumstance.

'But this train ends here, it doesn't go on … it's going right back.'

But I remained seated and Winterberg shook his head and sat back down with me.

The train dispatcher raised the signalling disk, the locomotive driver whistled, and the small, rickety train rode back to Strakonice with us on board.

FROM WINTERBERG TO PILSEN

I looked at the floor.

Winterberg looked at me and then looked out of the window and then back at me.

'What?'

'Nothing.'

'Why are you staring like that?'

'Nothing.'

'Please, leave me alone.'

'Yes, yes, it'll be all right.'

'Nothing will be all right.'

'Herr Kraus…'

'Leave me alone!'

The train was rattling and squealing again in the short, sharp curves. It was snowing and Winterberg looked out at the snow and then he looked back at me and then back at the snow.

Just before Strakonice, he said that he understood everything.

'Back then, when I came back to Reichenberg for the first time after the war, I couldn't do it either, no, no… I felt just as derailed as you, dear Herr Kraus. I couldn't manage to leave the bus, I stayed in my seat and everyone thought that I'd gone mad. But I hadn't gone mad. I was just afraid.'

* * *

In Pilsen, we left our things at the train station. It really did take us just three hours to see the city, like it said in the Baedeker.

We walked through the city in silence amid the flurry of snow.

Winterberg rambled every now and then about something.

I didn't listen to him.

It was cold and snowing and the snow lay gently over the roofs and the streets and was whirled up by the wind and everything was quiet.

The city.

The cars.

The trams.

And me.

We couldn't find the hotel *Zum Kaiser von Österreich*.

But we did find the inn *Zum Salzmann*.

We ordered roast pork with caraway and sauerkraut and dumplings and beer.

I drank beer and Winterberg told me about the dumplings his mother had cooked.

About napkin dumplings.

About bread dumplings.

About pork dumplings.

About potato dumplings.

About Karlsbader dumplings.

About fruit dumplings.

I drank the next beer and Winterberg told me about his theory of 'Dumpling-Central-Europe', according to which dumplings connected everything and everyone.

I drank the next beer and the foam was so creamy that Winterberg went on to only order glasses full of foam.

I drank the next beer and thought about my father, who always said that a Muslim was obliged to make a pilgrimage once in their life to Mecca, and a Czech to Pilsen.

I drank the next beer and thought about the war that my father constantly waged with the other men in the pub.

The war between Budweiser and Pilsner Urquell.

My father could argue for hours with the other men about which beer was the best beer in the world.

Pilsner Urquell or Budweiser?

I drank the next beer and started to feel better.

I told Winterberg about my father, who was an officer of the People's Army of Czechoslovakia.

I told him that my father wasn't a colonel like my grandfather, but just a lieutenant.

I told him about my mother.

I told him about my little sister.

I told him about the summer evening when she was run over by the Soviets.

I told him everything, and Winterberg listened to me.

And I thought:

For the first time, he's listening to me.

And then he said:

'You don't have it easy either, dear Herr Kraus.'

We wanted to go back to the train station to take the last train back to Budweis.

But then someone told us that the hotel *Zum Kaiser von Österreich* was actually still there, just under a different name.

We took a taxi to grab our luggage from the train station and drove over.

A short time later, we stood drunk in the snowdrift in front of the old, noble hotel, which was no longer called *Zum Kaiser von Österreich*, but now *Slovan*.

The Slav.

'And so time goes by, everything comes to an end, everything passes by, oh, how time goes by…'

FROM PILSEN TO LINZ

We were both hungover. Just as soon as the train left for České Budě-jovice, Winterberg sprang from his seat and ran to the toilet. He was violently ill.

'Damn beer.'

'It wasn't the beer. It was the schnapps you ordered.'

'I didn't order any schnapps.'

'Yes, you did. In the hotel bar, for us and two women.'

'For which women? I can't remember… my head… why does it hurt so much?'

'But then they left. Don't worry, there were no moral slips.'

'Moral slips?'

'That's what my father always said. When you drink, there's always the threat of a moral slip.'

'And were they beautiful, these women?'

'They were, indeed.'

'You see, then I'm not old yet, I'm not yet transparent… I've always had good taste. I've always had beautiful women… yes, yes, life is too short to spend with women who aren't beautiful. Lenka was a gorgeous woman. Well, the important thing is to smell nice, yes, yes, you can't underestimate scent… oh… Nepomuk!'

He grabbed his book and his magnifying glass and flipped wildly through the pages.

'I've always wanted to go to Nepomuk… Nepomuk… birthplace of St. John of Nepomuk, born in 1320… more on page 297… one moment…'

He flipped through the pages and the train slowly left the station of Nepomuk.

'Yes, yes, here, of course, the Charles Bridge in Prague, it had to be here… its picturesque impression is mainly thanks to its rich decoration with statues… on the right, in the middle, cast in Nuremberg based on a model by Brokoff in 1683, a bronze statue of St. John of Nepomuk, the patron saint of Bohemia, first canonised in 1729, to which many thousands make a pilgrimage all year round, but particularly on May 16… I feel so ill, dear Herr Kraus, I think I may have to vomit again… a small marble plaque with a cross on the right side of the wall, between the sixth and seventh pillars, indicates the place where, according to legend, the pious priest was thrown from the bridge in 1383 at the orders of Wenceslas IV, yes, yes, they didn't much like each other, Wenceslas and Nepomuk. And so Wenceslas ordered that Nepomuk be drowned in the Moldau, yes, yes, two fishermen fished him out of the river, water corpses aren't a pretty sight.'

He flipped back.

'Nepomuk… here… at the location of his parents' house stands the Church of St. John, consecrated in 1686, an alter indicates the birthplace of the saint, that has to be the church over there, do you see it?'

'Yeah.'

'Branch line to Blatná, yes, we're not going there… perhaps another time. We're heading to Vienna, yes, yes, finally. Now where did I leave off?'

'The women.'

'Yes, precisely… I feel so sick… why do I feel so sick… beer is no holy water… if you don't smell nice, everything is lost. You needn't even unpack your bags, you can just get up and go… oh, poor Nepomuk, truly a martyr, yes, yes, you can be hated, you can be tortured, you can be drowned, and only then can you be canonised, it's all mad… I feel so ill… I knew a tram driver in Spandau, he also wanted to be canonised, but right then, while he was still alive, he didn't want to wait, he said he wanted to enjoy it while he still could. He once saved two nuns from a tram accident, yes, yes, and he really did, if not for him, then both nuns would be dead. But the church didn't canonise him, the priest said it isn't that easy, first he has to die, ideally as a martyr, and only then would they consider it. And so he later hanged himself… as far as I know, he hasn't been canonised yet, no, no… I feel so poorly, Herr Kraus. I think I have to…'

Winterberg stood up and stumbled to the toilet.

And then he returned, looking very pale.

'The tram driver was such a pious man, yes, yes, he was the only Catholic tram driver in Berlin that I knew, he lived alone and yet he wasn't alone… yes, yes, he lived in a flat in Spandau with forty birds, yes, yes, with sparrows and tits and pigeons, but also with kestrels, which would hunt the pigeons and the other birds in his flat. I saw it, I visited him several times, he always sat in the middle of the room and watched the birds for days on end, yes, yes, he always had to keep the window closed, it stunk something awful in the flat, the birds shat on everything, and he too stunk something awful, yes, yes, I was the only friend he had, no, no, rope corpses aren't a pretty sight. He hanged himself in the living room on the light fixture, and when they found him, there were two pigeons sleeping on his shoulders as if on a statue, one pigeon on his left shoulder, the other on his right shoulder, yes, yes, that's how it was back then in Berlin, most people hanged themselves in Berlin, I'm quite sure of that… another colleague of mine, another one stranded by the war like me, collected old chamber pots, he wanted to open a museum when he retired, I had no idea there were so many types of chamber pots. He was looking so forward to his retirement, but one day he popped out to do the shopping, and a fire engine…'

Winterberg suddenly fell asleep, just as he always fell asleep.

The train travelled through southern Bohemia and I fell asleep too and only awoke in Budweis. It was snowing and we changed trains in the direction of Linz. Winterberg thought about travelling to Vienna via Gmunden, to see the Heldenberg, but then he settled on the route via Linz after all, as Budweis and Linz and Gmunden had once been connected by a horse-drawn tramway.

'Yes, yes, it was the first railway in Austria. We really must see it, we'd regret it otherwise.'

The train snaked slowly through the Bohemian Forest. It was snowing more and more and not much was visible. The train became emptier with each station and Winterberg told me about the horse-drawn tramway opened between 1827 and 1836.

About the first railway in Austria.

About the second-oldest railway in Europe.

He told me about the railway pioneers of Mathias Schönerer and Franz Josef Ritter von Gerstner and Franz Anton Ritter von Gerstner.

He told me that they weren't afraid of the mountains and the wilderness and boldly built tracks through the Bohemian Forest, as we can still see today.

'Yes, yes, look over there, the old bridge, those are the remains of the horse-drawn tramway, yes, yes.'

He looked out of the window, but I couldn't see anything.

'And there, a monument, do you see it?'

It was snowing and snowing and the conductor said that if it continued to snow like this, the trains would come to a standstill for a couple of days.

Just like last year.

'Yes, yes, that's exactly what will happen.'

Just like every year.

'Yes, yes, that's how it'll be.'

The conductor said that we were the only passengers today taking his train over the border, the others had already alighted. He said that on some winter days there would be no passengers travelling over the border at all, and then he would sit in his train all alone. He said it's actually like that on many winter days. He said he liked it. He said he liked winter in the Bohemian Forest. He said he had five kids at home so he enjoyed being alone in the train and reading books. He said he liked to read books about the Bohemian Forest most of all. He said that yesterday a colleague of his, an old shunter, fell asleep in the first train of the day after his night shift in České Budějovice and missed his station.

He said that he slept all the way to Linz and only there did someone wake him. He said he took the next train from Linz back to České Budějovice for his next night shift. He said that it won't happen to us, we can't sleep past our train station, after all, we were going to Linz.

And we don't have to work the night shift.

Then he continued on and Winterberg fell asleep, the train glided silently through the winter landscape. The snow was piling higher and higher.

I saw a village with derelict houses.

I saw a hunting perch on the edge of a wide clearing.

I saw the trees that had been toppled from the storm.

I saw a forest road that disappeared up into the woods.

Suddenly the train braked and came to a stop. I opened the window. It was snowing and it was so still that I could hear my heartbeat. Winterberg's heartbeat. The snow drifting down over the landscape.

It was snowing and the locomotive stood with our train in a long curve. It stood on a tall railway embankment before an entry signal which was glowing red in the snow. I saw a narrow culvert and a frozen creek. And then I saw something else. It was grey and white and red. It was bleeding. It was a deer that had been hit by a train and was now being gently buried by the snow on the embankment. The snow was falling and I looked for a long time at this snowy grave.

The locomotive whistled, released the brakes, and the train began to move. We waited briefly at the border station for the train coming in the opposite direction and then drifted onwards through the snow. We were in Austria. Winterberg cleaned his glasses, opened his book, and wanted to read something about Linz. But then he simply sighed and closed the book again.

He looked out of the window exhausted and resigned. As if it weren't him who was giving our journey direction and purpose. As if we were being driven forward without knowing where. Without knowing why. Without knowing if there was a purpose to it all.

And yet we were driving forward.

Winterberg said nothing and closed his eyes again.

I did too.

I thought about the two winter flies that I had awoken from their hibernation at the hotel in České Budějovice. That were alive and yet not. That were so lost and confused. That were awake and yet tired and drowsy.

We were the two winter flies.

* * *

And then we were in Linz.

And looked for a hotel.

And today Winterberg didn't care whether the hotel was in his Baedeker or not.

He was still tired and hungover.

And then we ate fish.

And then we stood on the long bridge and looked into the darkly gleaming Danube. The wind was blowing and we looked into the strong current. We heard the trams driving past us.

And Winterberg said:

'My mother always baked Linzer biscuits at Christmas.'

'Mine too.'

'Also pasted together with marmalade?'

'Yeah.'

We looked into the Danube and a freight ship was passing under us on its way to Vienna.

'With cherry marmalade?'

'Yeah. Mostly.'

'I didn't much like Christmas otherwise.'

'Me neither.'

'We're quite high up again, dear Herr Kraus…'

Winterberg stood on tips of his toes, gripped the handrail and looked into the Danube. Into the dark depths below us.

'Good thing this is such a sturdy handrail, just one foul step and you'd quickly become a water corpse, one they'd perhaps only fish from the Danube in Vienna or in Budapest, or possibly never… yes, yes, they fished out Nepomuk, Nepomuk is the most famous water corpse of the Moldau, perhaps the most famous water corpse in the world, yes, yes, everywhere in Bohemia and in Austria you find a church or a chapel or a statue of Nepomuk, including here in Linz… the Englishman always said that the three most important religions originated in the desert, yes, yes, but the water, the river, it also plays a role, what would the Catholic Church be without the Moldau, what would the Catholic Church be without the water corpse of Nepomuk, dear Herr Kraus. It'd be nothing.'

A train could be heard rattling over the bridge in the distance.

'Yes, yes, just as the religions are bound up with the desert and with the rivers, the history of war is bound up with the railway.'

We looked into the dark river.

'Why do you have that rope in your bag?'

'In case of fire.'

'What d'you mean, fire?'

'In case of fire, I can rappel to the ground.'

I lit a cigarette.

'And the pistol?'

'You never know what can happen, dear Herr Kraus.'

'Where did you get it?'

'From the Englishman.'

'Uh-huh. Okay...'

'He wanted to shoot himself back then in Berlin.'

'And you?'

'What, me?'

'Did you try to do the same?'

'Yes, but I couldn't do it. And you, Herr Kraus? Did you try to do it?'

'Yeah. I couldn't do it either. The only thing I could do, was drink.'

FROM LINZ TO VIENNA

The train to Vienna was full and raced over the new tracks. It travelled so fast that you could hardly see a thing. Just the snowy mountains off in the distance.

Winterberg didn't like the route. He said he would have preferred to travel via Krems with a change in St. Pölten, but the woman at the counter in Linz hadn't understood Winterberg.

She asked him multiple times why he wanted to take the longer way when the trains ran so quickly and comfortably on the new tracks to Vienna. Winterberg tried to explain it to her. At first rather calmly and then unfortunately less calmly and in the end not calmly at all.

He began to quiver and to yell that it he didn't care if he arrived in Vienna ten minutes earlier or ten minutes later, Vienna wasn't running off anywhere, Vienna had stood for hundreds of years where it was standing now, and where it would continue to be standing in another hundred years.

But she still didn't understand and attempted to explain it to him once more.

Winterberg capitulated and then did finally buy us the tickets for the faster connection without changing trains.

And so Winterberg was in a foul mood that morning.

He read his book to calm himself. But he read increasingly faster and became increasingly angrier.

'Vienna, the old capital and residence city of the imperial Austrian state, now capital of half the Austro-Hungarian Monarchy, seat of the highest imperial offices and the provincial offices of the Archduchy of Lower Austria, a Roman Catholic Prince-Archbishop, and the Command Centre of the Second Army Corps, yes, yes, it lays under 48° 12' north latitude and 16° 22' east longitude, not interested in that, average elevation of 170 metres at the eastern foot of the Vienna Woods, almost entirely on the right bank of the multi-streamed Danube with only the district of Floridsdorf on the left, not interested in that, the main stream was given a new riverbed 284 metres wide over a length of 13 kilometres as a result of the Danube regulation carried out in 1870–77, not interested in that, the city covers nearly 275 square kilometres, I'm not interested in that.'

A short, portly gentleman with a briefcase sat down next to us and listened intently to Winterberg.

'The urban area is surrounded by a wide belt of forests and meadows to the west and northwest, which ensures a supply of clean air amidst the prevailing western winds and is to remain protected from any extensive construction activity, not interested in that either, with 2,031,500 residents as of 1910, Vienna holds the fourth place among the great metropolises of Europe…'

'Excuse me… may I ask you something?'

'No.'

'I understand… I didn't want to bother you…'

'What do you want?'

'How old is that book?'

'Old.'

'How old then?'

'1913, the last edition before the war.'

'Lovely… but surely it's not all that accurate anymore, is it?'

'Why wouldn't it be?'

'I mean…'

'It's far more accurate than you can imagine.'

'Lovely.'

'Yes, it is lovely, or else it's awful. It depends on how you look at it.'

'There are newer guidebooks out there.'

'I'm only interested in this book. In 1913, the world was still in order.'

'But it really wasn't. The war happened right afterwards.'

'Exactly. I'm aware of that too, of course. But one can believe that it was in order… anything else?'

'No.'

'Good. The native language and social language of more than four-fifths of the residents is German. The rest are divided, with one half comprising Slavic immigrants, mostly Czechs, at 98,400, and the other half comprising peoples of the Hungarian lands as well as other nationalities, I'm not interested in that, only one-third of residents are not adherents of the Roman-Catholic faith, among them 73,400 Protestants and 174,500 Jews… the garrison is composed of four infantry brigades, each with two cavalry and artillery brigades, for a total of 26,560 men.'

'Excuse me, may I ask you another question?'

'No.'

'I just wanted…'

'What do you want?'

'Where are you from?'

'Berlin. But I was born in Reichenberg, if you know where that is.'

'Yes, yes, I know.'

'And this gentleman here is a proper Czech.'

The man froze and suddenly appeared very sad. He looked at me for a long time and I looked at him too.

'You're Czech?'

'Yes? And?'

'And what do you see?'

'What?'

'What do you see when you look at me?'

'I don't know.'

'You see a wreck. You can go on and say it. It's all the Czechs' fault.'

'Of course, it's always the others' fault.'

'My first car was stolen in the Czech Republic, they found it later without a motor, without wheels, without seats. A genuine wreck, just like I am now. But there's more. My first wife was a Czech woman from Znojmo. She set my house on fire and ran off with my best friend. But there's more. I invested together with a Czech partner in a winery in the Czech Republic. He cheated me and what do you think happened to the money?'

'Buggered.'

The man looked at me sadly.

'So it is. Buggered. It's all buggered. And it's all the Czechs' fault. But you know what the worst part is? My name is Sykora, 'great tit'. I'm from Bohemia myself. My grandfather came to Linz from Nymburk. That's my problem, I'm a Czech myself, I'm buggered myself, I'm a wreck, just like my first car that got stolen in the Czech Republic. No, I know I'm a wreck, you don't have to console me.'

He got up and left our compartment in tears.

Winterberg stared after him.

'And so time goes by, everything comes to an end, everything passes by, oh, how time goes by. You see, Herr Kraus, where it can lead when you lose one woman and can't find another? To mental derangement, to a tunnel with no end. That's not as easily overcome as the Alps by the railway… and you say that I wallow in self-pity.'

'I've never said that.'

'But you think it.'

'Yeah.'

'That's fine. It's true, too, yes, yes, and why can't you wallow in self-pity. Is it forbidden? But I'll tell you one thing, they shouldn't let that man walk near the train tracks unsupervised, yes, yes, I once nabbed a sad case like that with my tram in Berlin, he'd stood there all day, and in the end it was my tram he chose for his demise.'

'And, did he survive?'

'Well, as my father would say, it wasn't a pretty sight.'

Our train entered a long tunnel.

'That must be the Vienna Woods… the new train line isn't in my book, but it doesn't matter, I won't let it get to me. Once we're in Vienna…'

And then Winterberg fell asleep. Suddenly, as always.

And I did too.

. . .

We arrived in Vienna and Winterberg opened his eyes for a moment, gave a start, and then closed them again immediately. And then he placed a pair of sunglasses in front of his horn-rimmed glasses.

'What's wrong?'

'I can't stand to look.'

'What is it this time?'

'I can't bear it.'

'What is it?'

'This again.'

He told me about the new train station in Vienna.

He told me about glass and concrete, about the downfall of travel culture, about the Königgrätz of architecture.

'The main train station in Prague... that's a proper train station. But this here? A travesty. Just like in Berlin. Or in Linz.'

We exited the train.

'Herr Kraus, get me out of here immediately, please. Out! This is no train station. This is a shopping centre... get me out of here immediately, or else I'll die, yes, yes, or else that's it for me, please get me out of here immediately and let me know when we're finally in Vienna.'

'But we're in Vienna now.'

'No, no, we're not. Take me out of this dreadful department store, let me know when we're standing in front of a nice, old building. Train stations used to be cathedrals of transport. And now? Shopping malls. Thoroughfares. Nothing more than that. Yes, yes, Rudolf Bitzan always designed his train stations as places to stay and places to leave and places to arrive, yes, yes, and my father said he designed his Feuerhalles like that too. And now? Horrible. Bitzan would vomit in an instant here, this station would derail him.'

I looked at Winterberg, who facing the floor with his eyes closed. I took our luggage and Winterberg's hand and we walked through the loud new Vienna Central Station.

Past the clothing stores.

Past the bistros.

Past the ticket machines.

'How long can it take! How much longer is it! The demise of travel culture, yes, yes, poor Carl Ritter von Ghega would vomit in an instant too... back in his time, the stations were designed like cathedrals, even the smallest train stations in the Waldviertel or in Bohemian Paradise or in Galicia were built as little churches, and the platform stops as village chapels, poor Carl Ritter von Ghega, that poor hero, it's a good thing he didn't survive, it's a good thing he died of consumption... a train station like a shopping centre, a train station like a circus tent, yes, yes, it's the Königgrätz of railway architecture. You can't open the windows on the train these days, you can't even properly smoke there... the downfall. And yet another Königgrätz.'

'You don't even smoke.'

'But if I did smoke, it wouldn't be possible anymore in the train... nor here in the station either, tragic, tragic... but you smoke, it must bother you.'

'I can go without.'

'It bothers me.'

'Or I smoke in the toilets.'

'And it bothers me even more that it doesn't bother you, yes, yes, soon they'll forbid you from drinking beer in the train too.'

'I don't think so.'

'You'll think of me when they do. How much longer is it, Herr Kraus, why aren't you doing anything... I'm dying, how much longer? When will we finally be in Vienna?'

We were already out in front of the station.

I looked around. And then I saw it.

'I think we're here. We don't need to go any further, Herr Winterberg.'

'Yes, yes, Vienna.'

'No. Sarajevo.'

'What, Sarajevo?'

Winterberg took off his sunglasses and opened his eyes.

'Really. It's Sarajevo.'

We crossed the loud and groaning heavily trafficked street. And then we were there.

In Sarajevo.

THE IMPERIAL CRYPT

The coffee in *Sarajevo* was strong.

The beer sweet and cold.

The ćevapčići fatty and delicious.

Winterberg calmed back down.

'I'm looking so forward to Bosnia. It'll be such a lovely train ride.'

'Train ride?' laughed the barmaid, a Bosnian woman. 'No one takes the train to Sarajevo these days, only a crazy person would do that. Take the bus.'

'We're not taking the bus.'

'Then go by car. You don't have a car?'

'No.'

'Everyone has a car in Bosnia.'

'We're taking the train.'

'Or stay here. *Sarajevo* like Sarajevo… I'm telling you, my Sarajevo is the best and most beautiful Sarajevo in Vienna. And there are a few others… but what do you want in Sarajevo?'

'We're looking for someone there… a woman. It's a long story…'

A man sat down next to us. A large man built like a tank.

'I assumed you were heading there because of the war.'

'That too, you're right. Because of 1914.'

'1914… that's no war… let me show you something.'

He pulled up his t-shirt and showed us his torso. It was riddled with several bullet scars.

'That's war. I was hit eight times by those bastards, but a cat has nine lives.'

'And a tomcat too, Zlatko,' said the barmaid, and kissed him on his bald head.

The man told us how miserable it was. Every day, he had to fill in each of these eight holes, each of these eight tombs in his belly, with eight schnapps so that the wounds wouldn't burst and everything stayed where it was supposed to be.

Winterberg said the eight schnapps were on him.

'That's his trick. It always works,' said the barmaid.

'What trick? It's true!'

'I know, Zlatko.'

He drank the first schnapps and she kissed him again on his shiny, bald head.

She told us that she loved the eight little tombs in her husband's belly, but the most beautiful tombs in Vienna were the tombs in the Imperial Crypt. She knew that because she did the housekeeping there when she wasn't working at *Sarajevo*.

She told us that she wiped down the sarcophagi of the Habsburg family there three times a week.

She told us that she loved the massive sarcophagus of Maria Theresa the most, which the Empress had commissioned while she was still alive.

She told us that she also loved the modest sarcophagus of her son Joseph.

She told us her stories and Winterberg listened to her in fascination and said:

'You are a very interesting woman.'

'I'm really not.'

'Yes, yes, you are, you see through history.'

The barmaid smiled and her husband drank the next schnapps and said:

'What do you mean by that? "Interesting woman"?'

Winterberg didn't say a word and looked at the barmaid.

And the man turned to me:

'What does he mean by that?'

'He loves history. And his father built the first crematorium in the Monarchy, in Liberec, in Reichenberg. He's from an undertaker family, that's why...'

'It's not a crematorium, it's a Feuerhalle,' said Winterberg. 'The first Feuerhalle in Austria.'

The man drank the next schnapps.

'Reichenberg is in Austria?'

'Yes. In the Czech Republic. It used to be in Austria.'

'Why isn't it in Austria anymore?'

'Because then Reichenberg was in Czechoslovakia, and because now it's the Czech Republic.'

'But why?'

'What do you mean, why. Why isn't Sarajevo in Austria anymore?'

'Sarajevo was in Austria?'

'Yes.'

'Sarajevo was never in Austria. Sarajevo has always been in Bosna.'

'Yes, of course Sarajevo was in Austria, Zlatko,' said the barmaid.

'You taking the piss out of me?'

He drank the next schnapps.

'No. You know I love you, Zlatko.'

She kissed him again on his bald head and he hugged her and kissed her back.

'I don't want to end up in a crematorium. I don't want to be burned,' said the man. 'It must be so claustrophobic and so hot in there, no, no, we bury our dead in graves.'

'But Zlatko, if you're dead, you won't notice if it's too claustrophobic or too hot for you.'

'Still, still. We don't burn anyone in Bosna. It's against God.'

He drank the next schnapps.

'You won't notice anything when you're dead.'

'I'd rather be laying next to you in the Imperial Crypt. With you.'

He slapped her ass.

'Yeah, right, letting tourists take pictures of you all day like you're in the circus and waiting until the worms finally make it to you through the lead.'

'The worms don't bother me.'

He drank the next schnapps.

'But they won't get in, Zlatko, don't you understand? They can't get in, the sarcophagi are made of metal, how awful, how are the worms supposed to manage?'

'I'd manage it.'

'No, you wouldn't, Zlatko.'

'I always manage to get through everything, you know what I mean… back then… I managed to get through all of it.'

'I know, I know, but the sarcophagi of the Habsburg family are armoured, they're soldered shut, I've seen it all, they're lying there like a waiting room. No, I'd rather go to the crematorium.'

'Then do it. I won't.'

'It's called a Feuerhalle.'

'Is the crematorium still functioning?'

'Or a fiery tomb. I don't like the word crematorium, no, no, it feels too cold to me, I just don't like it.'

'Yes,' I said. 'It's still functioning.'

'Then let's go tomorrow, we'll go to… what was it called again?'

'Liberec,' I said.

'It's called Reichenberg,' said Winterberg.

'Right, we'll go there and check it out. Is it nice there?'

'It rains the entire time. Or snows. It's in a mountain valley.'

'Like Sarajevo… and is it easy to find, the crematorium?'

'It's called a Feuerhalle. I don't like the word crematorium.'

'Yeah.'

'And is it far?'

'Walk straight towards the city from the train station, then ask about the mountain of fire… everyone in Reichenberg knows where the mountain of fire is, yes, yes, you can't miss it either. It's the most beautiful hill in the entire city.'

'All right. Thank you. I've never been to the Czech Republic.'

'There's a crematorium in Vienna too,' I said. 'I mean, a Feuerhalle.'

'No, let's go to Reichenberg, do you want to come, Zlatko? The first crematorium in Austria is in the Czech Republic, and the first brewery in Sarajevo was also built by the Czechs.'

'Yeah, and you can go on and have yourself burned while you're at it.'
He drank the next schnapps.

'But Zlatko…'

'Dobro došli.'
He drank the next schnapps.

'To you. To the crematorium. To the Feuerhalle.'
He drank the next schnapps.

'Don't drink it all so fast, Zlatko… you know…'

'I won't let myself be burned.'

Winterberg opened up his book, read about Vienna and said:

'Mad. All mad.'

'What, mad?'

The man first looked at Winterberg, and then at me.

'The old man thinks I'm mad? Hey, mate – fuck off!'

Winterberg didn't react. He was reading about the museums of Vienna.

'He should watch his mouth!' The man turned to me. 'Is he taking the piss?'

'He's not talking about you,' I said. 'He's talking about himself.'

'Yeah, Zlatko, calm down.'

'Are you taking the piss?'

'No.'

'Exactly, don't go losing the plot,' said the barmaid.

Winterberg continued to read his Baedeker.

The barmaid told us that she believed some of the sarcophagi were empty, because when she tapped the metal coffins with her broom, many of them sounded as if no one were there. As if no one were home, as she said it.

She tapped on the table as if tapping on a coffin.

'So, you see? That's what it sounds like. There's nothing inside. They say that the bodies were stolen and sold off. My colleague, a Slovak, thinks they were sold to the Japanese, they collect quirky things like that.'

'To the Japanese!'

The man drank the next schnapps.

'Zlatko, don't drink so fast!'

The barmaid kissed him on the head and told us that the corpses lay in the Imperial Crypt without hearts or organs, since those were in the Augustinian Crypt. They were also lying there without viscera; those were in the catacombs under St. Stephen's Cathedral. She rambled on and Winterberg listened to her. She told us that an old retiree came to the Imperial Crypt every day and counted the sarcophagi to make sure none were missing, and every day he miscounted them. He told her that one day all the pieces would reunite and Old Austria would rise from the dead and perhaps the Crown Prince Rudolf really would become Kaiser. Rudolf, the murderer and self-murderer, but a bright young man, the cleverest in the Habsburg family.

She rambled on and Winterberg listened to her intently.

'You're an exceptional woman. You can tell such lovely stories.'

'I don't know.'

'Yes, yes.'

The barmaid smiled and her husband looked at Winterberg angrily.

'An "exceptional woman"? What d'you mean by that? Listen, you...'

He stood up and wanted to seize Winterberg by the collar, but he was already too drunk. He toppled over and passed out.

'You see, Zlatko? I told you, you shouldn't drink that stuff too fast. And we wanted to go to Reichenberg tomorrow... well, that's my husband. My Zlatko.'

Her husband slept and she kissed him on his bald head.

'But why do you work in the crypt? You have this place.'

'Because I like working there.'

She told us how she left Sarajevo during the war with her husband and started working in the Imperial Crypt, it was only several years later that she took over the *Sarajevo*. She told us how much she loved working in the Imperial Crypt, although the Slovak woman insisted that it was haunted, and that she once had to chase the ghost of Empress Elisabeth back into her coffin with her broom.

She rambled on and her husband slept with his head on the table and Winterberg listened to her.

She told us about the retiree who came to the Imperial Crypt every day, who said that he could also imagine Maximilian as the next Kaiser, the Emperor of Mexico, who was well-read and certainly wouldn't jump right into a war with Russia. She told us the retiree had once proposed to her in front of the sarcophagus of Empress Elisabeth, because he thought perhaps he wouldn't have to pay for the entrance ticket to the Imperial Crypt every day. She told us the Imperial Crypt was nearly full, there was only room for one more corpse.

'I'm excited to see who'll get to lie in the last sarcophagus, whose grave I'll be dusting next. Assuming the corpse isn't sold to the Japanese.'

She told us about the Slovak woman, who had just started dating a tour guide from the catacombs under St. Stephen's Cathedral and had been wondering the whole time what kind of lovely, strong perfume her lover was using, until it turned out that it was the scent of the catacombs, the musty perfume of the world under Vienna.

The barmaid rambled and her man slept and Winterberg listened to her. Then he motioned as if to say something. But in that instant, he dropped forward with his face in his book and fell asleep.

'What happened to him?' she asked.

'He's asleep. He likes to do that.'

And so both men lay there. Winterberg and her husband. Zlatko.

In the late afternoon, Winterberg and I went to visit the Imperial Crypt.

Winterberg looked around, and as soon as no one was in sight, he knocked cautiously on one of the sarcophagi. And then on the next. And then on one more.

'The Bosnian woman was right, dear Herr Kraus. They really are empty, no one's there. Or, what do you think? Is someone in there?'

Winterberg knocked on the beautiful sarcophagi of the Imperial Crypt and a group of Japanese tourists laughed and filmed him at it.

'No one here. Maybe someone here. No one in this one either. Here, I don't know... someone here. No one here. Someone here. No one here. No one here either...'

Winterberg knocked on all the sarcophagi of the Habsburg family as if they were a series of bells, as if the Imperial Crypt were nothing more than a massive chime, as if he were playing the chime in order to ring the dead back to life.

Then he set off the alarm. And one of the guards who then escorted us to the exit said that we were formally banned from the Imperial Crypt. He said that the loonies have no business among the dead.

LOVE

We were eating breakfast in the *Astoria*. That was the name of our hotel. It was in the Baedeker. And Lenka had stayed here too, as Winterberg said. She'd sent him a postcard from here.

We were eating breakfast and the city was still grey and the sky looked the same as it had yesterday.

It made me think of Carla's grey eyes, of the two small, deep pools in the soft, slender, protracted landscape of her face.

We were eating breakfast with a couple of Asian and Arabic tourists and I thought about our crossing, which lasted nearly a year and which was one of my first crossings, after I had left Bavaria, just as I had left Czechoslovakia before. Only less dramatic, and less bloody.

We were eating breakfast and Winterberg cleaned his glasses and read aloud from his book with the magnifying glass, a coffee and cheese roll sitting on the table in front of him.

'The main sight in Favoriten, near the Southern Station, sadly that one isn't around anymore, yes, yes, tragic, tragic, and the State Station isn't around anymore either, tragic, tragic, the Imperial and Royal Artillery Arsenal near Maria-Josefa-Park, built between 1849 and 1855, a 689 metre long, 480 metre wide rectangle with eight blocks of barracks, yes, yes, lovely, lovely. Enter through the northwest side of the beautiful commandant's building designed by architects Sicardsburg and van der Nüll, sandstone statues by Hans Gasser above the entrance... yes, yes, Sicardsburg and van der Nüll, from the Arsenal to the State Opera House, look at that, dear Herr Kraus, war and art are just as intertwined as the war and the railway, yes, yes, like the railway and the Feuerhalles, it's all mad, the two architectural friends are also victims of Königgrätz, just like you and I, we'll come back to that later,' he said, and drank a bit of his coffee.

I was reading the newspaper and Winterberg noticed that I was reading the newspaper and said: 'Of course, you find a newspaper from today more important and more interesting than a book from the past. Shallow journalism pitted against science, tragic, tragic.'

And he continued reading aloud from his book.

'In the inner courtyard, across from the commandant's building, the Imperial and Royal Military History Museum, built in a mixed Roman-Byzantine style by Förster and Hansen to house the collection of the former Imperial Armoury, with rich artistic decoration on the central block.'

'You've long since memorised all that. Why do you keep reading it?'

'You've already asked me that, and I've already answered.'

'But still.'

'Once again: I read it so I don't forget, yes, yes, so I don't forget the history, because someone has to do it, yes, yes, because no one sees through history these days. And don't interrupt me when I'm reading.'

'Then read it quietly. Read it to yourself. I'm reading too.'

'If I read it quietly then I won't remember it. I can only remember it when I read it aloud. That's always been the case. And don't interrupt me when I'm reading, all right?'

'Yeah, yeah,' I said, and set the newspaper down on the side table.

I looked out of the window. Everything was still grey, and it made me think of Carla again. She wanted to travel the whole world, but the only trip she took was our journey together.

Winterberg read so loud that the other guests were constantly looking over at us.

But Winterberg didn't let that bother him.

'Catalogue, 1.5 crowns. Curator Dr. John.'

I looked at him and ordered another coffee.

'320 cannon barrels on display outside the museum building. On the left, Austrian cannons from the 15th century onwards, on the right, foreign, mostly conquered cannons, yes, yes, probably from Italy or France.'

I thought about Carla and about the evening I returned from our joint crossing alone. I thought about how I tumbled into the pub in my home harbour to drown myself in beer. To forget. To move on.

'Of particular note, among other sights, is the massive iron mortar from the start of the 15th century, as well as the elaborately decorated barrels by Hilger, Christ, Löffler, Neidhart, Heroldt, Benningk, and other outstanding cannon founders of the 16th and 17th centuries, yes, yes, the cannon founders and the bell founders, the two were always waging an eternal foundry war, you can cast either cannons or bells, never both, no, no.'

I've forgotten many things.

'Of course you can also cast cannons from bells, but I've never heard of casting bells from cannons... we've certainly got to have a look at that.'

The names.

The faces.

The suffering.

'Next to the museum entrance on the right and the left, the 553 metre long chain with which the Turks blocked the Danube between Ofen and Pest from 1602 to 1643, how exciting.'

I never forgot Carla.

Maybe because she was so young.

Maybe because I was so young.

Maybe because she loved me.

Maybe because I loved her.

'Why don't you find it interesting, Herr Kraus?'

'I do, I find it interesting.'

'You're not listening.'

'I'm listening.'

'Well, not everyone can see through history.'

Winterberg drank a bit of his coffee and continued reading from the Baedeker.

'The magnificent entrance hall, supported by twelve clusters of pillars, is decorated with 56 marble statues of Austrian heroes by Kundmann, Costenoble, Gasser and others, yes, yes, in the next hall to the left, the library with a collection of prints on the history of the Austrian military, yes, yes, perhaps we'll leave that out.'

I thought about the days and nights when we told each other stories.

'On the right, the firearms hall, with over 500 firearms, and the artillery hall, with 200 artillery models, the munitions collection, and battlefield depictions, we won't leave that out.'

I thought about the evening when we held each other for the first time.

'Oh, it can't be, Herr Kraus, look at this! Sochor's *Cavalry Clash at Stresetitz* in the Battle of Königgrätz. I've always wanted to see that.'

I thought about the evening when we kissed for the first time.

'Sochor was always my inspiration in our Art Association of the Berlin Tram Drivers, where I was the only tram driver who could also paint a bit.'

I thought about the evening when we made love for the first time.

'Yes, yes, Sochor's landscape paintings always gave me inspiration for my model railway, although of course for Sochor it was just about the war, and for me it was about the landscape and the railway, but the railway is a war, too.'

It was still grey outside.

'Yes, yes, what a shame that I'll never finish my model railway.'

Winterberg fell silent for a moment, as if ruminating over his lost model railway.

I thought about our initially long and then increasingly shorter outings with her wheelchair through the Bremer Quarter. Carla always wanted to keep going. Keep doing her rounds through the city. But her illness grew more and more painful.

'Yes, yes, the old artillery, that's not so exciting, perhaps the organ gun by Kollman from Vienna from the year 1678, we could have a look at that. I knew someone who went mad from the nocturnes of the Russian organs, like my neighbour in Berlin... twenty years after the war, he still heard the music of the Russian organs, and when he suddenly stopped hearing their song, the silence was so overwhelming that he shot himself in the cellar, yes, yes, bullet-to-the-head corpses aren't a pretty sight.'

I thought about the many other evenings and nights we made love.

'Yes, yes, that's how it is in life, one shoots himself, the other hangs himself, the next throws himself from the window, yes, yes, I think perhaps I'd prefer to freeze to death somewhere out in the woods, if you ask me, that's not as painful as hanging yourself or shooting yourself, it might just take longer, yes, yes, you have to consider it all very carefully, dear Herr Kraus, frost corpses aren't a pretty sight, as my father said... so, what's next, yes, yes, back through the stairwell, which is supported by four clusters of columns, with allegorical frescoes by Rahl and marble statues of the military commanders Radetzky, Haynau, Windischgrätz and Jelačić … Benedek is missing, of course Benedek is missing, Benedek, the poor fool of military history.'

Carla could move less and less. She wanted to make love all the more.

'Yes, yes, tragic, tragic, he should have stayed in Italy… and yes, yes, another marble statue, Austria shielding her children, by Benk, you see, dear Herr Kraus, the Austria of Königgrätz, she's here too.'

'But you already know it all.'

'I don't know everything.'

'Yes, you do…'

'But I want to read it. Everyone should read it. And of course other historical literature too, like *The Construction of the Alpine Railways*, for example.'

Winterberg took a sip of his coffee and read more from his book.

And I knew that I wouldn't be able to stand him and the war and the fog in his head for much longer.

I thought more about Carla.

'In the middle of the first floor, the pantheon, a domed hall and two smaller side chambers, with memorial plaques for Austrian generals and colonels since 1618 who stood their ground before the enemy, with frescoes by Blaas, yes, yes.'

I thought about her long, fine hair, which I always washed, dried and combed.

'First hall of weaponry, the period from 1618 to 1788, case 52 contains trophies from the Thirty Years' War, make note of that, dear Herr Kraus.'

I thought about her lips.

'Stand 75, the sword of Tilly, Wallenstein's hand-written order to Pappenheim, found drenched in blood in the breast pocket of the fallen cavalry commander after the Battle of Lützen. Yes, yes, Wallenstein, perhaps next time we really should trace the steps of Wallenstein, he comes up in my book again and again.'

Her slender neck.

'Old sketches of the positions of the Imperial Army at Lützen, the collar that Gustav Adolf wore on the day of his death at Lützen, yes, yes, the fog of war once again, make note of that, dear Herr Kraus… I could talk for ages about Gustav Adolf as well, about his landing on Usedom, well, perhaps another time.'

Her small breasts.

'Stand 119, the sword of Kaiser Ferdinand III, make note of that, display case 170, mementos of Prince Montecuccoli, make note of that, Herr Kraus. In cabinets 203 and 204, Turkish trophies, make note of that, yes, yes, including a Turkish pocketwatch from 1664 scavenged near St. Gotthard, I can't possible remember it all.'

Her nipples.

'Case 240, mementos of Prince Eugene of Savoy. Cases 267 and 268, medals from the reigns of Leopold I and Charles VI. In window arches VII and VII, polearms from the time of Maria Theresa, trophies from the War of Austrian Succession and from the Seven Years' War, yes, yes, good thing we'll have the book with us… you think I already know and remember everything, but who can possibly remember all that? It's too much. Too much history! It drives me mad that I can't remember it all.'

Her ribs, which stuck out under her pale skin like a mountain range, like the Alps, as Carla said.

'Stand 298, the sword of Count Rüdiger von Starhemberg. Stand 363, mementos of Laudon, yes, yes, it's really impossible to remember that, second hall of weaponry, the period from 1789 to the present, yes, yes, I'm interested in that, the present, dear Herr Kraus, especially the present from 1866 to 1914, the present between Königgrätz and Sarajevo.'

Carla loved it when I kissed her lips.

'On the entrance wall, trophies from the last Ottoman War.'

When I nibbled her lips.

'In window arches I to II on the left and IX on the right, weaponry from the period 1789 to 1848.'

Tenderly.

'II and III, trophies from the war against France, 1792 to 1815.'

Roughly.

'Including the Montgolfier balloon captured near Würzburg in 1796.'

She loved it when I kissed her neck and licked her with my tongue like a dog.

'Perhaps we'll leave that out, I'm not interested in flying, flying is for fools, you get somewhere an hour earlier… and then what? I have time. I've tried so often to explain that to my daughter, but always in vain…'

Her ears.

'Stand 70, the cuirass of Leopold II, yes, yes, two Ottoman rifles from Belgrade, 1789.

Her breasts.

'The swords of field marshals Clerfayt and Wurmser. Who can remember it all?'

But Carla especially loved it when I kissed her ribs, her Alpine landscape, as she said.

'Stand 111, commemorative coins from the period from 1789 to 1848, cases 132, 134, 136, mementos of Austria's patriotic sacrifice in wartime from 1792 to 1794, it's truly impossible to remember that, dear Herr Kraus. It makes me a bit melancholy.'

But above all, Carla loved it when I kissed her between her legs.

'Case 158, mementos of Crown Prince Charles.'

She moaned and didn't want me to stop kissing.

'The banner of the Zach regiment, with which the Crown Prince led the Austrians to victory in that decisive moment at Aspern.'

Oh, my little puppy, she always said. My little puppy.

'Stand 160, mementos of Franz II and the Prince of Schwarzenberg.'

I didn't stop kissing her.

'Case 282, mementos of Radetzky.'

I kissed Carla between her legs. I licked her clean. And then her body arched, as if in that moment, she was healthy again.

'Stand 861, mementos of Hentzi and the Prince of Windisch-Grätz.'

She moaned. She screamed. She bit my finger.

'Yes, yes, they don't remember Windisch-Grätz too fondly in Prague.'

Oh, my little puppy.

'Nor in Vienna, really. Just in the Arsenal.'

Afterwards, she cried and screamed and bit down on the pillows, and I had to hold and comfort her. Take me away, she always said afterwords. Please, take me away, I don't care where, just take me away from here.

The only major journey we took together was our crossing.

'Case 362, uniforms from the middle of the 19th century.'

At the beginning of the crossing, Carla could still move a bit.

'Stand 383, commemorative coins since 1848, window arch VII. I just can't remember it, tragic, tragic, and you don't care at all, dear Herr Kraus.'

At the end of the crossing, she could no longer breathe. The only thing that she could still move were her beautiful lips.

Her face became increasingly pale and grey until the end, when it was much greyer than her eyes.

'VIII: Weapons from the period of 1860 to the present.'

Carla loved me and I loved her.

'VII: Trophies from the campaigns in 1859, 1864, 1866.'

To this day, I don't know if her parents knew that we loved each other.

'Between VII and VIII, the bust of Archduke Wilhelm, the founder of the military museum, by Haag.'

They knew that I'd been in prison.

I'd told them what had happened back then.

'Case 408, uniforms of the Archduke Albrecht. Too much history!'

But they didn't care.

'Uniforms since the middle of the 19th century.'

As I sat alone in the pub after Carla's crossing to drown myself in beer, her father suddenly appeared at my table. I didn't know how he knew where I was drinking. But he knew, and he had to drown himself in beer too. In beer and schnapps.

So we sat there together and drank and didn't say a word.

Since then, I haven't been to Bremen.

Since then, I have a drinking problem.

Since then, I haven't been in love.

'You just can't remember it, tragic, tragic … we should go, yes, yes … the coffee was terrible, by the way.'

I looked out of the window. The city was still grey and so was the sky.

'Herr Kraus, what's wrong? Were you asleep?'

'No.'

'Why are you crying?'

'I'm not crying.'

'Yes, yes, I see it.'

'You cry too sometimes.'

'Me? Never.'

I looked at him and thought that it wasn't just him, but that I, too, was lost. He was travelling with me through Europe and mourning Lenka Morgenstern, with whom he had wanted to take this trip, this honeymoon that never took place. But instead of Lenka Morgenstern, I was travelling with him through Europe, and mourning Carla.

Winterberg is mad and lost.

I'm mad and lost.

And then we briefly went up to our rooms.

And then we went back downstairs.

And then we sat in the tram.

And then we sat in the bus.

And then we stood at the entrance to the military history museum at the Arsenal in Vienna.

Winterberg and I.

And I knew that I wouldn't be able to take it much longer.

I can't help him.

And he can't help me either.

THE ARSENAL

The museum wasn't busy. The two guards looked at us in surprise, as if we'd mistakenly wandered into the Arsenal that day and actually meant to visit a completely different museum, or the Christmas market.

But this was exactly where Winterberg wanted to go.

He didn't bother with the Ottomans.

He didn't bother with Wallenstein.

He didn't bother with the field marshals Clerfayt and Wurmser.

He hurried through the empty military history museum directly to Königgrätz. In the large, high, quiet hall, he remained standing in front of a massive painting.

'Václav Sochor.'

He said that according to his Baedeker it should really be a different battle painting hanging here, *The Cavalry Clash at Stresetitz* in the Battle of Königgrätz, but he wasn't disappointed, not at all, perhaps the painting was hanging in a different part of the museum, perhaps there was another room on Königgrätz, he said, in fact it would surprise him if there was no other room on Königgrätz, for this battle that ran through his heart, that tore at him and destroyed him.

'*The Cavalry Clash at Stresetitz* is also a rather jovial painting. You don't see there how the battle ended, yes, yes, you see it much more clearly in this painting. *The Battery of the Dead*. How beautiful.'

He walked up to the painting, briefly stood very close, took two steps to the right, then five to the left, then three backwards and six to the left and another eight back, one more step forward, and finally remained standing and looked at the painting.

For minutes. For hours. For days.

'Mad, it's all mad.'

He sat down next to me on the red bench in front of the painting.

'The Battery of the Dead, yes, yes.'

And then he stood back up and walked back and forth and began to ramble.

'Look at it, dear Herr Kraus, perhaps you might understand now why the Battle of Königgrätz runs through my heart, this battlefield portrait by the battlefield painter Sochor is one of the most beautiful artworks ever produced in battlefield painting as a whole, it's a monument to death, to the downfall of the cavalry battery of the Imperial and Royal Field Artillery Regiment No. 8, which secured the retreat of the Austrian army to Königgrätz with a heroic drumfire, which transformed into a great, dense wall of fire. Yes, yes, tragic, tragic, the cavalry battery sacrificed itself entirely in the process… this painting is a monument to the whole fiery catastrophe, to the whole foolishness of humanity, to derangement, to downfall, yes, yes, to the defeat of Austria and the victory of Prussia, which transformed itself later into a defeat and into an even greater fiery catastrophe of the sort that can only be found in the history books, which lead to an even deeper derangement, this bloody battlefield portrait by the battlefield painter Václav Sochor, which he worked on for seven years, and visited the battlefields of Königgrätz several times and almost fell into derangement himself at the scene, just like me, just like you, just like us, dear Herr Kraus, this battlefield portrait is really a battlefield monument for all the battlefields of the world, yes, yes, a monument to the entire century of battlefields which followed Königgrätz.'

Winterberg rambled and began to sweat and shake and I knew that I had to stay alert and would shortly need to assist him.

'Do you see the death, dear Herr Kraus?' He marched back and forth and didn't speak to me, but rather to the painting.

To the dead Austrians.

To the dead Prussians.

To the dead horses.

'Look at how this defeat is celebrated here, only a battlefield painter from Bohemia could paint that, yes, yes… it's not a coincidence, dear Herr Kraus, a Prussian painter would rather take his own life than paint and celebrate such a defeat. Only a Bohemian is always in the spirit to do something like that, yes, yes, only a Bohemian loves his defeats, only a Bohemian is already looking forward to the next losing battle, to the next battlefield painting, and it doesn't matter whether he speaks

German or Czech. Yes, yes, that's how it is, dear Herr Kraus. Perhaps the ancestors of the battlefield painter Sochor had already fought in the Battle of White Mountain in 1620, that was also a splendid Bohemian defeat, yes, yes, you should know all that already. Perhaps Sochor's ancestors were beheaded on the Altstädter Ring in Prague in 1621 in front of thousands of Praguers, perhaps they were shot in Prague in March 1848, perhaps they fell at Königgrätz alongside my two ancestors, Karl Strohbach and Julius Ewald, one from Ottensheim on the Danube, the other from Tangermünde on the Elbe, both dead on the same foggy day, there's no escape, it's not as easily overcome as the Alps by the railway.'

Winterberg remained standing and was sweating and shaking and I stood up and went to him and had to hold him up so that he didn't collapse.

I brought him back to the bench.

He looked for a long time at the painting, the many dead, and the few survivors, and was silent.

And then he began to cry.

And I wanted to console him.

But he wouldn't let himself be consoled.

We sat there like that on the bench and I felt that Winterberg was right. There really is no hope and no escape. I looked at the crying Winterberg, at how he stared at the painting, and felt the cold wind that was pulling Winterberg back to Königgrätz, to the snowy, abandoned fields and meadows and into the forests, into the landscape of rolling hills where the earth shifted and rose and sunk and groaned and opened and struggled to breathe, because it can't stomach the dead and is constantly heaving.

Then he calmed down a bit.

He looked at the painting with exhaustion and was silent.

And then he began to ramble again.

'Only one man from the Battery survived, yes, yes, just the one… and so time goes by, everything comes to an end, everything passes by, oh, how time goes by. Not just in Königgrätz but all over Europe, the earth is shifting and trying to speak with us. But no one's listening, no, no… all of Europe is a deep, damp grave in the Svíb Forest near Königgrätz, where we'll all be buried, yes, yes, everywhere, the earth is shifting and trying to speak with us; everywhere, the countryside is unable to stomach all the dead and is constantly heaving; everywhere, the graves are opening; everywhere, the dead are crawling up and the living are falling down. Yes, yes, that's how it is, dear Herr Kraus, why aren't you interested in history? Why don't you see through history? Why haven't you read *The Construction of the Alpine Railways*? If only you were interested in history…'

And suddenly Winterberg conked out.

Cork pulled.

Air out.

Eyes closed.

Good night.

His head lay on his chest. His breathing was deep and regular, he suddenly sat there quite peacefully and fully reconciled with his history, with his madness, with himself. I sat next to him, looking at the dead of Königgrätz, and heard Winterberg begin to snore.

I sat there next to him for a long time.

I looked at Winterberg.

And I knew that it was now or never.

If I didn't take the chance now, then I too would soon be lying buried at Königgrätz. Just like him.

Very slowly, step by step, I distanced myself from the red bench.

Step by step, I slipped out of the hall.

In the doorway, I turned around once again and saw Winterberg as he sat on the bench and slept and snored.

The room was still and empty like a church. Still and empty like the battlefield at Königgrätz when we were there.

He should stay here. Among his dead. Nothing will happen to him here. They'll find him, he'll look at them, open his mouth, and then start to ramble about Königgrätz, about the Svíb Forest and the railway and Sarajevo, and someone will call the ambulance that will finally take Winterberg to the mental ward. Maybe it actually happens here often. Weapons and wars can only draw in the crazies.

I walked away and I knew that it was the right decision. Our crossing together had come to an end. The only crossing that I, as a soldier of the Army of Last Hope, broke off. The only crossing I didn't manage to complete.

Winterberg was the only sailor who'd come back with me alive.

Winterberg was the only one who now needed to continue alone.

And I knew he would do it, that he would haunt this world for a long time to come. I walked away and I knew that this was how it had to be.

Suddenly I felt elated. I had to do it. I couldn't help him any further, nor could he help me. And I couldn't go on. I'd had it up to here with this endless rambling, with this crazy journey through history, with his never-ending stories, with his history lessons, with his confusion, with his corpses and Feuerhalles and railways and battles and wars. I didn't want to go mad and end up like him. And yes, I didn't want to be arrested either, I didn't want to end up back in prison for his sake.

I wanted to be free. I wanted to go out into the uncertainty that lurks within freedom, as Winterberg once said.

I wanted to start again from the beginning.

It didn't matter where.

It didn't matter how.

It didn't matter with whom.

The most important thing was to get away from here.

Maybe I'll go to Vimperk. Maybe to Berlin. Maybe to Bremen, where I can get piss drunk with Carla's father and tell him we were sleeping together.

'Bon voyage,' I said finally.

And so I walked away.

Step by step, I left Winterberg.

Step by step, I left the battlefield of Königgrätz.

Step by step, on tiptoe, I left the museum.

In the door, I looked back at him one last time.

Winterberg slept, and I left.

I grabbed my things from the coat check and left his stuff hanging there. I pulled on my coat. And then I was standing in the door. And then I was standing outside.

It was raining and I looked out at the courtyard of the Vienna Arsenal, of this fortress that Kaiser Franz Joseph had built to protect Vienna and his empire from revolutions and from collapse from within, as Winterberg had told me.

I lit a cigarette and walked away.

I walked through the empty courtyard. I walked past the thick walls. I walked and lit another cigarette. I walked past the flagpoles where no flags were flying. I walked past the parked cars. I walked and no one came after me. I walked and felt freer with each step. I walked and couldn't remember the last time I had felt so good and so free.

I walked and looked forward to the first beer, with which I'd already start to forget this whole bonkers story.

I walked and the rain became heavier and heavier, and the wind, too.

Then I stood at the bus stop and lit another cigarette.

The bus came, the doors opened, I put out my cigarette and moved to the doors. But then I stopped. I didn't get on. I couldn't.

The driver looked at me in surprise and then shook his head, closed the doors and drove off.

It was raining and I stood at the bus stop and stared after the bus until it disappeared into the distance.

. . .

I went back.

Into the Arsenal.

Into the military history museum.

Into the museum of historical military failures, as Winterberg had said to me on the bus ride here.

Into the museum of downfalls.

Into the museum of catastrophes.

I rushed to Hall IV. But Winterberg was no longer sitting on the bench.

The room was empty. Only the bust of Benedek stared back at me. Benedek, who was damned to stare at his catastrophe of Königgrätz here for all eternity.

I asked a museum guard if she had seen an old man, but she hadn't seen anyone. We came in here together, I said, but she couldn't remember us at all. She hadn't seen a soul in the museum today, not a single one all day.

I wanted to go, but she held me up.

Who would go to the military history museum at a time like this, she said; certainly no normal person, a normal person would go to the Christmas market and have a mulled wine, only the truly mad sort would be interested in weapons and wars during the Advent, I was the first person she'd seen, and not just today, but in the last few days, I was perhaps the first person she'd seen in the military history museum in the last week, and I had to be mad.

Then she asked me if I had been baptised and if I believed in Jesus Christ, and I thanked her and continued on.

I ran.

I was afraid.

I looked for Winterberg in the toilets.

I looked for Winterberg in the café.

I looked for Winterberg in the pantheon.

I looked for Winterberg in the field marshals' hall.

I looked for Winterberg in the entire museum.

But I couldn't find him.

I looked for Winterberg between the uniforms and paintings and showcases and weapons and only found two gun nuts from Slovakia taking pictures of themselves in front of a cannon.

I looked for Winterberg in the old period from the Thirty Years' War up to Prince Eugene in Hall I and found Wallenstein and the organ of death.

I looked for Winterberg in the old period of the Spanish War of Succession at the time of Empress Maria Theresa in Hall II and found a Turkish state tent and the Mortar of Belgrade.

I looked for Winterberg in the old period of the revolutions between 1789 and 1848 in Hall III and found Napoleon and the French war balloon.

I looked for Winterberg once more in the old period from Field Marshal Radetzky and Königgrätz in Hall IV and again found just Benedek, the mute, black field cannon and the battlefield portrait of the battlefield painter Václav Sochor.

I looked for Winterberg in the old period from Franz Joseph and Sarajevo in Hall V.

And there, finally, I found him.

. . .

I saw Winterberg standing at an illuminated glass display case. His hands lay on the pane of glass, his gaze on the blue uniform.

I approached him.

He didn't turn around.

But he knew that it was me.

'Do you see, dear Herr Kraus, this small, almost invisible tunnel?'

Winterberg pointed to a small hole under the collar of the uniform.

'If you wanted to build a train tunnel, how would you do it?'

'No clue. I've never built a tunnel,' I said, and thought, Winterberg was beyond help, maybe it was a mistake to come back.

'Who knows, perhaps you'll need to build a tunnel someday, perhaps all of us will. There's a lot about train tunnels in my Baedeker, as you might have noticed. Every individual tunnel is mentioned in my Baedeker… of course there are also a lot of railway bridges and other railway structures, but it's about the tunnels above all. About loop tunnels and summit tunnels and spur tunnels, about mountain tunnels and city tunnels, about single-track tunnels and double-track tunnels, yes, yes, but it focuses particularly on the long tunnels, they write quite passionately about those, of course. But even the shortest tunnel is mentioned in my book, yes, yes, because any tunnel can lead to mental derangement, to a personal Königgrätz, and to the Reichenberg Feuerhalle… haven't you noticed how many people are afraid when the train enters a tunnel? They used to have entire wards in mental hospitals for tunnel-affected travellers, just as they did for unhappy romantics and casualties of war.'

Winterberg still didn't look at me.

He was fascinated by the blue, blood-smeared uniform.

'As a tunnel-builder you're immortalised in history forever, like the railway engineer Jan Perner, who built the train line from Vienna to Prague with a few beautiful tunnels, and three weeks after the line was finished, he died in an accident in one of those beautiful tunnels, when he went to Choceň to revel again in how well he'd constructed his tunnel. He looked out of the window on a sunny day in May 1845 and slammed his head into a signal post and so he became the first victim of the railway in Bohemia and now he's lying in the cemetery in Pardubitz, yes, yes, tunnel corpses aren't a pretty sight, as my father always said, tragic, tragic, the entire city gathered for his burial, even the Kaiser sent a wreath from Vienna for the tunnel-builder, by train, obviously. A few years later, they tore down the tunnel and carted the remnants away, it's all mad, yes, yes, tunnel-building is a wonderful and demanding profession. Perhaps you know the story of Louise Favre, who built the Gotthard Tunnel in Switzerland and died during a maintenance inspection, as a tunnel was bored through his own aorta, and now he's lying in the cemetery in Göschenen, buried just a few steps away from his piece of art, from this masterpiece of railway artistry, watching the trains of the Gotthard Line enter his tunnel in the crisp air, yes, yes, he's lying there, and 188 other workers who died during the construction are lying right next to him. Perhaps we should go there too, yes, yes, it's a dangerous job to be a tunnel-builder. And in this case, it was no different, dear Herr Kraus.'

He leaned against the glass case and now properly began to ramble.

He was once again swept up by this storm in his head and carried off far away.

He told me that there were multiple different options if you wanted to build a tunnel. You only needed to know if you were dealing with hard rock or soft rock; that was the decisive factor.

'Let's assume that a human body like this is more of a soft rock,' he said, and he briefly listed a few bones in the human body, mentioned the tissue and the muscles and the blood.

'And yes, perhaps the person through whom you'd like to bore a tunnel is also wearing a beautiful blue uniform like this one here, you see, Herr Kraus, the buttons and straps and badges and the collar, you can't forget that either, there are plenty of fault zones when you're building tunnels.'

Winterberg peered at the blue uniform in the glass case, which looked like a glass coffin.

'Yes, yes, the tunnel-builders say the fault zones are entirely unpredictable… there are many fault zones, and not just in tunnel-building, but also in life and in love, yes, yes, just ask my daughter, she suffers from so many fault zones that aren't as easy to overcome as the Alps by the railway… mad, it's all mad, you can't even imagine it, dear Herr Kraus, how complicated it can be to build a railway tunnel like that, often it all comes crumbling down, yes, yes, and you have to start all over again or even move the path of the tunnel and start again from the beginning, it can take entire years until a railway tunnel is finished, it can even take decades before the first train passes through, yes, yes, no one can imagine how complicated and dangerous it was and is and will be to build such a tunnel. Carl Ritter von Ghega had to rip rocks and entire mountains from Mother Earth for the Semmering Railway with only black powder, because they didn't have dynamite back then, yes, yes, who knows, perhaps his consumption came from the gunpowder, tragic, very tragic, consumption corpses aren't a pretty sight.'

Winterberg continued to look at the blue uniform in the glass case.

'Why haven't you read *The Construction of the Alpine Railways*, you would already know all this, and you wouldn't be afraid anymore, because almost every problem of this world, yes, even the most complicated problem, can be overcome like the Alps by the railway, yes, yes, that's how it is, dear Herr Kraus, you can even overcome consumption these days, it's no longer a hopeless disease, but back then, back then it was different, consumption wasn't just the disease of the poor, it was also the disease of the railway pioneers, the railway engineers. Consumption killed Carl Ritter von Ghega. Consumption also killed the other great railway pioneer Julius Lott, the architect of the Arlberg Railway and the Arlberg Tunnel, yes, yes, tragic, tragic, he didn't survive to see the opening, he died of his illness at just forty-six, that's how it goes in life, yes, yes. The breakthrough of the tunnel was completed in the year 1883 on the name day of Empress Elisabeth, whose corpse would be brought through that tunnel fifteen years later in the hearse wagon on the way from Geneva to Vienna for her burial. So if you, dear Herr Kraus, want to build a tunnel, it seems that it's all so complicated, all of nature fights back, and the people fight back too, people often become fault zones, there are always these fools turning up who have the feeling that they would find a much better path than you, yes, yes, a tunnel-builder is constantly fighting against the elements and against human stupidity. So if you want to build a tunnel, it all needs to be well thought-out, yes, yes, if you're planning such a great technical achievement as Carl Ritter von Ghega, the creator of the Semmering Railway, the creator of the world's first alpine railway, the creator of the Southern

Railway from Vienna via Graz to Trieste, you have to think it all through not just once, but ten times over.'

Winterberg rambled and still didn't look at me.

'Yes, yes, it all has to be well thought-out, because the Alps are standing before you like a great, black, impenetrable wall. Carl Ritter von Ghega spent weeks – no, months – no, years – studying the landscape of the Semmering, he lived in harmony with the landscape and the elements, until he became one with the landscape and the elements, with the mountains and the gorges and the cliffs, until he became a part of the alpine landscape himself. That's how he prepared himself for his fateful battle against the elements, yes, yes, I know what you're going to say, dear Herr Kraus, if Benedek had been able to enjoy that kind of time at Königgrätz, to become one with the landscape, he would have been much better prepared for his fateful battle, and Königgrätz wouldn't have turned into Königgrätz, into this fiery crypt, and he wouldn't have taken his leave from history as a fool of history, but Benedek didn't take the time, yes, yes, oh Benedek, but it wasn't all his fault… now where was I… too many stories, too much history, you can only lose yourself, you have to lose yourself…'

Winterberg began to tremble and I was prepared to prop him up, to catch him if he fell to the ground again, as he so often did after his historical fit.

'Yes, yes, I know… you have a lot of options if you want to build a railway tunnel, dear Herr Kraus. For boring a tunnel through soft rock, there's an old Austrian method, and a Belgian method, and an English method, and an Italian method.'

Winterberg coughed, as the air in the military history museum was dry.

And then he said nothing.

He trembled a bit and leaned over the glass case and looked once again at the blue, blood-smeared uniform, as if he were considering whether he shouldn't just purchase it and put it on himself.

The fine officer's uniform.

The blue-grey officer's coat.

The dark blue officer's trousers with two red lampasses.

The white leather gloves.

Winterberg looked at the uniform in fascination and I thought, perhaps he hasn't noticed at all that the uniform is smeared everywhere with blood, that the breast of the coat had been cut open and only quickly and sloppily sewn back together.

But Winterberg did notice.

'Blood everywhere, yes, yes, I know what you're going to say, dear Herr Kraus, there's blood everywhere. On the breast and on the abdomen and on the sleeves and on the legs. Blood everywhere. Mad, it's all mad, *Cornus sanguinea*.'

The blood was the blood of Franz Ferdinand.

Of the Archduke.

'Anyway, there are many options if you want to build a tunnel, yes, yes, but they're all arduous and complicated and take a long time, because the stone is usually tough, and the mountain and the elements fight back, the mountain is always like a fortress, and the fault zones are unpredictable. But there's another possibility, dear Herr Kraus. You simply take a pistol, a good old Browning, precisely, precisely, that's the famous Bosnian-Serbian method, and that'll take you a long way quite quickly, as you can see here.'

'I don't understand any of it.'

'I know that, of course, and I'm also not surprised. It's not easy. Even for someone who sees through history, just like I see through history.'

He still wasn't looking at me.

'No, it's really not easy at all.'

Winterberg told me that in this case, of course, it wasn't just any ordinary tunnel.

He told me that at the time, in 1914, the Monarchy had long since expanded the tunnels to include room for two tracks, even though often just one had been installed, because they believed in the railway.

'They believed in the strength and power of the locomotives, in the future; that is, the future of the railway. And in war, because ever since the Battle of Königgrätz, war was tightly bound with the railway, yes, yes, the railway and the war were married at Königgrätz and this union will never be split apart, a war without the railway, you can't imagine it, or can you imagine it?'

'No.'

'There you have it.'

'Yeah.'

'But this tunnel…'

Winterberg pointed again to the tiny hole right under the collar of the grey-blue coat.

'This tunnel is unusual.'

He told me that this tunnel was built for a very small railway, perhaps even for a narrow-gauge railway.

'Yes, yes, certainly, that's how it was, for the narrow-gauge railway of the Bosnian 760 mm gauge… they built such railways all over the Monarchy, many in Bosnia, near Sarajevo, but also in other places, in Austria and in Bohemia and in the Waldviertel and in the Zillertal and and in Wobratein and in Neubistritz and in Hotzenplotz… as a Bohemian you should already know all that, dear Herr Kraus. Everywhere there they swore on the narrow and limber Bosnian gauge, yes, yes, because the construction of a narrow-gauge railway was often significantly cheaper than the construction of a standard-gauge railway. Oh, why don't you know that, dear Herr Kraus?'

Winterberg coughed a bit and quickly polished his glasses.

'Why do you have so little interest in history and in the railway, dear Herr Kraus?' he continued, without looking at me the whole time.

And still he stared, as if spellbound, at the grey-blue and dark blue uniform in the museum's glass display case as if he wanted to put it on right then.

'All these narrow-gauge railways appear in my Baedeker too, of course.'

He continued to ramble and again gave a slight tremble.

'Even if the entries are a bit short, yes, yes, that's not right, of course, because the narrow-gauge railways usually travel through the most beautiful landscapes. Just like the narrow-gauge railway from Sarajevo to Uvac, the Bosnian Eastern Railway, as they called that line, yes, you only have to look it up in my Baedeker, yes, yes, how beautiful the long journey on this route with the many tunnels on the Drina was. The Bosnian gauge is not to be confused, however, with the other gauges of the other narrow-gauge railways, for example, with the Saxon gauge. That would be a fatal mistake, dear Herr Kraus, because the narrow-gauge railways in Saxony are only 750 mm wide, and so a Saxon narrow-gauge train from Zittau would immediately go off the rails in Bosnia or in Hotzenplotz or in the Zillertal or elsewhere in the Monarchy, and you wouldn't even be able to get a Bosnian or Austrian or Bohemian narrow-gauge train on a Saxon track in the first place.'

Winterberg fell silent for a moment and still didn't look at me.

His gaze remained fixed on the white leather gloves.

'I know what you're going to say, it's only ten millimetres, yes, yes, and you're right, dear Herr Kraus. It really is just ten millimetres, yes, yes, but those minuscule ten millimetres might as well be a kilometre in this case, they're like a threshold you can't pass without danger.'

Winterberg stared at the blood-smeared officer's uniform.

At the grey-blue officer's coat.

At the dark blue officer's trousers.

At the red officer's lampasses.

'Isn't it interesting, dear Herr Kraus? The lampasses, take a look at them, they're like two thick red railway tracks. They should've warned the Archduke, yes, yes, they should have advised him against leaving the train in Sarajevo. These two blood-red rails down his trousers were the last warning… isn't it interesting, dear Herr Kraus, this little war of the narrow-gauge widths of the Central European narrow-gauge trains, they never came to peace here, this narrow-gauge war between Germany and Bohemia and Austria continues to this day.'

He gestured again towards the small, nearly invisible hole under the collar of the uniform, which was slightly frayed at the edges.

'However, this case, dear Herr Kraus, this case concerns very particular gauge, yes, yes, as you can see, this here concerns an even narrower gauge than is otherwise common in narrow-gauge railways. It concerns a gauge that you could perhaps compare with a model train, yes, yes, precisely, with my model train… as you can see, it concerns a tiny, narrow tunnel under the collar of the uniform, which towers like a steep cliff over the beautiful, almost summery grey-blue landscape of the coat. It looks like a summit tunnel, if you'd ask me, or Ghega, or Perner, yes, yes, this tunnel struck the Archduke's jugular vein, yes, yes, it tore it open, and the windpipe along with it, yes, yes, as you see, dear Herr Kraus, it was a good, surprisingly clean piece of work, a quick, nearly perfect breakthrough. No initial fault zones, those didn't come until later, shortly afterwards, that's often how it goes in life, yes, yes, that's often how it goes in tunnel construction, the fault zones are treacherous, go and read something by Carl Ritter von Ghega on tunnel construction already. It happens so often that you hit water and the whole construction is quickly flooded by a powerful water surge, yes, yes, I know what you're going to say, the fault zones, it's all mad, nature strikes back, precisely, precisely, you've learned something after all, the fault zones are the greatest enemies of the tunnel-builders, the fault zones are our greatest enemies, because fault zones can quickly lead to a Königgrätz, yes, yes, how lovely our lives would be without fault zones, dear Herr Kraus. And how dull. Yes, yes, you're right, dear Herr Kraus, you always have to account for water inflow in tunnel construction, the water has to be redirected quickly, otherwise you can't continue the work of detonating charges and laying concrete, and you can't even begin to think of timbering and refractory lining and ballasting, let alone laying the tracks, yes, yes, tunnel construction can be delayed for entire weeks or months or years due to a water inflow. But in this case, as you can see, it happened quite quickly. A perfect breakthrough! And it wasn't a surge of water, but rather a surge of blood that occurred in the throat of the Archduke Franz Ferdinand, after this tiny tunnel was bored on June 28, 1914, in Sarajevo.'

Winterberg was trembling.

I thought, now, now it's finally over.

Now he'll collapse again after his historical fit.

Now he'll fall back asleep.

But it wasn't over yet.

He was silent for a moment and continued to look at the little hole under the collar of the uniform.

'What we see here, however, is just the portal. We don't see the jugular the tunnel bored through, no, no, we don't see the damaged windpipe. This tunnel has the particularly narrow Bosnian gauge of just 7.65 mm, yes, yes, and the arteries of the throat, dear Herr Kraus, were the worst fault zone of this tunnel construction in Sarajevo in 1914, as you can see all over the uniform.'

He rambled and rambled and didn't look at me the entire time.

'The tunnel-builder was called Gavrilo Princip. He wasn't a construction engineer, no, no, he was a ne'er-do-well, a fool, a poor, clueless kid, yes, yes, he likely had no clue about proper tunnel construction, no clue about trains and history, he was just lucky and unlucky at the same time, otherwise he had no clue in general, if you ask me, yes, yes, a poor boy, a fool, not even the Serbian Army wanted him, much too small and much too weak. He wasn't even capable of offing himself after the assassination, and so the cold and damp of the basement cell in Theresienstadt took him first, yes, yes, and his consumption. Yes, yes, dear Herr Kraus, it wasn't just the great railway pioneers and tunnel-builders and train people like Ghega or Lott, even the tunnel-builder Princip died of consumption, yes, yes, this disease of all tunnel-builders around the world, no, no, his corpse wasn't a pretty sight, consumption wasn't as easily overcome back then as the Alps by the railway.'

Winterberg trembled for a moment in silence.

'I always wanted to show this uniform to Lenka. Yes, yes, she was very interested in the accidents of history, just like the Englishman. Yes, yes, Lenka understood me, just like the Englishman, yes, yes, *"the beautiful landscape of battlefields, cemeteries and ruins"* ...'

He stopped talking and coughed.

And then he rambled on.

'Isn't it interesting how the fools and ne'er-do-wells of history constantly keep attracting each other, dear Herr Kraus? This fool met another fool, and then yet another fool joined the mix with the brilliant idea to murder the Archduke during his visit to Sarajevo. The Archduke took the train to Sarajevo from the resort town of Ilidže, and I'll tell you, yes, yes, he should have just stayed sitting on the train. Train travel is, as you know, much safer than car travel, and that was already true back then, yes, yes, this narrow-gauge tunnel is the best evidence of that, dear Herr Kraus. But no, the Archduke didn't want that, he didn't want to sit in the train, he wanted to see Sarajevo from the car, and that's how it came to be that Gavrilo Princip bored a narrow-gauge tunnel through his throat, and while he was in the business of tunnel-building in these Habsburg mountains, he bored the second narrow-gauge tunnel through the mighty abdominal landscape of his pregnant wife, yes, yes, they discovered that during the autopsy, dear Herr Kraus, tragic, tragic, the things you find out during an autopsy, when you open up the body, in Reichenberg they once found ten golden teeth in a man's stomach, no one ever found out what had happened… now where was I, yes, yes, I know… in the belly of Sophie Chotek, who was born in Stuttgart, where they also have a lot of experience with tunnel construction. Two breakthroughs on one day, yes, yes, it doesn't happen often in tunnel construction that you make such swift progress, yes, yes, through both of these narrow-gauge tunnels, the two quickly bled out, and half of Europe along with them shortly after, marching into the First and then twenty years later into the Second World War, drawn in by the colour of the Archduke's blood, by the red hue of *Cornus sanguinea* from the Svíb Forest near Königgrätz… the rails of all different gauges then brought the soldiers to the front for their own bleeding-out, yes, yes, mad, it's all mad, Benedek was a fool because he didn't know his way around Königgrätz, Gavrilo Princip was a fool who wanted to kill, Franz Ferdinand was a fool because he didn't stay in the train and wanted to see Sarajevo from the car, the driver of Franz Ferdinand, a certain "Lojka" from Brünn, was also a fool, a man who was made a fool of history after he took a wrong turn at the intersection and drove in front of a coffeehouse where the other fool Princip happened to be drinking a coffee and wondering if he shouldn't just take his Browning and bore a tunnel through his own head… and then from there, the history really gets going. Fool for fool for fool for fool. The fog of war. It's true to this day. There's no escape, dear Herr Kraus, you can't hide yourself or save yourself from the fools of history… you have to grit your teeth and press on through the foolishness these fools have unleashed. You have to try to overcome it, but it's not easy, tragic, tragic, yes, yes, I know what you're going to say, dear Herr Kraus, history isn't written by the victors, but by the fools. Yes, yes, and so now we're here, in the Arsenal in Vienna.'

Winterberg trembled more and more and I was ready to catch him.

Finally, he turned around.

But not to me.

Winterberg looked at the large, old car.

'You see here how dangerous car travel can be, yes, yes, that's why we're taking the train.'

And then he finally looked at me.

'Mad, it's all mad, I know. *Cornus sanguinea.*'

And I saw that Winterberg had been crying the whole time.

'Are you all right?'

'Yes, yes.'

'Really?'

'Where were you, then? I looked everywhere for you.'

'Stepped out for a smoke.'

'You shouldn't smoke so much. Lung cancer isn't as easy to overcome as the Alps by the railway.'

And then Winterberg stopped rambling.

He was tired.

And I was, too.

He was exhausted.

And I was, too.

He was trembling.

And I felt that I was trembling, too.

Another historical fit.

We looked at the old car of the brand Gräft & Stift by Graf Franz von Harrach with which Franz Ferdinand was driven through Sarajevo. We looked at the hole above the back tyre from the gunshot that had killed Sophie Chotek von Chotkova.

And Winterberg began to tremble so violently that I had to support him to make sure he didn't fall to the ground.

'Mad, it's all mad. You can't overcome it.'

. . .

We sat in the museum café and Winterberg had a brief nap.

He lay there as always, with his head in the open pages of his little red book, on the pages about Vienna and its environs.

I let him sleep and thought about Carla. About how it would have been if it had been different. If she hadn't gotten sick, but was healthy, how things would have been. We wouldn't have met each other at all if she hadn't gotten sick.

The illness brought us together, just as a school classroom or a disco or an office or a trip brings others together.

The illness brought us together and tore us apart.

But I was still grateful to this illness.

I thought about Carla and looked at the sleeping Winterberg and felt my heart racing again, as if it wanted to leap out of my chest and go on alone, as if my body was holding it back. I started to feel slightly dizzy.

When our journey is over, I'll go to the doctor.

And then we left.

It had stopped raining. The sky was grey and so was the city. The sun was setting. I lit a cigarette and Winterberg said: 'You really shouldn't smoke so much, dear Herr Kraus.'

And then we saw her in front of the museum.

She was wearing a red coat. A tight black skirt. High heels. And sunglasses. Despite the fading sunlight.

Silke. Silke Winterberg.

'Papa!' she cried, and started walking towards Winterberg. 'Papa!'

'Do something, Herr Kraus.'

She was getting closer.

'Do something… otherwise it's all over.'

'What do you expect me to do?'

'It doesn't matter. Just do something, otherwise we're lost.'

'Papa!'

'Why aren't you doing anything?'

'Papa…'

'What do you expect me to do?'

'Hello, Miss Winterberg,' I said.

She came to us. She took off her glasses. She gave me a dirty look. She had tears in her eyes. She hugged Winterberg. She kissed him.

He let her hug him.

He let her kiss him.

'What are you doing here?' asked Winterberg.

'I've been looking for you. I missed you so much.'

'What are you doing here?'

'Didn't you miss me?'

'What are you doing here?'

'I missed you so much.'

THE DAUGHTER

We were sitting in a taxi. Silke Winterberg was in the front. Winterberg and I in the back. The radio was playing and the presenter said that the winter would be long and cold. Silke said that she had visited the Arsenal the day before. And the day before that, too. She knew we would come there. Her father didn't tell her all that much, but he often talked about Vienna and the museum in the Arsenal. She said she was sure that we would come to Vienna. She said most tourists came to Vienna for the art, for the many museums, for theatre and opera, but she knew we wouldn't be going to the opera. Sooner or later, we would show up at the Arsenal.

'At Königgrätz. In your war museum.'

'It's a military history museum, not a war museum.'

'It doesn't matter, papa.'

'It does matter. It's not a war museum, it's about history. And about art.'

'About art?'

'Yes, yes. Herr Kraus and I are very interested in art, aren't we, Herr Kraus?'

'Yes. Very interested.'

'You should stay quiet.'

'Okay.'

'We went together to see the Habsburgs in the Imperial Crypt and tomorrow we want to visit the Central Cemetery… that's all there is that's worth seeing in Vienna. Vienna is dead. Or do you disagree, Herr Kraus?'

'No.'

'But what are you doing here, Silke, how did you find us?'

Silke said she'd left a photo of Winterberg at the entrance along with her phone number and a ten euro banknote. Someone had recognised us and called her that afternoon. A medical student, she said.

'The medical students were always traitors. And the worst braggarts…'

'He was very nice.'

'For ten euros. Pitiful. Am I not worth more?'

'I gave him twenty.'

'Tragic. How many beers is that, Herr Kraus? Not many… I'll give you fifty if you leave me alone.'

'Papa…'

'Or five thousand euros, yes, yes, or the entire flat. I don't care, yes, yes, I just want to finally have my peace and quiet.'

'Papa… I'm begging you.'

'I'm begging you, too. Leave me alone. Why do you ruin everything?'

'Me?'

'Yes, you.'

'Papa!'

Winterberg was silent and stared out of the window.

Silke was crying.

And me – I was somehow just relieved that it was over.

'And now? Are we going to the police?'

She looked at me. 'Yes, we are.'

'Fine. I just want to say…'

'You don't have to say anything to me, you can tell it to them.'

'Sure. I'm happy to tell them everything.'

'But first, let's have something to eat.'

'I don't want to have something to eat,' said Winterberg. 'And we're not going to the police. It was all my decision.'

'Yes, yes, papa, sure… he kidnapped you, that's that.'

'He did not. I don't want to go to the police, Herr Kraus.'

'I'm telling you we'll stop and eat first and discuss everything.'

'What do you want to discuss?'

'Everything.'

'Good. I'm hungry. Let's have schnitzel,' said Winterberg.

'Yes,' she said, stroking his hand. 'A really big, really good Wiener schnitzel, that'll do us good. You've earned that. You know I really love you, papa.'

'I know. I love you, too.'

'We can go to a lovely Viennese coffeehouse. I'm sure you know some from your Baedeker.'

'Yes.'

'I'm looking forward to it.'

'Herr Kraus, did you see the chain?'

'Which chain?'

'Which chain, papa?'

'The chain in front of the Arsenal, the one the Turks used to block the Danube.'

'No, I didn't.'

'Me neither. Maybe someone stole it.'

. . .

We drove to *Sarajevo* at the main train station.

Silke was a bit surprised by the small, smoky locale.

'Is Sarajevo really in your Baedeker?'

'Of course.'

The Bosnian barmaid recognised us immediately and was glad to see us. Her husband didn't recognise us. He was asleep at the counter.

The schnitzel was large.

The beer was good.

And the potato salad was pleasantly sour and well soaked through, as Winterberg said.

Winterberg told us that it really wasn't that easy to prepare a good potato salad. He told us that it all started with the choice of potato. He told us about the potato war between Prussia and Austria, which took place in Bohemia in 1778 and 1779, although Bohemia hadn't been responsible for the war, as happened so often in history, like in the war of 1866 or the war of 1744 or the war of 1755, which also took place in Bohemia.

Silke was listening to him and I thought, please, please, not again, what do you have to do to get Winterberg to shut his trap, to stop rambling.

But once again, Winterberg could not be stopped. On the contrary, the train of history in his head was only just leaving the station, and soon Winterberg was racing like an express train of the Empress Elisabeth Line on the schedule from 1913.

He told us that the potato war wasn't really about potatoes, but about Bavaria.

He told us that his ancestors had perhaps already killed each other in this war, as they did later at Königgrätz.

He told us that the Prussian soldiers were so starving that they ate unripened potatoes right from the fields in the Great Mountains of Silesia to quell the endless hunger of the soldier.

He told us that the hunger of the soldier wasn't easy to quell, and any man who had been a soldier knew that.

He told us that the potato tubers were green.

He told us that you really shouldn't eat green potatoes because they're poisonous, and that was known to every child, though evidently not to every soldier.

He told us that the Bohemian farmers thought that this was the source of the terrible stomach pains and intestinal cramps which many soldiers suffered.

He told us that the soldiers suffered above all from shigellosis, from endless diarrhea.

And in fact I was curious to hear what came after the diarrhea, but then, all of the sudden, his head fell forward and Winterberg fell asleep.

In the middle of a sentence.

In the middle of a word.

As always.

He lay with his head on his open book, on the page for Vienna in 1913. And one hand lay on the plate with the rest of the potato salad.

Silke was so shocked, she jumped to her feet and wanted to call an ambulance.

I stopped her.

'Let him be, he always does that... just let him sleep for a bit, that's the best thing to do. We'll wake him up when we leave.'

'Does he always ramble like that?'

'Yeah.'

'That's strange. He didn't use to talk so much.'

'No?'

'No. I can't remember him ever talking like that.'

'I thought he'd always been so…'

'Mad?'

'Yeah.'

'He was. But he didn't say much, he just looked after my mother and his trains. I wanted him to talk to me, but he never told me anything. This is the first time. What does he talk about?'

'About history. About the war.'

'World War II?'

'No. Well, that too, but mostly about the war in 1866. And Sarajevo. And about the railway and the trains and so on. About tunnels and locomotives. But above all about the war in 1866 and Sarajevo in 1914. About Königgrätz.'

'Königgrätz?'

'Yeah, the Battle of Königgrätz, 1866. He says that battle "runs through his heart".'

'Wild. I have no idea about Königgrätz. He's never talked about it.'

'One day with your father and you'll know everything about Königgrätz. And Sarajevo. And the railway history of Austria-Hungary. And the crematorium in Reichenberg, he talks a lot about that, too. About the corpses.'

'What?'

'He prefers "Feuerhalle".'

'But that's crazy.'

'He was born in Reichenberg.'

'Yeah, I know… but…'

'Have you ever been there?'

'No.'

'We were there just now.'

'In the crematorium?'

'Yeah. His father founded it. He was the first director of the Feuerhalle.'

She looked at me as if I were mad.

'What?'

'That's what he said.'

'"Feuerhalle"? I've never heard that. That sounds sort of… Nazi-ish.'

'That's what they used to call it.'

'Was he a Nazi?'

'I don't know.'

'I don't either.'

'But he probably was.'

'I don't know anything about him.'

We clinked glasses.

'He never talked to me much about anything. My mother, she did, even when she was already sick. But he never did.'

'His father built the crematorium, the first Feuerhalle in the Austrian Monarchy.'

'I don't know anything about that at all.'

'Maybe you didn't ask.'

'I did, I wanted him to talk to me. But he never told me about anything like that. Why would he tell you?'

'I don't know. Maybe he just needs to get it out. I don't want any part in it, I really can't listen to any more, but he doesn't care, he just rambles on. He rambles and rambles and rambles and reads from his book and gets everything jumbled up.'

'He just talks, just like that?'

'Yeah.'

'And do you talk to him, too?'

'Not really.'

'Does he ask you anything?'

'Rarely. Most of the time he just rambles.'

'I didn't matter to him. He was never interested in me.'

We ordered another beer.

And Winterberg continued to sleep with his head in his book.

The Bosnian barmaid brought him a pillow.

'This trip isn't good for him. He's going mad.'

'He's already mad.'

'But maybe it's good that he's travelling, that he's doing this, that he's talking.'

'I dunno…'

'Maybe it really is a good thing.'

I looked at her.

'I know I fucked it up. I know that. Your father offered me money if I went with him, and I thought, okay, then I'll have a bit of cash for something. I don't want the money. Take him, take the money, and take him back home. He needs your help, I can't help him anymore.'

The city behind the window was dark, cold and wet.

I told Winterberg's daughter where we'd already been.

I told her about Reichenberg.

About the Feuerhalle on the hill in the middle of the city that was just as old as the Czechoslovak Republic and just as old as her father.

I told her about Jičín.

About Königgrätz.

I told her about the journey to Prague.

To České Budějovice.

To Vimperk.

To Pilsen.

To Linz.

I told her again about Königgrätz.

About the battle that ran through his heart like flames of fire.

About the snowy battlefields.

About the deathly silent Svíb Forest, where the earth was unable to stomach the many July corpses, as Winterberg's father would say, and is constantly spewing them back up.

I told her about the search for the dead. For his ancestors. For her ancestors. I told her where we were headed. To Sarajevo.

I told her everything that Winterberg had told me.

I told her that her father is probably genuinely mad and truly needs help.

I told her everything and she listened to me and nodded, and she drank one beer after another from Sarajevo in *Sarajevo* and didn't say a word and Winterberg slept with his head in his book between the two of us.

'Why didn't he ever tell me any of that?'

'I don't know.'

We ordered another beer.

'You have to travel with him to the end.'

'What?'

'You have to do it for him.'

'I don't have to do anything.'

'I'm asking you to do it.'

'You can see it yourself, he's old, it's not good for him, and not for me either. He should be taken right back home.'

'You have to continue.'

'He's mad. He's mad.'

'Please, I'm asking you.'

'No. You should take him back to Berlin tomorrow.'

'Herr Kraus, you continue on with him. Or else I'll go to the police right now and tell them I've found you.'

'Good. Let's do that.'

'I know you were already in prison.'

'Hm.'

'It wasn't so hard to find out what you were there for.'

'That was more than thirty years ago. And I didn't do anything.'

'That's what they all say.'

'What's that supposed to mean?'

'It means you'll go back to prison for a few years, and this time for longer, I can guarantee you that. My father may not have told me much, but I studied law, I know how it works.'

'Kiss my ass.'

'What?'

'You heard me right.'

'Excuse me?!'

'You have no idea what happened back then. No idea, you hear me? You have no idea how fucked it all was. I'm leaving.'

'Whatever you want.'

'A daughter who doesn't know a damn thing about her father. That's sad.'

I grabbed my coat and stood up to leave.

'Bye, then.'

'No, please stay… we'll do things differently… please, Herr Kraus… I'll go to the police and say that my father wasn't kidnapped, that he went with you willingly, everything's fine, you're both on your way back to Berlin and it was all a mistake, a misunderstanding. You and my father – you're best friends.'

'Best friends? Ha, ha.'

'It's true. You're his only friend.'

'No thanks.'

'And you don't have many friends either.'

'That's none of your business.'

'Call it charity. Or sympathy. Empathy.'

'Empathy. You really have no business talking to me about empathy.'

'I know.'

I looked at her and she looked at me and Winterberg slept with his head in his book.

'Why should I do it?'

'Because my father really does need to make this trip. I think it's not about Sarajevo. Or about Königgrätz. Or about a crematorium somewhere in Reichenberg. About a Feuerhalle. I fear it's about something else. About a lot more, about something completely different.'

I sat back down. 'About what, then?'

'I don't know. I don't know much about him. You already know more than I ever did. The story with Reichenberg and Königgrätz, yes, maybe he did talk about that at some point, I don't know anymore, I thought it was all just a joke.'

'So he did tell you about it?'

'Yes, maybe... but I thought it was a joke, we all thought it was a joke. "The battle of Königgrätz runs through my heart", that does sound like some mad joke. You have to find out what's really behind it, Herr Kraus.'

Silence.

'I'm begging you.'

Silence.

'Another beer?'

She nodded.

'What do you do, by the way? Professionally?'

'I sit at the office.'

'Hm.'

'And travel a lot.'

'I know that much... but what exactly do you do?'

'I'm a lawyer.'

'Divorces, et cetera.'

'More like marriages.'

'Marriages?'

'But divorces too, you're right about that.'

'I don't understand.'

'I work in mergers and acquisitions. When a company wants to marry another company, I'm something like the maid of honour and make sure it's all legitimate. When a company wants to split, I'm also there.'

'Do you enjoy it?'

'Yes… but you've got the more exciting job.'

'You mean, with the crossing?'

'Yes.'

'Your father is the first one I haven't managed it with. The first to survive the crossing.'

'"Crossing"? By that, you mean…'

'Yeah, exactly, the first one that I haven't brought to the other side. It really only goes in one direction in our business. No one comes back.'

'But he came back.'

'Yeah.'

'You know, we might as well be on a first-name basis. I'm Silke.'

'I know. Jan.'

'Jan, the Czech.'

'Hm.'

'I've never been to Prague. I've been to Warsaw, and Budapest, and to Vienna before, but never to Prague. And never to Reichenberg or Königgrätz.'

'No need. You've been to Vienna. Prague is like Vienna, just smaller. But the beer is better. But that means the schnitzel is smaller, as your father would say.'

She laughed.

'Why don't you live there? Why are you in Germany?'

'I made a break for it, didn't I?'

'What happened back then?'

'Doesn't matter. Read the file, Miss Law Professor.'

'I know what your file says, I read it. But I'd like to know how it really was. How it was for you.'

'It doesn't matter. Another beer?'

She nodded. 'Why do you do this job?'

'Because I didn't study law.'

Between us, Winterberg began to snore.

'I don't know. I knew someone else who did it. I gave it a try and decided to stick with the crossing, with the Army of Last Hope.'

We drank our beers and the old Bosnian woman began to close up *Sarajevo*.

'"Army of Last Hope." Did you come up with that?'

'No, that was Agnieszka.'

'Your wife?'

'No, a friend of mine. But a nice woman. We were together for a bit.'

'Frau Sikorska, the one who recommended you?'

'Yeah, exactly…'

'I called her, of course, when I didn't find the two of you at home… she was worried…'

'Hm…'

'You lot have a hard job.'

'Not at all, sometimes it's really entertaining. It's entertaining with your father. Sometimes.'

'Yes, sometimes it is.'

We laughed and clinked glasses.

'I wouldn't be able to take much more entertainment anyway.'

We ordered another round.

The *Sarajevo* was empty. As was the city outside. The Bosnian barmaid was wiping down the tables. We were the last guests. Me, Silke, and the snoring Winterberg between us. And the barmaid's husband, who was still asleep at the counter.

'He was quite old, I mean, as a father.'

'Over sixty. He once told me that he never wanted to be a father.'

'He said the same to me. He'd already been married twice, after all. At some point you're just too old for children.'

'Do you have kids?'

'No.'

'Are you sure?'

'Pretty sure.'

'And you… do you want kids?'

'I don't know. I always thought there would be time. And now I'm too old for it.'

I looked at her. She was a bit drunk. So was I.

'I'm afraid your father didn't really love any of his wives. Including your mother.'

'I know.'

'It's all about this Königgrätz. Maybe he actually had the right idea.'

'He never really loved my mother.'

'But you're his kid.'

'It happens pretty quickly, having children.'

'Not that quickly.'

'He knew that if he didn't give her a child, my mother would leave him. He had a lot of other women…'

'Really?'

'Yes, a lot… my mother knew about it… he was already quite old when he met my mother.'

'I'm asking myself how he managed all that. Maybe he's just bragging.'

'I don't think so. Maybe he wasn't afraid of women, even the strong and beautiful ones like my mother. He's an egotist. I thought he wanted to have her so that he'd have someone to take care of him when he was old. And look at what happened, she didn't take care of him, but he took care of her for years.'

'Then he did love her, if he did that.'

She cried. She looked at me. And then at her father.

'What happened?'

'She had a stroke, something in her brain snapped.'

'Probably an aneurysm.'

'Yes. Just like something in his brain snapped after my mother died.'

'But your father isn't dead. He seems pretty lively – I mean, when he's not asleep.'

'Thank you.'

'No, that's ridiculous.'

'Really, I mean it.'

'Nonsense. He was lucky. I've never seen something like that.'

We ordered the last round of beers. And asked for the cheque. I wanted to pay, but it was Silke who took the bill.

'Lenka. Lenka Morgenstern. Does the name mean anything to you?'

'No.'

'Hm.'

'Lenka Morgenstern?'

'Yeah.'

'I have no idea. Who is that?'

'The first "woman in the moon".'

'What?'

'That's what your father says.'

'I don't understand.'

'Me neither, not really.'

'Who is she?'

'I think your father was in love with her.'

'The first woman in the moon.'

'I think that's who he's looking for.'

'What do you mean?'

'That's why we're on this trip. Lenka Morgenstern is the one woman he truly loved. And he's in love with her to this day. He says this trip is a honeymoon trip that he'd planned for himself and Lenka. A honeymoon trip that never was, a farewell trip, you know?'

'No.'

'I didn't understand it either…'

'But that's completely crazy.'

'Yeah. I didn't understand it at first, but now I do.'

'The first woman in the moon. Is Frau Morgenstern still alive?'

'No. Otherwise he'd be making this trip with her and not with me.'

'A honeymoon to the battlefields and to the graves, that's really mad, no woman would want that. Not even one from the moon.'

'He said she'd like it. Even his model train in Berlin, he didn't make it for himself, he made it for her, it's our journey in a microcosm.'

'Mad.'

'He says that quite often too. And it's true.'

'But what isn't mad these days.'

'Yeah.'

'A honeymoon and a farewell trip, huh.'

We sat in silence.

'Did he ever talk to you about the Englishman?'

'What?'

'He says he was his best friend.'

'No idea. I thought he didn't have any friends. An Englishman?'

'Yeah.'

'I don't know.'

'It doesn't matter.'

We sat in silence for a moment and then ordered one another beer after all. And schnapps. I paid for that.

'This "Lenka"… your father said she was murdered, she was a Jew, she had fled from Liberec to Brno, Vienna, Budapest, and Zagreb, then to Sarajevo, he said she'd sent him postcards, and the last one was from Sarajevo, so that's where he wants to go. She wanted to flee to Palestine. He thinks something happened in Sarajevo, or shortly afterwards.'

'Something happened?'

'Yeah. That's what he says. We're looking for her murderer.'

'Murderer?'

'Yeah.'

'And who was he, or she…?'

'He doesn't know.'

'The Germans?'

'I don't know. Maybe… probably.'

She was silent.

She cried.

'Shit.'

'Yeah.'

'Just look, he's my father and I don't know anything about him. Not even what he did in the war.'

'I don't know that either.'

'I don't know who this woman in the moon was. Lenka Morgenstern. I don't know anything about Königgrätz.'

'Well, as I said, I can tell you a thing or two about Königgrätz these days…'

She laughed.

'I'm being serious.'

'I know.'

'1866. The Prussians, the Austrians and the Saxons... the Saxons are so often forgotten in history, unfortunately...'

'Why the Saxons?'

'That's how he always says it...'

She laughed.

She looked out of the window.

She looked at her sleeping father.

'And you?'

'What, me?'

'Are you looking for someone too?'

'No. Why do you ask?'

'Just because.'

'I'm happy enough alone.'

'Everyone's looking for someone.'

'I'm not looking for anyone.'

'No one's happy on their own.'

'I am.'

'No matter how often they insist otherwise.'

'I'm not alone. I've got him. You're right, he's my best friend, in a sense. My only friend.'

Winterberg suddenly awoke. For a moment he didn't know where he was. He looked at us. He looked at his book. The pillow. The half-empty glass with the stale beer. He drank the rest and gestured to the barmaid.

'Three more schnapps, for good digestion.'

Then he turned to us.

'The Sarajevsko beer is surprisingly good, don't you think?'

'The brewery in Sarajevo was founded by the Czechs, according to the barmaid.'

'Of course, the best beer in the Monarchy always came from Bohemia, yes, yes, from Pilsen... the best beer for the people and also the best weapons for the army, and the most beautiful women overall... oh, it doesn't matter.'

The barmaid brought us three schnapps. Silke looked at her father in surprise.

'Now where was I... right, yes... what I wanted to say earlier... yes... so... the Bohemians also called the potato war the "plum war". Because when the Prussians stole and ate all the potatoes from the Bohemians, they went after the plums, but the plums weren't ripe either, and so their intestinal cramps were much worse, yes, yes, and their shigellosis too. Dear Herr Kraus, you should really read something about history. And you too, Silke.'

He held up the shot glass and looked at both of his with his small, green, and suddenly so vibrant eyes.

'Cheers.'

. . .

We picked up Silke's things with a taxi and then returned to our hotel. The city was empty and wet, the streets glimmered, the soft, hazy lights of the streetlamps reflected off the asphalt, and the city made us soft and hazy as well. We were all a bit drunk. A bit too drunk.

Silke, Winterberg and I.

'The Burgtheater, look, you see that?'

He pointed to the theatre.

'It always started around seven o'clock, just like it does today, I read that in my book. What a shame that there's still no play about Königgrätz, that would fit right in with the Burgtheater, or in the Opera, yes, yes, a musical piece about Königgrätz in the Königgrätz of architecture, perhaps I'll have to write it myself. No one knows as much about the battle as I do, about the history, about the fog of war, about the construction of the Alpine railways. I am the battle, I am Königgrätz, yes, yes, tragic, tragic…'

'Papa, your battle wouldn't interest anyone in the theatre.'

'You have no idea. You don't see through history.'

'Yeah, yeah.'

'My play about Königgrätz would interest everyone! I know everything. Everything! But I can't write a play, tragic, tragic.'

We exited the taxi.

The hotel door was locked.

'Look at that, dear Herr Kraus, just like in 1913. The doors are locked after 11 pm, that's what it says in my Baedeker. Nothing has changed in Vienna, yes, yes, only a few thousand more corpses are resting in the Central Cemetery, only a few more water corpses and arson corpses and noose corpses, yes, yes, you can't rely on anything these days, only on my old book, on the railway, and on death, which is always hungry, yes, yes, just as Gustav said, but not Gustav Adolf, the Swedish king, another Gustav, a colleague of mine from the Berlin tram, who certainly didn't know Gustav Adolf, he didn't see through history at all… and so our Gustav was always hungry, he ate so much that one day he couldn't fit in the driver's cabin, yes, yes, that made him very melancholy, and Gustav drowned himself in the Landwehrkanal not long afterwards, yes, yes, Gustav's water corpse wasn't a pretty sight, as my father would say… in my Baedeker the world is still in order and so is the hotel *Astoria*, but where's the night porter, ring him again, dear Herr Kraus, unfortunately I'll have to… yes, yes, the beer from Sarajevo, you understand, dear Herr Kraus, the beer from Sarajevo is good, but… yes, yes, finally, someone's coming, why does everything take so long. Tomorrow we'll go to the *Café Hawelka* and eat Bohemian dumplings.'

'Yeah, sure, we'll do that. But for now, go to sleep.'

'The *Café Hawelka* is also recommended in my Baedeker, you plum head.'

'Plum head?' said Silke.

'That's what they said in Reichenberg before the war about the Czechs. Before the war, during the war, and after the war. It's not a bad thing, I like plums, especially in dumplings, my mother always made them like that.'

The night porter yawned, unlocked the door, and yawned again.

Winterberg wanted to give him a 20 heller tip, he said, as was recommended in his Baedeker. But he didn't have any hellers. He swayed and wanted the porter to convert it into cents. He didn't quite understand him. Silke gave him two euros.

* * *

I lay in bed and couldn't sleep.
I thought about Winterberg.
About Silke.
About Carla.
My chest was burning. My heart was burning.

Someone knocked on my door.

It was Silke.

'Did something happen with your father?'

'No. Can I come in?'

We sat on the sofa. We drank another beer. And she told me about Winterberg. And about her mother. And about herself. About her childhood. About her time at university in Munich and in Paris. About a man she'd once loved. About her job.

She told me about the loneliness.

About the loneliness in school.

About the loneliness at university.

About the loneliness in the office.

About the loneliness in meetings.

About the loneliness in phone conferences.

About the loneliness at the airport.

About the loneliness in Brussels.

About the loneliness in Paris.

About the loneliness in Warsaw.

About the loneliness in Berlin.

About the loneliness in English.

About the loneliness in German.

About the loneliness in her hotel room.

About the loneliness on the internet.

About the loneliness while shopping.

About the loneliness of eating in front of the television.

About the loneliness of vomiting in the bathroom.

About the loneliness of walking in the park.

About the loneliness in the gym.

About the loneliness at Bikram yoga.

About the loneliness at Kundalini yoga.

About the loneliness at gravity yoga.

About the loneliness in the sauna.

About the loneliness in the morning.

About the loneliness in the evening.

About the loneliness on the weekend.

About the loneliness in her apartment.

About the loneliness in the shower.

About the loneliness in bed.

She embraced me and I embraced her. We kissed. We made love. On the sofa. In bed. In the shower.

We made love, and I thought the entire time about Carla, and I knew that Silke was thinking the entire time about this man whom she had loved. And I also knew that we were just as lost as Winterberg, who looked for Lenka Morgenstern in every woman. It's not the Battle of Königgrätz that runs through Winterberg's heart, that tears him in two and rips him apart, it's his love for Lenka. A wound that can't be healed but remains forever.

Lenka Morgenstern.

Carla.

And the man whom Silka loved.

A great emptiness. A great loneliness.

Cornus sanguinea.

It's not as easily overcome as the Alps by the railway, as Winterberg would say.

. . .

We lay in bed and looked up at the ceiling and listened to a fight between a man and a woman in the next room over.

'What's it like to die?'

'It's terrible.'

'What do you think comes afterwards, after the crossing?'

'I'm constantly asking myself the same question.'

'And?'

'My father thinks there's a pub there. It's always open, the beer is free, and those you've known in life are all sitting at the table waiting for you, your family, your friends and so on.'

'Funny.'

'I don't know. I don't want to sit down with all the people I've known. I really don't. And some certainly wouldn't want to be sitting with me, I'm sure of that.'

'Hold me again.'

I wrapped my arms around her.

'Yes, just like that. Just hold me like this, yeah?'

'Sure.'

'It's so strange. You really do know more about him than I do.'

'Come with us, then you'll learn more too.'

She looked at me.

'You think I should come?'

'Why not?'

'But… well… I don't know, do you really think so? Maybe it's not such a bad idea. I could do with a holiday, anyway. Yeah, I'll come, all right? You think it's really fine?'

'Yeah, why not? He's your father.'

'Yeah, you're right, I'll do it. I'll come. I won't go back.'

'Great. We'll go to Sarajevo together.'

'Yes. I'll call the office tomorrow. It won't be the end of the world if I'm gone for a few weeks. I haven't gone on holiday for two years. Great. I'm really looking forward to it.'

'You see? It's that easy.'

'Hold me again.'

I wrapped my arms around her.

'Yes, just like that. Hold me tight.'

She closed her eyes and drifted off to sleep. So did I. But the fight between the man and the woman next door didn't stop.

THE NOOSE

When I awoke in the morning, Silke was gone.

She wasn't at breakfast, either.

Winterberg sat alone in the dining room and read his book through his magnifying glass.

'Yes, yes, when we're in Brünn, we have to find the house where my Lenka stayed … she sent a lovely postcard to me in Reichenberg with the old city hall, a crocodile and Spielberg castle, yes, yes, we have to see Spielberg, I've always wanted to go there. And the inn where the saddest fool of history, Lojka, drank himself to death, perhaps it's still there. And we also have to see the Central Cemetery and the Feuerhalle, yes, yes, that always cheers me up. And ride around a bit with the tram, that'll also do me good, that always relaxes me.'

'Where's Silke?'

'Who?'

'Your daughter.'

'My daughter?'

'Yeah.'

'Yes, exactly, where is Silke?'

'I don't know.'

'Oh, yes. Yes, yes… Silke had to get back. To Munich or Madrid or Paris, I don't know, back to a wedding or to a divorce, as she always says.'

'But she said…'

'What did she say?'

'Nothing.'

'I'm supposed to give this to you.'

Winterberg handed me an envelope. Inside was a small mobile phone and a note.

'Thanks for doing this. Call me when you get there. Or if something happens. Or if you need money. Much love, -S.'

'Maybe we should go to the theatre, too, in Brünn. Why not? Or to the opera… I haven't been to the opera in ages, when was the last time you went to the opera, dear Herr Kraus?'

'I've never been to the opera.'

'Ah, well, you haven't missed all that much. But perhaps we should go. Or, you know what, we should go to Austerlitz instead, that was also a fateful battle, of course not as fateful as Königgrätz, but fateful enough to be worth the trip to Austerlitz, yes, yes, Austerlitz has surely also mangled a few hearts just as Königgrätz mangled mine, yes, yes, the legendary "Sun of Austerlitz", perhaps we'll get to experience it.'

'Mm…'

Winterberg ordered an omelette with ham and cheese.

'I think you've fallen for her a bit, Herr Kraus, if I may be so bold.'

'For who?'

'For Silke.'

'No, I haven't.'

'Yes, yes, I see it, you've gone all red.'

'I'm not red.'

'It won't amount to anything, sadly, sadly, I know my daughter. It never has, yes, yes, too many fault zones… I've always thought that every problem can be overcome just as Carl Ritter von Ghega overcame the Alps with the Semmering Railway. But this problem can't be overcome, yes, yes, we can't overcome ourselves, our heart problems, any longer, yes, yes, we're dying out, dear Herr Kraus, that's what I see when I look at my daughter.'

'Maybe that's for the best.'

'Yes, perhaps it is. Perhaps we don't deserve any better.'

'Has it always been this complicated with women, Herr Winterberg?'

'Yes… but with men, too. The fog of war prevails everywhere, you should read Clausewitz. *The Fog of War*… that's all it is.'

'The fog of war? All right, sure.'

'The fog of war envelops every battlefield and every relationship. It's not so easily overcome.'

'I really don't understand you.'

'Poor communication. That's the fog for you… You only have yourself to rely on, yes, yes, even worse than the fog of war is the fog of love, tragic,

tragic, we're simply dying out, not today, not tomorrow, but the day after – certainly. You're right, it's not much of a tragedy, life will go on, just without us. But it's nice that you're not yet completely transparent.'

'Transparent?'

'Yes, like glass. Many men your age, dear Herr Kraus, are already transparent, if not all men, yes, yes, when you're twenty, every young woman is looking your way, at thirty, perhaps every third, at forty, perhaps every fifth, but then all of the sudden, you, as a man, are as transparent to them as a pane of glass, tragic, tragic… the women simply look through you, you're not there any longer, you don't exist anymore, dear Herr Kraus. But my daughter is proof that you still exist at least a bit, yes, yes, that you're still somewhat there.'

'And how is it at ninety-nine?'

'Well, then you start to become visible again.'

'You're visible again? To the women?'

'Yes. Haven't you noticed?'

'No.'

'Women are looking at me all the time. Young, old, blonde, brunette, all of them.'

'Because they're afraid you'll collapse at any moment. I'm looking at you all the time for the same reason.'

'No, no, that's not it… the ladies know that I'm still young, I'm still all there.'

'Young, you say?'

'Or rather… young again. Young and fit as a fiddle, as if reborn. I've never felt as young and healthy as I do now, yes, yes, we can give it a try, and then I'll show you how visible I am and how invisible, yes, yes, how transparent you've become, even though you're so young, even though you could be my son, no, my grandson, no, my great-grandson.'

. . .

Shortly before noon, we got into a tram and rode in circles.

We kept riding and Winterberg didn't want to get out and look at anything, he wanted at most to transfer between trams in order to ride another ring line, as he called it, onwards or backwards.

And so we spent whole hours riding in a circle, in the tram circle of Vienna, as Winterberg called it, in this noose of trams that the centre of Vienna carried around its neck like a noose, like a cord, which is constantly being tugged and pulled, as he said, until the city centre one day hangs itself on this belt of trams.

'Yes, yes, like the poor souls who hang themselves… noose corpses aren't a pretty sight, my father really didn't like the noose corpses, the swollen faces and the swollen eyes and the swollen tongues and the swollen lips and the damp trousers, no, no, my father always wanted to dispense with those ones quickly, send them swiftly to the Feuerhalle to reconcile them with their fate.'

We rode on and Winterberg rambled and looked out at Vienna and read aloud from his book and looked out of the window again and rambled again and read aloud from his book again.

'Yes, yes, dear Herr Kraus, and yet those poor souls are the freest people on earth, yes, yes, I know what I'm talking about, I've so often wanted to hang myself or shoot myself, and I think you know that, too… look at that, the Ringstraße, built over former fortifications like the old boulevards in Paris, along with the Franz-Joseph-Kai, encircles the entire old city centre over a length of 5.5 kilometres and a width of 57 metres, with magnificent state buildings, plush tenements, monuments, gardens and parks, the pride of modern Vienna… yes, yes, yes, dear Herr Kraus, my father didn't particularly like suicide corpses, but he still prepared a lovely cremation for every one… look at that, dear Herr Kraus, that must be the Deutschmeister monument, so, so, a soldier with a banner atop a granite pedestal, the figure of Vindobona underneath, Bravery and Camaraderie in two groups on the sides, just as it says in my book, yes, yes, the victory over the Turks at Zenta, the victory over the Prussians at Kolin, we've already been there, dear Herr Kraus, my father said the water corpses were even worse than the noose corpses.'

We rode on and Winterberg rambled and looked in bewilderment at a woman who was looking back at him with equal bewilderment and listening to him, and as he noticed this, he began to speak even louder.

'Yes, yes, that's right, I know what you're going to say, dear Herr Kraus, they love to eat water corpses with beer in Bohemia, yes, yes, look at that, that must be the stock market, but I'm not interested in that… there's where the Ringtheater used to be, I am interested in that, tragic, tragic, many fire corpses, that's why I always keep my rope on me, yes, yes, to be able to save myself, fire corpses aren't a pretty sight, as my father said… back in the war, I was in a terrible fire.'

'In Reichenberg?'

'No.'

'Where?'

'It doesn't matter… but it's nice to know you're listening. I thought you'd stopped listening to me… now where was I… anyway… yes.'

He looked out of the window. Then he looked at a woman who also looked back at him. And then he looked back at his book.

'Yes, yes, there's the university, yes, yes, the birth of Athena, the oldest German university after the one instituted in Prague in 1348, yes, yes, only founded in 1365, the first university in Prague, the first Pilsner brewery in Pilsen, the first Feuerhalle in Reichenberg, the first electric tram in Tábor, the first electric Feuerhalle in Semil… yes, yes, the Bohemians have a lot to be proud of, but who remembers things like that these days, I remember it, Vienna only came afterwards, over 530 professors and private lecturers, 8,500 students and 1,800 visitors, nearby the 7th Commando Corps, it has to be somewhere around there… my father didn't like water corpses, he said water corpses weren't a pretty sight, lovely, lovely, look at that, the lovely city hall park, but the fire of the Feuerhalle reconciled even the water corpses with their fate, my father said… no, no, he didn't like water corpses and he couldn't eat water corpses with his beer in the Ratskeller either, those sausages that often lay for weeks in vinegar stock reminded him too much of the human corpses that often lay for weeks in the water, the ones they fished out of the Neisse or out of the Reichenberg Reservoir… oh, look at that, dear Herr Kraus, the Hofburg and the Heldenplatz, really a bit smaller than one would expect, don't you think? Prague Castle might be the largest castle complex in the world, but the Vienna Hofburg seems much greater and more powerful than all the castle complexes in the world, yes, yes.'

He read and rambled and Vienna passed us by and he again looked at a woman, this time an older woman, and the women looked back at Winterberg, and he said to me: 'Look at that, dear Herr Kraus, I'm not transparent… sometimes the faces of the water corpses could hardly be recognised, said my father, sometimes with the water corpses you couldn't even tell if it was a young or an old man, a young or an old woman, yes, yes, sometimes you couldn't even tell at a glance whether it was a man or a woman at all, tragic, tragic… after a certain period of time in the water, the water corpses would start to lose their skin, yes, yes, water corpses always made my father a bit melancholy.'

Winterberg briefly looked at me.

'Do you like to eat water corpse sausages?'

'Yeah, I do. But you can't get them in Germany. I always make them myself.'

'Really? With your own recipe?'

'Yeah.'

'Would you make them for me sometime?'

'Sure, why not?'

'I'll look forward to it.'

And then he looked back out of the window.

'Oh, look at that, dear Herr Kraus, the Vienna city hall, maybe it has a Ratskeller too, maybe there you can order water corpses with your beer, a lot of Czechs have lived in Vienna after all, perhaps we can find a Bohemian inn tonight with beer and water corpses… my father didn't eat water corpses with beer, only brawn, brawn didn't remind him of any corpses, at least that was the case for a long time, but then my father had to cremate a shunter who had been squashed by two wood freight carriages, yes, yes, shunter corpses aren't a pretty sight, and afterwards my father couldn't eat brawn for a long time… I actually like brawn, it doesn't make me think of shunter corpses… the Vienna city hall, the most prominent building of the city after St. Stephan's Church, it's like that in Reichenberg with our city hall by Franz Ritter von Neumann, who based his designs on the Vienna city hall.'

We rode on and Winterberg told me that in Reichenberg they were always trying to keep up with and imitate Vienna, just like in Gablonz they were always trying to keep up with and imitate Reichenberg. He told me that in Prague it was the same. He told me that the Praguers were masters in imitation and keeping up. And it's surely the same to this day.

'Yes, yes, always this battle, this competition between Gablonz and Reichenberg and Prague and Vienna... the mighty 97.9 metre high tower is crowned with a bannerman wrought in iron, so, so, the Iron Man, yes, yes, just like in Reichenberg, you see... our city hall is crowned with the knight Roland to protect the city from enemies and idiocy... Franz Ritter von Neumann was unfortunately a victim of railway travel, he collapsed in Vienna's Southern Station as he wanted to travel with the Southern Railway towards Semmering, but the train was delayed by hours due to an accident at a previous station, he got himself all riled up and then collapsed on the platform of a heart attack, yes, yes, you should never get riled up over a delay, heart attack corpses aren't a pretty sight, wasn't that just the equestrian statue of Radetzky? In Prague they blew it up and forgot him; here, Radetzsky lives on.'

We rode on and then exited the tram and then entered another tram.

And the next tram also travelled in a circle around the centre of Vienna, and it felt to me like the circle was increasingly closing in. I felt as if someone were holding their arms tightly around me, and it made me think of my dream where Carla had held on to me so tight. I felt hot and dizzy and I had to open the window.

'Are you feeling unwell, Herr Kraus?'

'No, no.'

'Perhaps you have a fever?'

'I'll be fine.'

The tram travelled on as if caught in a loop, and Winterberg rambled on as if caught in a loop. In a loop of his stories and of the greater history that refused to let him rest. He looked again at another woman, quite young and elegant; and then a slightly stiff and stern woman in uniform who reminded me of Silke. She also looked briefly back at him and listened and Winterberg was thrilled that she was listening, and so he rambled much louder than usual.

'My father didn't like shunter corpses, and yet he eventually started eating brawn again with his beer, because you've got to eat something with your beer... he loved brawn with vinegar and onions and a bit of pepper. Yes, yes, my father liked his brawn with a lot of onions and a lot of vinegar, he said life isn't sweet, life is sour, just like brawn, and bitter, like a good, hoppy Pilsner, yes, yes... Olmützer Quargel, the cheese, my father liked to have that with his beer too, but not too strong, because the smell reminded him too much of his work, of his corpses in the cellar of his Feuerhalle, yes, yes, the strong Olmützer Quargel sometimes reminded him of the damp and rotten forest corpses, the ones that often weren't found until months later, mostly suicides or lost tourists, yes, yes, that can happen in the Iser Mountains... forest corpses aren't a pretty sight, as my father always said, yes, yes, forest corpses always made him very melancholy, then he'd have to have schnapps with his beer, usually an herbal spirit of the brand Jan Becher from Karlsbad.'

Winterberg rambled and the woman looked at him and turned pale and quickly left the tram.

Winterberg read on and our tram continued to circle the city centre of Vienna, and I had the feeling of a cord encircling my neck. A noose. With every circle, the noose was getting tighter. I felt feverish and dizzy. I had to open the window.

And Winterberg rambled and rambled. There was no noose around his neck growing tighter and tighter.

'Look at that, Herr Kraus, the Hoftheater designed by Semper and Hasenauer, auditorium built for a capacity of 1,532 persons, lovely, lovely, the auditorium of the Reichenberg Stadttheater is much smaller, let alone the auditorium of the Reichenberg Feuerhalle... yes, yes, the hall was kept in the style of Louis XVI, marble busts of actors from the old Burgtheater by Tilgner on the loge parapets, and charming camaïeu paintings by Hynais.'

He was silent for a moment and looked out of the tram.

'The Volksgarten, yes, yes, and there, the parliamentary building, seat of the house of representatives and the house of lords, yes, yes, here the Czech-speaking Bohemians and the German-speaking Bohemians fought a few linguistic battles in German and Czech, which were much worse than the beer battles in the Reichenberg Ratskeller, as my father always said, beer brings many people together, but it makes some a bit melancholy, too... now where was I...'

Winterberg continued to read from his book and looked again at a woman, about seventy years old, who also looked back at him.

'Yes, yes, I know... a mighty building in the Greek style erected by Hansen between 1874 and 1883... a wide ramp with four bronze horse-tamers by Lax and eight marble seated statues of Greek and Roman chroniclers by Kauffungen and Seib and others, leading to the eight-pillared portico, marble relief by Hellmer, "Conferment of the Constitution", in the tympanum… on the right, the chamber of representatives with 516 seats, on the right, the chamber of lords with 261 seats, yes, yes, the German and Czech representatives had quite passionate battles here, neither of them won, everyone lost, one Königgrätz after the other, and when the Hungarians or the Bosnians tried to intervene, yes, yes, there would be more than a few slaps across the face, they'd be chasing each other with their trouser belts between the benches, all much worse than in the Reichsberg Ratskeller, my father said, because in the Ratskeller, the last beer always reconciled the Czechs and the Germans, at least until the next day, at least until Henlein showed up, my father said, after that, the beer no longer sufficed to bring the Czechs and the Germans back together… that didn't just make my father a bit melancholy, that made him very melancholy, this Henlein, this swine, this village idiot, who had scratched his Bohemian mother, Frau Dvořáčková, whom my father knew well, out of his life, just like the Saxons scratched the architect Bitzan out of the Leipzig main train station, yes, yes, this Henlein, this poor, untalented sportsman, as my father said, who like all poor, untalented sportsmen didn't become a good sportsman, but a poor sports instructor, this little worm Henlein with his squeaky voice and predilection for uniforms and tall boots… Henlein made my father very melancholy, Henlein made him far more melancholy than all the water corpses and shunter corpses and forest corpses and noose corpses that my father had tended to in the cellar of his Feuerhalle all together, because my father knew that Henlein couldn't be overcome as easily as the Alps, no, no, just as human stupidity can't be overcome.'

And then it was quiet.

Winterberg yawned.

I thought, it's over, now he's tired, now he'll fall asleep. Or we'll go back to the hotel and he'll lie down and I'll go out for a beer.

But Winterberg didn't want to go to the hotel.

He looked at another woman. He looked out of the window. He cleaned his glasses silently. He yawned again. And then he began again to ramble and read aloud from the Baedeker and jumble it all up. Just like always. I wanted to leave, but the tram looped again around the Vienna city centre.

'I know, it's mad, it's all mad... the 15-metre-high Pallas Athene Fountain has stood in front of the Imperial Assembly building since 1902... the Inn and the Danube by Haerdtl and the Elbe and the Moldau by Kundmann, yes, yes, the four fateful rivers, Austria was just the "Danube Monarchy", what rubbish, I've been saying it the whole time, my book has got it a bit wrong there, yes, yes, four fateful rivers like the four fateful railways, the Southern Railway and the Northern Railway and the Western Railway and the Eastern Railway...'

Winterberg once again couldn't be stopped and I was once again feeling hot and dizzy and I once again had to open the window.

'Not far from the northern tip of the park is a monument to Empress Elisabeth placed in 1907, yes, yes, her last railway trip was to Geneva in 1898, not everyone is happy to take the train to Switzerland, but for train people like you and I, of course, Switzerland is a railway dream, yes, yes, a railway paradise, but you can perish even in paradise, yes, yes... architecture by Ohmann, the seated image of the Empress by Bitterlich, yes, yes, the Olmützer Quargel can really stink quite terribly, back in school we made little stinkbombs out of the Quargel and hid them in the staff room... there, that's the Maria Theresa monument, well, well, the Empress, seated on a granite pedestal bound by four double pillars, is portrayed as a 35-year-old woman, holding a sceptre and the Pragmatic Sanction to her left, around the pedestal are equestrian statues of the field commanders.'

He read on and looked again at another woman who looked back at him. A young woman with a tattoo of a Chinese dragon on her face.

'You see that, Herr Kraus, I'm not transparent... one of the commanders is General Laudon, I thought as much, the victor over the Prussians at Kolin in 1757 and in 1788 over the Turks at Dubitza and Belgrade, the loser at Liegnitz in 1760, although that wasn't his fault.'

Winterberg rambled and I again had to open the window for a moment because I was feeling hot and dizzy.

'My father also didn't like the suicides that were mangled by the trains, they often had to be put back together, like pieces of a machine that wouldn't work again, and there were always one or two or even several pieces missing, but even the railway corpses mangled by the

trains were reconciled with their fate by the flames of the Feuerhalle...
oh, the Kunsthistorisches Museum, yes, yes, beautiful, although Vienna
only came to grow in importance as a centre of fine arts at the end of
the 15th century, and yet the museum is one of the first art collections
in the world, its treasures were multiplied many times over, all as an
adulation of the Habsburgs as patrons of the arts... when there wasn't
any braun or Olmützer Quargel to have with his beer at the Reichenberg Ratskeller, my father liked to eat simple sausages with onions and
vinegar, the sliced pork wieners didn't remind him of water corpses...
perhaps we should go in, but not today, statues of artists and patrons
on the balustrade, yes, yes, busts of the artists, well, well, allegorical
portrayals, yes, yes, the only suicide corpses that my father really liked
were the frost corpses and the corpses of those who'd offed themselves
with gas or with medication, with morphine for example, they were
a lovely sight, said my father, those corpses didn't have to be pieced
back together, the dead looked as if they'd just fallen asleep, said my
father, but unfortunately suicide corpses like these were rather rare
in Reichenberg, said my father, most suicides had hanged themselves,
most of the men and most of the women too, or cut open their wrists
with a knife or a razor-blade or shot themselves or thrown themselves
out of the window, but all of them were reconciled with their fate by
the fire of the Feuerhalle, yes, yes, look at that, dear Herr Kraus, the
Naturhistorisches Museum matches the façade and the dimensions of
the Kunsthistorisches Museum, except for its depth, which is 70 metres
shallower, who would have thought...'

Winterberg continued to ramble and continued to look out of the
window.

'Who knows how it is with the suicides in Reichenberg today,
whether most people still hang themselves, next time we'll have to ask
around, who knows how it is in Vienna, in Königgrätz, in Sarajevo, in
Winterberg... most people hanged themselves in Reichenberg in the
late summer during the crisis years, a lot of Germans, and then in the
late summer of 1938, a lot of Czechs and Jews, yes, yes, then from that
point I don't know, because my father died shortly afterwards, he, the
staunch and loyal republican and citizen of Czechoslovakia, yes, yes, the
last German republican in Reichenberg, the last democrat, tragic, tragic,

I know, perhaps the most loyal Czechoslovak among all the Germans in Reichenberg, Czechoslovakia had gifted him his Feuerhalle on the Mountain of Fire in Reichenberg, and it was a gift that he appreciated.'

Winterberg rambled and looked out of the window of the tram, which was running in an eternal loop. I was feeling hot and dizzy, I tried to open the window again, but it didn't work this time, it was a newer tram.

'The collapse of Czechoslovakia in 1938 made my father very melancholy, yes, yes, human stupidity is endless, yes, yes, people are often stupid when they're young, but many are still stupid when they're old, take a look around at what's happening now, yes, yes, human stupidity is winning on all fronts... yes, yes, and so time goes by, everything comes to an end, everything passes by, oh, how time goes by...'

We got off the tram and right into another one and continued to travel in a loop, and Winterberg rambled and rambled and began to tremble.

The next historical fit.

'Yes, yes, look at that, the Imperial Opera, the Viennese didn't like the new opera house. When the Imperial Opera was opened three years after the Battle of Königgrätz with *Don Giovanni*, the papers called it a Königgrätz of architecture, no one liked the new opera house, the first new building, this sunken crate on the Ringstraße was too small, too tiny, too simple for the population of Vienna, yes, perhaps that shack would have been fine for Reichenberg, Budweis or Laibach, but never for Vienna, the Kaiser didn't like the new opera house either, the new opera house was nothing but a Königgrätz of architecture, and so the architect van der Nüll hanged himself in his flat even before the opening, yes, yes, the swollen face and the swollen eyes and the swollen tongue and the swollen lips and the damp trousers, yes, yes. What a shame that my father couldn't reconcile van der Nüll with his fate by the fire of his Feuerhalle, now van der Nüll is lying in his grave of honour in the Central Cemetery, shortly before his death the Viennese hated him, shortly afterwards they honoured him, his funeral was a party and the opening of the Imperial Opera was an event, but that's not all, dear Herr Kraus, his best friend and partner, the architect Sicard von Sicardsburg, collapsed over his desk a few weeks later of a heart attack, he couldn't bear the criticism of the

Imperial Opera either, and the horrible death of his friend as well, yes, yes, the life of an architect can be arduous, the Bohemian architect Bitzan was scratched out of history by the Saxons in Leipzig, the architect van der Nüll hanged himself in Vienna, the architect Sicard von Sicardsburg died in Vienna of a heart attack just like the architect von Neumann, the student of von Sicardsburg and van der Nüll, that's what my father told me, he was interested in architecture and good friends with Bitzan, and that was all because of Königgrätz if you ask me, yes, yes, you're right, there's no escape, dear Herr Kraus, and so my father was also reconciled with his fate by the fire of the Feuerhalle in his fiery crypt, *Cornus sanguinea*, and so Czechoslovakia lost one of its most loyal republicans, and so my mother became a widow, and so my life became a Königgrätz, yes, yes, it makes me a bit melancholy, today we're drinking beer and eating water corpses, all that remains is *"the beautiful landscape of battlefields, ceme-teries and ruins"* and the trams and the trains, always heading forward, always on the move, no exits, only transfers, always pushing forward, to Sarajevo, perhaps that'll help, always chasing freedom up until death.'

And then Winterberg closed his book, looked out of the window and said nothing more for a good long while.

After some time, he turned to face me, and I saw that he had again been crying throughout.

'What do you think, dear Herr Kraus, is the Naturhistorisches Musuem really 70 metres smaller than the Kunsthistorisches Museum?'

'I don't know.'

'Nor do I. Did you notice a difference?'

'No.'

'Nor did I. Perhaps not everything in my book is right.'

'Perhaps.'

'Perhaps not everything's right with me.'

'Perhaps.'

We rode in another circle around the centre of Vienna. We rode the tram and Winterberg fell asleep and I felt the loop around my neck growing tighter and tighter, and I thought I'd soon have to get up and get out and get some fresh air.

But then we were suddenly freed as the tram freed itself from this tight loop, from this noose.

THE CENTRAL CEMETERY

We had been in the tram for an eternity, and I was already tired, but Winterberg was beaming again.

And I thought, no, it can't be, I can't take any more.

Winterberg rambled on and read his book and looked out at the city. And the women. Young and old and locals and tourists, those with loose hair and those with headscarves.

He was looking to see if they were looking at him. And they really were looking at him, which might have been due to the particular way in which he was looking at them. With a slightly open mouth and with a look as if he wanted to undress them in an instant, take them to bed and bore a tunnel.

We sat in the number 71 tram towards the Central Cemetery and Winterberg was pleased, because the number 71 tram was also warmly recommended in his Baedeker for the trip to the Central Cemetery.

'Nothing's changed, yes, yes, nothing's changed.'

He said he thought it was wonderful that aside from the main sights and train stations and hotels and cafes, the Central Cemetery also played a particular role in his Baedeker. Every major city in the Monarchy had adorned itself back then with a train station and barracks and a brewery and a church and a museum and an opera house and a theatre and with a central cemetery. A city without a central cemetery or an opera or a theatre or a museum or a church or a brewery or barracks or a train station was a city no longer, but was condemned to a fringe existence as a note in the margins, as a meaningless small town.

Ideally, he would love to see all the train stations and all the cemeteries and all the battlefields, and of course all the Feuerhalles, he told me, while looking out of the window.

'Yes, yes, dear Herr Kraus, I hated the graves, this whole funerary establishment of my father's, which my mother continued to operate after his cremation up until her death in Karlsbad, up until the entire Feuerhalle perished in the flames of war… and look at where we are now, dear Herr Kraus.'

The journey took forever. Winterberg read aloud from his book and looked out of the window and said yes, yes, no, no, yes, yes, and then continued to read, or looked at the women in order to convince himself that he wasn't transparent, that he was young, in order to convince me, in order to humiliate me, that it was me who was old and transparent.

An elegant woman around forty years old entered the tram and sat down diagonally across from us. She was on the phone.

'But that's good, mum.'

Winterberg looked at her legs, which she had crossed.

The woman looked at him and then looked out of the window.

'Yes, but that's good that it's negative. Right. Yes, mum…'

Winterberg looked at her breasts.

The woman looked at him again and then looked again out of the window.

'That's how you have to think about it, mum… it's positive that it's negative.'

Winterberg looked at her tall, thin neck.

The woman looked at him again and then looked again out of the window.

'Mum… mum!… mum!!!… No. Mum, please, that's not what negative means.'

Winterberg looked at her red lips.

The woman looked at him again and then looked again out of the window.

'No, no, mum, they would tell you if it were actually positive.'

Winterberg looked her in the eye. And she really did look back at him.

'It's positive that it's negative, mum… and you also have to be positive. What does it help to be so negative… no… no, mum… I'm not negative. I'm positive, too… oh, mum, it's not easy.'

Winterberg again looked at her breasts.

The woman looked at him again and then looked again out of the window.

'I'll talk to you later, mum.'

Winterberg was still looking at her breasts.

The woman suddenly stood up. Winterberg smiled at her, but she wasn't smiling at all, she slapped him in the face and left the tram.

'You see, Herr Kraus? I'm really not transparent, yes, yes, that was the best evidence.'

'I see that.'

'You're unfortunately quite transparent, dear Herr Kraus, I've noticed that, the women don't notice you, and not just this one, yes, yes, unfortunately I can't help you. That was a lovely slap.'

He turned around as if wanting to look again at the woman who had just slapped him in the face, as if wanting to thank her.

'That must be Simmering, don't you think? We're almost there, the Feuerhalle must be somewhere around here, yes, yes, I know what you're going to say, dear Herr Kraus, the Hofburg and Schönbrunn and the museums and the Arsenal and the Burgtheater and perhaps the Imperial Crypt as well, that's all wonderful, that's why it's worth visiting them in Vienna, and that's true, you're right, they're all certainly recommended in my Baedeker, but anyone who wants to visit the first Feuerhalle in Austria needs to travel to Reichenberg, not Vienna, yes, yes, as far as Feuerhalles go, Reichenberg really achieved something, Reichenberg pulled ahead of Vienna, and so Vienna had to catch up with Reichenberg, and it'll be that way forever, the Reichenbergers must be proud to this day of this victory over Vienna, where the first Feuerhalle wasn't built until 1922.'

Winterberg glanced out of the window, polished his glasses, and then continued to read from his book.

'Yes, yes, the Central Cemetery, built in 1873 by Bluntschli and Mylius, a beautiful name, Mylius, a very unusual name, noteworthy, I've never heard it, Bluntschli, also a beautiful name, also very unusual, I've never heard that one either, perhaps he was Swiss, yes, yes, Swiss or perhaps from the Egerland…'

He looked again briefly out of the window and then continued to read from his book.

'Central Cemetery… repeatedly enlarged since then, yes, yes, certainly enlarged yet further since 1913, yes, yes, we have to use the second gate towards the arcades, nearby to the left, the Memorial for the Victims of the Ringtheater Fire, yes, yes, a trip to the theatre can always be hazardous, my father always said, he also incinerated the best-known theatre critic of the Reichenberger Zeitung, Franz Reimann. Reimann had suffered a stroke during a performance of Schiller's *Wallenstein* in the first row of the Reichenberg theatre, yes, yes, because the performance riled him up so much that a little vein popped in his head, tragic, tragic, theatre corpses aren't a pretty sight… of course all the actors attended his cremation as well as the manager and the director, Nowotny was his name, said my father, and Reimann's widow accused him of having purposely murdered her husband, a father of five, with his atrocious production of *Wallenstein*, yes, yes, she said his production was a devious attack on Reimann, the theatre critic and husband and father, the widow screamed that Nowotny's attack was just as villainous as the attack on the Archduke in Sarajevo in 1914, yes, yes, as you can see, dear Herr Kraus, Reimann's widow could see through history quite well indeed… she said, Nowotny's attack on Schiller's *Wallenstein* was plotted as an attack on her husband, Nowotny's attack on Schiller's *Wallenstein* and on her husband was just as coldly calculated and orchestrated as the attack on Wallenstein himself in Eger in 1634, in Eger, where Wallenstein had withdrawn after all his allies had abandoned him, and his only remaining hope was the Swedes, whom he had previously fought with gusto, yes, yes, precisely, in the fog of Lützen, for example… but the Swedes didn't come, and so Wallenstein was to die, just like her husband, the widow cried, yes, yes, dear Herr Kraus, the director Nowotny left the theatre after the performance of *Wallenstein* in Reichenberg, he went over to the railway and was listed as missing in action after Stalingrad, tragic, tragic, he was a great talent, my father said… now where was I again, dear Herr Kraus?'

'The Ringtheater Fire.'

'Yes, yes, thank you, I know, too many stories, too much history, you can always lose yourself so quickly in the history, yes, yes, but perhaps you have to lose yourself… in Vienna it was truly terrible, much worse than the fire in the Czech National Theatre in Prague that same year, four hundred dead, if not a thousand… that evening they were playing *The Tales of Hoffmann* by Jacques Offenbach when the Ringtheater transformed into a theatre of fire, yes, yes, into a fiery crypt, Lenka and

I once saw *The Tales of Hoffmann* in the Reichenberg Stadttheater, yes, yes, Lenka loved theatre, the theatre in Reichenberg was always known for its musical theatre and also for the curtain by Gustav Klimt.'

The tram rattled on and he continued to ramble. The next historical fit.

'Yes, yes, the Viennese always envied Reichenberg because of the Feuerhalle. For the Friends of Fire Burial and the Hygienic Movement, Reichenberg was the capital of progress, the capital of the future, the capital of hope. There were always many friends of cremation in Vienna, but when the Feuerhalle was opened with great fanfare in Reichenberg on October 31, 1918, the old Austria had ceased to exist as of a few days, the Feuerhalle in Reichenberg was no longer in Austria, but in Czechoslovakia, which was founded on the 28th of October, yes, yes, that's how life goes. That made the Friends of Fire Burial in Vienna very melancholy, many took their own lives, yes, yes, there were many noose corpses and bullet-to-the-head corpses and defenestration corpses after that in Vienna, said my father.

Winterberg yawned a bit and I thought, now, now he's getting tired again, finally a moment of peace.

But he wasn't tired yet.

The tram screeched in the curve, I was feeling hot and dizzy again, I had to open the window, and he continued to ramble.

'The Ringtheater transformed into a ferocious Feuerhalle that evening, yes, yes, into a fiery crypt… there was never a fire in the Reichenberg theatre, but of course my father had to cremate the victims of various fire accidents in his Feuerhalle, yes, yes, he always said that the charred fire corpses were a difficult fare for the ovens of his fiery crypt, it took longer to turn the fire corpses to ash. He didn't know why that was so, but it was so, yes, yes, life is full of mysteries, the once burned resisted the second burning, mad, it's all mad, I know.'

Winterberg rambled and read aloud again from his book.

'The Central Cemetery… yes, yes… the graves of honour are located behind the arcades, and no, no, it can't be… Carl! Carl Ritter von Ghega! Look at that, dear Herr Kraus, von Ghega is mentioned in my Baedeker, right next to Mozart and Beethoven and Brahms, yes, yes, the railway pioneer is in a league with the great artists, yes, yes, the great railwayman von Ghega on the same level as the greatest composers, back then it was possible, today it would be unthinkable, yes, yes, the trains create a beautiful, soul-soothing railway music of their own, everything breathes a sigh of relief, all the wrongs of the world are forgotten… that's why I love to take the train, yes, yes, in Prague before the First World War, a gynaecologist and psychiatrist tried to heal the hysterical fits and neuroses of women with long train rides, yes, that's right, dear Herr Kraus, to overcome hysterical fits and neuroses and derangement like the Alps by the railway, he believed that long mountainous stretches with many bridges and gorges and tunnels were the best medicine, because the narrow mountain valleys make you feel like a child in a cradle, the narrow mountain valleys create a particularly beautiful railway music, especially in the darkness of the tunnels, you often hear such a lovely melody there that it can bring you to tears, the gynaecologist said. But unfortunately, his train cure didn't work very well. And he wasn't a gynaecologist and psychiatrist but a veterinarian, as the newspapers later reported, and he was sued several times, not by the women he treated, no, no, but rather by their husbands, all fine wealthy gentlemen who had no time for their wives, many of the women fell in love with the doctor, and they didn't care that he wasn't a proper gynaecologist or psychiatrist, but a veterinarian… when he later perished in the war at the Piave, yes, yes, that's right, in the Feuerhalle of artillery, there were many tears in the cafés of Prague. Yes, yes, dear Herr Kraus, the beautiful mountain railways, the high bridges and the deep gorges and the long tunnels, yes, yes, like the Semmering Tunnel and the Semmering Railway of Carl Ritter von Ghega, yes, yes, we're going there just for von Ghega, because only Carl Ritter von Ghega, the son of Albanian parents from…'

And finally it happened.

Winterberg suddenly fell asleep, just as he always suddenly fell asleep.

Cork pulled.

Air out.

Eyes closed.

Goodnight.

There was still some time to go and the tram on line 71 was getting emptier with each stop. No one wanted to come along to the Central Cemetery today.

Winterberg slept with his head against the window and his book open on his lap and his magnifying glass in his hand. He was snoring. Then the tram turned, screeching and sighing and groaning in the curve, and came to a stop.

The door opened and the cold air rushed in. I woke Winterberg and we exited the tram.

We looked at the massive white gate of the cemetery and walked past the stands where people were selling candles and wreaths.

Winterberg bought a wreath and asked the seller if she knew where we could find the grave of Carl Ritter von Ghega, but the seller didn't know. She only knew where the children's cemetery was, and where the singer Falco was buried. A lot of people asked about Falco, but no one had ever asked her about Carl Ritter von Ghega.

We walked through the gate and entered the cemetery. Winterberg held the wreath and looked around and saw the building of the funerary museum. He said Carl Ritter von Ghega wouldn't be getting away from us in the cemetery and that he was interested in the funerary museum because he had never been in a funerary museum.

And so we went in.

. . .

Winterberg wanted to leave the wreath for Carl Ritter von Ghega at the coat check. He complained that the lockers at the Central Cemetery weren't large enough, and the museum attendant offered to look after the wreath while we visited the exhibition. And so, the wreath for Carl Ritter von Ghega lay on the black table in front of the round, reddish face of the museum attendant, who was in the middle of falling asleep, since aside from us there were no other visitors in the Museum of Funerary Arts in Vienna, whose building and atmosphere reminded Winterberg of the Ratskeller in Reichenberg.

'After midnight it always looked just as dead.'

We walked through the empty museum and looked at the exhibits. But we stopped already at the first picture with the first grave.

'Yes, yes, what a shame that my father isn't with us, he would love this exhibition, much more than I, because all my life I wanted nothing more than to get away from the graves and Feuerhalles and funerary arts, I didn't want anything to do with death, and where am I now, dear Herr Kraus, look at where I've ended up… our journey is nothing more than a funeral procession through *"the beautiful landscape of battlefields, cemeteries and ruins"*, as the Englishman always said, yes, yes, no one spoke as beautifully about Bohemia and Central Europe as the Englishman, it's all mad, *Cornus sanguinea*, there's no escape, the Englishman said it best, the Englishman saw through history, not like you, why don't you read any books about history, dear Herr Kraus, the Englishman would have been the right companion for my historical journey, but the Englishman has probably already become history himself, a corpse, yes, yes, he's probably already been reconciled with his fate in a Feuerhalle somewhere… so now we're here, travelling together from battlefield to battlefield and from grave to grave, yes, yes, I thought I'd be able to free myself from history, but there's no escape, why doesn't anyone understand, the Englishman would understand, why don't you understand, dear Herr Kraus?'

Winterberg was already trembling a bit.

'My father would love it here, and hate it at the same time, because there's so little about the Feuerhalles here, that has to change, I'll write a letter to the museum, no, I'll do something here and now.'

As Winterberg told the museum attendant, who was trying to sleep, the man simply nodded shortly and said: 'Just straight ahead.'

We were the only ones in the entire museum, us and the chubby museum attendant about my age in his much-too-tight uniform, with his hands clasped over his massive belly.

On his black table were no books or newspapers, only Winterberg's wreath. Otherwise, nothing.

'Just straight ahead.'

And so we walked straight ahead through the funerary museum of funerary arts in Vienna. Straight ahead through history, as Winterberg said.

We walked straight ahead and were very quiet and Winterberg enjoyed the hearse tram that used to take the dead across the city to the Central Cemetery.

'My father may have built the first Feuerhalle in Austria in Reichenberg, but his dream of a hearse tram all the way to the gates of the

Feuerhalle and a tram loop on the front plaza and a tram connection to the 1000 mm rails in the cellar of the Feuerhalle, which are surely still cemented in to this day, yes, yes, down in the fiery crypt, this dream of his was unfortunately never fulfilled, tragic, tragic, I know what you're going to say, dear Herr Kraus, the rails and the trains and the Feuerhalles, I know… but it's not my father's fault, he didn't mix up the signals, there's nothing he can do about the fact that humanity is constantly getting derailed, not him.'

We walked straight ahead and Winterberg enjoyed the Viennese funerary costumes and said his father also dressed the dead in fine clothes before the cremation.

'He made even the ugliest corpses a pretty sight.'

We walked straight ahead and Winterberg enjoyed the little train carriage that had been built for Empress Elisabeth of Austria, who, just like me, just like us, enjoyed travelling frequently by train.

'Always in motion, always moving forward, yes, yes, always longing for freedom, for a long train journey, for a new adventure. Just like me, just like us.'

I saw that Winterberg again began to tremble, and that he spoke increasingly louder, as if he wanted to wake the dead. And I knew that he couldn't be stopped, that he had once again been swept up in the storm.

He looked at the photo of the little carriage and told me that this carriage had been built for the Empress in the carriage factory in Sanok, and not for her train journeys with the Empress Elisabeth Railway, not for her train journeys to Bad Ischl, not for her train journeys to Gödöllö. He told me that a second, much nobler salon carriage had been prepared for the Empress for these trips, which she used less often after a derailment in 1889.

'Yes, yes, I know, dear Herr Kraus, for the Empress and the Kaiser, the year 1889 was not a happy year, the Crown Prince Rudolph had shot his lover and then himself in Schloss Mayerling, yes, yes, their corpses weren't a pretty sight, and then another derailment en route from Wiesbaden to Vienna, terrible, terrible, one Königgrätz after the other, I know, this slim black carriage we see here was built in Sanok.'

Winterberg looked at me and said: 'Sanok, I hope the name rings a bell… laying tracks over the Carpathians was no less difficult, by the way, than laying tracks over the Alps or the Bohemian Forest. Does the name Sanok ring a bell for you?'

Winterberg didn't wait for my reply and said he hasn't surprised that Sanok didn't ring a bell for me.

He told me that no one knows these days about Sanok in Galicia. He told me that before the First World War, it was different. He told me that many freight trains and passenger carriages were built in the railway factory in Sanok. He told me that even the most modern hearse carriages for the railway were built in Sanok, which made the transportation of corpses significantly easier and more convenient. He told me that before that, the soldiers' corpses were brought back from the battlefield in the standard open wagons used for coal and wood and sugar. He told me that the soldiers' corpses were stacked on top of each other as if in a massive open coffin. He told me that the introduction of the hearse carriage was a railway revolution. He told me that after the Second World War, they stopped producing railway carriages in Sanok. He told me that the railway factory was turned into a bus factory. He told me it was yet another sign of the downfall of the railway.

'Yes, yes, another Königgrätz, dear Herr Kraus, a Pole told me about it in the *Heidelberger Krug*… there's nothing I hate more than buses, bus transportation is the Königgrätz of passenger transport, the worst is when buses are used for rail replacement services, there's nothing I hate more than buses, but I hate rail replacement services even more, now that's the true downfall of travel culture, it makes me physically ill to think of it.' Winterberg trembled and continued not to look at me, but stared ahead, at the hearse carriage and beyond. Into a wide emptiness.

'Before the First World War, that's when the railway world was still in order, that's when they built a lot of freight carriages and military carriages and hospital carriages and hearse carriages in Sanok, and this beautiful and one-of-a-kind salon carriage for Empress Elisabeth was also built in Sanok on the San in Galicia, it was only used for a single rail journey from Geneva to Vienna, yes, yes, back then, when a narrow tunnel was bored through the Empress's breast with a file on the promenade along Lake Geneva in front of the hotel *Beau-Rivage*, an even narrower tunnel than the one in the throat of the Archduke in Sarajevo later, at first the Empress didn't even notice this tunnel construction of the anarchist Luigi Lucheni, another of these fools of history, it was only when the ship departed for Caux that Elisabeth felt herself bleeding from this narrow railway tunnel in her breast, tragic, tragic.'

Winterberg rambled and continued to look at the black salon carriage.

'This salon carriage, dear Herr Kraus, was only built for her last rail journey, yes, yes, this salon carriage, really a salon hearse carriage, as we can read, isn't it lovely, this salon hearse carriage of the first Railway Carriage Leasing Company in Vienna, lodged at Vienna's Western Station, as it says here... who knows, perhaps the carriage is still sitting unnoticed on the siding there, yes, yes, at a dead end. But what I'm asking myself now, dear Herr Kraus, and perhaps you're asking yourself the same thing, is how the railwaymen managed to climb these steep stairs into the carriage with the coffin, perhaps the coffin wasn't particularly long or wide, perhaps they managed it through the window, or perhaps they lowered it through the roof.' Winterberg continued to look at the very modest black salon hearse wagon in the photograph.

'You see? The one railway employee is already waiting, the coffin with Empress Elisabeth should be arriving any moment, yes, yes, and there's the other. He's preparing to hook up the salon hearse carriage at any moment to a locomotive, yes, yes, so that the hearse train can head straight for Vienna, yes, yes... the switches had surely already been set.'

Winterberg was trembling, he was exhausted again, I had to support him. But he didn't want to sit down, he wanted to continue. As we left the Funerary Museum of the Viennese Funerary Arts, Winterberg asked the attendant, who was still attempting to fall asleep in his chair and in uniform, where we could find the grave of Carl Ritter von Ghega.

'Just straight ahead.'

And when we were back outside, Winterberg said: 'I hope that man has settled all his accounts, did you see his red face, dear Herr Kraus? High blood pressure. Just like you... high blood pressure corpses aren't a pretty sight.'

I lit a cigarette.

'You shouldn't smoke so much... the inside of your lungs surely must look like the chimney of the Reichenberg Feuerhalle.'

* * *

We kept walking straight ahead and then we really did find the grave of Carl Ritter von Ghega.

The sky was grey and so was the cemetery. It was still, only in the distance could trains be heard passing the cemetery. The fast trains and the heavy freight trains, loaded with coal or steel or gravel, as Winterberg said, and every time a train went by, he perked up his ears. He looked like a curious little dog picking up a scent in the wind.

'Yes, yes, that's surely a coal train, at least thirty wagons.'

Winterberg looked at the narrow white grave monument of Carl Ritter von Ghega, which loomed over Vienna's Central Cemetery like a signal box, high above the main cemetery, the Central Station of the Viennese Dead, as Winterberg said.

'Yes, yes, his grave stands like a central signal box in this great train station, which isn't a shunting station or a freight station or a passenger station, but a holding station, yes, yes, a holding station of the dead, a holding station is often underestimated, some say that a holding station isn't a proper station, it's more like a sub-station, but for the railway, a holding station is of great importance...'

He rambled on and again praised the construction and the architecture and the location of the grave of Carl Ritter von Ghega, the hero of the Semmering, the son of Albanian parents from Venice, who had been knighted after the construction of the Semmering Railway.

He looked to the sky and thought for a moment.

'For the heroic construction of the tunnels and bridges on his line.'

He followed a squirrel with his gaze.

'Or the dilapidation of the tunnels and bridges in his lungs.'

He watched a woman carrying a bouquet of flowers.

'For his incredible prowess.'

He looked at me.

'Or for his consumption.'

And then he looked again at the grave.

'Perhaps for all these stories, yes, yes, that's quite possible... so this is where he rests, the victor and the loser, pride and downfall, cheers and tears, this is where he lies, buried in Vienna's Central Holding Station Cemetery in Simmering, yes, yes, I always wanted to see his grave, I always wanted to show it to my Lenka too, she was interested in the railway as well, not just for my sake, as you might think, Lenka was simply a railway woman… it's only thanks to Carl Ritter von Ghega that we met in the train between Prague and Reichenberg, I still remember the exact train station, it was in Münchengrätz, yes, yes, where Wallenstein is buried today, yes, yes, we must go visit his crypt too, Wallenstein lived his imperial dream and Carl Ritter von Ghega his railway dream, after his death in Eger they buried Wallenstein three times, first in Mies, then in Walditz near Jitschin, and finally in Münchengrätz, yes, yes, so far they've buried Carl Ritter von Ghega twice, in the Währing Cemetery and then here in the Central Cemetery… my Lenka was never buried because no one knows where exactly it happened, yes, yes, there you have it, tragic, tragic, but I believe it was in Sarajevo, that's why we have to get there, yes, yes… now where was I again, yes, yes, I know, Lenka had gone to visit her aunt back then and was looking for a seat, and in our compartment there was still one spot free, it was summer, a terribly hot summer day, and I can still see the long, slanted rays of soft evening sunlight on her beautiful face, on her dress, on the book that she was reading, yes, yes, dear Herr Kraus, Lenka read a lot, yes, yes, dear Herr Kraus, it was Carl Ritter von Ghega who brought us together, who made us into railway people, because he came up with the entire thing, he drafted the whole railway network of the Monarchy, yes, yes, that's how it was… thanks to Carl Ritter von Ghega, today anyone can travel quickly from a village along the Semmering to the Feuerhalle in Simmering, yes, yes, to the Central Cemetery, to the grave of Carl Ritter von Ghega.'

Winterberg rambled, and he didn't care whether I was listening or not.

He rambled and I knew that he couldn't be interrupted.

He was sick.

He had to ramble.

He had to get it out.

I knew that soon he would start to shake again. I knew that soon he might topple over. I knew that soon I would have to hold him up and rescue him.

I stamped out my cigarette and waited.

A freight train passed the cemetery and Winterberg said they were tank wagons, surely at least twenty-five wagons filled with oil. He recognised a train with tank wagons right away, even in his sleep he could recognise tank wagons from the sound.

All the while he continued to look at the grave of Carl Ritter von Ghega and said that from every signal box, one should have a good, no, a perfect, no, an unimpeded overview of rail traffic, yes, yes, a signal box is just as important for the railway as a pulpit in the church, a command bridge on a ship, a hunter's perch in the woods, a counter in the pub, or an observation post in a battle, because from the counter just as from the pulpit or the observation post, it was important to have a good overview of the battlefield.

'It doesn't matter whether it concerns beer or God or trains or soldiers… you need to have an overview, yes, yes, it's the only way to see through the fog of war… this signal box is the most fortunate case, from here, you can observe and direct the train operations across the entire Central Cemetery of Vienna, there's no risk of fog here… yes, yes, the trains pulling in with the corpses, all the shunting work with the dead and with death, you get a very good overview from here.'

Winterberg was holding the wreath in his hands.

'If you ask me, dear Herr Kraus, signal boxes are the most important railway constructions of all, because decisions affecting the entire railway are made in a signal box like this, this is where they set the switches and signals, yes, yes, this is where everything is set in motion, yes, yes, but this is also where traffic is stopped, as you can see if you just look around.'

I looked around, but Winterberg did not.

He was still looking at the tall and noble and silent grave of Carl Ritter von Ghega, and once again I had the thought that our journey couldn't possibly come to a good end, because the switches for this train were set poorly from the start, buried in snow, and frozen.

As if he heard what I'd said only to myself, Winterberg said: 'Precisely, precisely, the switches… you have to take care that the switches don't get snowed in and freeze in the winter, because winter is the greatest foe of railway traffic. A single frozen switch can halt railway traffic for hours, if not days, and bury it under snow… oh, it's so beautiful here. Not just Ghega, but also Riepl and Etzel and Gerstner and Lott and Perner and many other railway pioneers deserve such a lovely grave of honour, such a lovely signal box of honour in Vienna's Central Cemetery, don't you think, Herr Kraus? I think so.'

Then Winterberg finally lay the wreath at the foot of the grave. He tried to light the candle, the wind was faint, and yet too strong, and the candle refused to light easily.

He looked at the crests of Vienna and Laibach and Graz and Trieste and Zagreb. He looked at the crests of the cities that Ghega had linked with the railway, and that Winterberg had also linked with his life. With his railway life. He looked at the crest of Venice, where Ghega was born. He looked at the dedication on the side of the monument to the genius architect of the Semmering Railway. He looked at the grave, at the sarcophagus, which lay atop the structure like a wide bathtub under a small roof. He looked at the pale face of Carl Ritter von Ghega on the wall, which was staring down at him.

I waited for the next eruption of the history volcano, but Winterberg remained calm and and said nothing more. He only looked at the grave, briefly listened at the next freight train, and was silent.

'And?'

'And what?'

'Why aren't you saying anything?'

'What do you expect me to say?'

'I don't know. Anything.'

'But why?'

'You constantly ramble on about everything. And suddenly...'

'I don't ramble at all.'

'So it's been someone else rambling on this whole time.'

'That's right. What do I have to ramble on about?'

'That thing about time, for example, that'd be fitting... "and so time goes by, everything comes to an end, everything passes by, oh, how time goes by."'

'But here, everything has already been said, dear Herr Kraus. I'm listening to the music.'

'What music?'

'You don't hear it?'

'No. You hear music?'

'Yes. Quite clearly.'

'What music?'

'The prelude to *Parsifal*.'

'Oh, I see. Right. The music from the Feuerhalle in Reichenberg.'

'Precisely.'

'But there's no music playing. Really. I don't hear anything.'

'How lovely that you hear it too.'

'I don't hear anything.'

'How lovely that you hear it too, dear Herr Kraus.'

'Yeah, lovely.'

I nodded like I always nodded and thought what I always thought.

And then Winterberg laid two dried red leaves at the foot of the grave. *Cornus sanguinea*. I don't know where he got them. Perhaps from the Svíb Forest near Königgrätz. Or perhaps he plucked them somewhere in Vienna.

Winterberg looked up again at the sarcophagus of Carl Ritter von Ghega.

'Lovely, lovely.'

Suddenly he turned and stalked off. And then stopped just before the two white pillars that formed the gate to the Central Cemetery.

'Precisely, precisely, a signal box and here the two signal masts that secure the entry to the station, it's like that at every proper train station. I can already hear the beautiful music of the levers and switches and buttons, yes, yes, it's a much more beautiful music than *Parsifal*, that just makes me melancholy. Oh, what a shame I can't play music.'

Then he perked up his ears and said: 'Another freight train, probably wood, at least thirty wagons, yes, yes, I'd know a freight train with wood in my sleep.'

I thought we would go to the tram stop and ride back into the city, but Winterberg turned around.

We walked through the cemetery and Winterberg was silent.

We walked without a destination and without a plan.

And soon we were lost.

And every time a train drove past the cemetery in the distance, Winterberg paused for a moment and perked up his ears.

In this part of the cemetery, there were no graves of honour. The graves that we saw were not signal boxes.

The graves were crumbling

Decaying.

Destroyed.

Winterberg was constantly stopping and reading the names of the dead aloud.

'Horváth. Musil. Kraus. Like you, Herr Kraus, perhaps you're related.'

He walked past the graves and read out the names as if he were paging through an old telephone book.

'Bloch. Morgenstern. Morgenstern. Look at that, like my Lenka, perhaps they were related.'

It was icy cold and Winterberg walked on and on through the sleepy and abandoned Vienna Central Cemetery.

'Lenka loved strolling through cemeteries, especially the cremation cemetery at the Feuerhalle in Reichenberg, where there was a lovely view over the city centre, and where of course there were no graves like these with coffins under the ground, because in Reichenberg they were already well past that, in Reichenberg they were already progressive a hundred years ago, in Reichenberg they weren't as old-fashioned as in Vienna, in Reichenberg they just buried the little urns with the ashes in the crema-tion cemetery, it saves a lot of space, said my father, it saves money, said my father, it also saves the hard work of grave-digging, said my father, yes, yes, it also saves on the schnapps that you had to give the grave-diggers as compensation later, said my father, you can re-train the grave-diggers to be gardeners for the cemetery, said my father, and I say, the earth can stomach the ashes much better than the corpses and doesn't have to spew them back up like the ground near Königgrätz... yes, yes, I know what you're going to say now, dear Herr Kraus, you're right, it also makes me think of the forests at Auschwitz and Treblinka, I can't imagine that the landscape has found any peace with the dead, the earth there must also be constantly spewing them up, the earth can't be placated there either, there's no treatment for this disease, for this human derailment, but in Reichenberg in the cremation cemetery it's different, it's at peace there, we saw it ourselves, no one's spewing up anything there.'

Winterberg kept walking and the snow crunched under his feet.

'Look at that, Herr Kraus, there's a row of Bohemians buried here, Polacek, Nowotny, Sykora, and Duch. What does "Duch" mean again? I knew a Duch back in Gablonz.'

'*Duch* means "spirit".'

'Yes, precisely, I knew a spirit, a Duch… his father was an optician in the Prager Straße, he lost his way in the Iser Mountains and wasn't found until spring, yes, yes, you can't underestimate the mountains, not even small ranges like the Iser Mountains, yes, yes, forest corpses really aren't a pretty sight… the architect Rudolf Bitzan designed the cremation cemetery together with the Feuerhalle, the cremation cemetery was an important part of his artistic vision, just like the furniture of the Feuerhalle, as my father always said, yes, yes… now where was I…'

'The forest corpses.'

'Yes, yes, that's right, Lenka loved walking through the cemetery, she looked at all the graves and always calculated how old they were, yes, yes, she was always deeply affected when they died young, look at that, Lenka would cry, he was only nineteen, that's terrible, look at that, she was only seventeen, that's so sad, she always said, and then wanted me to hold her and promise her that I would never leave her and that I'd grow old so that she wouldn't have to cry at my graveside, yes, yes, Lenka truly loved me, tragic, tragic, and I truly loved Lenka too, tragic, tragic, my Lenka, the first woman in the moon, who has no grave, no tombstone, where someone could be deeply affected when they calculate how young she was when she died. And so I promised her that I wouldn't leave her and that I would grow old, and look at that, dear Herr Kraus, that's precisely how it turned out, I really did grow old, I'm as old as the Republic of Czechoslovakia, as old as the Feuerhalle in Reichenberg, which is now called Liberec, now where was I…'

'The woman in the moon.'

'Yes, yes, so I promised Lenka and held her and looked with her at the graves of those who died young, but at the same time, I was looking at the surprisingly small chimneys of the Feuerhalle in the background, which Rudolf Bitzan had very skilfully hidden at the back of his construction, as my father always said, from the front you can't see the chimneys at all, only from the back, from the cremation cemetery, but Bitzan couldn't hide the smoke from the ovens, yes, yes, dear Herr Kraus, the smoke would rise into the air and dissipate over the city of Reichenberg and mix with the clouds, yes, yes, they say there's no other city in Bohemia where it rains as much as in Reichenberg, perhaps it's related to the smoke that rises from the Feuerhalle and mixes with the clouds in the sky, yes, yes, you can't hide the smoke of the Feuerhalles, that's where Heydrich and Himmler and Hitler and Henlein misjudged and miscalculated, yes, yes, just like you can't hide the smoke of the steam locomotives, as the Englishman told me, and he had to know, he shot up a number of steam locomotives with his plane and his machine guns, yes, yes, numerous locomotive drivers and stokers were scalded by the hot steam when the boilers exploded and died of their injuries, scalded corpses aren't a pretty sight, my father always said, yes, yes, scalded corpses and fire corpses and water corpses, my father didn't like them… for Freital in Saxony, Rudolf Bitzan designed a modern Feuerhalle very similar to the one in Reichenberg, including furniture and a cremation cemetery, but he went even further, Bitzan designed an entirely new city concept for Freital which would enthrone the new Feuerhalle like a castle at its centre, as the core of Freital, but the Saxons rejected him and that made him very melancholy, yes, yes, it's no wonder the Saxons are so often forgotten in history, just like at Königgrätz, the Saxons are often the ones responsible for their own 'forgottenness', yes, yes, dear Herr Kraus, always so rejecting, tragic, tragic, it's no wonder the Saxons are so often forgotten… now where was I, too many stories, too much history, I know… you can so quickly lose yourself and lose your way, but perhaps you have to lose yourself and lose your way to understand it… now where…'

'The scalded corpses.'

'Yes, yes, precisely, that's how my Lenka was, I loved her long nose and her long legs, my Lenka so often loved to be moved in the Reichenberg cremation cemetery, as if she herself knew how young she would be when she died, yes, yes, it still makes me melancholy to this day, it leaves me derailed, we have to nab the murderer, perhaps we'll still find him, perhaps he still lives in Sarajevo, Lenka loved these cemetery strolls and I hated them, because perhaps I already knew back then what was coming for us, what would happen to Lenka, what would happen to me, yes, yes, I know what you're going to say, dear Herr Kraus, many people look at the graves and the tombstones and calculate how old the living were when they turned into the dead, and hope that they'll die older, and don't want to accept that there's no escape, yes, yes, and

I'll tell you, that's for the best, in that moment they know that they too will soon be just a number on a tombstone and nothing more, yes, yes, there's no escape, just like here, look at this, Richard Scharf, independent gentleman, Elisabeth Scharf, wife of an independent gentleman, Alexandrine Scharf, wife of an editor, Alexander Scharf, owner of the Sunday paper and Monday paper, yes, yes, if I recall correctly, the chief editor of the newspaper *Die Einäscherung* in Reichenberg was also a certain Scharf, yes, a good name for a journalist, yes, yes, the only thing you can do is keep going, always moving forward, always chasing freedom, otherwise you can only shoot yourself or hang yourself and let yourself be cremated in the Reichenberg Feuerhalle, yes, yes, you always have to move forward, always onwards and onwards, just like we're doing, dear Herr Kraus, and yet you'll also eventually end up in a graveyard or a cremation cemetery or a battlefield or a Feuerhalle, tragic, tragic.'

Winterberg moved on and stopped in front of the next gravestone, which had almost sunken into the earth.

'*Die Einäscherung* was a good newspaper, my father always said, even in Vienna many people read *Die Einäscherung*… he wanted *Die Einäscherung* to become one of the great papers which wouldn't appear once a month, but once a week, and perhaps later even daily, right from the start *Die Einäscherung* was known for its excellent feuilletons, and also for its good sport section, yes, yes, my father once wrote about the performance of *Parsifal* in Prague and also about Rapid Reichenberg, he loved *Parsifal*, as you know, yes, yes, although he loved Smetana's *Vltava* even more, I know what you're going to say, none of that is true, I've made it all up, but it is true, that's exactly how it was, if you want we'll go together to the Austrian National Library tomorrow, they must have at least a few copies of *Die Einäscherung* lying around, yes, yes, even in Berlin I've found some copies, the whole story is true… look at this here, Frau Goldberg née Wolff, widow of a medical doctor, born in Warsaw, died in Vienna, yes, yes, widow, that used to be a popular women's profession in Reichenberg as well.'

Winterberg trembled and continued down the long, narrow path between the silent, forgotten graves, and I walked with him and made sure to support him in case he stumbled or slipped or lost himself in history for good.

He stopped again in front of a grave and studied the mouldy names that remained of the dead.

'Look at this, dear Herr Kraus, it reads almost like a poem! Yes, yes, Lenka loved poetry, just like many women, she would surely love this poem too, this graveyard poem with the missing letters, this graveyard puzzle, this graveyard play of time and the elements, yes, yes, Knöpflmacher, Pflmacher, Nöpflmacher, Plfm… what a shame it doesn't continue, yes, yes, put perhaps it doesn't have to continue, perhaps that's the whole poem right there, Knöpflmacher, Pflmacher, Nöpflmacher, Plfm, yes, yes, Knöpflmacher is quite an uncommon name, and so time goes by, everything comes to an end, everything passes by, oh, how time goes by, dear Herr Kraus, yes, yes, you can hang yourself, you can shoot yourself, you can throw yourself from height or you can keep moving forward, battle with time and history, just as we're doing battle with it, and yet we too are lost, yes, yes, I know, it's all mad.'

He continued forward with his head bent forward, he walked on with his stubby legs and trembled and was suffering again from a historical fit and kept rambling to himself just like he always rambled, and I thought what I always thought, and looked out for him.

'I was never interested in graves and in death, I hated it all, the Feuerhalle, the cremations, the slightly sweet scent of death on my father's clothes that my mother could never wash out, you can't imagine how I hated it, dear Herr Kraus, yes, yes, and yet my father taught me everything, and I resisted, but he still managed to do it, he overpowered me, yes, yes, violated me with his funerary knowledge, he raped and infected me with his Feuerhalles and the sweet scent of death, madness, madness, I only ever wanted to get away, away from the dead, away from him, away from my family, away from the funerals, away from the Feuerhalle, away from the Friends of Fire Burial and the Friends of the Hygiene Movement, away from Reichenberg, I dreamed the entire time of endless train tracks, and I managed to do it, I got away, not to the railway unfortunately, just to the tram, but I managed to free myself from my family, from the sweet scent of death, yes, yes, but then came the war and the next dead and the next graves that I saw, yes, yes, that I had to dig and saw being dug, yes, yes, that's how it was, the war almost buried me just like it buried Lenka, but I managed to overcome even that and leave it behind me, I freed myself again, yes, yes, I became interested in history, I even wanted to study history in Berlin, but they didn't take me, yes, yes, that made me very melancholy, and then I thought, I'll become all the more interested in trains and history, but now, when I think about it, I see that the more I became interested in trains and history, the more I also became interested in graves and in death, the more I know about history, the more I lose myself in history, yes, yes, *"the beautiful landscape of battlefields, cemeteries and ruins"*, as the Englishman always said, because do you see, dear Herr Kraus, where I am now, where we are now?'

He looked at me. We were standing in the Central Cemetery of Vienna under a tall oak.

'Mad, it's all mad. *Cornus sanguinea.*'

He looked at me again and I looked back at him.

'There's no escape, dear Herr Kraus. No, no, there's no more hope, there's only a grave in the Svíb Forest or the Feuerhalle in Reichenberg, tragic, tragic, but we still have to fight, we still have to continue to Sarajevo and find Lenka's murderer.'

It was cold and starting to snow, and we continued on. The path was icy and I had to assist Winterberg so that he wouldn't slip.

And suddenly we saw something in the bush.

It was a deer.

A little deer in the snow.

It approached us and stopped in the middle of the path, between two rows of graves.

It looked at us.

And then came another, and another, and suddenly a small herd of deer had gathered around us.

It was snowing and freezing and we stood between the abandoned graves and stared at each other.

Winterberg.

Me.

And the deer.

We stood there as if captured in an old painting by Václav Sochor, as Winterberg said.

A freight train passed by the cemetery. The locomotive whistled and in a single instant, the deer disappeared between the graves and copses.

Winterberg stared after them for moment.

'Another coal train. Probably from Poland, or from Ostrava, yes, yes, they only built the Northern Railway for the coal, yes, and for the steel of course, yes, yes, if I were a deer, I would hide away here too, here the deer are safe, here they won't be shot, here they won't be killed or slaughtered, here all the people are dead already, yes, yes, and the deer look after the dead. My grandfather was a hunter, and he always told me it isn't good to kill animals, but if you have to kill an animal, do it quickly. I've never killed an animal, not a single animal, dear Herr Kraus. When my grandfather came to visit us, we often had deer goulash, sometimes deer schnitzel too, but mostly deer goulash … the animals will have their revenge on us someday, my grandfather always said, one day the deer will take revenge for everything, yes, yes, and so will the people we've killed.'

And as I looked at him, I saw that he was crying.

∗ ∗ ∗

I thought Winterberg would want to see the Simmering Feuerhalle while we were here. But he didn't want to see anything else. He was tired and exhausted and trembling, and I had to help him walk.

We went to the tram stop. It was cold. The cars drove past us in two unending queues. The drivers spoke on the phone and cursed and smoked and stared glumly ahead and smoked and cursed and spoke on the phone.

Then the tram finally arrived. We got on board and sat down across from two elegant women in their forties for whom Winterberg and I were transparent. They were talking about a man they'd both loved who was now lying buried at the Central Cemetery, and at whose grave they came to meet every two weeks.

Another woman next to us was speaking to a different woman about the crematorium.

Winterberg leaned towards me.

'Crematorium is an ugly word … what a shame the word "Feuerhalle" didn't catch on, or fiery crypt, I hated these words because my father loved them, but that's how it is in life, now I like them … my father was a proud republican, a proud citizen of Czechoslovakia, because it was Czechoslovakia that gave him and his friends of Fire Burial and Hygiene the Feuerhalle and the first cremations, yes, yes, and because I didn't just love my father, but hated him too, as all boys can and must hate their fathers in order to free themselves and move on, I also hated Czechoslovakia and even supported Henlein, yes, yes, it's mad, I know, I loved Lenka and supported Henlein, I thought it was all a misunderstanding, I thought it would all be fine and Lenka would come back, just like the others who had to flee would come back, not just the Jews, but also the Czechs and Germans who were communists, yes, yes, when the drunken labourer from the cement factory cracked my father's skull in the Ratskeller, I even thought the same as my mother, that it was my father's own fault, that he brought the whole tragedy on himself.'

'That is mad.'

'I know.'

'What did you do in the war?'

'I painted.'

'Sure.'

'Really, though unfortunately not as well as Václav Sochor. And so I had to do what one does in war.'

'What's that?'

'Dig graves.'

'Hm. And where did you paint?'

'It doesn't matter.'

'Hm.'

'I became a locomotive driver in the war.'

'A locomotive driver that dug graves.'

'Yes, I had to do that too. In the war it didn't matter that I had bad sight. I was a locomotive driver for the S-Bahn.'

'In Berlin?'

'No.'

'Where?'

'It doesn't matter.'

'But Lenka, Lenka was a …'

'Yes … I loved Lenka.'

'And the Englishman.'

'That has nothing at all to do with anything. Leave me be.'

'Well, I mean…'

'Leave me be.'

'It's really not easy.'

Winterberg went silent and I started to feel a bit dizzy again and had to open the window.

I looked at him and thought, I don't care.

These are his problems.

His war.

I just want my money.

My ship.

When we get to Sarajevo, I'm going to take it and go.

To America.

I don't care where.

Just away from here.

I'll take to the sea.

I'll disappear.

Forever.

We rode back into the city centre. It was pleasantly warm in the tram and Winterberg fell asleep. And I thought about all the things I'd experienced during the crossing. Nothing surprised me anymore.

I looked at Winterberg and he made me think of Hildegard, who called me Karl after her dead husband, who stood framed on her night-stand in a black SS uniform. A young, blond man with a stern, angular face. A grenade had blown open his belly in Kursk.

She called me Karl and I didn't care.

She said to me, Karl, Karl, it's so wonderful that you're back, how was it, tell me. And I told her that Russia was beautiful, especially the countryside, and the deep forest. The taiga. And the lakes. And the people, too. They were very nice to us. And I didn't care.

She asked me if I hadn't been too cold.

And I said, no, not at all. And I didn't care.

She asked, weren't you afraid? I was so afraid for you.

And I said, I wasn't afraid. When you're a soldier, you're not allowed to be afraid.

And I didn't care.

She asked, weren't you starving?

And I said, no, not at all, we were spoiled for cooking. We had goulash and pork chops and schnitzel.

And I didn't care.

She asked, did you think about me? I thought about you the whole time.

And I said that I had thought about her the whole time.

And I didn't care.

She said that we could have a baby now, a beautiful German baby, that she wanted it so badly.

And I said, sure, that's a wonderful idea, I want to have a beautiful German baby with you, too.

And I didn't care.

None of it mattered to me, because it can't matter.

There's no sympathy. There's no hope. There's no mercy. There's no compassion. There's no altruism.

There are only lies. It's the lies that bring comfort. That comfort others. That comfort us.

None of it mattered to me. And yet I sat there and held her hand, just like I held Winterberg's hand.

That's how it is on the crossing.

⁂

That night, I dreamed of the hunt.

We were in the forest. Winterberg and Carla and Lenka and I. And then I saw Silke, too. And Josefa.

Winterberg said that everything was falling into ruin, but here, the world was in order. Just like it is in my book.

The trees were tall and thin and naked, with almost no branches.

The tree bark was completely smooth. As if polished. As if made of glass.

We walked through the forest.

In a clearing, we saw several deer.

The snow was fluttering down.

It was quiet.

And then we heard the shots. And the barking dogs. And the hunters.

The deer ran.

We ran.

We were the deer.

We ran through the woods.

We stumbled and fell and climbed back to our feet.

We kept running.

We were surrounded.

The hunters wore grey uniforms and carried rifles.

They were looking at us and smoking and laughing.

One of the hunters said, it isn't good to kill animals, but if you have to kill an animal, do it quickly.

And pulled the trigger.

I held Carla and Carla held me.

She squeezed me so tightly that I couldn't breathe. That she was crushing my heart.

I woke up sweating and couldn't catch my breath.

FROM VIENNA TO BRÜNN

We drifted on.

On and on.

Always in motion, as Winterberg said.

Always chasing freedom.

Always on the run.

From the major history.

From the minor history.

From his history.

From my history.

We sat in a northbound train, in a Railjet en route from Vienna to Prague.

Winterberg wanted to go to Brünn.

To Brno.

He wanted to visit the city of Leopold Lojka, the city of the driver from Sarajevo, who, after his misadventure in the streets of Sarajevo, bought a pub in Brno and drank himself to death there, because the one side told him he was a fool for taking a wrong turn and driving the Archduke to his death, and the other side told him he was a hero for taking a turn and driving the Archduke to his death.

And so Lojka was now lying in the Central Cemetery of Brünn, near the Brünn Feuerhalle, and was still hated and loved to this day, as Winterberg said.

He wanted to seek out his grave in Brno, just as he had sought out the grave of Carl Ritter von Ghega in Vienna, and lay flowers there. He also wanted to find out what had happened to Lenka in Brno.

She had been in Brno, that much he knew.

She had sent him a postcard.

The train was racing across the flat countryside and my heart was racing too and Winterberg read aloud from his book and two older women and I were forced to listen.

'Brünn, train station restaurant, of course, that's self-evident, perhaps we can grab a bite to eat there, it's not a long journey, capital city of Moravia with a population of 125,000, two-thirds of whom are German, yes, yes, that's probably a bit different today, yes, yes, at the foot of the Spielberg hill between the Schwarzawa and Zwittawa… like two sisters, these rivers, don't you think? If I were to have more children, that's exactly what I would name them, Schwarzawa and Zwittawa, yes, yes, amid lovely, fertile surroundings, are you feeling unwell, Herr Kraus?'

'I'm good, thanks.'

'Shall I open the window a bit? Damn it, damn these new trains, the windows don't open.'

'I'll be fine, I'm just a bit tired.'

'You're looking rather flushed again.'

'Yeah, I know.'

'Now where was I… yes, yes, the city centre is located within the old fortifications, torn down in 1860, surrounded by parks and ring roads, with handsome suburban districts… Brünn is one of the most prominent industrial cities in Austria, yes, yes, textiles and machinery and leather, Brünn was known for that, but also for weapons, yes, yes, pistols and cannons, Brünn was known for that too… the factories lie in the southern and eastern suburbs, probably due to the wind and air quality conditions, oh… wasn't that Dürnkrut? That must have been Dürnkrut, next time we should take the local train and alight at Dürnkrut, yes, yes, precisely, dear Herr Kraus, the Battle of Dürnkrut in 1278, the famous battle of knights on the Marchfeld, yes, yes, precisely, this is where King Ottokar II of Bohemia met his death, here the infamous Lion of Bohemia was conquered by ambush… no, no, it wasn't pretty, it was the Königgrätz of the thirteenth century… are you really quite well, dear Herr Kraus?'

He looked at me with concern.

We were in Břeclav, back again in the Czech Republic, and continued on, and the train was racing and my heart was racing too. My heart wanted to outrun the train.

The train travelled on.

'Vranovice, was that Vranovice just now, Herr Kraus?'

'I don't know.'

The train was racing so quickly through countryside that it was hard to distinguish individual stations and stops.

'I think that must have been Vranovice, what a shame the train doesn't stop there… Vranovice is also a fateful town, yes, yes, no one would know Königgrätz if not for the Battle of Königgrätz and no one would know Vranovice either if not for the railway accident, yes, yes, you have to imagine, this is where the first railway collision in Austria took place, and of course it had to happen on the inauguration day of the new rail line between Vienna and Brünn, sixty people injured, and all that due to a couple of loose screws and due to the locomotive driver, who wanted his ceremonial train to make up its delay and forgot that another ceremonial train was ahead of him on the tracks, which had a minor mechanical issue, yes, yes, they had to tighten a few screws on the locomotive… and so the train had to stop halfway, and the other train ran into it, yes, yes, tragic, tragic, sixty people injured on such a beautiful and summery and important day in railway history. But the railway isn't to blame, just as the Feuerhalles aren't to blame, no, no, it's the people, they're always to blame for such catastrophes and derailments, for our downfall, it doesn't matter what they say, it doesn't matter what excuses they find, tragic, tragic… the seventh of July, 1839, in Vranovice near Brünn, was a sad day for the railway, a sad day for all train people, a sad day for the many injured, a sad day for the driver of the locomotive christened "Gigant". By the way, the locomotive driver, or the machine engineer, as they tended to say back then, was an Englishman, yes, yes, the first locomotive drivers in Austria were often Englishmen, just like the Bohemians were the first brewers and cremators in Austria, what a sad day in railway history, yes, yes, poor communication, poor visibility on the tracks, poor braking, yes, yes, and so the calamity took its course… I know what you're going to say, dear Herr Kraus, once again the fog of war has come down over history, just as Clausewitz described, it's all so precarious, so incomplete, so uncertain, yes, yes, once again you can only rely on yourself and your own wits, on your own eyes, it's difficult, so difficult, the eyes often see nothing, they become lost, they don't see through the fog, just as many people don't see through history, unfortunate, but that's how it is, that's what happens in life, it's no surprise that things constantly end in catastrophe, whether it's in rail transport or on the battlefield or in a relationship, yes, yes, dear Herr Kraus, you can't underestimate the fog of war in a relationship either, I know what I'm talking about, I've been married three times, and yet I loved the woman I couldn't marry, my Lenka, Lenka Morgenstern from Reichenberg, the first woman in the moon, yes, yes… now where was I, yes, well, yes, yes, precisely, I fear that a railway accident is waiting for all of us, our own personal railway catastrophe, our own personal Königgrätz, and unfortunately it often doesn't stop with one Königgrätz, that's how it is, in life you often have one Königgrätz lining up after another, there's no escape, history has us tightly in its grasp, the major history and the minor history too, it's not as easily overcome as the Alps by the railway, are you really feeling well, Herr Kraus? You don't look well.'

'Yes, yes.'

'But you're looking quite derailed. You should relax, perhaps try a bit of yoga, like my daughter, perhaps that might help a bit. Or simply find yourself a woman…'

'I'm fine,' I said, and I felt so tired and exhausted.

'Yes, yes, Moravia, look at that countryside, lovely, lovely, the low mountains in the distance, that must be the Pollauer Highlands, my father was there once, yes, yes, good white wines, I don't really drink white wine, it always gives me heartburn, it's too acidic for me, it often makes me sick, but today I'd have a glass of Grüner Veltliner from the Pollauer Highlands, Nikolsburg must be somewhere around there, yes, yes, just as it says in my Baedeker, with the handsome hilltop castle of the Prince Dietrichstein-Mensdorff, known for the Preliminary Peace of July 26, 1866, in fact a pre-capitulation of Austria was determined in Nikolsburg in 1866, the capitulation before the capitulation, yes, yes, it's complicated, I know, but no one says that history and human life are uncomplicated, no one says it'll be easy, no, no, why does everyone believe that our lives have to be easy and uncomplicated? That everyone has to be happy? Why is that?'

He looked out at the low mountains on the horizon.

'Yes, yes, we really should go to Nikolsburg, since we're already here, yes, I know what you're going to say, dear Herr Kraus, that's precisely our problem, to many stories, too much history, too many tracks and only one lifetime, which always seems too short to us, even if you're as old as the Republic of Czechoslovakia, as the Feuerhalle in Reichenberg, just like me, yes, yes, you're right, you really are starting to see a bit through history, that's our problem, that's our Central Europe, yes, yes, *"the beautiful landscape of battlefields, cemeteries and ruins"*, as the Englishman always said, it all makes me so melancholy, it's no wonder that so many people here are mad and suffer from mental derangement... there's no escape.'

Winterberg fell silent for a moment and looked out of the window. The low mountains were no longer visible. Only the fields. The black, endless fields. And the many black birds.

'The Moravian lowlands, lying at the southeastern foot of the Bohemian massif, form a strip of land about 70 kilometres wide, narrowing towards the northeast, between the aforementioned massif and the Carpathians, yes, yes, the White Carpathians, they have to be somewhere in that direction, yes, yes, composed in part of the upper tertiary sediments of the Carpathian Foothills, where Austerlitz... yes, yes, we must go there, yes, yes, the inauspicious Battle of Austerlitz in 1805, as it says in my book, yet another glorious Austrian defeat, just like Wagram in 1809, oh, Wagram, we have to go there too, just like Solferino in 1859, we really have to go there too, just like Königgrätz in 1866... really, we need to visit all the great historical defeats in order to understand our own defeats, yes, yes... I know what you're going to say, dear Herr Kraus, it's almost hard to remember the last time Austria won a battle, but of course Austria won many battles, including many fateful battles, but in Bohemia and in Austria we only remember the defeats, yes, yes, it's like that in life too, the defeats always come to the forefront, we can't stomach them and overcome them as easily as the Alps with the railway, we keep spewing them back up, that's exactly how it is, dear Herr Kraus, and above all, the two of us already know that a defeat is a victory and a victory is a defeat, yes, yes, even the most glorious victories are nothing other than glorious defeats, yes, yes, there's no escape. The next time we visit the military history museum, we should look more closely at the exhibitions on Austerlitz and Wagram and Solferino, you can't do it all, too many stories, too much history, that has to make everyone melancholy, and not just those who see through history... as

long as we're in Brünn, we absolutely must go to Austerlitz, yes, yes…
now where was I again, you can't go on interrupting me like that… yes,
yes, look at that, yes, the high population density is a testament to the
fertility of the soil… are you not feeling well, dear Herr Kraus? You're
quite pale, just a moment ago you were red, and now you're all white.'

And then we were in Brno. We saw the church on a hill over the city,
a few tall new buildings, a train heading in the opposite direction. Our
train was no longer racing but travelling increasingly slower and rattling
over the switches.

My left arm was convulsing in pain and a fire was burning in my
chest.

As if in a battle.

As if in a Feuerhalle.

As if in a fiery crypt.

I felt like someone was calling my name. It was Carla. I heard her
calling for me. I felt her. She took me into her arms. She held me so
tightly that I couldn't breathe. Carla wanted me to come to her.

I felt sick.

I wanted to get out.

Everything was spinning.

The moment I stood up, I collapsed on the floor. The last thing I
could remember was the two women looking at me and screaming.
And Winterberg, who leaned over me, and I had the feeling that he was
pulling a heavy black blanket over my head.

I didn't see anything else after that.

My heart was no longer racing.

We were in Brno.

In Brünn.

ST. ANNE'S

Around me was nothing, and that nothing was white and still.

I looked around me and saw only endless white emptiness.

I was floating in the air and thrashing around with my arms and legs. I turned around. I thought I was moving. But I hadn't moved. I kicked my legs and remained stuck.

I called out.

I screamed.

I only heard the silence.

I fell asleep.

And was awoken by a sound. At first it was hardly discernible; it came from somewhere in the distance.

But then it grew increasingly more distinct, and clearer, and stronger.

And suddenly everything around me was filled with this sound. I knew what kind of sound it was. I saw the aeroplane. It was coming right at me and then flew just over my head.

And then I heard a shot.

And then I heard Hanzi shouting.

And then I heard the others shouting.

And then it was quiet.

I was alone.

And then I heard Carla calling for me. From the distance. From the emptiness. From the nothing.

Take me with you. Take me with you.

I don't care where, just take me with you.

* * *

The first thing I saw were five bottles of beer. They were standing in a row on my bedside table. In green glass and brown glass, tall and short.

I didn't know if it was day or night.

I didn't know where I was.

I looked at the beer bottles and also noticed the cables and the small monitors which were blinking and beeping. Through the window, I could only see the grey sky. It was snowing, and my chest was no longer burning. The fire had been extinguished.

'So, you're finally awake. Good morning.'

It was a nurse.

'Where am I?' I asked in German.

'At St. Anne's.'

'Where?'

'In the hospital. In Brno.'

'Where?'

'In Brno. At St. Anne's Hospital.'

'In Brno?'

'Well, you're certainly not in Prague.'

'Why are you speaking Czech?'

'What else would I speak?'

'We're in Brno?'

'Yes.'

'And you're from Brno?'

'Yes, yes.'

'How did I get here?'

'How do you think? Like everyone else. With the corpse taxi.'

'Corpse taxi?'

'That's what we call it. With the ambulance, of course… you've had a heart attack, dear… and quite a bad one, the head physician thought that might be it for you, especially with the coma afterwards, but you've pulled through. Take a look at the next bed over…'

I looked at the bed.

'…there were two there who didn't pull through. And one of them was much younger than you, Mr Kraus.'

'Hm.'

'Yes, the heart can collapse so quickly, and you don't even need to be unlucky in love. I'm always saying that people need to get more exercise, but who wants to get more exercise these days? They all just sit in front of the television and let themselves stew, even my husband, and when he gets up, it's just to go to the pub with his mates… but you'll be fine. You'll probably have to stay here for a couple of weeks.'

'I can't.'

'Yes, you can. You have to.'

'I have to… we have to keep…'

'You'll probably have to spend Christmas in Brno, it'll be nice, I'll bring you something from the Christmas market… don't worry, you'll manage, we've cleaned out the pipes.'

'Which pipes?'

'Well, your pipes… your heart! Your arteries were clogged and we've cleaned them out. It's nothing more than a clogged drain in the bath. You pour a bit of that chemical stuff in, it eats everything away, and the water can flow through. Our station is really nothing more than a cleaning crew.'

She laughed. I wanted to laugh too. But I couldn't. I was too exhausted.

I looked at the beer bottles.

'Your father brought those.'

'My father is dead.'

'No, no, he's not.'

'He is.'

'My father is dead, he's buried in the far back on the right side of the Central Cemetery here in Brno, if you know it… but your father, he's not…'

'Oh, I get it, the old man… he's not my father…'

'He comes in every day and always brings a bottle of beer. It's for my son, he always says, he loves beer, he's even learned how to say it in Czech. Your father is a funny old fart, I would have never thought that a German could be so funny… oh, and the stories he tells… I don't completely understand him, but he doesn't seem to care. He rambles on and on and on.'

'He's not my… whatever, it's complicated. But yeah, he tells some stories, that's for sure.'

'I can't understand him very well, unfortunately. I had German in school but, oh, that was so long ago… where did you learn German?'

'In Germany.'

'I see… well, you can't drink these beers, you can only look at them, that should be clear.'

She looked at the collection of beers on the bedside table.

'We've never had anything like it. Flowers, of course, family photos, teddy bears… but bottles of beer, I can't remember anything like that.'

I fell back asleep.

And when I awoke, a sixth beer was standing on my bedside table. And Winterberg was sitting on my bed. He sat there with his arms resting on his stomach and with his head bent a bit forward and was cleaning his glasses. Outside it was already dark and Winterberg was smiling at me.

'I thought you'd enjoy the little beer collection, dear Herr Kraus.'

'Yeah…'

'The last beer is from Austerlitz.'

He looked at the last beer in the row.

'Yes, I have to tell you about that, have you ever been there?'

'No.'

'I was there today, on the fields of the Battle of the Three Emperors, yes, yes, I thought, as long as I'm in Brünn, and as long as I have some time, I have to go to Austerlitz, yes, yes, I know, dear Herr Kraus, of course, the Battle of the Three Emperors was a fateful battle, but not as fateful as the Battle of Königgrätz in the broadest sense, and that doesn't have to do with the fact that the Battle of Königgrätz runs through my heart and tears me to shreds, no, no, that's not it… I travelled to Austerlitz very early in the morning, I'm not far from the train station, I found a room in the *Grandhotel* across the street, the *Grandhotel* is also recommended in my Baedeker, it's the first hotel listed, they gave me a quiet room in the back, but I wanted a room at the front, facing the train station, yes, yes, now where was I… yes, yes, I know, I took the first train to Austerlitz, because I wanted to experience *le soleil d'Austerlitz*, yes, yes, the sun of Austerlitz can only be experienced here, although Napoleon was of a different opinion, of course, but that's how it goes in history.'

Winterberg rambled like he always rambled, and I thought what I always thought.

I couldn't retain any of it, I was too tired and kept falling asleep. But that didn't bother him.

'The train was almost empty, it was still dark and Austerlitz was blanketed in fog, yes, yes, precisely, you're right, just like on the second of December, 1805, yes, yes, I know what you're going to say, dear Herr Kraus, the fog of war, that's right, that's right, you are starting to see through history, the fog of war, just like in Königgrätz on the third of July, 1866, and just like in Lützen on 16th of November, 1632, oh, I'm so happy that you're alive, dear Herr Kraus, I was a bit worried about you, and so were the doctors.'

Winterberg rambled as if he'd encountered no one in these last days to whom he'd been able to tell his stories. And I thought about my dream, about the sounds I'd heard in that empty space without walls. About the sounds that sounded like an aeroplane, and which really were the sounds of an aeroplane.

'In Austerlitz I met two Austrians, yes, yes, right at the station, a retired secondary school instructor from the Burgenland and his very lovely wife, yes, yes, what a wonderful coincidence, they also wanted to experience *le soleil d'Austerlitz*, and the secondary school teacher, who had been a history teacher, opined that the Battle of Austerlitz was the greatest and most important and most fateful battle that had taken place in Bohemia and Moravia and Austria in the nineteenth century... you should have heard, dear Herr Kraus, how long and how brilliantly we argued over the history, it was a fateful battle of our own that we waged at the battlefield of Austerlitz, and of course this battle, this Austerlitz, was won by myself... this history teacher didn't see at all, and I mean not at all, though history, and when I say not at all, I mean truly not at all, I've never meet a history teacher so void of history, but he's from the Burgenland, and the Burgenland is the only state in Austria that doesn't have a single Feuerhalle to this day, to this day they still dig these deep, laborious graves, yes, yes, and it's hard work, and not just in winter like now, yes, yes, that really says something about the country, as my father would say, there's even a Feuerhalle in Carinthia, yes, yes, my father and Rudolf Bitzan received many hostile letters from Carinthia and the Burgenland when the Viennese newspapers reported that the first Feuerhalle in Austria was being built in Reichenberg, Rudolf Bitzan and my father and the entire city of Reichenberg were cursed by the Catholics, and if it had been possible, if all the soldiers hadn't already been on the front or in their graves or in the infirmary, the Carinthians would have surely called up another crusade to punish the Reichenbergers, yes, yes, that's how it was, my father said, his Feuerhalle had many enemies in Austria, but Rudolf Bitzan and my father received much more hostile letters from the Burgenland, a priest from Eisenstadt even wanted to crucify my father, yes, yes, as you can see, dear Herr Kraus, it wasn't easy to live together in Austria, and that wasn't even a dispute between the Slavs and the Germans… now where was I, yes, yes, I know, the history teacher… we argued about the battle and about the weapons and about the uniforms and about Clausewitz and ultimately about everything that one can argue over, and his fine, beautiful wife said that she worked in the city library, yes, yes, his lovely wife, who reminded me of my first wife, yes, yes, the same somewhat shy blue eyes, the same somewhat shy look, what a shame that my first wife also didn't see through history… now where was I again…'

Winterberg rambled and I heard the droning of the aeroplane engines.

'So, yes, his lovely wife… she wanted to calm us down, she wanted to say something too, and surely she had something meaningful to say, a lady from the city library, I mean, yes, yes… but her husband, the old history teacher, didn't let her get a word in edgewise, horrible, horrible, I don't understand it, this ignorance, this arrogance, you can't have a conversation with a person like that, you can only argue with a person like that, and I did argue with him, but he lost himself in long, boring, empty monologues and didn't even allow me to get a word in, you can't imagine it, dear Herr Kraus! But I attacked him again and again with my thoughts and arguments, with my entire historical knowledge, yes, yes, I batted him around with my knowledge, and in the meantime, the sun rose up out of the fog, I swear, it was just like that day on the second of December in 1805, yes, yes, *le soleil d'Austerlitz*, the sun of Austerlitz, unfortunately I didn't notice it and the history teacher didn't notice it either, because we were fighting and screaming at each other the whole time, yes, yes, like two dogs, but fortunately his wife saw it, and so suddenly we were standing there, on the little hill of Santon, yes, yes, that's right, just like Napoleon and his artillery, we so we stood there and looked out at the countryside, all three of us blinded by the red-yellow sun on the horizon, by the sun of Austerlitz, yes, yes, suddenly everything was quiet, suddenly we were all blinded by *le soleil d'Auster-litz*, the fog had dissipated, the entire wintry landscape lay before us, the entire battlefield of Austerlitz, like it did back then on the second of December, 1805… what a shame you weren't there, dear Herr Kraus, *le soleil d'Austerlitz*, yes, yes, if you like, we can go back to Austerlitz when you're feeling better, perhaps we'll get lucky and experience *le soleil d'Austerlitz* together…'

Winterberg rambled.

I heard Carla calling from somewhere in the distance.

Take me away, take me away from here.

Please take me away.

'It was so beautiful, yes, yes, I've never experienced something so beautiful in my life, *le soleil d'Austerlitz* over *"the beautiful landscape of battlefields, cemeteries and ruins"*, as the Englishman would say, yes, yes, what a shame you weren't there, what a shame the Englishman wasn't there, what a shame Lenka wasn't there… the sun was red and then red-yellow and then yellow-red, and the whole white, snowy landscape transformed along with it, we saw it bleed beneath us, yes, yes, *"the beautiful landscape of battlefields, cemeteries and ruins"*, it made me very melancholy, and I'll admit, in that moment I began to cry, and you, dear Herr Kraus, would surely cry too… I was deeply moved, and you would have been deeply moved too, I'm sure of that, even the attractive wife of the history teacher was deeply moved and cried, I thought, the retired history teacher will also shut up for a moment, he must be moved by this too, if we were so affected… but no, he ruined everything, the entire mood, the entire morning in the sun of Austerlitz, he started again to argue about the history, and so I slapped him across the face and his wife threatened to call the police, yes, yes, what else could I have done, I was fully in the right, what a horrible person, and not just because he didn't see through history… compared to this history teacher void of history, dear Herr Kraus, you're a Ph.D. historian…'

Winterberg rambled and the voice of Carla broke off and the droning of the aeroplane engines became louder.

'On the way back in the train I kept asking myself how it can be that people who don't see through history can become history teachers… no, no, it's no surprise then that the mistakes of history keep being repeated, the historical accidents and coincidences and dead-ends and stalemates that always lead to catastrophe, yes, yes, that always lead to the Feuerhalles, to the graves with corpses that the earth can't stomach and is constantly spewing back up, yes, yes, you, dear Herr Kraus, you would understand, the Englishman too, and Lenka too, and perhaps even my daughter would understand, but the history teacher simply didn't understand.'

The droning of the aeroplane engines was so loud that I thought at any time a jet would crash into the room and take me away.

I heard the jet and then I heard Carla calling for me again.

Take me away.

Take me away.

And then I heard the shot again and felt the bullet come at me and drill through my skull.

I heard Carla screaming and the shot was still echoing.

I felt sick.

'Just imagine, dear Herr Kraus, the history teacher had never been to Königgrätz, yes, yes, I know what you're going to say, how can someone who doesn't see through history become a history teacher, I was a tram driver my whole life and I still see through history, tragic, tragic, I've read much more about history than he has, he didn't even know *The Construction of the Alpine Railways*, nor my Baedeker… but otherwise it was very lovely at Austerlitz, yes, yes, *"the beautiful landscape of battlefields, cemeteries and ruins"*, the Englishman would have loved it, as would you, and surely Lenka as well, Lenka loved long winter walks, yes, yes, and then a nice glass of hot grog afterwards… it was lovely at Austerlitz, a beautiful, hilly, and very placid landscape, which reaches out to grasp at every passer-by, which wants to embrace every person, embrace and strangle and entomb them, yes, yes, I saw many lovely monuments and graves, yes, yes, all just as lovingly maintained as at Königgrätz, I just wonder, who maintains all the graves today? They must all be long since lying in graves of their own, I mean, all the relatives… yes, yes, lovely, lovely, it was just a bit too cold and too windy on the battlefield at Austerlitz, but surely it was the same on December 2, 1805 … the beer should be quite good, that's what a railwayman told me at the station in Austerlitz, yes, yes, the station is of course much smaller than the *gare d'Austerlitz* in Paris, which I visited with my second wife, my second wife suffered from France, she was sick from and addicted to that country, we were there quite often, no one in France knows where Austerlitz is, just like no one in France knows anything about Königgrätz, yes, yes, I know, too many stories, too much history, you can only lose yourself, you have to lose yourself, there's no escape … from a technical point of view, I found the train station in Austerlitz much more interesting than the *gare d'Austerlitz*, because in Austerlitz, they still pull the switches by hand, yes, yes, just like in 1913, just like in my Baedeker, I watched them do it … yes, yes, I know what you're going to say, dear Herr Kraus, too many switches, far too many stories, yes, yes, I know, the switches of history are always pulled by hand, with human hands and with human stupidity, yes, yes, much too often it's unfortunately the fools who set the switches of history, no, no, I know, the railway switchers are no fools, of course, just as the shunters are no fools … yes, yes, I know what you're going to say, dear Herr Kraus, the old man is off his rocker again, the old Winterberg is mad, yes, yes, there you have it, you're right, I'm mad, I really do suffer from history, I suffer from Königgrätz and from Sarajevo and from the Feuerhalle in Reichenberg and now from Austerlitz too, I suffer from historical fits, yes, yes, there you have it, the shunting of history has left me fully derailed … I'm sorry, dear Herr Kraus, that you're so often the victim of my historical fits, but I do think that perhaps it's better to suffer from historical fits than from hysterical fits, yes, yes, like my second wife, she could never be soothed, she only found her peace beside the wall of the Heerstraße Cemetery in Berlin, where she lies next to my first and my third wives, yes, yes, a lovely spot in the sun right behind the rubbish bins, no one wanted that spot so it was quite affordable, a really lovely spot, who are the rubbish bins really bothering when you're already dead, yes, yes, it's especially lovely in the late afternoon, yes, yes, I'll find my own peace eventually in the Heerstraße Cemetery, very soon I'll be lying there and listening to the beautiful music with my three wives, yes, yes, the railway music, the music of the trains, yes, yes, the ones that drive past both sides of the cemetery, yes, yes, I know what you're going to say, dear Herr Kraus, as a Bohemian in Berlin you're obliged to find your peace in the Bohemian churchyard in Bohemian Rixdorf, yes, yes, I wanted that too, it's a very beautiful cemetery, quite modest, quite hidden, just like the Bohemian fraternity... but the trains, I would have missed the trains, Bohemian Rixdorf was just too quiet for me... I looked at all the cemeteries in Berlin before I decided on the Heerstraße Cemetery, and I don't regret this difficult decision... because without the music of the railway, I find it hard to fall asleep, I have to take sleeping pills like my daughter... yes, yes, I'll lie there, but sadly without Lenka... yes, yes, I would trade my three wives for Lenka, I know, it's mad, I'm truly mad, you're right, dear Herr Kraus, but there you have it, I am truly mad... but I want to be cremated in Reichenberg and not in Berlin in the Crematorium in Ruhleben, where my three wives were cremated, no, no, I want to be cremated in the Feuerhalle of Rudolf Bitzan and my father, you have to promise me that now, dear Herr Kraus, that you'll bring me to Reichenberg to be cremated, with the train of course, perhaps the railway still has a couple of hearse carriages on the siding on a dead-end track somewhere... yes, yes, that would be lovely, travelling as a corpse to Reichenberg and as ashes back to Berlin, to my wives... but please don't play any Wagner, not in Reichenberg and certainly not in Berlin, I don't want the graves to open, yes, yes, that can happen when you play Wagner at a cemetery, the music is too beautiful for a cemetery, too great, the graves will open up, the earth will spew them up, I prefer something from Smetana, yes, yes, that won't open the graves, that won't make the earth spew them up, so preferably Smetana, dear Herr Kraus, something from the *Vltava*, you have to promise me that... or perhaps Wagner after all... I don't know... so, Wagner for the cremation in Reichenberg, yes, yes, precisely, please do that for me, the prelude to *Parsifal*, just like in 1918, and Smetana for the burial of the urn in Berlin, that's a lovely way to link Bohemia and Germany, yes, yes, just like the Pilsner Brewery in Pilsen links the Bohemians and the Bavarians... that would be lovely... and please, no flowers, no, no... or perhaps yes, *Cornus sanguinea, svída krvavá*, only that, from the Svíb Forest near Königgrätz, if I can make such a request... and no speeches, you have to promise me that, at most you can read a few lines from my Baedeker, no, preferably something from *The Construction of the Alpine Railways* … yes, yes, that would be nice … something about the construction of the Semmering Railway … and then perhaps something on the subject from my Baedeker, yes, yes, for the cremation in Reichenberg something from The Construction of the Alpine Railways and in Berlin something from the Baedeker, the description of the Battle of Königgrätz for example, that section moves me deeply, it's so reticent, so cold, and yet so strong and warm … now where did I leave off again, yes, yes … I know … what I really wanted to say is that I was in Austerlitz and I brought you a bottle of Austerlitz beer. How are you faring? I was very concerned for you, dear Herr Kraus, you look quite derailed … how do you feel?'

And suddenly the droning was gone.

I heard only Winterberg.

And the beeping of the monitors and devices that were linked to my heart.

'Good.'

'Good?'

'Yes.'

'I'm happy to hear that. I was really very worried.'

'Were you really here every day?'

'Yes. Of course. And every day I brought you a different beer. If you go to the supermarket here, you can find so many beers … but you were always asleep and I didn't want to wake you, I tried it once but it didn't work, you were calling for someone … for Carla, yes, for Carla.'

'For Carla?'

'For Carla, yes … who is Carla?'

'Carla is … Carla was … it's a long story.'

'And you said something about an aeroplane in your sleep.'

'Yes …'

'The doctor told me today that he was also quite concerned about you … I was very happy to hear that you were doing better. You know, two people died on the bed here next to you, and one of them was much younger than you, a computer engineer, yes, yes, computer people often suffer from fault zones, yes, yes, from heart failure, the doctor told me … the other man was older, but not as old as me, a retiree, a communist, no, he was a Stalinist, he didn't like that I was speaking German here, yes, yes, he was still at war… and yet he still called for a priest, yes, yes, even a Stalinist wants to get into heaven… a heart attack isn't as easily overcome as the Alps by the railway, but I knew you would overcome it, dear Herr Kraus. Since I'd already managed it myself.'

'Did you tell them you were my father?'

'No. That's what they said, that's what they assumed. I didn't want to complicate things. If you want, I'll tell them who you are and who I am.'

'No, no.'

I wanted to say something else to Winterberg, but suddenly everything felt so heavy

My eyes.

My lips.

My tongue.

My heart.

It was all too much.

Too much Winterberg.

Too much life.

I fell back asleep.

. . .

That night I dreamed about the plane again.

I was the only person on board and I didn't know where it was headed.

I woke up and looked at the ceiling, which collapsed down on me.

Then I fell back asleep.

. . .

The next day, the seventh bottle of beer was standing on my bedside table.

Winterberg told me about how it had snowed the entire day and rained and then snowed again and he'd had to spend the entire day at the hotel, but it didn't bother him or ruin his mood, because he stood all day at the window and watched the trains on the bridge at Brünn Central Station.

He told me about how he had borrowed the current railway time-table of the Czech Railways from the reception. He told me about how happy he was that the reception even had a copy of the railway timetable, that he hadn't expected it. He told me about how he then stood at the window with a copy of the railway timetable.

He told me about the trains to Prague.

To Budapest.

To Vienna.

To Berlin.

To Ostrava.

To Uherské Hradiště.

To Přerov.

To Znojmo.

To Austerlitz, which was now called Slavkov.

He told me about how he hadn't just watched the trains, but also the trams. He told me about how he went over to the train station just before noon to get something to eat and saw a man on the platform who was dispatching the trains, although he wasn't a railway employee. He told me about how the man gestured around him, not wild and chaotic, but deeply concentrated and intentional. He told me that the man stood there like the conductor of an orchestra of trains. He told he about how he saluted the trains and the locomotive drivers, and how he riled himself up when the trains arrived or departed late. He told me about how this man moved him deeply.

He told me about how he slept every night with his hotel window open despite the cold, because the trains didn't bother him. He told me about how the railway composed the most beautiful music in the world, and when the railway music mixed with the music of the tram, it created an even greater and more beautiful music. An opera of the rails. He told me that the music was so beautiful that it seduced him from his sleep and called to him, drawing him to the window at 4:30 am to sit on the ledge with his feet over the edge to listen to the music of the rails. He told me that it was quite high up because his room was on the third floor. He told me about how he sat on the window ledge and listened to the beautiful opera of the rails and looked down at the drop below.

He told me about how a woman with a plastic bag had screamed at him from the ground because she thought he was about to throw himself from the window. He told me about how the woman had alarmed the hotel concierge and how the concierge had alarmed the police and the fire rescue and how the hotel concierge suddenly stood in his door with the police and the fire rescue and he had to reassure them all that he didn't want to jump, because he just wanted to listen to the rail opera from his window sill, but that no one heard him or wanted to hear him.

He told me that after this minor incident, he went back to bed and slept until nine.

• • •

That night I dreamed about Carla.

I saw her sunken face.

I saw her big, grey eyes.

I heard her crying.

Take me away.

Take me away.

I don't care where, just take me away.

I didn't know how to help her, just as I didn't know how back then.

I held her.

Kill me.

Kill me.

Then came the aeroplane, it took me away and I heard the shot and saw the blood.

A lot of blood.

I woke up and thought I was dead.

But I wasn't dead.

• • •

The next day, the eighth bottle of beer was standing on my bedside table.

Winterberg told me how he had gone looking for the former Deutsches Haus, which was recommended by his Baedeker and which was supposed to have a good beer hall, and that he didn't find it and couldn't have found it, because at the end of the war all the Germans were expelled from Brünn and the Deutsches Haus was blown up, as an older woman explained to him.

He told me that it made him melancholy.

He told me how he had been looking for the bronze statue of Kaiser Joseph II by Brenek from 1892 which had stood in front of the Deutsches Haus and was mentioned in his Baedeker, which he didn't find and couldn't have found, because they blew up the statue back in 1918 right after the collapse and revolution and birth of Czechoslovakia, as a man explained to him.

He told me that it made him even more melancholy.

He told me how he had gone to the Ringstraße looking for the city theatre built by Fellner and Helmer in 1882, the first electrically lit theatre in Europe with its own steam generator, and how he was so happy when he found the theatre and that no one had blown it up, and so he decided to buy a first-row ticket for the performance of Schiller's *Wallenstein*.

He told me that he didn't understand any of it because the play was in Czech. He told me how he thought about Lenka the whole time because one of the actresses looked like her. He told me that Lenka loved to go to the theatre and had secretly dreamed of becoming an actress like Gerda Maurus.

He told me how during the performance he also thought about the Ringtheater fire in Vienna, because the theatre in Brünn was the first theatre to be built in Austria after the Ringtheater fire and had such modern fire protections that another theatre fire wouldn't be possible. He told me how he still had to reassure himself multiple times that he had his rope in his bag in case the theatre burst into flames anyway. He told me that the fact that he had the rope in his bag was comforting to him.

He told me how he had thought the entire time about the loneliness of Wallenstein in Eger, who waited there undeterred, abandoned by everyone, for the Irishman who would then run him through with a spear.

He told me how he had also thought about the Saxon locomotive flight to Eger in 1866 and wondered to himself how long it had taken until all the locomotives were able to be used again in Saxony.

He told me how he had also thought about the theatre critic Riemann from the Reichenberg newspaper, who always sat in the first row of the Reichenberg Stadttheater, until a little vein in his head popped out of sheer agitation during Schiller's *Wallenstein*.

He told me how everything suddenly seemed so close to him, as if it hadn't happened decades or centuries ago, but yesterday. He told me again about Wallenstein and Austerlitz and Königgrätz and Sarajevo and *"the beautiful landscape of battlefields, cemeteries and ruins"*. He told me how it had agitated him greatly to realise that he was also sitting in the first row and also watching Schiller's *Wallenstein*.

He told me that he was very relieved that he could leave during the Intermission and that no vein had popped in his head and that he hadn't fallen over dead on the spot. He told me that he actually enjoyed the performance quite a lot. He told me that maybe tomorrow he would go to see the second half of *Wallenstein*.

. . .

That night I dreamed about Carla.
She was healthy.
She could move.
She could run.
She could walk.
She could make love.
I was the one in the dream who couldn't move.
I was the one waiting for a slow death.
I was the one who said, take me away, take me away.

. . .

The next day, the ninth bottle of beer was standing on my bedside table.

Winterberg told me about how he had spent the entire day on the tram and went to see all the tram loops in Brünn, because the tram loops are the most important part of the tram line, because the tram loops stand for the eternal recurrence, which every tram driver and every railway person knew, of course.

He told me about how he had observed the women in the trams and was forced to come to the conclusion that he was unfortunately more transparent to the women in Brünn than to the women in Vienna, and how that made him melancholy.

He told me that the most beautiful tram loop in Brünn was the tram loop at the Central Cemetery. He told me that a tram driver there, who could speak a bit of English, told him about how a heartbroken colleague had once hanged himself on the edge of that tram loop.

. . .

That night I dreamed about Johann and Franjo and Eugen and Hanna and Simone and Hildegard and Andrzej and Jonas. I dreamed about the sailors I'd bought over to the other side during the crossing.

I saw their pale, decrepit faces.

I heard their cries.

A storm came and brought them all back to life.

When we arrived at the harbour, they didn't want to leave my ship.

I had to finish them off with an oar.

Then I was brought before the court and sentenced to death.

To suicide.

I threw myself into the sea and swam deeper and deeper.

But I couldn't kill myself.

I began to breathe underwater, and I knew that I would remain in the water forever.

Until I became a water corpse.

. . .

The next day, the tenth bottle of beer was standing on my bedside table.

Winterberg told me how he'd found Lenka's last address at the Augustiner Straße 17, which was now called Jaselská ulice. He told he how he'd tried to speak with multiple neighbours, but no one knew anything about Lenka, just as no one knew anything about the Bohemian Theatre, which according to the Baedeker had still stood somewhere nearby in 1913 until someone blew it up.

He told me that it made him melancholy.

He told me how at the end of Jaselská ulice a man approached him who spoke a bit of German and told him that the earth wasn't round, but flat, and if not everywhere, then at least certainly in Brünn.

He told me that the man told him that the real city of Brünn lay under the city of Brünn and that the city we saw was only a reflection of the city under the city. He told me that the man told him that the entrance to the city of Brünn under the city of Brünn lay somewhere between the main train station and the cabbage market, and that he would soon find out exactly where it was.

He told me how he had visited the Imperial Crypt in Brünn, where no one from the Habsburg family was buried, but instead many mummies of monks, all terribly grey and dried out for all time by the air of the deepest depths of the Brünn. He told me that he wanted to see the coffin with the mummy of Baron Franz von der Trenck, which had been heartily recommended in his Baedeker.

He told me that it was cold in the crypt and he was the only one there, until he met a Japanese man at von Trenck's coffin who thought that the grey-black mummy wasn't the Baron von Trenck, but Wallenstein. He told me how the fact that the Japanese man was standing at the wrong grave in the wrong city had deeply affected him and made him very melancholy. He told me how outside in front of the crypt he realised that the Japanese man was actually a Korean man and was a professor of modern history at the university in Seoul.

He told me how he and the Korean man had gone to the cabbage market to view the late Baroque Holy Trinity column in the snowdrifts and how the saints at the top had looked down on them with peace and tranquility, including Nepomuk, the most famous water corpse of the Moldau. He told me that despite the conciliatory and merciful gaze of the saints of the Holy Trinity Column, it made him think the entire time about Clausewitz's curious trinity of war, because this trinity knew no conciliation and mercy, and that made him melancholy.

He told me how he and the Korean man went behind the high altar in St. Jacob's Church to see the funerary monument for the field marshal Radwit Graf von Souches, who had heroically defended Brünn against a superior number of Swedes with just a handful of soldiers in 1645. He told me that he had knocked on the coffin and was quite sure that the field marshal was still in there and hadn't been stolen and sold to the Japanese like the corpses of the Habsburg family in the Imperial Crypt of Vienna.

He told me how he and the Korean man drank hot punch at the Christmas market and then mulled wine. He told me that they looked at the lights of the Christmas tree. He told me that the Korean man actually saw through history quite well, in any case far better than the history teacher from the Burgenland. He told me that the Korean man told him in a worried tone that he couldn't understand how he could have confused Brno with Münchengrätz and the coffin containing the mummy of Baron von der Trenck with the coffin containing the corpse of Wallenstein, and that he wasn't sure whether he could come back to Europe to visit the actual grave of Wallenstein, because he was retiring soon and had to save money, and as a Korean he only expected to visit Europe once in his life anyway.

He told me how he and the Korean man had then parted ways, and that he really did want to see the second half of *Wallenstein* in the theatre, but the theatre wasn't playing *Wallenstein* anymore, *Wallenstein* wouldn't come back to Brünn until January.

He told me that this made him even more melancholy than anything else he'd experienced in Brünn that day.

Even more than the fact that he was so transparent to the women in Brünn.

. . .

That night I dreamed about my little sister.
It was a summer evening.
I stood in the bend and saw the green Soviet lorries coming.
I saw her walking down the side of the street.
She was singing a song.
It was an old song.
I saw the lorry coming.
I screamed for her.
But my little sister didn't hear me.

. . .

The next day, the eleventh bottle of beer was standing on my bedside table.

Winterberg told me about how he found the green tavern in Husovice where Leopold Lojka drowned himself in beer at just forty years old, the unlucky driver of Franz Ferdinand in Sarajevo, the unluckiest fool of history. He told me that he talked to an older gentleman who repeated to him what his grandfather had told him about how Lojka told the story of the attack to all the guests every night and how he began to drown himself in beer and tears, and how his grandfather always had to help Lojka back up to his flat.

He told me about how he rang the doorbell and the woman who opened the door thought that he was there for the yoga session, because the inn where Lojka used to draw beer was now a centre for yoga, meditation, healthy pregnancy and positive energy. He told me that his daughter did a lot of yoga and was still not happier than himself, who did no yoga.

He told me about how he then walked to the top of the Spielberg hill to visit the old castle and the penitentiary, which was one of the most famous penitentiaries back in Austrian times, and that many rebellious Magyars and Italians and also the Baron von der Trenck could have surely told us many stories about it if they weren't already long dead and if von der Trenck hadn't withered into a grey mummy.

He told me that it was very windy up there, but because the day was so clear, he could see the Alps and the towers of Vienna, because Brünn had always been far closer to Vienna than to Prague, and that if you looked down at the city from the Spielberg, you really could get the impression that you were in Vienna.

. . .

That night I dreamed about Hanzi.

He came to my bed.

Hanging around his neck was the shoelace he'd used to hang himself.

Hanzi wanted to know how I was doing.

I wanted to say something to him.

I tried several times.

But I couldn't say anything.
My mouth was sewn shut.

. . .

The next day, the twelfth bottle of beer was standing on my bedside table.

Winterberg told me how he had met the history teacher from the Burgenland at the market square in front of the plague column, greeted him cordially and tried to start a conversation, but the history teacher acted as if he didn't recognise Winterberg and kept on walking, but his lovely wife recognised him and greeted him very warmly, at which point the history teacher from the Burgenland began to fight with his wife.

He told me that the plague columns belonged to Central Europe just as much as the train stations and battlefields and Feuerhalles and cemeteries and mental asylums and castle ruins, just like the water corpse of Nepomuk, because you didn't just find a train station or a battlefield or a Feuerhalle or a cemetery or a mental asylum or a castle ruin everywhere in Central Europe, but also a plague column and a statue of Nepomuk, because everywhere in Central Europe, the people swear by death and hope for redemption.

He told me how afterwards he rode the tram to the Brünn Central Cemetery and examined the tunnel that connected the platform to the Central Cemetery. He told me how he thought that his father would have loved the platform, because he had dreamed of having a direct tram link between the Reichenberg train station and the Reichenberg Feuerhalle. He told me the tunnel seemed to be quite practical. If there were to be a mass event at the Central Cemetery or at the Feuerhalle, for example a mass funeral, then the masses of mourners would simply pass through the tunnel and no one would get hurt, because no one would be run over by a tram and turned into a tram corpse while crossing the tram rails. He told me that his father always said tram corpses weren't a pretty sight.

He told me how he had bought some flowers and a candle. He told me how he had looked for hours for the grave of Leopold Lojka in the wind and cold and in the falling snow until he finally found it. He told me how he laid the flowers on Lojka's grave and lit the candle, which wasn't easy in the strong wind. He told me that on the flat, black tombstone stood the inscription 'Here lies the head driver of the automobile of death', which made him angry. He told me that Lojka hadn't driven the Archduke and his wife to their deaths. Lojka was perhaps a fool and a drinker, but not a murderer, as the inscription implied. Lojka was, above all, a victim of history. He told that on top of that, Lojka was the driver, not the head driver, since there was no other driver besides Lojka, because there couldn't have been another driver since cars only have a spot for one driver.

That's how it was back then.

That's how it is now.

That's how it will be in the future.

He told he how he had to spend hours at the Central Cemetery in Brünn, which was of course much smaller than the Central Cemetery in Vienna, marching through the snow to calm himself down.

He told me how he had been watched in all this by an elderly woman, who was still, however, about thirty years younger than him. He told me how she followed him through the empty cemetery paths and between the graves and how she told him that she came to the cemetery every day to look after the grave of the composer Leoš Janáček to make sure that no one was stealing his flowers.

He told me how they then entered the Feuerhalle together to warm up, and watched four cremations in rapid succession, which reminded him of the rapid succession of trams in the Berlin tramways. He told me how he had the feeling that he wasn't transparent to this woman, because she leaned her head on his shoulder and fell asleep.

He told me how the visit to the Brünner Feuerhalle had calmed him, and how it made him think that the architect Ernst Wiesner must have come to Reichenberg to seek advice and inspiration from his father and from Rudolf Bitzan, because the Feuerhalle in Brünn hadn't been built until 1929.

He told me how he promised the woman, who had previously worked as a music teacher, that he would meet her at the cemetery tomorrow at 11 o'clock at the grave of Leoš Janáček so they could both watch over it and make sure that no one stole his flowers. He told me that he wasn't going to go there tomorrow morning. He told me that he didn't want to give the woman, who could have been his daughter and who said to him that she'd been waiting an eternity at the Central Cemetery for someone like him, any false hope. He told me he didn't want to make life any more complicated for himself, because he knew that while it might be nice to fall in love, the same often can't be said for what comes after.

He told me that it would surely make the woman very melancholy tomorrow. He told me that it was already making him feel a bit melancholy. But that's how it is in life and in love, one or the other always ends up disappointed.

. . .

That night I dreamed about Carla.
We sat on my ship and I was bringing her to the other side.
The waves were small and the sea calm and the air clear.
The sun was shining and Carla was asleep.
Suddenly she had reconciled with everything.
She didn't fight anymore.
She didn't hit me anymore.
She didn't hurt herself anymore.
She didn't scream anymore.
She didn't cry anymore.
Then she woke up and said, I know I'm going to die.
In the distance, we could already see the other shore and our harbour.
And then the aeroplane swooped in like a big black bird with talons and took me away from Carla.
I woke up several times in the night screaming and covered in sweat, and I knew that I had to get away, that I couldn't take it here much longer.

. . .

The next day, the thirteenth bottle of beer was standing on my bedside table.

Before Winterberg began to speak, I told him that I couldn't stand it any longer and needed to get out of here, that I needed to keep going, otherwise I would die here.

'Well, look, I wanted to tell you that we're heading back.'

'What?'

'Yes, yes, we're ending the journey here and not going to Sarajevo…'

'Why not?'

'It doesn't make sense. You have to recover your health… yes, yes, I thought, perhaps we'll head first to Bad Ischl, I looked in my Baedeker for a good health resort for heart problems, and I thought Bad Ischl could be the right place for you, although the treatment in Bad Ischl didn't help Empress Elisabeth with her heart problems, no, no, she was always on the run with her sick, heavy heart, with her heart problems, and so are we…'

'No, I don't want to go to Bad Ischl…'

'We could also go to Karlsbad.'

'No.'

'Or to St. Joachimsthal, to Jáchymov, that's also in western Bohemia… give me a moment…'

Winterberg opened his Baedeker.

'Yes, precisely, here… St. Joachimsthal… inns, annex of the radium spa house not far from the train station with a café-restaurant, yes, yes, it's supposed to be quite good, then *Stadt Dresden*, *Kaiser von Österreich*, I'm sure it has a different name today, if it's even still standing… both on the market square, train station hotel, rather modest, yes, yes, then let's not take that one, we'll take the *Stadt Dresden* instead, yes, yes, Dresden, look at that, the Saxons haven't been forgotten here… the question is only whether *Dresden* is still there, you never know today, I'm afraid… there's more… town of 6,000 inhabitants, uraninite ore mine, precisely, highly radium-laced springs… with an imperial and royal tobacco factory… the silver mine, quite rich in the sixteenth century, has been closed since 1900… Count Schlick minted the first Joachim taler here in 1520, yes, yes, interesting… from the train station, continue straight downhill, not that interesting… ah, here it is… the sanatorium for radium therapy, yes, yes, with a radium laboratory and with the large radium spa house built in 1911, do you hear that, dear Herr Kraus?'

I wanted to say something, but Winterberg wouldn't let me get a word in.

'Yes, yes, St. Joachimsthal has the oldest radium spa in the world, yes, yes, radium was new and very popular in 1913, radium does wonders for people to this day, radium is good for all that ails you, even heart problems… what a shame that Empress Elisabeth couldn't take regular radium baths, perhaps it would have helped with her heart problems, yes, yes, and then she wouldn't have been on the run so often, and the Kaiser wouldn't have been so lonely and sad and the Empress wouldn't have been stabbed in Geneva and brought back to Vienna in a black salon hearse carriage that had been built for the Empress in Sanok, yes, yes, perhaps my daughter should take regular radium baths too, because Silke has been alone and heartsick for too long, perhaps it would help her overcome her fault zones, yes, yes, her personal Königgrätz, yes, yes, perhaps we should all take regular radium baths, yes, yes, perhaps it would help me to forget Lenka… now where was I again…'

'What's this about a radio in the bath?'

'Not radio. Radium! I'm talking about a radium bath, not a radio bath.'

'I don't want…'

'Yes, yes, a bit of radiation can't hurt… perhaps everyone should take a radium bath in St. Joachimsthal, yes, yes, perhaps it even works for human stupidity… perhaps there would be a few less fools on this earth. Yes, yes, we'll go to Jáchymov, I'm already looking forward to it.'

'I don't want to go to Jáchymov.'

'Oh, no?'

'My grandfather was interned there… the other one, on my mother's side, he wasn't a communist.'

'In the spa house?'

'In a labour camp.'

'Ah, I see… there's nothing in my book about a labour camp.'

'It became the uranium mine later under the communists. A communist concentration camp. He got ten years for trying to flee the country. He had to mine uranium for the Russians, for their nuclear bombs.'

'I see… so, you'd prefer Karlsbad?'

'No.'

'Marienbad?'

'No.'

'Or Franzensbad? Although all the inns are closed there in winter, as I'm reading now… what a shame… the theatre for operetta and comedy is also closed in the winter, unfortunately… the mud baths and chalybeate baths are surely also closed…'

'No.'

'So Bad Ischl after all? It's beautiful in Bad Ischl, there weren't any camps there…'

'No.'

'Although… who knows. It's not that far by train from Bad Ischl to Ebensee or Mauthausen, unfortunately… yes, yes, dear Herr Kraus, you're right, *"the beautiful landscape of battlefields, cemeteries and ruins"*… the camps are unfortunately part of that, part of the beautiful landscapes and part of us, yes, yes, there's no escape, it grows everywhere, the *Cornus sanguinea*, yes, yes, *svída krvavá*, it's enough to make you vomit, or drown yourself in the radium bath, or drown yourself in beer, just as you do, dear Herr Kraus, yes, yes, I'm understanding your affection for alcohol better and better… I'll just have to check whether it's true that all the inns and spa houses in Bad Ischl are closed in the winter, as it says in my Baedeker, it could be the case, but perhaps we'll have luck and find accommodation after all… the Kaiser also only stayed in his imperial villa during the summer, and he was always hunting all summer from morning to evening, yes, yes, in his love letters to the Empress he always wrote extensively about the hunt, the hunt was his Empress, the hunt meant everything to him, just as it did for the Archduke, yes, yes, but it's not right, if you bring down animals for fun and entertainment, you'll be brought down yourself one day, you become fair game yourself, as my grandfather always said, and he had to know, he was a hunter… now where was I…'

'Stop!'

'What's wrong?'

'Just stop for a minute, goddammit! I can't take it any more! I want to keep going… I want to go to Sarajevo.'

'To Sarajevo? You?'

'Yes… I have to get away, I have to get out, I can't stand it here. I can't go back. I have to get away. I can't stand it here. Please, take me away from here. Take me away… we have to keep going.'

'But you're ill.'

'No, I feel fine. I just want to get away from here. I can do it. They've cleaned out the pipes.'

'Which pipes?'

'My pipes, dammit.'

'Good. That's good, the pipes need to be in good working order, that's right, nice and clean… that's what a retired brewmaster told me in the *Heidelberger Krug*, otherwise even the best beer in the world will taste off, yes, yes, unfortunately in Berlin it's often underappreciated and forgotten that you have to clean out the pipes…'

'Herr Winterberg…'

'And that's why the beer in Berlin tastes so dreadful…'

'Herr Winterberg… I…'

'Yes, yes, precisely, Herr Kraus, I know what you're going to say, too sour, no, no, what they sell as beer in Berlin isn't beer at all, it's no holy water or baptismal water like it is in Bohemia, as my father said, it's corpse water, yes, yes, the grave water that you see when you open up an old crypt…'

'I…'

'I don't understand why Berlin is so popular these days, I don't understand the masses of tourists who come here, the brewmaster always said, the beer here is just so appalling, he told me…'

'Herr Winterberg…'

'Yes, yes, that must have been at least forty, if not fifty years ago… the brewmaster was a terribly gloomy man, another stranded veteran, just like me, he was actually from Bamberg, yes, yes, in Berlin he went from one pub to the next and campaigned everywhere for clean pipes, but always in vain… yes, yes, tragic, tragic, Berlin has long been in a state of downfall, the downfall of beer culture, he said, after a beer in Berlin, the brewmaster often had to spew it right back up, yes, yes, he couldn't stomach the dreadful beer just like the earth at Königgrätz can't stomach the corpses…'

'Please, not now…'

'It's no surprise that the brewmaster hanged himself, yes, yes, noose corpses aren't a pretty sight…'

'Herr Winterberg…'

'In Berlin you can only really drink the beer in the *Heidelberger Krug* in Kreuzberg. They clean the pipes there… I believe they clean the pipes everywhere in Brünn… of course I'm not expert like you, dear Herr Kraus, but last evening…'

'I can't take it anymore…'

'What?'

'I can't take it anymore.'

'Yes, I know, yes, yes, please excuse me, too many stories… it'll be all right… I'll be right back.'

He stood up and left. A few moments later, he returned with a wheelchair.

'I told the nurse I was taking you down to the dining room. Where are your things?'

FROM BRÜNN TO BUDAPEST

Winterberg pushed me in the wheelchair through the dark, grey city. It was snowing. It was icy. People turned to look at us.

I was craving a cigarette, but Winterberg didn't want me to smoke. I wanted to get up and walk, I would have managed it, but Winterberg didn't want me to get up and walk. He pushed me through the cold, wet city. And then he couldn't push me any further, so we took the tram.

And suddenly Winterberg hid behind the wheelchair.

'That woman there, you see her? That's the old widow.'

'Which widow is this?'

'The widow who haunts the Central Cemetery... good thing we're leaving tomorrow... otherwise she'll catch me and marry me.'

We arrived at the train station. It was snowing even harder and the square was flooded by dim yellow light. And then we were at his hotel.

We ended up staying another two days there after all.

Winterberg brought me warm beer.

He said it helped against everything.

And then we drifted on.

* * *

We were sitting in the train to Budapest. Winterberg had also received a postcard from Lenka there. The train arrived late due to a snowstorm and the heat wasn't working. Winterberg looked out of the window. He didn't want to miss the train station in Vranovice, where the first railway accident in Austrian history occurred. But the train was fast, and he missed Vranovice this time too. And I noticed that it made him melancholy, as he would say. But he didn't say anything and continued looking out of the window.

We returned to Břeclav and then instead of taking the right track to Vienna, we took the left track towards Bratislava. The train rattled over a short bridge and we were in Slovakia.

We travelled through the snowy forest, and it wasn't Winterberg who started to ramble that morning.

It was me.

I told him about my journey from Vimperk to Karlovy Vary. About our meeting at the colonnade. I told him that I only knew Hanzi and none of the others. I told him that we were all young, but I was the youngest. I told him how Hanzi said he would take care of everything himself. I told him about the first and last flight of my life. I told him about the flight to Prague that didn't fly to Prague. I told him how Hanzi got up shortly after take-off, went to the pilots in the cockpit, pulled his pistol and said, we aren't flying to Prague. I told him how one of the pilots of the small craft refused to change course. I told him how they fought and how the pilot then reached for Hanzi's gun. I told him about the shot that I still hear today. I told him about the blood.

On the pilot's throat.

On his hand.

On the floor.

On the hands of Hanzi.

On the hands of Pítrs, who joined him.

On the hands of Kamil.

On the hands of Blackie, which was what Hanzi called his girlfriend, because her hair was dark and long like a winter night.

I told him about the blood on my hands.

I told him about the panic. I told him about the fear. I told him about the screams from the passengers. I told him about the shock in Hanzi's eyes. I told him how we flew over the Bohemian Forest to Bavaria, and I saw Vimperk from above for the first and last time.

The train travelled on and on through the plains and it was snowing. It was cold and I was tired, but I had to talk. And Winterberg listened to me.

I told him about the landing in Weiden. I told him how we all perhaps thought for a moment that we were free, although it was clear to us that we were not. I told him about how we were immediately arrested.

I told him about my detention.

About the trial.

About prison.

I told him how I learned German with the Duden from 1938. I told him about the day when I learned that Hanzi had hanged himself in his cell. I told him about the day when I learned that Blackie had died, too. I told him about the Soviets and about my little sister, who was run over by a Soviet lorry on a summer evening. I told him about my father, who was demoted after my flight and then properly hit the drink, until he started to see ghosts, as my mother later wrote to me in prison, shortly before disappearing among the ghosts himself. I told him about my mother, who was still allowed to work in the hospital, but no longer as a nurse, and instead as a cleaning lady. I told him about the day when the news reached me that my father was dead. I told him about the day when the news reached me that my mother was dead.

I told him about the fights.

In the cell.

In the toilets.

In the workshop.

I told him about the knives.

About the scars.

About the silence.

I told him about my release. I told him about my training to become a geriatric nurse. I told him about my training to become a general nurse. I told him about the fear that I would be pulled off the street into a car and brought back to Czechoslovakia in the boot. I told him about the day when I found out about the Velvet Revolution, and that it wouldn't affect me in the slightest.

I told him everything and Winterberg listened to me. He didn't look out of the window. He didn't flip through his book. He didn't talk and didn't get lost in history nor in his stories.

I told him about my first crossing.

I told him about Carla.

About our nights and secrets.

About our love.

About our crossing.

About her long, slow death.

I told him how Carla grasped at me in my dreams and screamed and cried.

I told him about my drinking. I told him how I'd tried to kill myself. I told him that I had never loved any woman as much as I'd loved Carla.

I told Winterberg what I'd never told anyone before.

And Winterberg listened to me, until I had nothing more to tell him.

The train kept travelling on and I said nothing else and cried.

'Yes, yes, Herr Kraus, how well I understand you… yes, yes, our human life is nothing more than a grave. When you're young, you dig it out, and then you fill it in with all the rubbish… but the deepest grave isn't deep enough, yes, yes, the earth shifts, the earth can't breathe, the earth can't stomach it, the earth has to spew it back up, yes, yes, our life is nothing more than a damp, nameless grave in the Svíb Forest near Königgrätz… I know very well what I'm talking about, I know very well how you're feeling… perhaps you should take a radium bath, but I'm not sure whether it will help, it wouldn't help me… only this book helps me sometimes to forget… I'm glad that we're travelling together.'

'Yeah.'

'I'm truly happy to hear it, dear Herr Kraus. Should I fetch you a beer from the dining car?'

'Maybe later.'

But he stood up and left to fetch me that beer.

. . .

I drank the beer and looked out of the window and Winterberg opened up his Baedeker.

'At Blumenau, *Lamacs* in Magyar, the train reaches the Little Carpathians, which border on the Danube, yes, yes, that must be the mountains on the horizon there, yes, yes, Blumenau is a lovely name, don't you think? Then comes a tunnel… unbelievable, in my book they really do list all the tunnels in Austria-Hungary, the poor man who had to write them all up back then surely went mad, just imagine if he'd forgotten one tunnel, that wouldn't do at all, a Baedeker is like a train schedule, like a Bible, it all has to be correct, even the number of tunnels, yes, yes, we should be in Pressburg soon, *Pozsony* in Hungarian, now Bratislava, state railway station, *Államvasúti indóház* in Magyar, no, I won't be able to remember that, 78,000 inhabitants including 33,000 Germans, seat of the Command of the 5th Army Corps, I can remember that, the previous capital and coronation city of the Hungarian kings of House Habsburg, guesthouses *Savoy, Deák*, that one is supposed to be nice, *König von Ungarn, Goldener Hirsch*, yes, yes, wine and warm cuisine in the evening at Schmidt-Hansl, beer at Horváth, well, we don't really need to know that, we're continuing on to Budapest anyway, perhaps another time, what do you think, dear Herr Kraus? Or would you like to stop in Pressburg?'

I looked at me, but I didn't say anything and just drank my beer.

'Please excuse me, dear Herr Kraus, I know I'm a bit mad.'

'Me too.'

'We're both mad … but that's nice.'

'Yeah.'

'And both lost … that's nice, too.'

'Yeah.'

'Lunatics have to stick together. And lost souls, too.'

We both looked out of the window at the cold, flat, endless Slovakian landscape passing us by, blurry and uncaring.

I said nothing more and neither did Winterberg.

Suddenly the train began to brake violently.

Trat-trat-trat-trat-trat.

It rattled as if we had run over a tree.

Trat-trat-trat-trat-trat.

The train stopped.

We saw the forest. A farm lane. The wreck of a car in front of an abandoned guard house. The masts of the catenary. A signal mast. The second track. And the glaring red streaks and drops in the white snow along the railway embankment.

It was still.

It stunk of burning brakes.

The conductor ran past us with a first aid kid and Winterberg looked after her.

And then he said:

'Railway corpses aren't a pretty sight.'

. . .

After an hour, we were evacuated from the train.

'Don't look right, just look left. Don't look right. Keep moving,' the conductor repeated in Slovak.

We walked along the long train, stumbling with our baggage in the gravel and snow, I helped Winterberg, and he helped me, and suddenly he stood still and stared under the train to the right. An arm was lying between the tracks.

'Don't look right, just look left. Keep moving. Keep moving.'

The arm lay there as if someone had just left it for a moment with the intent to pick it right back up. To put it back on. I could see a wedding ring on the hand. I could see the red nail polish at the end of the long, slender fingers.

'Don't look right, just look left.'

We saw the fire and rescue service. We saw the police. We saw a doctor. We saw the ambulance. We saw the snow sprayed red.

'Please keep moving!'

The red was just as red as the red nail polish.

'Don't look right, just look left.'

We saw the tattered bits of clothing. Pieces of a blue winter coat. Shoes. Trousers. A handbag.

'Don't look right, just look left.'

We stumbled through the red-speckled snow and walked past the Slovakian train driver. He was standing beside his blue-white locomotive, gesticulating restlessly and speaking in an agitated voice with the conductor, who was listening to him and saying nothing. Only nodding and smoking. I was suddenly hit with a formidable craving for a cigarette.

'I can't keep driving. Even if I could keep driving, I can't do it, I can't, they'll have to have someone take over, I can't keep driving, this is the third time it's happened now, I don't get it, why is it always me? Alois has been doing it far longer than I have and it's never happened to him... do you understand it? I don't understand it. Why always me? What have I done? I can't keep driving, even if I could keep driving, I can't, they'll have to have someone replace me, it's in the regulations. I can't keep driving...'

The railway employees led us to a small railcar that was waiting on the second track. We could still hear the train driver talking.

'It always happens to me in winter, always right before Christmas…
I can't keep driving, I would probably manage it, I'm sure, I've always
managed it, but I can't, I can't keep driving, it's in the regulations.'

⋅ ⋅ ⋅

The small, overfilled train slowly took us in the direction of Bratislava.
    We saw many black birds on the bleak, black-and-white fields.
    We saw small train stations.
    Farmhouses.
    Gardens.
    Fruit trees.
    'Railway corpses are really not a pretty sight, yes, yes, no corpses
are a pretty sight, in fact… perhaps the poison corpses and gas corpses
and frost corpses and pill corpses, as my father said… the only corpses
that are truly a pretty sight are the moor corpses, which look like proper
people, my father said, yes, yes, although he only ever cremated one
moor corpse that they found in the moor high up in the Iser Mountains, she was at least one thousand years old and a victim of murder
or manslaughter, as the doctors discovered, yes, yes, and the police
officer, a certain Schulze from Tannenwald, lost his mind afterwards,
because he couldn't find out what had happened back then a thousand
years in the past, who the murderer of the moor corpse was… he had
caught all the murderers in the Iser Mountains, except for this one
single murderer, and so he spent his final years in the mental asylum…
now where was I again…'
    'What do you do when something like that happens? I mean, as the
driver?'
    'What else can you do… brake and pray… but I can't pray. You can
drink schnapps, yes, yes, you can do that… you have to do that.'
    The railcar wobbled and the engine droned and the travellers were
looking at their phones.
    'Were you really the last tram driver in West Berlin?'
    The travellers were looking at the pictures they'd taken of the
accident.
    'Yes. You don't believe me?'

'I do.'

They sent the pictures of the accident to their relatives and partners and friends.

'You don't have to believe me, but that's how it was, yes, yes, I drove the last number 55 tram on October 2, 1967.'

And with each picture sent, they began to forget the accident.

'It was a lovely route, but then it was over… yes, yes, back then no one believed in rail travel, yes, yes, unfortunately human stupidity can't be as easily overcome as the Alps or the Bohemian Forest.'

Winterberg told me that the second of October 1967 was a Monday, and people were standing everywhere on the streets to say goodbye to the tram. He told he about how it reminded him of a mass funeral, like the kind that took place when a president or a great artist died.

And yet the people weren't sad, they were excited for the new buses.

For the new cars.

For the new era.

He told me that only the tram people like him were sad. He told me that tram people are very sensitive people. He told me how the Orchestra of Berlin Tram Employees played the overture of *Parsifal* by Richard Wagner from an open-top wagon hitched to the back. He told me how deeply the music had moved him. He told me that as he drove his tram through the gates of the hall in the tramyard for the last time in the red-yellow afternoon sun, it was as if he were in a coffin driving through the gates of the ovens into the fiery crypt of the Reichenberg Feuerhalle. He told me that as he saw the gates of the hall slowly closing, he felt as if the gates of the ovens were slowly closing behind him. He told me he suddenly felt so warm that he needed to drink one beer after the other, but he wasn't able to extinguish the fire in his body.

He told me how he had collapsed.

He told me how they had offered him the opportunity to switch over to the U-Bahn. He told me how he had quit the public transport services and spent the last few years before retirement as the custodian at a school, where he met his third wife, who was freshly divorced and whom he had comforted. He told me about the night that Silke was conceived. He told me about the night when she was born. He told me about the day when his wife fell apart. He told me about how he began to care for her. He told me about the day when she died. He told me about the day when she was cremated in Ruhleben. He told me about the day when he buried her next to his first and second wives along the wall in the Heerstraße Cemetery in Berlin.

'Three lines and three wives. That was my tram life in Berlin, dear Herr Kraus, yes, yes, the number 53, the number 54, and the number 55. The number 55 was the most beautiful line.'

'But the most beautiful of the beautiful lines was the number 1, right?'

'Yes.'

'Lenka.'

'Yes. There you have it.'

Suddenly we were plunged into darkness.

'Aha, look at that, dear Herr Kraus, this must be the tunnel before the main train station in Pressburg, lovely, lovely, we didn't want to alight in Pressburg and yet we have to alight in Pressburg, yes, yes, that's how it goes in life, that's how it always is, you want something and then something else happens that you don't want, yes, yes, back at the Berlin tram there was a man who always wanted travel south to Italy, to the Mediterranean, he was also a bit of a romantic like you, dear Herr Kraus... he wanted to cross the Mediterranean as the captain of a yacht, and ended up drowning in the North Sea on an inflatable mattress in Holland, his water corpse washed up after three days on the beach of Scheveningen near The Hague, a fluke really, most water corpses in the North Sea are lost, yes, yes, the water corpses are swallowed by the sea, yes, yes, the strong current, yes, yes, the North Sea is miserly, the North Sea is always hungry, the North Sea wants to keep all the water corpses to itself, yes, yes, you can't underestimate the North Sea... I know it well, I was in Holland, yes, yes, unfortunately I was there back in the war, yes, yes, my personal Königgrätz... but the only thing that interests me is how they've built this tunnel, was it the Austrian method or the Belgian or the English or Italian? What do you think, dear Herr Kraus?'

* * *

In Bratislava, we had to wait for the next train to Budapest.

We sat in the pub right across from the train station. I was drinking beer from eastern Slovakia and studying the menu with the various types of schnitzel on offer.

Tatra schnitzel.

Fatra schnitzel.

Bear schnitzel.

I started with a goulash soup.

Winterberg was studying the map of Austria-Hungary from 1913 in his Baedeker. He was contemplating whether it would be worth travelling from Bratislava to Vienna and then from Vienna via the Semmering to Graz or Villach and Maribor or via Ljubljana to Zagreb and then onwards to Sarajevo.

In fact, he really did want to see the monument to Carl Ritter von Ghega at Semmering station. In fact, he wanted to visit the grave of the general Benedek in the St. Leonard Cemetery in Graz to lay down the last branches of *Cornus sanguinea* that he still kept in his luggage. In fact, he wanted to return to the military history museum in Vienna to have another look at Václav Sochor's painting of the Battle of Königgrätz.

'Perhaps we've missed something, a small detail… perhaps we'd understand it differently the second time, yes, yes, understand and interpret and perceive the Battle of Königgrätz and the whole downfall and collapse differently, you should view every painting at least twice, yes, yes, if not three times, yes, yes, or four times, in fact you should really see every painting at least ten times, that's what I learned in the Art Association of the Berlin Tram Drivers, yes, yes, I know what I'm talking about, I was also a bit of a painter, no, no, not as successful as Sochor, of course. Whose idea was it anyway for us to travel to Sarajevo via Budapest and not via Vienna and Graz?'

'Yours.'

'Mine? No, that must have been your idea.'

'No. You didn't even ask me. You wanted to go to Budapest. You said that Lenka had been there…'

'Yes, that's right, but still… was it really my idea?'

'Yes.'

'Maybe I really am getting old.'

A man in a railway uniform was seated next to us with a goulash and beer in front of him. The goulash was already cold and the beer stale. The man was sleeping.

And Winterberg once again couldn't be stopped. He was once again like a heavy freight train, one that couldn't be held back by the shunters, one that had come free, that was tossing out one brake shoe after the other, that was racing down the mountain to the next station, until he derailed in a curve, until he came to cork pulled, air out, eyes closed, good night.

Winterberg couldn't be stopped.

Couldn't be steered.

The next historical fit.

He told me that he actually wanted to see the Busserl Tunnel near Gumpoldskirchen, the oldest tunnel in Austria, which was of course more a poor joke of a tunnel than a proper tunnel.

'Yes, yes, a tunnel for Kaiser Ferdinand's amusement, as they said back then, a short tunnel for a quick kiss.'

The man in the railway uniform woke up, ate a bit of his cold goulash, took a sip of his warm beer, stared vacantly ahead, and fell back asleep.

'Yes, yes… I know, the first travellers on the Semmering Railway were screaming in terror, and so they always had to lock the doors of the carriages so no one would come to any physical harm during the trip, yes, yes, but many of the passengers did come to harm, not physically, but psychologically, they didn't think about that, what the darkness of the tunnels does to the soul, that travelling through a tunnel can end in complete derangement, yes, yes, we absolutely must stop in Semmering on the trip back and look at the monument to Carl Ritter von Ghega, breathe in the cool, fresh mountain air, it'll be good for your smokers' lungs, fresh mountain air is much better than a radium bath… yes, yes, and yet the fresh mountain air didn't help Ritter von Ghega and he died of consumption…'

The railwayman awoke again, ate a bit of his cold goulash, took a sip of his warm beer, and stared vacantly ahead with a sad look.

I ordered a bear schnitzel.

And a beer.

'I'm glad that you're already feeling better, dear Herr Kraus… please order a small beer for me too, and a goulash with dumplings, just like that gentleman has… what I'm still wondering is, his grave in Vienna, I mean the sarcophagus, you remember, Herr Kraus… how did they get his corpse up there? It's a good few metres. Perhaps with an elevator? Or with a little crane? What do you think? I'll have to find out, of course it would have been much less complicated with an urn, an urn saves space and money and also the effort of the gravediggers, my father always said, yes, yes, many grave-diggers in Austria protested the construction of the Reichenberg Feuerhalle back then, there was even a grave-digger strike.'

The waitress brought me the schnitzel and the man in the railway uniform fell back asleep. The bear schnitzel was gigantic, like the paw of a bear. I started to eat and Winterberg rambled on and on.

'The grave-diggers were afraid they'd be out of a job if all the corpses were cremated, because any fool can dig a grave for an urn, yes, yes, and most people will choose the columbarium anyway, yes, yes, for the little glass cases, staged like the loveliest scenes from life, like the loveliest theatre scenes, as my Lenka always said, she loved the columbaria and the theatre… the grave-diggers hated my father and his friend Rudolf Bitzan, yes, yes, just like the Catholic Church and later Henlein's goons hated my father, yes, yes, the grave-diggers were very insecure back then, they felt their existence was being threatened… now where was I just now, dear Herr Kraus?'

I ate my schnitzel and drank my beer and the man in the railway uniform fell asleep again.

'Yes, yes, what a shame that we're not travelling via Vienna, yes, yes, too many possibilities, too many train lines, too many stories, too much history, you can only lose yourself, you have to lose yourself to understand it, to try to understand it, and yet in the end it'll only drive you mad, tragic, tragic, the only way is a tunnel trip through to mental derangement, there's no escape, the fresh mountain air doesn't help with that, the radium bad doesn't help either, yes, yes, and neither does yoga, just think about my daughter, she…'

Winterberg suddenly passed out and lay with his head on his open book. On the fold-out map of Austria-Hungary from 1913.

The man in the railway uniform awoke again and looked over at Winterberg, who was asleep, then stared vacantly ahead, and then he looked at me. The rings around his eyes looked like two deep, grey-black ashtrays.

I lifted my glass and nodded to him.

We raised our glasses to each other.

We didn't say a word.

The railwayman gave a slight smile and cut off a bit of his dumpling. But then he suddenly fell asleep again, with the unchewed dumpling in his mouth. He leaned forward over the plate as if he were trying to read the cold goulash.

And so we sat there in our corner.

At one table, the sleeping Winterberg.

At the other, the sleeping railwayman.

And in the middle, me.

A plate of goulash landed in front of the sleeping Winterberg. And a beer.

It was quiet and I pulled the book that Winterberg had given me in Liberec out of my rucksack. *Chronological Notes on the History of Winterberg and its Surroundings 1195–1926, written by Josef Puhani, the Forester of Schwarzenberg*. I looked at the old photo of the city on the cover. I saw the church and the belltower, the sloping market square and the castle, which looked much larger in the photo than it did in reality. I opened the old, grey German book. I wanted to start reading. But in that moment, there was a crash.

The railwayman landed with his face in the goulash.

And Winterberg woke up.

'Yes, yes, now where was I…'

He looked at the railwayman asleep in his goulash.

'Probably the victim of a night shift… yes, yes, it isn't easy to be a railwayman, the young people today always want some kind of experience and nothing is enough for them, one goes swimming with the sharks, the other goes climbing in the Alps without a rope, yes, yes, just like my daughter, always this yearning for adventure, yes, yes, for new experiences, always this dissatisfaction, always these fault zones, and really it would be enough if my daughter would go to the railway, there she'd experience so much during a single night shift that she'd have stories enough to tell for two months at yoga, yes, yes, or to her doctor, who prescribes her these pills every month to make her less deranged... have you noticed, dear Herr Kraus, how all railway people are similar in a sense? That comforts me... not much has changed. The train dispatcher in Pressburg could surely start working seamlessly in Winterberg or in Laibach and they'd immediately know what to do and what the life is like, yes, yes, that comforts me, railwaymen are the only true Europeans, the train employees and the train people, yes, yes, only when the train people perish will our Europe perish with them, yes, yes, and that won't happen all too quickly, yes, yes, that comforts me... we'll continue via Budapest. But on the way back we have to visit the monument to von Ghega in Semmering, yes, yes, the Semmering Railway... are you reading the book?'

I shook my head.

'What a shame... but perhaps you'll come to it later, I think it's terribly interesting, a standard work on the history of Winterberg, I'd say, just like *The Construction of the Alpine Railways* is a standard work on the history of the railway.'

I put the book away.

'Of course, we have to take the Semmering Railway... yes, yes, perhaps we'll spend Christmas together at a nice hotel there.'

Winterberg started to eat his goulash.

'Christmas?'

'Yes, why not?'

'I don't celebrate Christmas.'

'I don't either, but I thought, with you...'

The man in the railway uniform awoke again and looked over at us. His face was smeared with goulash. He stood up and made his way to the toilets.

'And then we'll go to Krakow and Lemberg, I've never been there either.

'I thought you wanted to stay in Sarajevo.'

'Yes, yes, perhaps I will stay. But perhaps not... I'll see. The most important thing is to find Lenka's murderer.'

'But why there? It could have happened somewhere else.'

'It happened in Sarajevo, that's where the last postcard came from, she wrote that she was in the *Hotel Europe*, she was waiting for me there, that's where it happened.'

'Why didn't you just go after her right then?'

But he wasn't listening to me anymore.

'The goulash is sublime, a little bit cold, but well-seasoned.'

He didn't want to listen.

'And your schnitzel? May I try a piece?'

I cut him off a chunk.

'What did you do in Holland?'

He didn't want to answer.

'Great. It tastes wonderful. You think it's really bear meat?'

'Probably pork.'

'No, no, surely it's bear meat. There are bears in Slovakia... I'm sure that we'll also get a good schnitzel in Sarajevo too, yes, yes, you can forget about that in Holland, there's not just a Dumpling-Central-Europe, but a Schnitzel-Central-Europe, I'm sure about that.'

The man in the railway uniform returned and asked for a coffee and the bill.

'And what about you, what will you do, Herr Kraus, when we get to Sarajevo?'

'I'm going to take the money, travel to Bremen, build a ship and sail away.'

'Where to?'

'America.'

'America?'

'Yes, we were trying to get to America back then.'

'You have to fly to America.'

'I can't fly.'

'But this America business is ridiculous.'

I took a sip of beer. And so did Winterberg.

'I know.'

'Come with me... travelling helps.'

'What do you mean, it helps?'

'Well, to forget. We could spend another two hundred years travelling with the train... America makes no sense, not like Austria-Hungary. It's our history, yes, yes.'

'Hm... why not, I guess.'

'Good, I'm happy to hear that.'

'But you have to promise me one thing.'

'What?'

'You have to rein it in with the rambling.'

'Me? But I don't ramble. It's history. I know, I'm a bit historically ill, yes, yes, my historical fits, I know… but that's not rambling, that's not nonsense, this is serious, I beg your pardon, Herr Kraus.'

'Yes, but it's too much.'

'It can never be too much when you're talking about history.'

The man in the railway uniform drank his Turkish coffee slowly and stared tiredly ahead.

. . .

We travelled on. And were both so tired that we fell asleep immediately. We were awoken by the old, bumpy switches at the station in Nové Zámky. The conductor noticed.

'The line is going to be modernised in ten years. But that's what they said ten years ago.'

He continued on his way.

And Winterberg said that it didn't bother him at all.

'I don't care, the important thing is that the trains are running… yes, yes, in 1913 you could probably get to Krakow and Lemberg quite quickly, and certainly also to Sarajevo or Hermannstadt as well, yes, yes, that was certainly the case, you'd surely have gotten there much faster than today, you just have to compare the train schedules, I used to do that often… but I've always been in favour of slowing down, as a tram driver in Reichenberg you always had to drive slowly, and that was true for Berlin in any case, the rails were so crooked after the war, so dilapidated, so out of sorts that you'd derail every day, yes, yes, I recently heard on the radio that young people are looking to slow down, yes, yes, just like my daughter, tomorrow she's in Madrid, the day after in Paris, and the day after that, she has to slow down, and so she lies completely broken down in the bath and gets sick and has to take pills, yes, yes, my daughter takes far more pills than I do, then she always has to do yoga and only eat healthy, yet she's no happier for it, yes, yes, she should also take the train to Sarajevo sometime or take a radium bath, but that won't happen, I know my daughter... everyone wants to reach their destination more quickly, but what for? I hate fast trains, yes, yes, I'd prefer just to travel with the local trains, yes, yes, there's no point in arriving an hour earlier, but there isn't a point to any of it, it's all mad. The things that interest me aren't going anywhere... the history, the railway, the battlefields, the graves, yes, yes, *"the beautiful landscape of battlefields, cemeteries and ruins"*, the corpses and the ghosts aren't going anywhere, dear Herr Kraus.'

He opened up his Baedeker. And I closed my eyes, I was tired again. I was already feeling the weight pressing on my heart again. But I couldn't sleep.

'The train stations in Budapest are the Eastern Station, the state railway station, in Hungarian *Keleti pályaudvar*, please make note of that, with connections to Vienna via Bruck, Graz via Raab and Fehring, and to Bosnia, yes, yes, so probably to Sarajevo, and to Kronstadt and Siebenbürgen and Bucharest via Predeal, and Fiume and Lemberg and Ruttka, and the Tatras and Oderberg, and probably our arrival station, too, for this train from Prague, if we alight there... yes, yes, then the Western Station, yes, yes, like in Vienna, also part of the state railway, in Hungarian *Nyugati pályaudvar*, make note of that, I won't be able to remember it, for Vienna via Marchegg, the Orient Express to Constantinople, either via Belgrade... the Orient Express, those were the times, dear Herr Kraus, with the Orient Express to Budapest, and onwards...'

Winterberg was rambling and there was no holding him back. I thought about Carla. About her young, pale, and delicate body, which got increasingly paler and more delicate the longer our crossing went on.

'Aha, a word of caution, dear Herr Kraus, an important note, the other trains leave from the Eastern Station, yes, yes, I just read about that, or via Orşova-Bucharest-Konstanza, also to Sillein and the Tatras and Oderberg and Gran... then there's the Southern Station of the Southern Railway, *Déli vasúti pályaudvar*, no one can possibly remember that, hopefully there's bilingual signage in Ofen...'

I opened my eyes and looked out at the black trees.

'By "Ofen" here they don't mean the oven, *der Ofen*, like the ones in a Feuerhalle, they use "Ofen" here in German to refer to Buda...

but that's not without interest, don't you think? Maybe it refers to the cremation culture in Hungary, what do you think?'

The empty branches of the tall, bare, black trees reached out for the clouds.

'The Southern Station offers connections to Pragerhof and Graz or Trieste, we have to go to Trieste, the coffee harbour of the Monarchy…'

They reached out for the train.

'Yes, yes, we absolutely have to travel to the coast, to Trieste. Or to Fiume.'

Winterberg flipped quickly through his book and I continued to look out of the window.

'Yes, yes, here… Trieste, *Tergeste* to the Romans, part of Austria since 1382, capital of the coastal region and Austria's only major maritime trading port, population of 230,000, Italians and Slovenes and Germans, yes, yes, a largely modern city…'

Large birds were everywhere.

'Without the benefit of a natural harbour, Trieste owes its initial significance to the benevolence of Kaiser Charles VI, yes, yes, we met him in the Imperial Crypt, who granted the city status as a free port in 1719, and its economic boom to the construction of the Semmering Railway, yes, yes, *The Construction of the Alpine Railways*, I've been saying it this whole time, I found the book in a rubbish bin, by the way, yes, yes, a standard work on the history of the railway, on the history of humanity, yes, yes, the things you find in the rubbish these days, isn't that right, dear Herr Kraus?'

The birds spread their wings.

'Yes, yes, you're right, you shouldn't let yourself be put off from rooting around in the rubbish, I actually quite enjoy it, it calms me down, I've found entire sections of my model railway in rubbish bins… there are seaside resorts in every locale, but sharks, though rare, are everywhere to be found, and endanger swimmers even in Trieste, yes, yes, we'll have to look out for the sharks.'

There were more and more birds.

'I found a new frying pan in the rubbish for my first wife, I have it to this day, yes, yes, it's terribly heavy, you could beat someone to death with it, yes, yes, that happened once in Reichenberg, a woman beat her husband to death with a frying pan because her schnitzel wasn't good enough for him, he told her his mother's schnitzel was better… yes, yes, frying pan corpses aren't a pretty sight, my father always said… when someone is looking to slow down these days, they should travel with the train and root through rubbish bins, but could you even imagine my daughter digging around in the rubbish? She prefers to do yoga and take pills… yet she's still not happy.'

They sat on the black fields.

'Yes, yes, the Semmering Railway and Trieste… the Semmering Railway expanded its trade area to include Germany, lovely, lovely, competition from German maritime traffic in the Mediterranean, which favoured Genoa, was hoped to be countered through the opening of the Tauern Railway in 1909, yes, yes, the Tauern Tunnel and the Dössen Tunnel, always up and then down, panoramic views.'

They sat in the trees.

'The Tauern Tunnel was an important breakthrough to cross the High Tauern, at the time it was the fastest connection between Berlin and Trieste via Halle and Nuremberg, twenty-two hours, but who travels from Berlin or Halle to Trieste these days, only the lunatics, only the historically ill, only those who suffer from historical fits, only railway people like me, like you, dear Herr Kraus, yes, yes… we have to take the Tauern Railway too, from Villach to Salzburg.'

They were circling in the air above.

'Port traffic in 1912 comprised 12,614 ships, importing coffee, rice, wool, spices, ore, coal, and olive oil and tropical fruits from the Levant, yes, yes, exporting sugar, beer, and industrial products, yes, yes, precisely, good beer and modern weapons from Pilsen, those were the hit exports from the Monarchy, and also the mentally ill, they could have exported those by the tonne, but they didn't export them.'

The birds were all black.

'We could also travel to Pola… the waitress at the *Heidelberger Krug* was also called Pola, but she wasn't from Pola, she was from Königsberg, yes, yes, Pola was my age, she's certainly dead now, at my age you know very few people still alive who are just as old as you, at my age most people are already dead, you don't have any more friends, you don't have any more lovers, they've all long since been cremated and buried, yes, yes, I know what you're going to say, dear Herr Kraus, it's tragic, and it really is tragic, but I'm not sorry for the dead, I'm only ever sorry for the living, yes, yes, for the survivors, yes, yes, the ones left behind, yes, yes, I'm only sorry for the ones carrying sorrow, yes, yes, I'm not sorry for the soldiers buried at Königgrätz, I'm sorry for the soldiers who survived it and spent the rest of their lives with all that misery and death before their eyes... yes, yes, Pola made the best Königsberger Klopse, she had such lovely legs and no luck with men...'

The birds glistened in the late afternoon sun.

'Her first husband was a drinker and her second husband was a drinker and her third husband was also a drinker, Pola didn't have any luck until the fourth husband, but then he cut his throat with the razor while shaving, yes, yes, razor corpses aren't a pretty sight, my father always said... wait!'

And then I saw the deer. Ten, twenty, thirty deer in winter. Winterberg didn't see the deer. He was flipping through his Baedeker.

'Pola... Pola was beautiful, Pola deserved a good man... Pola... the main military harbour of Austria-Hungary since 1866, 36,200 inhabitants and a strong garrison, yes, yes, one of the most important naval bases on the Adriatic Sea as far back as Roman times, as you can see, dear Herr Kraus, here's the year 1866 again, yes, yes, the downfall at Königgrätz on one side, the founding of the main military harbour on the other, yes, yes, the world has to remain in balance, Austria had many glorious victories in Italy in 1866, and lost everything in the glorious defeat at Königgrätz, yes, yes, that's how it has to be, that's how it all balances out, you don't have to do yoga, it's enough just to see through history, and you do see through history, dear Herr Kraus... now where was I again... yes, yes, balance... we certainly have to go to Pola, a good friend of my father, Sedlatschek, was stationed in the navy at Pola as a petty officer, second class, my father cremated him in his navy uniform in Reichenberg, he said that petty officer Sedlatschek was quite a lovely corpse.'

Winterberg rambled and couldn't be held back and I looked out of the window which held his reflection.

'The harbour is well-divided, as you can see on the map, *porto di commerzio* and *porto militare*, yes, yes, *porto militare* looks to be much larger than the *porto di commerzio*.'

Which held my reflection.

'Yes, yes, we'll go to the hotel *Zentral* in the Via Arsenale with the courtyard garden and a good restaurant and café frequented by officers, yes, yes, in the Via Arsenale we'll also visit the Maritime Museum with the model ships and trophies and weapons… and then we'll take the train to Abbazia, I've always wanted to go there.'

Winterberg flipped through his book.

'Yes, yes, we'll alight in Abbazia-Mattuglie and can get a room right at the train station, yes, yes, with a magnificent view of the sea, that's really what it says here, to the northeast the town of Castua with church ruins, lovely, lovely, but we don't have to go there, we've seen enough ruins already… the station is the stop for Abbazia, six kilometres to the south, precisely, precisely, that's where we'll go, electric tram, unfortunately they don't say which gauge, pedestrians can follow the new Kaiser-Franz-Joseph-Jubilee-Empire Street.'

I looked out of the window and I saw the black fields and the black trees and the black birds.

'Abbazia… hotels… pre-booking advisable, shared beaches for men and women, warm water beaches at the Archduke Ludwig Viktor Spa, also offering hydropathic cures, next to the hotel *Stephanie*, Dr. Schalk's New Spa House and the Hydropathic Institute of Dr. K. Szegő, both at the North Beach, probably no radium baths.'

I saw myself and Winterberg reflected in the window.

'Abbazia… seaside resort and winter spa, listen to that, dear Herr Kraus, a winter spa! Finally, a place where the inns aren't closed in winter, a place where they dance and eat and heal and love, yes, yes, the right place for us, yes, yes, Abbazia lies in a sheltered area on the west coast of the Quarnero at the foot of Monte Maggiore, with stately houses, beautiful park facilities, and large bay tree groves, when my second wife made goulash, she always threw in some bay leaves, yes, yes, just two leaves are plenty… Abbazia is visited each year by 42,000 resort guests, bay leaves are always good, for soups, for roasts, but not so much for fish, according to my second wife, the average temperature is 13.2 degrees Celsius year-round… Lenka had a small birthmark between her shoulderblades that looked like a bay leaf, I loved to kiss Lenka on her bay leaf, Lenka was afraid that if we had a child, it would have to carry her birthmark on its forehead, because birthmarks wander, yes, yes, just like the stars in the sky, but we never had a child... now where was I... yes, I know... east of the Angiolina Park, the new spa hall with a theatre under construction, the theatre must have long since been completed, don't you think, Herr Kraus?'

And suddenly I saw something else.

'Not far from the hotel *Quarnero*, a bust monument to the Director of the Southern Railway and Founder of the Seaside Resort, F. Schüler, died in 1894, that's right, that's right, the railway doesn't just connect cities and harbours and battlefields and Feuerhalles and people and histories and stories, but also resort towns.'

I saw in the window's reflection that someone was sitting next to us.

'Yes, yes, more panoramic views from the windows, as it says here.'

Next to Winterberg sat a young, beautiful woman. And I knew it was Lenka.

'The high mountains, the blue sea, the deep gorges and forests.'

Next to me sat Carla.

'Yes, yes, that's right, Herr Kraus, we have to keep travelling on over the bridges and through the tunnels, we just can't stay too long in one place, we have to keep moving through *"the beautiful landscape of battle-fields, cemeteries and ruins"*, as the Englishman said.'

All four of us were sitting on this train towards Budapest.

Towards Sarajevo.

Towards endlessness.

Towards the end.

And in that moment, it was also clear to me that our journey really couldn't come to a happy ending.

I felt a heaviness around my heart.

And yet I also felt happy.

'The most popular stroll is the beach promenade, which stretches along the many cliffs of the coastline for ten kilometres from Volosca to Lovrana... another worthwhile stroll leads from the Slatinabad via the Kaiser Franz Joseph Facilities, the Queen Elisabeth Rock, the Aurora Heights, how beautiful that sounds, hopefully the Aurora Heights aren't all that high, my Lenka wouldn't like that, you know, her fear of heights.'

The train braked and came to a stop. We were in Štúrovo and suddenly there was nothing more to be seen. The whole train station lay in a thick fog. The whole city. The whole country.

I only saw two police officers with a dog standing on the platform. They were smoking. The dog was barking.

And then I fell asleep.

* * *

When I awoke, we were still drifting onwards.

'We're already in Hungary.'

Winterberg was thumbing through his book. He still wasn't tired. A Hungarian family sat next to us. The man was looking warily at Winterberg.

'In Hungary, the natural attractions are generally limited to the Carpathians.'

Winterberg briefly looked out into the mist and looked riveted, as though we were somewhere in the Carpathians, but all that could be seen was the fog.

'Yes, yes, of course, the High Tatras, known for its small narrow-gauge railways, unfortunately I don't know which gauge, the Baedeker doesn't specify, we'll find out when we get there… now where did I leave off again… yes, yes, the natural attractions.'

The train was travelling slowly and it became possible to make something out.

It was a river.

The Danube.

'Yes, yes, the Danube Gorge between Baziaş and Orşova, Siebenbürgen, the great, fertile Hungarian plain is terribly monotonous and often oppressively hot at the height of summer, it's a good thing we're travelling in winter, dear Herr Kraus, yes, yes, no tourists, no heat, I can't stand tourists and I can't stand the heat either, when the summer days turn into Feuerhalles, it always makes me very melancholy, I feel very derailed, yes, yes, isn't it lovely we're travelling in winter, dear Herr Kraus?

The Danube was smooth and dark and wide. The trees reflected in the water.

'Look at that, dear Herr Kraus, the trees look like old widows. My father loved widows, especially the young ones. He enjoyed comforting them, yes, yes, I know, I've comforted many women myself, yes, yes, I know what you're going to say, it wasn't exactly kind as far as my own wives were concerned.'

Winterberg wanted us to learn a bit of Hungarian.

He said it always made a good impression when you came into a country as a foreigner and already knew at least a few words.

He said he'd always wanted to learn Hungarian anyway, because only when he understood Hungarian could he fully understand his Baedeker as well.

His Baedeker.

Our Central Europe.

Our world.

'If you don't speak Hungarian, you only understand of half our world.'

The man was looking at him in irritation. But Winterberg didn't notice. Or didn't want to notice.

He read aloud from his Baedeker:

'Railways... at the stations, the place names are announced in Magyar, prior communication with the conductor is therefore advisable, the fast trains run slower than in Germany and are often overfilled, yes, yes, delays in passenger transport, especially on branch lines, are not uncommon, well, I'm eager to see what's awaiting us, this train is also a bit late already.'

He asked me if I knew any Hungarian words and I said I knew one: *pálinka*. In Regensburg, where the Danube wasn't yet as smooth and wide as it was between Szob and Nagymaros, in Regensburg in the Bachgasse, Herr Horváth loved to drink pálinka. He was another one of my sailors. I brought him to the other side, too.

Our crossing took nearly two years, it was one of my longest crossings to date. Herr Horváth always said that if he'd started drinking pálinka at ten, he wouldn't have gotten ulcers and stomach cancer later. And so, at seventy years old, Herr Horváth drank a full bottle of pálinka every three days. And so, I always had to toast his health with him at his insistence, so he wouldn't have to drink alone, because those who drink alone are alcoholics, and those who drink in company are not. And I already knew a thing or two about that.

I never had to finish the pálinka, he always took care of that himself. I preferred to drink beer. It was just the toast that he cared about. The little ritual. You learn things like that during the crossing.

His cancer really did retreat from the depths of his body, perhaps it disappeared somewhere in the Hungarian puszta, where the pálinka was from, or even further afield. Herr Horváth died of a stroke after learning that Bayern Munich was slated to play against Honvéd Budapest, and it tore his soul apart, because he knew that Bayern Munich would win and Honvéd Budapest would lose and then he would have to cry like only a Hungarian can, as he told me.

I told Winterberg that I knew another Hungarian word, *jelen*, which meant "present" in Hungarian and "deer" in Czech. We Czechs often said *jsem z toho jelen*, which meant "I'm confused", or "I have no idea". Herr Horváth told me right at the start of our crossing, right on the first day of our journey together to the other side of his river of life, that *jelen* meant "present", and that was how you responded when called upon in the Hungarian army.

'So "I'm *jelen*", I'm present, doesn't mean that you're lost and confused like a deer in the woods, but rather lost and confused like a Bohemian soldier in the Hungarian army.'

The man looked warily at me.

And Winterberg said:

'Look at that, Herr Kraus, wonderful, you're seeing more and more through history, Herr Horváth was a smart man, what a shame we can't drink pálinka with him, I am feeling a bit peckish.'

He opened up his book.

'In larger cities there are hotels everywhere which are up to modern standards. In the larger lakeside and summer resorts, there are often just simple inns, with food served in a particular café-restaurant, yes, yes, room prices are always displayed, dining is best done in hotel restaurants or in the station restaurants of larger cities, yes, yes, a national idiosyncrasy which may not be to the liking of every foreign guest is the gypsy music, common in many inns, which may run late into the night… I have nothing against music, nor against gypsies.'

The man looked at me and Winterberg with increasing agitation.

'What did Herr Horváth do professionally?'

'In Regensburg he was a locksmith. But before that, in Budapest, he lived in a tunnel directly on the Danube.'

'What do you mean, in a tunnel?'

'He was a tunnel warden. He had a flat right in the tunnel… or so he told me.'

Winterberg shook his head and then began to learn some Hungarian from his Baedeker.

Szálloda.

Sör.

Szappan.

Sörház.

Tányér.

Pohár.

Villa.

Kés.

Kanál.

Pályaudvar.

Váróterem.

Bejárat.

Kijárat.

Állomásfőnök.

Állomásfőnök, Állomásfőnök, Állomásfőnök.'

Winterberg repeated the word and the Hungarian looked over at us with an increasing scowl, as did his wife, and his kid played with a phone.

'*Állomásfőnök* is a stationmaster… *Állomásfőnök*… I fear it's impossible to learn, dear Herr Kraus… or this here… *ennyibe kerül a vezető X-től Y-ig*… "What does a *Führer*, a driver, cost from X to Y"… perhaps we shouldn't use the word *"Führer"* in Hungary either… *beszél itt valaki németül*… does someone here speak German… *kérem vezessen hozzá*… please take me to him, can you make note of that, dear Herr Kraus? I won't be able to remember… at least *sörház*, "beerhouse", I can remember that, or "beer", *sör*… I won't be able to remember more than that, but how is Hungarian beer, what do you think, as the expert? Be honest. Perhaps we should drink pálinka instead… was Herr Horváth really a tunnel warden?'

'Yes. He said it was the tunnel under the castle.'

'Really? Across from the Chain Bridge?'

'I don't know.'

'There's a tunnel there.'

'I don't know if there is.'

'I don't either, I only know it from my book… *Állomásfőnök… Állomás-főnök*… I'll never remember it… who came up with something like that?'

The man turned to us.

'I don't like when someone mocks Hungary,' he said in German.

'We're not mocking it… I want to learn some Hungarian.'

'You're mocking it.'

'No, I'm quite serious.'

'I don't like it.'

'He's just learning Hungarian,' I said.

'Exactly. I'm learning Hungarian.'

'I don't like it when someone ruins our language.'

'I'm not ruining it. I want to learn it.'

'You're making fun of us.'

'You're speaking German too, and really quite well. I think so, don't you, Herr Kraus? It sounds good, not silly.'

'You don't have to listen to us.'

'Where did you learn German?'

'In school.'

'Lovely.'

The man grumbled.

And Winterberg saw a castle on the other bank of the Danube. He flipped through his book.

'That must be Visegrád, in German *Hohe Feste*…'

The man spoke up again.

'What do you mean, Hohe Feste. It was always Visegrád.'

'Yes, yes, well… that's what it used to be called in German…'

'It was always Visegrád.'

Winterberg remained unperturbed. He continued to read aloud from his book.

'Market town with 1,500 Magyar and German inhabitants, you see… hotel *Gisela*… I also knew a Gisela, although she wasn't from Hohe

Feste-Visegrád, but rather from Thuringia, she worked as an account-ant for the tramways, a very beautiful woman… but this is probably referring to Gisela of Austria, she was just as adored in Hungary as her mother Empress Elisabeth, yes, yes, in Austria they even named a small railway after her, the Gisela Railway, we have to take that one too, just like the Rudolf Railway… what a shame we can't alight here, I'd be interested to know whether it refers to this Gisela or a different Gisela, perhaps the hotel *Gisela* is still there in Hohe Feste, I'm starting to get hungry, but soon we'll be in Budapest and we'll go eat paprika chicken, or *halászlé*, or *gulyás*, we should really be there quite soon, there's only Vác left, called *Waitzen* in German, guesthouse *Curie*, diocesan town, cathedral, Roman votive panels in the city museum, yes, yes…'

The man looked increasingly angrier at Winterberg. He began to roll up his sleeves.

The train sighed in the curve and leaned towards the Danube and Winterberg read on.

'A prison on the Danube… look at that, Herr Kraus, isn't that the Vác prison, there, surely you must be able to tell whether it's a prison, you do have a bit of experience with prison architecture, after all…'

And the man listened to him and looked at us angrily. And I wanted to say something, but Winterberg was faster.

'There's no need to fear. It was just a small matter, he hijacked an aircraft and gunned a man down in the process. Do you know that expression? "Gun down"?'

The man looked at me in shock.

'That's enough, Herr Winterberg.'

'Herr Kraus here is a hardened criminal, but there's no need to fear…'

'Won't you finally just shut up?!'

Winterberg stared at me.

I stared at him.

And the man stared at me too. As did his wife. Only their child continued to play on the phone.

'What, you want one in the face?!?' I screamed at him.

'No…'

'Good, then piss off!'

He grabbed his things, his wife, and his child and left for another carriage.

'You did a fine job, dear Herr Kraus.'

I said nothing. I grabbed my things and left for another carriage. My heart was racing. I walked through the entire train, opening one door after the other, and then remained standing in front of the last door and looked through the window at the tracks running underneath me. At the stretch of rails disappearing into a long curve.

I lit a cigarette. And put it right back out.

* * *

I was the last one to exit the train. I had run out of steam. I was tired. My chest was burning again. The platform was empty. I walked alongside the train and saw Winterberg standing at the very front. He was waiting for me.

'The man really did get a fright, that's why I said it, yes, yes, I think he would have thrown us from the train otherwise, he didn't care that his wife and son were there. We didn't do anything, after all, we were just learning Hungarian.'

'You were learning Hungarian, not me. I can't deal with this... you were clearly provoking him.'

'I know, I'm sorry... let's find a place to stay. My apologies, Herr Kraus.'

'Hm.'

'But first, the tickets...'

We went to the counter and Winterberg asked for two tickets to Sarajevo.

'Sarajevo?' said the woman in surprise.

'Yes, Sarajevo.'

'Sarajevo?' she repeated.

The woman shook her head. She typed on her keyboard. And then shook her head again. Then she typed again. There was a little plastic Christmas tree on top of the refrigerator.

'No Sarajevo.'

'What do you mean, no Sarajevo?'

'Sarajevo don't exist.'

'Sarajevo doesn't exist?'

'Yes, no Sarajevo.'

Winterberg showed her the book.

'Sarajevo yes, Sarajevo exists… Sarajevo is here. In Bosnia.'

He flipped through his Baedeker and showed her the old city map of Sarajevo.

'This is Sarajevo.'

'Yes, but in the system no Sarajevo. Sarajevo nicht existiert. Hier gibt es no Sarajevo. No trains to Sarajevo.'

'Then where are there trains to Sarajevo?'

'In Vienna, maybe.'

'In Vienna…'

'Or Belgrade? Zagreb? I can sell you a ticket to Zagreb. Then you will see.'

'Fine.'

'From *Déli*, South Station, tomorrow?'

'Fine, please do that, thank you,' said Winterberg, and then turned to me. 'What do they mean Sarajevo doesn't exist, of course Sarajevo exists, we're travelling to Sarajevo, it has to exist if we're travelling there, or do you also think Sarajevo doesn't exist? Of course it exists… it's in my book after all, it has to exist, Lenka also sent me a postcard from Sarajevo, from the *Hotel Europe*, why the hell didn't we just travel from Vienna?'

It was already late. We walked past an Arab family with children sleeping on a blanket in the station. The man looked grey and tired and exhausted and even greyer. So did his wife. We walked past a Roma family. Past two drunks. Past two police officers who were checking papers.

We stood out on the square in front of the train station and Winterberg turned around to look at the large station building, which was glowing in the night.

'Like a shrine,' he said. 'Like a cathedral, yes, yes, like a grand hotel, yes, yes, like a crypt, yes, yes, like a Feuerhalle, yes, yes…'

Then he looked at the city map. We headed towards the Kerepesi Cemetery, which was supposed to be right next to the station.

Winterberg was delighted by the outstanding location of the cemetery, he was excited that we could pop right over to look at the graves of Batthyány and Deák and Kossuth and the other great

Hungarians. He told me that he could also imagine being buried in the Kerepesi Cemetery next to Batthyány and Deák and Kossuth and the other Hungarian heroes, because you would certainly be able to hear the trains from Keleti pályaudvar, from the Eastern Station. He told me that when night fell over Budapest, you would certainly be able to hear the beautiful railway music of shunting and braking and whistling of the trains and locomotives, just like at the Heerstraße Cemetery in Berlin or at the Vienna Central Cemetery. He told me that the Central Cemetery in Brünn was also beautiful, but you unfortunately couldn't hear any trains there, only the trams, and so he couldn't imagine being buried in the Brünn Central Cemetery. He told me that Lenka had also sent him a postcard from Budapest, but unfortunately, he couldn't remember the name of the hotel where she had stayed. He told me that he didn't know what Lenka did in Budapest before continuing her journey, but he was sure that Lenka went to see the Kerepesi Cemetery and had certainly been deeply affected at the graves of the ones who died young. He told me how he always found it a bit ridiculous back then. He told me how the memories of Lenka crying over the graves of those who died young now affected him all the more and made him melancholy.

We walked to the entrance of the Kerepesi Cemetery, but there we were left standing with our luggage.

The cemetery was already closed.

It was cold and we continued walking in a detour around the Kerepesi Cemetery. Winterberg didn't want to take a taxi. No trams. We walked through the dark city along the cemetery wall with clouds of fog forming from our breath until Winterberg finally chose the hotel *Bristol* from his Baedeker.

But he didn't want to go to sleep.

He wanted to eat something first.

He wanted to experience something first, now that we were in Budapest.

But above all, he wanted to see the tunnel where Herr Horváth had lived and worked. Since he still didn't believe me.

And so, sometime later we were standing on the old Chain Bridge and staring into the Danube. It was already night and the city was black and so was the river and it was cold and other than us there was no one there. The bridge trembled slightly whenever a car or bus drove by. And Winterberg pressed himself against the railing, stood on the tips of his feet and peered down into the void. Just as he had done in Linz. Just as he had done on the hotel balcony in Hradec Králové.

We walked to the tunnel at the end of the bridge. We passed the two large lions who watched over the bridge. I could see their paws and their teeth, they were looking from the bridge towards the tunnel. We approached and saw that there really was a small flat just past the entrance of the tunnel.

There was a light on in the window. And Winterberg looked at the doorbell, which had no sign and no name. And then he rang it.

An elderly woman opened the window. She had a white scarf around her head, she looked small, much smaller and more fragile than Winterberg, who was already quite small, and said something to us that we couldn't understand. It was in Hungarian. She spoke to us and the cars roared in the tunnel. It stunk of petrol and diesel and smoke and the woman spoke on and on and Winterberg nodded and nodded, as if he understood her.

And then the woman closed the window and remained standing behind the window and looked down at us. She didn't move. She simply stood there and stared down at us. Like a statue. Like a sphinx.

We walked away and Winterberg said:

'Do you know if Herr Horváth was married?'

'Yes, I looked after his wife first, and then him. It happens often, one dies and then the other becomes sick from it and also dies. I was in Regensburg for a long time.'

'And before that, in Hungary, was he married?'

'I don't know.'

'Something tells me that the old woman is waiting for someone, and we weren't them. Perhaps that was the old Frau Horváth.'

We walked back across the bridge and I turned around again to look. The light was still on in the window and I had the feeling that the old woman was still standing at the window and watching us leave.

We walked back to the city centre.

And then we sat in a pub and didn't eat gulyás or pörkölt, but regular old schnitzel sandwiches. The schnitzel was good. So was the beer. I was already tired and wanted to sleep, but Winterberg wasn't tired, he wanted to ramble. He was once again overcome by a historical fit.

He told me again about Ludwig von Benedek, who was a Hungarian. About the tragic hero of the Battle of Königgrätz. About the fool, as Kaiser Franz Joseph said of him after the battle. Because those who lose are always fools, even if they're often heroes, as Winterberg said.

'Those who win are also fools, dear Herr Kraus, because there's no victor in a Battle like Königgrätz, which runs through my heart, through my body, through my soul, I still feel it, even here in Budapest, yes, yes, there's no escape, yes, yes, Benedek would understand how I'm feeling, he should have stayed in Italy, he should have resisted when they ordered him to take over command of the Northern Army, and now he's the tragic hero of this battle, a tragic victim of history, the tragic fool of Königgrätz, just like me, just like you, just like all of us, yes, yes, we're all perpetrators and victims and fools, someone really ought to write an essay about the fools of history, someone ought to write a whole historical volume about the fools, a stage play, or an opera… because it's often the fools who lead history into a dead-end or a stalemate, who pull the wrong switches and drive history into the abyss, into the grave, really the fools are the true heroes of history, yes, yes, we must go to Graz to visit Benedek's grave and leave flowers there, yes, yes, *Cornus sanguinea*, yes, yes, *svída krvavá*… in Graz we can also visit the place where Archduke Franz Ferdinand was born, Palais Khuenburg, yes, yes, we can leave flowers there too… born in the Sackstraße in Graz, died in a dead-end street in Sarajevo, which isn't actually a dead-end street, as you'll see in Sarajevo, but the driver Leopold Lojka turned it into a dead-end street, yes, yes, into a trap, into a Feuerhalle, yes, yes, that's how life is, it's enough to make one wrong turn in the car, and then you end up at a dead-end street in front of a café, and then you're dead, and your wife is lying dead beside you, and you, dear Kraus, have bled out on the outside, and your wife has bled out on the inside, yes, yes, it wasn't one, but two tunnels of this particularly narrow Bosnian narrow-gauge railway gauge that the tunnel maker Gavrilo Princip bored through the Habsburg Mountains, yes, yes, with these two tunnels he overcame the powerful High

Habsburg Range... two small tunnels were all he built, and yet he built so much more, he laid the tracks for the First and the Second World Wars and for the Cold War, yes, yes, one fool takes a wrong turn because another fool fails to tell him that he should drive straight ahead. And another fool just so happens to be sitting in front of that café and thinking about killing himself, and sees the automobile that the other fool has driven up right in front of his nose, in front of the barrel of his pistol, what a tragic coincidence of history, what a tragic accident of history, just like my case, just like our case, just like my accident, dear Herr Kraus... why is it that such fools so often stand at the start of a catastrophe? But the whole story had already started much earlier.'

'At Königgrätz.'

'Precisely, precisely, Herr Kraus! Look at that, you're slowly starting to really see through history.'

'It's not that hard.'

'I thought you weren't listening, that you weren't paying attention, but you're not lost yet, dear Herr Kraus.'

'Thanks.'

'You're certainly no fool.'

I nodded like I always nodded and thought what I always thought.

Winterberg had been swept up by his storm again, he was only concerned with himself, with his journey through history. He rambled on and on.

'Yes, yes, there you have it... all these catastrophes are bound up with these fools. And so Benedek is the tragic victim of Königgrätz and lies buried in Graz, and the Archduke Franz Ferdinand was born in Graz and is the tragic victim of the attack in Sarajevo.'

A drunk young man came over to us, held his balance on the wooden table, and wanted to know where we came from, and I said, from Berlin, and he replied in English, good, Hitler was good, he did a good job with the Jews and the gypsies. The gypsies are a big problem, he said. And the Jews. And the Romanians. And the Slovaks. They're the major problem we have today.

And suddenly it was quiet.

Winterberg stopped talking.

He looked at the man and said that he should leave. But the man didn't want to go. He wanted to drink schnapps with us.

'Hitler was good.'

'Is that so?' said Winterberg, looking at the man who was now leaning over our table.

Winterberg smiled at the man.

And the man smiled back at him.

Winterberg picked up his glass as if to drink from it, as if he meant to raise a glass to the man. He smiled at him again and then bashed the glass down suddenly with full force on his fingers, and I swear that I could hear them break under the heavy beer mug.

The man screamed, grabbed his hand and tumbled to the floor.

And I grabbed Winterberg.

We ran for the door.

We were out on the street.

I was pulling Winterberg and Winterberg was thrashing and laughing.

'Did you see that? Did you see that?!'

'Yeah, yeah.'

'The fool. Did you see that?'

I took a deep breath.

'Where did you learn that?'

'In the war.'

We kept walking and Winterberg was still laughing.

'Did you see that? It's an old trick, that's how you deal with fools, yes, yes, did you see that, Herr Kraus?'

We kept walking and I was looking behind us the entire time. The man rushed out onto the street with two others, they were looking for us, and I pulled Winterberg into an entranceway, into a club where young people were dancing, and ordered us two beers.

We were the oldest ones there.

'You did a fine job,' I said, and laughed.

He laughed too.

We clinked our glasses.

The people around us were dancing. The music was loud and the lights were harsh and glaring.

We stood in silence and looked at the young women.

Winterberg and I. Both no longer young. Both transparent. Both invisible. Both old, only the one a bit older than the other. Both lost, as he said, and I knew that he was right.

We looked at the young, beautiful, dancing women and searched in their bodies and movements and gestures and looks for the two women with whom we really wanted to dance. Carla de Luca and Lenka Morgenstern.

FROM BUDAPEST TO ZAGREB

The next day, we took the metro to Budapest-Déli train station. The entire way under Budapest, I was staring at a man who wasn't wearing shoes.

Winterberg was flipping through his Baedeker.

'Yes, yes, the electric underground railway, look at that, built back in 1896 and of course mentioned in 1913, a whole five lines, it was a novelty, a revolution in railway travel, a much more important revolution than the Revolution of 1848, if you ask me, yes, with the underground railway, Budapest really showed Vienna what modernity is, yes, yes, what progress is, just as Reichenberg showed up Vienna with the Feuerhalle, in Vienna they were all still travelling on foot, but in Budapest they'd already built a metro, and in Reichenberg a Feuerhalle.'

His feet were wrapped up in two plastic bags, just like his life was wrapped up in two other plastic bags lying on the floor.

'Running from Gizella tér under the Andrássy út to the Artesian Baths in the City Park in 15 minutes, a distance of 3.7 km, every 5 to 7 minutes in the summer.'

The man stunk.

'Unfortunately, they don't say how often it ran in winter.'

A large dog lay at his feet.

'Quite a shame, really.'

The plastic bags that were wrapped around his feet had holes at the heels.

'Yes, yes, my Baedeker is unfortunately written more for summer travellers, they really should have written one for the winter travellers too back then, you always get the feeling that the summer travellers get more from travel than the winter travellers, like us.'

He had bloody, festering sores.

'Yes, yes, the world was and is unfair.'

The dog was licking at his sores.

'Now where was I again…'

The man was looking at his hands. They were black and looked like they were covered in dirt. So did his face.

'Yes, yes, here… the last train at 11 o'clock, of course that's quite early for a city like Budapest, yes, yes, early to bed, early to rise, just like the Kaiser in Vienna, yes, yes.'

The man, who could have been thirty or forty or sixty years old, was talking to himself. But then he looked up and smiled a bit, as if he were surprised to have suddenly run into someone on the metro, a former lover or a friend, and spoke with them.

'Stations: Deák tér, *tér* means "square" …'

But there was no one in front of him. There was only the dog laying at his feet, licking his ailing heels though the holes in the plastic bags.

'Váci körút, Opera, Oktogon, Vörösmarty utca, *utca* is "street" … Körönd, Bajza utca, Arena út, what's *út*, yes, yes, I don't know… the City Zoo.'

We alighted at the terminal station. The man took his bags and stood up. The dog danced around his feet, continuing to lick at his sores as he walked. The man got into the train heading back to the city centre. He walked in small strides. He slowly shoved one foot in front of the other and the dog ran around him with its snout at his heels and danced and lapped at the sores on his heels.

The Déli train station appeared gloomy. The old building that Winterberg had expected was already long gone. The socialist-era train station was grey and cold. Only the sky over Budapest was greyer.

We got on the train.

Winterberg fell asleep immediately, as did I, and when I awoke again, Winterberg wasn't reading about Hungary in his Baedeker, but about the Semmering Railway.

'The Semmering, 980 metres in elevation, a mountain pass on the border between Lower Austria and Styria, 80 kilometres south of Vienna, yes, yes, initially a bridle path, then a proper road completed in 1728… the only mountain pass in the eastern Alps aside from the Brenner road and the road through the Radstadt Tauern, a new Semmering road was completed in 1841, but lost its earlier significance due to the railway, yes, yes, and that's how it should be, dear Herr Kraus.'

Winterberg read out of his Baedeker about the construction of the railway through the Alps and looked out of the window at the flat dark Hungarian winter landscape.

'The Semmering Railway, part of the Southern Railway from Vienna to Trieste, we really should go to Trieste, yes, yes, was the first great mountain railway and was built by Ghega between 1848 and 1854, yes, yes, we know that already... although newer Alpine railways exceed the Semmering line in terms of technical sophistication, the infrastructure was groundbreaking at the time, and it still inspires awe through the boldness of its structures and its splendid panoramic views, the route is 55 kilometres long from Gloggnitz to Mürzzuschlag, 15 tunnels and 16 viaducts, steepest gradient 1:40, the highest point of the line at 897 metres is located in the 1,430-metre-long Semmering Tunnel, yes, yes, then it all goes downhill from there, yes, yes, the apex of the Semmering Railway lies in the Semmering Tunnel and the apex of railway history in Central Europe lies in the year 1913, yes, yes, precisely, that's the year of my Baedeker, the year it all tipped over, after that it only went downhill with the railway and with history and with Central Europe too, dear Herr Kraus, it went straight downhill into complete derangement, yes, yes, many passengers plunged into derangement after that, some sooner, others later, and no, no, no one could help the passengers, many of them hanged or shot or drowned themselves and many were hanged or shot or drowned, and noose corpses and gunshot corpses and water corpses aren't a pretty sight, as my father said... the highest point of the line lies about one hundred metres lower than the highest point of the Bohemian Forest Railway at the station of Kubohütten between Winterberg and Wallern, dear Herr Kraus, yes, yes, but no one remembers that these days.'

Winterberg read and rambled about the mountain railways, and we drifted through the cold, flat fields. The sun appeared briefly behind the thick clouds, but then quickly disappeared again.

'Yes, yes, you shouldn't just read *The Construction of the Alpine Railways*, you also need to read *The Construction of the Bohemian Forest Railways*, but that book doesn't exist, that book still needs to be written, yes, yes, perhaps you should write it, because I probably won't manage to write it myself anymore, yes, yes, we should absolutely return to

Winterberg and then continue towards Kubohütten, perhaps you'll feel better this time and manage to leave the train, yes, yes, and you can show me the city, just like I showed you Reichenberg, actually, is there also a Feuerhalle in Winterberg? Probably not, I'd think? The town is probably too small for that, although sometimes even smaller towns have been graced with beautiful Feuerhalles, like Semil, for example… no, no, I know, it's not easy, too many memories, and not all good ones, all memories are just horrible really, I know how you feel, dear Herr Kraus… you've already told me after all, yes, yes, our own history is constantly making us sick, I know, oh, how well I know it… the best view is on the right up to Gloggnitz, then mostly on the left… the Semmering Railway begins at Gloggnitz, the mountain locomotives are pre-loaded, the rails begin to climb, what an image, I'm already looking forward to when we get there, lovely, lovely, perhaps we should get out in Gloggnitz and watch the pre-loading of the mountain locomotives more closely, yes, yes, you're unhappy, dear Herr Kraus, I can see it, yes, yes, the Bohemian Forest Railway receives much less attention in my Baedeker than the Semmering Railway and the other Alpine railways, and you're right, it isn't fair, and we have to do something about this injustice, perhaps we should write a book together about *The Construction of the Bohemian Forest Railways*, yes, yes, we should really think about it, when you read books, you're less mad, so if you write books, that ought to heal a madman, perhaps it'll help us to overcome the fear and grief, yes, yes, in the Schwarzatal Valley, the large paper factory Schlöglmühl can be seen on the left, then the Sonnwendstein mountain, with the Rax in the background to the west.'

And suddenly he fell silent. I thought at first that he might have fallen asleep. As he did so often after his historical fits. But he was just looking out at the great, flat lake.

'That must be the Plattensee… yes, yes, the largest lake in Hungary and in Central Europe, as it says in my Baedeker, like a sea, it's beautiful, don't you think?'

'Yes, like the North Sea.'

'No, like the Baltic Sea.'

'The Baltic Sea?'

'Yes.'

'I've never been to the Baltic. I've only ever been to the North Sea.'

'I was on the Baltic.'

'I thought you were on the North Sea, in Holland.'

'Yes, but before that, I was on the Baltic, too.'

And suddenly Winterberg went quiet.

He put down the book and looked out of the window. The train ran directly along the lake and stopped in one resort town after another. Winterberg was quiet and contemplative.

I didn't know yet at the time what he really saw.

What he was really contemplating.

I fell asleep and only know that we were checked later by the Hungarian and Croatian border police in Gyékényes. The train stopped for half an hour at the platform and we weren't allowed to exit. We had to stay in the carriages and couldn't even smoke at the door.

The train then continued very slowly through the gate in the barbed wire fence from Hungary to Croatia and Winterberg looked back at the fence and the barbed wire for a long time.

The conductor checked our tickets and asked us in German if we were travelling to Zagreb for the Christmas market, because it was the largest and most beautiful Christmas market in the world.

'Yes, yes, that's right, the Christmas market! That is why we're travelling to Zagreb, in fact… we're already looking forward to it, my son and I,' said Winterberg, smiling at the conductor.

And then we were in Zagreb and on the square in front of the train station there really was a Christmas market with many kiosks where it was possible to eat and drink, and the entire city was shining.

But in Zagreb, too, it was not possible to buy tickets for a train to Sarajevo. They told us that there were no more trains to Sarajevo. We should take the bus.

FROM ZAGREB TO SARAJEVO

It was early in the morning, it was raining, and the bus station was packed.

Everyone was tired.

Everyone wanted to leave.

Everyone wanted to get home.

Just like Winterberg.

Just like me.

Just like this day, which didn't want to start, which was clinging to the bedposts.

The men yawned and smoked, the women yawned and watched over the luggage and awkward, overfilled canvas bags, the children yawned and played with their phones.

I bought us the tickets. We were lucky, they were the last free spots on the next bus to Sarajevo.

And then it was finally time.

The bus pulled into the terminal.

We packed our bags into the luggage compartment.

We got on the bus.

Except for ourselves and two young Americans, all the travellers were Bosnian, mostly men with rough hands and coarse voices and wrinkles in their face so deep that you could lose your way, like in the valleys of the mountain ranges that we'd already passed on our journey, as Winterberg would say. You could lose your way and lose yourself just as you can in history, just as you can in your history, as he would say.

But Winterberg said nothing.

Nothing at all.

He was quiet.

And he wasn't doing well.

He was pale.

He was agitated.

He was staring out of the window.

I looked at the men. They were loud and laughing.

A bottle of schnapps was making the rounds, it passed from hand to hand and from seat to seat and from mouth to mouth. The bottle also made its way to me, and I took a small sip.

It burned in my mouth.

It burned in my throat.

It burned in my stomach.

I wanted to pass the bottle on, but Winterberg suddenly snapped the bottle from my hands and took a long swig.

Then he took a deep breath and took another swig, which was even longer than the first.

Longer and thirstier.

And one of the men said to us in German:

'Oi, oi, oi! Good, good! I always say that those who drink, die, oi, oi, oi, those who don't drink, they die too, oi, oi, oi. But those who drink, they die happier, oi, oi, oi, because they feel less when it happens, oi, oi, oi.'

He laughed and the others laughed too.

The man told Winterberg that he was travelling from Munich, where he worked on a construction site, he hadn't seen his wife and grandchildren for two months, oi, oi, oi, and every time he came back, his grandchildren weren't two months older, but two years older, oi oi oi. He wanted to know where Winterberg came from, but Winterberg said nothing.

He sat there in his old wool coat and continued to stare out of the window.

At the fast-food kiosk.

At the platform.

At the street lamps that were still burning, although the sun had long since risen.

I knew this look well. I knew that he was looking through these things, he was looking through this world, he was looking beyond, he was staring into the void, just as he often stared into the void, into this void where he saw so much, into this void where he saw what others didn't see and wouldn't see.

And then he said: 'Mad. It's all mad. *Cornus sanguinea.*'

And the worker turned to him and said:

'And you're right about that. Two months in Munich, oi, oi, oi, two weeks in Sarajevo, oi, oi, oi, and then two more months in Munich, oi, oi, oi. It's mad. And my boss says it's normal. I say, oi, oi, oi, let's trade places then. He said no.'

He laughed and wanted to know why we were going to Sarajevo. I said we wanted to spend Christmas there. He wanted to know if we had someone there waiting for us, someone we were visiting, and I said, yes, her name is Lenka.

He said, Lenka, Lenka, oi, oi, oi, there's no woman in Sarajevo called Lenka. And I said, but this Lenka is called Lenka, and he said, good, good, then it must be true, oi, oi, oi.

The bus driver was smoking his last cigarette with the relief driver and three other Bosnians. They finished the joke they were telling, laughed, and put out their cigarettes on a pillar near the platform.

The driver started up the engine.

The bus shuddered and sighed.

And slowly backed out of the platform.

It drove to the crossing.

And then onto the main street.

The worker said that he didn't know anyone who wanted to spend and celebrate Christmas in Sarajevo, at least no foreigners, because at Christmas you should be sitting on your arse at home, only the Americans had to be running around, oi, oi, oi, just like the two on the bus who were also going to Sarajevo, perhaps they didn't celebrate Christmas at all, oi, oi, oi, who knew what Americans celebrated. His neighbour didn't celebrate Christmas, he was Muslim after all, oi, oi, oi, but they'd always gotten on well, oi, oi, oi, he said, who knows if Americans believe in God, oi, oi, oi, perhaps Americans have no home, perhaps they don't need one and that's why they travel around so much. Even back then, in the last war and after the war, many Americans came to Sarajevo, oi, oi, oi, he said if we didn't have a home in Sarajevo and Lenka wasn't there, we could come to him, he'd write down his address for us. And he really did write down his address on an empty cigarette package.

'Thank you,' I said.

'Not at all,' he said.

His wife was very sweet, he continued, oi, oi, oi, he was looking forward to seeing her again, she always loved having guests and cooked so well that every guest came back. He had once brought a Croatian home, oi, oi, oi, he had been sleeping on the steps of the market hall.

Without a blanket.

Without money.

Without anything.

'He loved it so much at our place that he stayed for a week.'

He told us that the Croat might have stayed longer if he hadn't suddenly remembered that morning that his child had been born two weeks ago in Rijeka.

'So he had to go back.'

We drove on and Winterberg continued to stare out of the window.

The worker said that the Croat worked at the railway, oi, oi, oi, the Yugoslav State Railways, oi, oi, oi, back then the trains were still running, long, beautiful trains, you could travel from Ljubljana as far as Skopje, he said, and to Vienna and Budapest and of course to Munich as well.

I asked why the Croat had travelled to Sarajevo, what he was planning to do there.

And he said, oi, oi, oi, that's the thing, it's a secret. The railwayman couldn't remember, he didn't know anything, and certainly nothing about how and why he came to Sarajevo and why he was sleeping on the steps of the market hall.

'He had a hole in his brain,' he said. 'Ah, well, life is nothing but secrets, who would have thought. But he did know the train schedules, oi, oi, oi, you only needed to say "Rijeka" and he instantly knew how all the trains ran. Or Bar. Or Zagreb. Oi, oi, oi, we all have a hole in our brain, and that's why we need to drink, oi, oi, oi, to fill that hole, but it doesn't work, because you can't fill that kind of hole, that's how it's always been. Before the war, oi, oi, oi. After the war, oi, oi, oi. And that's how it is now. And that's how it'll be when it breaks down again, oi, oi, oi, but back then, he said, back then in Yugoslavia, back then we were young, oi, oi, oi, we were so young and so handsome, oi, oi, oi, our women too, oi, oi, oi, young and beautiful, we all slept together in one bed, oi, oi, oi, all of Yugoslavia was one big bed, and it was all great, everything worked out, oi, oi, oi, only then we hated each other, oi, oi, oi, perhaps we were all just envious, I don't know. In Munich I shared a room with a Croat and with a Serb, the rent is far too expensive, oi, oi, oi, and so we founded Yugoslavia anew in Munich. And it worked out well, you just can't eat too many onions with your ćevapčići, otherwise it'll cause another fight, oi, oi, oi.'

And Winterberg looked out of the window and said: 'Mad. It's all mad.'

And the man said:

'You're right, it's all mad, oi, oi, oi, and the bottle is empty, oi, oi, oi, and the journey is long, there's surely snow already in the mountains, and in Sarajevo too, Sarajevo isn't Munich, oi, oi, oi, in Munich they get three centimetres of snow and everyone talks about the end of the world. They have no idea what the end of the world looks like, what it's like for us.'

And Winterberg continued to look out of the window and said: 'Mad. It's all mad.'

And the man said:

'Yes, yes, that's how it is, you're right, it's all mad, the Germans are mad, we're mad, a hole in our brain, you have to drink a lot and forget a lot, oi, oi, oi, but you just can't drink enough to forget everything. Now I have to sleep. Good morning. Good night. Have a good trip.'

He turned around, sunk into his seat and instantly fell asleep.

And Winterberg continued to look out of the window and said:

'Mad. It's all mad. Just like at Königgrätz, just like in the Svíb Forest, the bus is like a coffin… Croats also lie buried at Königgrätz, yes, yes, we're all lying in a deep, damp grave. It's all mad.'

I said nothing and looked at two women of about fifty sitting two rows in front of us.

They were both sharing a cake that they had baked for the journey home, probably a recipe from their homeland.

I thought, that's how it is, the recipes always travel with you, whether you want it or not, just like the memories and fears and the first and last loves that you had or haven't had.

They were showing each other the gifts they'd bought for their children and grandchildren and husbands.

Christmas chocolate.

Children's dolls.

Bottles of schnapps.

I saw their tired faces. I saw the sleepless nights reflected in them, and I knew that it wasn't children or grandchildren or husbands robbing them of sleep, nor was it the long, arduous journeys by train or bus.

It was the brutal fight against the high waves.

Against the strong winds.

Against the dangerous currents.

I was certain that they worked for the same company as me.

For the crossing.

For the Army of Last Hope, as Agnieszka always said, which brought no hope, and at most a bit of comfort.

I was certain that they knew just as well as I did that there is no hope.

Only the journey.

The crossing.

Only the other side.

The fog.

The storm.

The waves.

The wind.

The current.

The finite.

The infinite.

The uncertainty.

The love.

The death.

We slowly made our way through Zagreb. There was heavy traffic. Too many cars. Too many construction sites.

Winterberg was staring out of the window at the cars and trams and construction workers and sweating.

'You don't want to take off your coat?'

'No.'

'It's going to be a long journey.'

Winterberg didn't respond. He was breathing heavily.

'Are you not feeling well?'

His face was completely flushed.

'Is everything all right?'

He was panting for air.

'You know I hate rail replacement services. I hate bus transport.'

'There aren't any trains, there isn't any other way… it isn't a rail replacement service if there's no rail to replace, right? It's just normal bus transport.'

'It's a rail replacement service, full stop.'

'It's not replacing anything. There aren't any trains here, and where there aren't any trains, there's no replacement service.'

'You can look up yourself which one of us is right. I just want to travel this way…'

He handed his Baedeker to me.

'Yes, that might have been the case back in 1913, there weren't any buses back then. But today it's different. You just have to live with it.'

'I don't just have to live with it, no, no, I don't want to live with it.'

'And maybe that's the whole problem.'

He looked at me in a rage.

'The problem? The problem?! I'll tell you what our problem is… when someone today wants to travel to Lemberg – rail replacement services. To Trieste – rail replacement services. To Sarajevo – rail replacement services… soon there won't be anything left in Europe but rail replacement services. We've brought this to the absolute brink, yes, yes, rail replacement services, that's the true Königgrätz of our time, the rail Königgrätz of travel culture, do you really not see that? I despise rail replacement services like the plague, yes, yes, soon you'll be able to burn all the train schedules and the Baedekers too, lovely, lovely, set all of history aflame… poor Carl Ritter von Ghega, good that he's not around to witness it, this demise of travel culture, this decay of his railway dreams, good that he had bad lungs, good that he died so early of consumption, good that he's lying buried in the Central Cemetery in Vienna, the poor man.'

He was speaking increasingly louder and the people in the bus were turning to look at him.

'Yeah, yeah. Keep it down a bit… we're not alone here.'

But I already knew he wouldn't keep it down.

'I don't care… you have no idea how I feel.'

Winterberg was sweating and was once again swept up in the storm.

He had been attacked by the next historical fit, and this one was very serious and very severe. Winterberg was the storm.

'You have no idea about history.'

A storm that painted the sky black.

'No one today has any idea about history.'

A storm that was gathering over our heads and flexing its muscles.

'No one today sees through history.'

A spring storm.

'No one today has any idea about the railway.'

A summer storm.

'No one has any idea how I feel.'

An autumn storm.

'Rail replacement services!'

A winter storm.

'Tragic, tragic.'

The next spring storm.

'We dug our own grave in the Svíb Forest, yes, yes, we're all cannon-eers of the Battery of the Dead in the mountain of fire in Chlum, yes, yes, in just five hours we'll all be dead.'

The next summer storm.

'We're all hanging today in the Arsenal in Vienna in the painting by Václav Sochor, yes, yes, the dead men and the dead horses, eight metres long and five metres high.'

Black clouds.

'A field kitchen of human meat and horse meat.'

Strong wind.

'Benedek wasn't the only fool!'

Torrential rain.

'My father was a fool too when he believed that a Feuerhalle could reconcile the people… yes, yes, and I am too, I'm a fool as well… we all are. Perpetrators and victims and fools.'

Hail.

'And now we have it, now we have to eat all the soup we've cooked, yes, yes, the soup from the field kitchen.'

Lightning.

'Rail replacement services!'

Thunder.

'It makes me want to vomit.'

The bus was still moving very slowly and the other passengers had turned to look at Winterberg.

'Maybe it'll be enough for you to just take off your coat and shut up for a moment.'

'I don't want to.'

'It's warm here.'

'I'm cold.'

'It's warm. You're sweating. And you're shouting.'

'Leave me alone.'

'Maybe you've got a fever. You're sick again.'

'No, no! I'm fine. Despite the rail replacement services, yes, yes, despite Königgrätz, yes, yes, despite the assassination in Sarajevo. I'm fine, I'm just cold.'

'If you're sweating like that, you clearly have a fever.'

'I'm not sweating.'

'Yes, you are.'

'I'm not sweating.'

'Yes, you are.'

'Fine, I'm sweating.'

'Then take off your coat.'

'I want to sweat, goddammit.'

'Well, then, go ahead and sweat, I don't care. But please just shut up for a bit.'

'If you didn't care, dear Herr Kraus, then you would let me sweat, but no, you won't let me, you clearly do care, you always have to be caring, that's a very serious diagnosis, it's a professional illness, yes, yes... I'm not a small child.'

'Maybe it was the schnapps. It does burn a bit.'

'Leave me in peace. Why do you always have to be worrying about me, dammit? Leave me alone... you're sweating too, by the way, and are quite red in the face, yes, yes, like the crayfish we always used to catch in the Iser, your face is that red, yes, yes, you should have stayed in the hospital in Brünn, yes, yes.'

Then he calmed down a bit.

We sat in silence.

And I thought, yeah, you're right, mate, why I am I doing this to myself. I'll bring you to your dead-end street in Sarajevo, maybe Franz Ferdinand and Leopold Lojka and Gavrilo Princip will be waiting there for you, then I'll take my money and then it's Tschüss and Auf Wiedersehen and ahoj and ciao and bye-bye and then you can kiss my ass and find another idiot to bring you home.

Or into the mental ward, where you belong anyway, with your Archduke and Benedek and Ghega and the Englishman and the corpses in the Svíb Forest.

I'm pissing off, I don't care what happens to you.

But where I would piss off to, even I didn't know.

Maybe to Josefa.

Yeah, maybe.

There, where the graves open up, there, where they see the ghosts, there, in the forest of the dead, that was certainly a good place to hide, I told myself, and thought about the deer in the Central Cemetery in Vienna, who no one was hunting and who lived among the dead in peace. And anyway, I haven't done anything wrong.

Kidnapping?

Bullshit.

That's all a bunch of bollocks.

He kidnapped me.

Not I him.

He forced me. I didn't want to go to Sarajevo.

I was feeling tired and closed my eyes.

But in precisely that moment, Winterberg sprang to his feet, shoved me from my aisle seat and ran towards the front of the bus.

'Stop. Stop! Open the doors!' he screamed at the driver in German.

I ran after him.

'I have to get out of here. I have to get out!'

'Are you crazy?' said the bus driver.

'Stop. Stop! Open the bloody doors, dammit!'

The driver shook his head and pulled over to the kerb.

'Deutsche crazy. Deutsche Krieg.'

Winterberg jumped out of the bus, bent over on the side of the road and began to vomit.

I tried to calm him, but he couldn't be calmed.

He was in a bad way.

He was knelt on the cold street underneath an ad for holiday travel to Dubrovnik and spewed everything up. The schnapps. The breakfast. His fear. The days of our journey. His entire history.

The bus driver left our luggage on the side of the street and said:

'No money back for the ticket.'

And I said: 'Okay.'

'Next time you walk to Sarajevo.'

'Sorry.'

'How sorry? No sorry. Germans crazy.'

'I'm Czech.'

'Czechs are crazy, too. You Czechs are more German than Germans are Germans. You are the worst. I was in Prague once, I know it. You are lost. You are like Germans. You just drink and make these stupid jokes all the time, just like this.'

The driver glared at me and shook his head. Then he climbed back into the bus and pulled away. I saw the two women from the crossing looking at us through the window. I wondered whether they recognised me too, whether they knew that I was a fellow traveller from the crossing.

I saw the older Bosnian, the worker, with whom I'd spoken earlier.

He laughed and held up the empty bottle of schnapps.

THE SHARK

It was raining and we were walking along the main street back to the city. I carried our bags and stopped every ten minutes to turn around and check on Winterberg, who was following me exhausted and limping on the side of the road, to make sure he was still there and hadn't yet been run over by a car.

I'd had it with him.

I wanted to go to the police.

To the German embassy.

I wanted to finally get away.

Without him.

I wanted to finally be free.

Free and alone.

We were walking and I thought about the earth at the battlefield of Königgrätz which can't stomach the dead and still spews them up to this day, just like this bus couldn't stomach us now and spit us back out. I'm not surprised. Winterberg is hard to digest.

No beer can help with that.

No schnapps.

No Slivovitz from Moravia.

No Becherova from Karlovy Vary.

No apricot schnapps from Wachau.

No rakija from Sarajevo.

Nothing can help with that.

We walked past a gas station where two men were having a brief argument and then started a longer fistfight. Winterberg watched the two men and didn't say a word. We were the only ones who paid attention to the screaming, fighting men. The others simply filled their tanks and paid and drove off.

We walked past a shopping centre that only sold cheap beds and mattresses. Past the first single family homes. Past the last stop of the tram, which we then took back into the city.

Not to the bus station. To the train station.

Winterberg fell asleep in the tram and I thought about Josefa, what she was doing now and how she was spending Christmas, whether she was making carp schnitzel with potato salad on Christmas Eve, whether she already had a Christmas tree at home, whether it came from the Svíb Forest. I hadn't had carp for Christmas in a long time, so long that I couldn't even remember when it would have been. I haven't celebrated Christmas in a long time. I thought, when all this is behind me, I'll go to Königgrätz and to Josefa and get a drink with her.

. . .

We sat on a bench in the hall of the Central Station. People were rushing past us.

To the trains. From the trains.

With luggage. Without luggage.

We sat on a bench in the middle of the hall. It was cold. I looked at a couple of pigeons that came to us thinking we might give them something. They kept approaching and then flying back and then approaching again, just like the sea, just like little grey waves, like gulls that would come up to us and then fly a few feet back, the grey pigeons of the Central Station of Zagreb. In the middle was a pigeon with only one leg, it hopped on its single leg towards us and then flew back with the other pigeons. Winterberg stared the entire time at this one pigeon, at this war-wounded pigeon of Zagreb, which was called Agram in the Baedeker, with 79,000 inhabitants, including 4,450 Germans and 4,000 Magyars, two train stations connected by one stretch of track, the State Station for Budapest, Fiume, Banja Luka, Sarajevo, and Belgrade, and the Southern Station for Steinbrück, Vienna, and Trieste, as I read in the book.

And suddenly everything was silent, and it made me think about how we had sat just like this on the bench in the military history museum. There hadn't been any pigeons nor any other people, just Winterberg and I and the silence after the Battle of Königgrätz, which we were looking at in the painting by Václav Sochor. The silence of dead soldiers. The silence of dead horses. The silence after the storm. This silence which felt so similar now to the silence of the Central Station in Zagreb.

Winterberg was shivering from the cold and from his historical fit. I stood up and walked to the bakery. The pigeons flew into the air, circled over our heads in a long, gentle curve, and disappeared. I brought back a couple of teas with rum.

'Thank you.'

''Course.'

The tea was warm and the rum was strong. It did us good.

A man approached us. He looked as if he had just been beaten within an inch of his life.

'What do you search here? Can I help you?'

He looked at us and spoke in broken English.

'No.'

'What do you search? I can help you.'

'No, I'm afraid you can't help us.'

The man left and sat down on a sleeping bag next to the door. The door was constantly opening and closing, and every time it opened, I could see the Christmas market as well as the equestrian statue of King Tomislav in the station square, and it seemed almost as if the first King of Croatia could ride into the station on his horse at any moment, carrying the lance with the cross in his hand, as if he would bring things to order. Or catch the train to Rijeka.

'I owe you an apology. I feel a bit derailed.'

'It's all right.'

'I can't hold my schnapps.'

'I noticed.'

'We all drank schnapps when we dug those graves.'

'Which graves?'

'We weren't actually allowed to have schnapps, but we got schnapps.'

'Which graves were these? At Königgrätz? In Sarajevo? Which graves, dammit?'

'In Holland … it doesn't matter. It doesn't make any sense.'

'Yeah, you're right … it hasn't made any sense from the start.'

'I know.'

'At least that's something, that you know it.'

'And so time goes by, everything comes to an end, everything passes by, oh, how time goes by.'

'Please stop. I don't want to hear it anymore.'

'It's from an old soldier's song. We used to sing it often.'

Then Winterberg fell silent and stared into the distance, he was again staring through the people and the buildings and the objects, he was staring into his own void, where he saw things that others did not.

And then he said that he had known from the start that this journey would become his personal Königgrätz, his personal catastrophe, his personal downfall.

I asked why we had departed at all when he already knew, and he said that he had to go. He had to make this journey, his European journey with the Baedeker for Austria-Hungary from 1913. He had to experience his personal Königgrätz, because only after experiencing your personal Königgrätz can one finally die.

'Revenge for Sadowa, yes, yes, revenge for my life, yes, yes, revenge for me. Revenge for her. For my Lenka.'

'I don't understand.'

'You haven't understood me the entire time.'

'It's not exactly easy to understand you.'

'Yes, I know, you're right, I don't understand myself all that well either. You'll get your money. But we're not travelling any further.'

'What?'

'There's no point.'

'No, we'll keep going.'

'No.'

'Yes, we'll keep going. We're almost there, after all. I have no idea why we have to go to Sarajevo or why you need to get there, but we're getting there.'

'There's no point.'

'We can do it. I want to go to Sarajevo now too, I'm curious. If the bus tomorrow is full, we'll take a taxi.'

'No. We're staying here… there's truly no point.'

'There isn't, but we're going to do it anyway, now that we've come so far.'

'I see her, Herr Kraus.'

'Who… the holy virgin Mary? Believe me, I know plenty of people who've seen her.'

'I see her every night, Herr Kraus, and I see her now. She's been with us the whole time.'

'Lenka?'

'Yes. Lenka. My Lenka.'

'Lenka is dead, Herr Winterberg.'

'I know. But I see her, I have to go to her, I have to follow her… up until now she's been the one following me, but now I need to follow her, yes, yes…'

'Lenka is dead, Herr Winterberg.'

'No, she's not, I see her.'

I placed my hand on his forehead. He was sweating.

'Herr Winterberg… you have a fever. Let's go to the hotel and have you lie down. And then tomorrow we'll continue to Sarajevo, it'll be good for you…'

Winterberg was silent and stared into the distance. He stared into his void. Who knows, perhaps he really did see his Lenka. The pigeons returned to us. Even the pigeon with only one leg came hopping back towards our bench.

I looked in the Baedeker. I found the pages on Agram. Zagreb. I looked at the map of the city. And then I read that Zagreb isn't just the capital of Croatia, but also the seat of the Command of the 13th Army Corps. That seemed to be particularly important to the writers of the Baedeker, just like it was important to Winterberg too.

It talked about the train connections.

It talked about the tunnels.

It talked about the attractions.

It talked about accommodation and food and drinks and spas.

It talked about the army.

It talked about war.

It talked about death.

I read about the electric trams. About the post and telegram office in the Jurišićeva ulica. About the Diana Spa and the beaches along the Sava River to the left of the railway bridge. I read about the Upper Town and the Kaptol and the Lower Town. I read about the busy Ilica, the main artery of Agram, as it said in the book. I read about the Franz Joseph University endowed by the Kaiser and about the Well of Life.

'It also says here that there are beautiful mountain landscapes from Agram onwards… maybe we should go to Fiume, I mean Rijeka, and from there to Sarajevo, that's supposed to be a lovely trip… picturesque views… maybe there's a train there that can take us further.'

'Picturesque views… that also makes me want to vomit… there aren't any picturesque views anymore.'

'But the sea would do you good. If it's not possible with the train, we'll rent a car and drive to Sarajevo.'

'No.'

I looked in the Baedeker.

'Let's head to the hotel.'

'No.'

'But before that, we'll go to the Budweiser Beer Hall and have something nice to eat, a good, strong beef soup or goulash or Wiener schnitzel and wash it down with a Budweiser, that'd be nice, you did like Budweiser… Preradovićev trg 2. Maybe it's still there.'

'No.'

'Yes, that's what we're going to do. We can stay here over the holidays too, why not? Christmas in Zagreb, I'm sure that'll be nice.'

The pigeons approached and then flew away. Only the one-legged pigeon remained and was looking at Winterberg.

And then I took the Baedeker and started to read about Bosnia. And about Sarajevo.

'The Russo-Turkish War of 1878 did not affect Bosnia immediately, Austria-Hungary was first permitted to occupy Bosnia and the Herzegovina at the Congress of Berlin… Austro-Hungarian troops under the high command of quartermaster von Philippovich entered the country on July 30, 1878, but it took months of fighting before the country was subdued. On October 5, 1908, Bosnia and the Herzegovina were annexed to the Monarchy as a jointly-administered territory…'

I read and Winterberg listened.

'The best time of year for a trip to Bosnia and the Herzegovina are the months of May, June, and September, in July and August the heat in the Herzegovina is often sweltering... the oriental character of towns and villages has been splendidly preserved... a well-organised gendarmerie corps provides security throughout the country... inns... in Sarajevo, Ilidža, Mostar, Banja Luka, Jajce, and in other locations where municipal offices or garrisons are present, it's possible to find good inns at moderate prices. Further afield, one may be dependent on simple but clean gendarmerie barracks... Bosnia has its own postal stamps... the local language is Serbo-Croatian, part of the southern group of Slavic languages, but with significant influence from Turkish vocabulary. Officials, hospitality workers, and almost all merchants in the larger cities speak German... *svjetlo* is light, *vatra* is fire, *rakija* schnapps, *pivo* beer, *voda* water...'

I read and Winterberg started to calm down.

He closed his eyes.

'Yes, yes, please read more, dear Herr Kraus, a bit louder, please... I can see it...'

'Okay.'

'Read more, I want to go to Sarajevo, I really do have to go, you're right...'

'Sarajevo, 537 to 682 metres elevation, capital of Bosnia, seat of the national administration, Chief of the General Staff, Command of the 15th Army Corps, a Roman Catholic Archbishop, a Serbian Orthodox Metropolitan, and a Muslim Reis-ul-Ulema, with 51,900 inhabitants... including 18,500 Muslims and 6,400 Jews... with a garrison of more than 5,000 men...'

'Five thousand men, look at that, and it still didn't help the Archduke and his wife.'

'Sarajevo lies in a narrow valley traversed by the Miljacka river, with partly forested sloping heights of up to 1600 metres.'

'Yes, yes, I can see it.'

'The numerous minarets and small houses surrounded by gardens lend the sprawling city a highly picturesque skyline.'

'Oh, I'm sure Lenka loved that.'

'There are multiple bridges over the river, which emerges from a deep gorge in the mountains above the city. The streets closer to the river are predominantly inhabited by Serbs, Catholics and Jews, as well as immigrants, while the Muslims tend to have their residences higher on the mountain slopes.'

'I'll have to remember that…'

'Between the train station and the city centre, the military barracks are to the left, the national museum on the right, built in 1908–12 based on designs by Pařík…'

'Yes, yes, precisely, Karel Pařík, born near Jitschin, a Bohemian, a good friend of Rudolf Bitzan, yes, yes… Pařík designed many buildings in Sarajevo.'

'For travellers with limited time: visit the bazaar and the Husrev Beg Mosque, the national museum… hike up to the fortress… excursions to the Goat Bridge, the Koševo Valley, Miljevići…'

'Limited time… we're not limited. We have time. Please read more.'

'It's preferable to plan a trip around the first half of the week, particularly Wednesday, for the markets; on Friday, Saturday, and Sunday, the city is less busy due to the Islamic, Jewish and Christian days of rest.'

'Lovely, lovely.'

'Guides can be recommended by inns, 80 hellers per hour.'

'I know it all already, I've read it a thousand times, but please read more, it comforts me, yes, yes, you can't imagine how much it comforts me.'

I read about the six buildings of the museum and about the botanical gardens. About the Bogumil Cemetery. About the electric trams. About the state tobacco factory. I read about the three main streets on the right bank of the Miljacka. About the Franz-Joseph-Straße, where the Serbian Orthodox church was. About Ćemaluša street with the old Serbian Orthodox church. About Ferhadija alley with the national bank and the market hall. I read about the bazaar, the centre of trade and industry. I read about the fact that the bazaar is busiest on Wednesdays, when the inhabitants of the surrounding areas from far and wide stream into the city. I read about the maze of more than fifty alleyways. About the wooden kiosks and stone warehouses. About cobblers and tailors and botanists and saddlers and coppersmiths and pawn shops. About silver and gold and copper products and metallurgy and carpentry and embroidery and rose oil and carpets. I read that many of the so-called oriental products came from Austria. I read about the

Husrev Beg Mosque. About the modern painting of the front hall and the interior. About the 50 hellers needed to pay the warden to open the mosque. About the overshoes that one had to don before entering the mosque. I read about the front courtyard with a beautiful well for religious washings under an old lime tree. I read about the corpses of the Muslims who were briefly displayed here, covered by a green sheet. I read that a turban on top signifies that it was a man. I read about the cathedral square and the Roman Catholic cathedral with two towers that was consecrated in 1889. I read about the city hall, built over 1892–95 in the Moorish-Byzantine style. I read about the Sinan Tekija, where the Whirling Dervish held their *Zikr* on Thursday evenings after nine. I read that entry is not allowed. I read about Franz Joseph Square and the Franz Joseph Barracks and the Konak, the seat of the national leader and the Chief of General Staff. I read about the military mess, mandatory guide. I read about the clubhouse with the gentleman's club, mandatory guide. I read about the Turkish bath and the other seat bath with a gentle massage.

I read while Winterberg held his eyes closed and smiled.

'The Central Train Station, a terminus station, lies three kilometres west of the bazaar… Bistrik Station for the railway to Vardište and Uvac on the southern side of town, local train station to Ilidže between the Central Station and the city. Recommended inns include the hotel *Europe*, Franz-Joseph-Straße 40, with electric lights and central heating, 120 rooms from 3 to 6 crowns… or hotel *Zentral*, recommended, or hotel *Royal*… restaurants… hotel *Europe* and hotel *Zentral*, the clubhaus with courtyard garden and a good restaurant and *Friedrich*… cafés… hotel *Europe* and hotel *Zentral* and hotel *Czezner* across from the national bank… *Tabory* and *Marienhof*, across from the tobacco factory…'

Winterberg no longer had his eyes closed. He was staring into space. And began to cry.

'That's where it happened, Herr Kraus, right there…'

'Where?'

'In the hotel *Europe*, that was Lenka's last address, her last postcard. That's where she was waiting for me, yes, yes, and because I didn't come… Lenka threw herself from the window.'

'What?'

'Yes. From her room on the third floor... Lenka overcame her fear of heights and threw herself from the window.'

'That can't be true.'

'It is, unfortunately it's entirely true. A friend of hers told me after the war.'

We were silent. People passed us by.

The beaten man approached us again.

'What do you search? What do you need? I can help you.'

We said nothing and he walked away.

'I see her... I see her again. I see my Lenka... I have to go to her, soon.'

I snapped the book shut. The pigeons flew into the air and disappeared. Even the pigeon with only one leg.

'I can't manage, dear Herr Kraus. I have to go to her... no, no, I don't want to go to Sarajevo. It's all nonsense. It's mad, I already know who murdered Lenka. It was me, Herr Kraus.'

'What?'

'I betrayed Lenka, Herr Kraus, yes, yes, it was me who handed her over, yes, yes, it's my fault... and I've been seeing her the whole time, yes, yes, I have to say goodbye to her now, I have to go to her, or else I'll keep seeing her forever... I wanted to go to Sarajevo, I wanted to stay in the hotel *Europe*, I also wanted to take a room in the third floor, I also wanted to also jump from the window... for the worst case scenario I also packed the rope, and my pistol, yes, yes, in case the hotel *Europe* was fully booked, in case I got a room on the first floor, in case I couldn't jump, yes, yes, because I'm a coward, dear Herr Kraus... I already tried to do it in Brünn, but I'm a coward, I'm not as strong as my Lenka, my woman in the moon. Yes, yes, how often I've imagined it, how often I've wanted to do it... but I'm a coward, dear Herr Kraus, there you have it... Lenka, Lenka was brave, yes, yes, defenestration corpses aren't a pretty sight, just like all suicide corpses, my father always said, but those who took their own lives were the only true heroes of our time, they were no failures, they were no fools, they actually did something, dear Herr Kraus... yes, yes, the bullet-to-the-head corpses aren't a pretty sight, the noose corpses aren't a pretty sight, and defenestration corpses aren't a pretty sight either, often it breaks their skull, often their whole brains leak over the pavement, often they break their legs, my father always said, but Lenka's corpse was surely a very pretty sight, dear Herr Kraus, she was surely the most beautiful of all defenestration corpses… I know where we have to go now, I know where we can find her.'

I listened to him and thought, Winterberg is beyond help.

'We should call your daughter.'

'No.'

'Yes.'

'No… we'll go back.'

'To Berlin?'

'No. To the Baltic.'

'To the Baltic. Okay, all right… first Sarajevo. Now the Baltic.'

'That's where we'll find her. I know where, she's there and waiting for me. I have to go. She's waiting.'

'Sure. And all the other dead people will be waiting there too.'

'Yes, precisely… you once told me about that pub, where your father said everyone was waiting for him… this is like that.'

'Okay, well, the trip to Sarajevo was crazy enough. But this here, this is truly unhinged. I'm not going, we're going to call your daughter. Right now.'

'No. Please, don't.'

'Was this whole trip for nothing?'

Winterberg was silent and stared again into the loud void, where he saw and heard what others couldn't see and hear. He again looked at the one-legged pigeon.

'This whole honeymoon trip with Lenka?'

Winterberg was silent.

'This whole crackpot farewell trip?'

Winterberg was silent and shared into the depths of his void, into the depths of his loneliness.

'This funerary trip?'

Winterberg was silent and looked up at the ceiling.

'It was all nonsense?'

'Yes.'

'You're a sick man.'

Winterberg was silent.

'What happened back then?'

Winterberg remained silent.

People came and went.

To the trains.

From the trains.

Just like yesterday.

Just like the day before yesterday.

Just like a hundred years ago.

Just like a hundred years in the future.

And then suddenly Winterberg stood up and ran for the platforms. I ran after him. A train was arriving. Winterberg ran directly in front of the train.

I tackled him to the floor.

People screamed.

Winterberg lay on his back and was breathing hard. Someone wanted to call a doctor, I said, no, no doctor, someone wanted to call the police, and I said, no, no police, he just slipped, no, everything's okay, this is normal, an old man, a little bit crazy.

* * *

It was raining and we walked through the empty Christmas market.

'Are you all right?'

'Yes.'

We walked up to the equestrian statue of King Tomislav.

'There, there it is.'

'Yeah.'

We crossed the ulica Baruna Trenka, which was named after the Baron Franz von der Trenck, who was lying buried as a mummy in the Imperial Crypt in Brünn, as Winterberg said.

'Look out, a car... should I help you?'

'No.'

We entered the café of the hotel *Palace*, where we'd been staying for the last few days.

'What do you want to drink?'

'A tea.'

'Do you want something to eat?'

'No.'

We were the only guests and Winterberg stared for a long time at his cup of tea and at my beer.

And then he said:

'There are seaside resorts in every locale… sharks, though rare, are everywhere to be found, and endanger swimmers even in Trieste.'

'What?'

'Page 378 in my Baedeker.'

'We're not in Trieste…'

'I know.'

'We're not even on the coast. We're in Zagreb. In Agram.'

'I know.'

'We're not going swimming. It's almost Christmas.'

'I know.'

'Are you in any pain?'

'No.'

'Maybe we should go to the hospital, maybe you broke something…'

'No, I haven't…'

'Why did you do that?'

'My grandfather was a hunter and always said that it wasn't good… to kill animals…'

'But if you have to kill an animal, do it quickly.'

'Exactly, that's exactly what he said, Herr Kraus, look at that, you have remembered something.'

'Hm…'

'Sharks… I'm the shark, dear Herr Kraus, I'm the one who murdered Lenka, I betrayed her. I have to go to the Baltic. To Usedom.'

FROM ZAGREB TO BERLIN

We travelled through the night.

The night train to Vienna wasn't full. Winterberg looked out of the window and then pulled it open. He took his Baedeker and threw it out into the darkness.

'My father was right after all, this world doesn't exist anymore, it's all just a fairy-tale… it's all just a lie.'

He wasn't agitated.

He was calm.

And tired.

He closed the window and lay down in bed.

I couldn't sleep. I stood out in the corridor and looked out of the window. Only individual lights were visible. A bridge. A street crossing. Smaller and larger train stations with dispatchers who stood in the door and smoked. And then I saw myself reflected in the window.

I bought a beer from the night conductor and went back into our compartment to grab the book that Winterberg had given me. Winterberg was sleeping. I closed the door, sat down on the floor of the corridor, and began to read.

Chronological Notes on the History of Winterberg and its Surroundings 1195–1926, written by Josef Puhani, the Forester of Schwarzenberg.

I read about the year 1195 and the construction of Winterberg Castle by the Bavarian Count Albrecht III of Bogen. I read that Winterberg was also briefly known as 'Windberg'. I read about the Golden Path. I read about salt and tropical fruits and wine and fine fabrics which the merchants from Bavaria brought to Bohemia. I read about hops and lard and butter and wax and fish and glass and beer and brandy and silver that the merchants brought from Bohemia to Bavaria. I read about the many raids. About the Hussite Wars and the Destruction of Prachatitz. About the many fires. I read about April 24, 1479, when Winterberg received city status from the King.

We travelled through the night and could only see the night.

I drank my beer and read about the first glassworks. About the founding of the brewery. About Catholic Winterberg and about Protestant Winterberg and again about Catholic Winterberg. I read about the German population and about the Czech population. I read about the Thirty Years' War. About Wallenstein. About the construction of the palace. About the Great Fire of 1665 and the impoverishment and emigration. I read about forests and moors and bears. About hunts and hunting accidents and poaching and marksmen from Bohemia and Bavaria. About the last lynx to be shot. I read about gold. About the new trading routes. I read about the discovery of chalk glass by Michael Müller and the rapid boom of the glass industry. I read about the businessmen from Prague and Vienna and Hamburg and Danzig and Moscow and India who travelled to Winterberg because of its glass.

The train stopped and we were in Ljubljana.

In Laibach, as Winterberg would say.

I peered back into the compartment.

He was asleep.

We travelled through the night and I drank the next beer and read about the year 1694, when someone first planted potatoes in Winterberg and initially just used them to feed cattle. I read about the churches and chapels. About brawls and murders and accidents in the forest. About the soldiers who marched through Winterberg in 1801 and 1804 and 1805 and 1806. I read about how the soldiers plundered the forests. I read about how severely the game stock suffered as a result. I read about the founding of the Territorial Army as a complement to the line troops. I read about Napoleon's campaign against Austria in 1809 and about the mobilisation. I read about the construction of the Passau Causeway. I read about the new Eleonora glass factory and about the world-famous crystal glass.

And then I saw it. I saw claws and tongues and contorted faces. They were bright and red and yellow. They were flames. On a small hill I saw a burning house. The flames were high and they were creeping ever higher, they were reaching for the sky, they wanted to get higher, they were reaching for the stars and the comets, they licked at them and wanted to grow ever higher, they wanted to set the entire universe aflame.

Set it aflame and burn it.

And us with it.

I felt the heat of the flames. I was sweating.

We travelled through the night and I saw no people, no firefighters, I only saw the old, burning house on a small hill in the snow.

Somewhere in Slovenia.

Somewhere in Austria.

Somewhere in Europe.

Somewhere in the night.

I drank my beer and stared for a long time out into the dark night and still saw the tongues and claws and contorted faces.

Then I read on. I read about the new Nepomuk altar. About the death of the glass factory owner Johann Mayr by a stroke while dancing at a ball. About the first pharmacy in 1817. I read about failed crops and hunger and oat bread and diseases and emigration to Poland. I read about the new glassworks. I read about tonewood and the first soundboard factory in the Bohemian Forest by Franz Wienert, who later became known as "the Old Man of the Bohemian Forest". I read about the last wildcats, who were killed in 1827. I read about the winter of 1840, which arrived so early that the people had to shovel snow to harvest the potatoes in September.

The train travelled through the night and I fetched another beer.

I read about the revolutionary year of 1848 and the founding of the national guard. I read about the disappearance of big game and the last deer, which was shot in 1848. I read about the year 1856 and the prince's order to implement Saxon forestry methods in the dominion of Winterberg. I read about the start of systematic forest management in the Bohemian Forest. I read about storms and hail and fires and frights and fears and confusion and death.

The train stopped in Villach and remained at the platform.

It was snowing.

The platform was empty.

No one got off and no one got on.

And then the conductor whistled again and we travelled onwards into the night.

I read about the war in 1866. About the defeat at Königgrätz. About the demise of the Austrian Northern Army. About the fear of the Prussians among the population. I read about the Saxon soldiers in Winterberg fleeing to Linz. I read about the corpse of Nepomuk, which made a secret stop at the inn *Zum Goldenen Stern* on its clandestine journey from Prague to Salzburg. I read about the high beer prices and lard prices and wheat prices. About the new streets and woodlands and foresters and timber and firewood. I read about the flood on May 30, 1868. About typhus and the typhus deaths. About the Holy Innocents. About the princely deer hunts. I read about June 1, 1869, when the gunpowder factory exploded. I read about how the entire workshop including eight workers was blown to pieces, how the blast could be heard up to four or five kilometres away, and how the shredded corpses were buried at a solemn funeral. I read about the primeval forest. I read about Franz Fuchs, who was stabbed at a dance on Easter Monday by a certain Spitzenberger, a dreaded ruffian.

The train stopped again. Klagenfurt. It remained at the platform for some time. The conductor said it had to wait here, otherwise we'd arrive too early in Vienna.

We travelled onwards into the night and I read about September 6, 1870, when the 500th birthday celebration of the magister Jan Hus was held in Husinec, at which about 30,000 people were in attendance, including scholars and academics from England and Russia and Prussia and Serbia and Poland and even one from North America. I read a lot about Prince Schwarzenberg. I read about the founding of the printing house by Johann Steinbrenner in 1870. I read about the earthquake and a dreadful crack, which, however, caused no damage. I read about the great cold in winter. About the heavy snows. About the people who froze to death. About the beautiful auroras on February 4, 1872. I read about the last wolf, which was killed in 1874. I read about the flooding and about even more snow and about a comet in the sky. I read about the six deaths after an arsenic poisoning. I read about the new boys' school. I read about the opening of the local train line from Winterberg to Strakonitz on October 14, 1893. I read about a terrible deluge. I read about the opening of the new, modern slaughterhouse. I read about the construction of the local train line from Winterberg to Wallern in 1899. I read about the establishment of the first telephone lines from Winterberg Castle to the police station in the Bohemian Forest. I read about the year 1900 and the first car in Winterberg, which was the personal automobile of the glass factory owner Albert Kralik. I read about the catastrophic fire of July 27, 1904, which took five human lives and reduced 48 houses and the entire Ringplatz to a heap of rubble in just two hours. I read about the firefighters and the hoses and the extraordinary performance of Winterberg's steam fire engine, which pumped and pumped and pumped without stopping for 38 hours, and yet the fire engine still couldn't save Winterberg. I read about death and despair and destitution and donations.

The train came to a stop somewhere, it was snowing more and more heavily and I wasn't tired and kept drinking beer.

I read about the visit of Kaiser Franz Joseph I, who was attending a major military manoeuvre in the area, on September 8, 1905. I read that the ruler arrived with the train and then left with the train after a couple of hours. I read about the Winterberg sculptor and woodcrafter Franz Igler, who spent weeks alone in the forest doing reconnaissance on the deer, and then carved a piece of this secret knowledge in true-to-life renditions. I read that one of the most beautiful fruits of these studies is the 'Belling Stag in Rut'. I read that Kaiser Franz Joseph I bought some of his carvings. I read that Igler couldn't find proper support in Winterberg and struggled with poverty and resettled in Vienna in 1910. I read about Johann Steinbrenner, the founder of the world-famous calendar and devotional press, who died on May 6, 1909. I read about the catastrophic weather of May 18, 1911. About thunder and downpour and masses of water and bridges that were washed away. I read about the electric power plant Elektra in 1913. About the cinema of Felix Pohl in 1914. I read about June 28, 1914, when the Austrian Archduke and his wife were murdered in Sarajevo as the result of a great Serbian conspiracy. I read about the dreadful World War that arose afterwards. I read about the mobilisation and the dutiful and courageous and dependable soldiers of the Bohemian Forest in the 91st Regiment. I read about the horrible battles in Serbia and the appalling deprivation and the many hardships and the tremendous losses. I read about the Carpathians and Galicia and Italy. I read about how the regiment was eventually sent to Bulgaria, but then the revolution and the collapse came. I read about musters and enlistments and Russian prisoner of war camps and Siberia. About the wounded soldiers in Winterberg Castle. About bread rations and war bonds and refugees and the introduction of daylight savings time on May 1, 1916. I read about the confiscation of four bells for military purposes. About the rage and devastation of massive battles. About the dead and missing and captured and wounded and disabled and crippled. I read about the confiscation of the funeral bell from the Winterberg city tower for military purposes in 1917. I read about misery and sorrow and tears and grumbling and complaining and inflation and shortages and hunger and diseases and epidemics and suffering and hardship and death and the moral breakdown of the youth, which the people, and particularly the people of the Bohemian Forest, were forced to endure. I read about the overthrow and collapse of the 600-year-old Habsburg Empire, which crumbled into small states.

We travelled through the night and it was snowing and a man came out of another compartment and looked out for a moment into the darkness. And then went back to bed. And for a moment I didn't know where we were or where we were headed.

I read about October 28, 1918, and the establishment of the Republic of Czechoslovakia with the President T. G. Masaryk at its head. I read about how there was complete confusion in Winterberg after the over-throw and collapse, how for some time no one knew to whom the city belonged, whether to the Czechoslovak Republic or to Austria or to Germany. I read about how people found this situation very unset-tling, how uncertainty and looting spread, how finally a local guard of ten decommissioned soldiers was established. I read about how, on November 23, a battalion of Czechoslovak troops swiftly moved in to occupy the city.

We travelled onwards and onwards through the night. I could hear when the train was swallowed by a tunnel and spit out the other side. I could hear the loud, iron rattling when the train crossed over a bridge.

I read about how the Czech National Church was founded in 1929. I read about the census in Czechoslovakia. About the 8,760,957 Czechs and Slovaks and the 3,129,448 Germans and the 747,096 Magyars and the 461,466 Ruthenians and the 75,852 Poles and the 180,535 Jews and the 23,052 of other nationalities and about the 232,943 foreigners. I read that there were 15,686 Germans and 11,786 Czechs and 58 Jews and 212 foreigners living in the judicial district of Winterberg. I read about the last soldiers of the World War who returned to Winterberg from Russian captivity with the train on June 2. I read about the black arch moths which suddenly appeared in the surrounding forests in massive swarms on July 27.

We travelled through the night and the train came out of the next tunnel and in the snow I saw the illuminated monument to Carl Ritter von Ghega at the Semmering train station.

I read about the death of the fully blinded glass factory official Julius Blechinger, who had been a jovial poet and a capable musician of the Bohemian Forest and paid homage to local pride and the green forest in his work. I read his poem "Peaceful Wood".

I read about the dissolution of the rifle club due to the adverse political conditions and the construction of the military barracks behind the train station. I read about the dedication of the four new bells. I read about April 1, 1924, when the land registry cancelled Prince Schwarzenberg's dominion over Winterberg. I read about the dedication of the new funeral bell. I read about the association "Winterberg in Vienna". I read about the opening of the newly constructed Israelite temple on January 3, 1926, and the fire in the city ice chamber on the same day. I read about the storm winds and a great deluge. I read about October 28, 1926, the eighth birthday of the Republic, when a red-and-white flag fluttered at the top of the 36-metre-high city tower that morning. I read about the assistant saddler Eduard Lepschi, who climbed up along the lightning arrester cable for the fourth time at midnight. I read about how he fell while climbing down and died the same day. He wanted to be famous.

We travelled through the night and I read about the history of Winterberg, which had also been called Windberg and was now called Vimperk. I read about the city that I so hated and had to leave. I read about Winterberg and thought about my father, my mother, and my little sister.

We travelled through the night and I felt how I was becoming one with the city.

With the whole history.

Page by page.

Year by year.

Note by note.

Story by story.

Event by event.

I felt how I was becoming this book.

How I was becoming Winterberg.

And then we were in Vienna. And out of the night, the new day had started. A dreary day.

We travelled onwards to Prague. It was snowing and the train was late and I slept the entire time and Winterberg looked out of the window and didn't say a word. And when I wasn't sleeping, I saw again in front of me the old man in bed, who was simply lying there and waiting for someone to take him to the other side. I saw the old man with the grey face. I saw Winterberg as my sailor on the crossing again.

We travelled from Prague to Dresden and then to Berlin and the snow was coming down harder and the train was overfilled and the people were wishing each other Merry Christmas and a Happy New Year.

In Berlin we took a taxi to Winterberg's flat.

I went out to get us something to eat, and when I returned, I noticed that Winterberg had taken down all the old Austrian maps and pictures and city maps and battle maps from the walls. They were standing out in the hall and Winterberg was sitting in the kitchen and handed me an envelope.

'This is the money for Sarajevo… you don't have to come along tomorrow… but I must, yes, yes, I must do it.'

'I'm coming.'

'You really don't need to; I can manage alone.'

'Yes, I'm coming, that's my Christmas gift.'

'I don't like Christmas.'

'Me neither.'

'This Christmas cheer always made me want to vomit.'

Winterberg gave a small smile and looked at a picture. A small, old black-and-white photo that he had never shown me before.

It was a photo of Lenka. Lenka Morgenstern.

A young woman with long, dark hair, a long, narrow face and dark eyes. Lenka was smiling in the picture, and outside it started to snow.

'She had such beautiful eyes, yes, yes, and I also loved her hair, her breasts, her legs… but what I loved the most was the bay leaf, yes, yes, the birthmark between her shoulderblades. I loved to kiss her there, and Lenka loved it when I kissed her there, too.'

The radio was reporting about war and displacement and murder and crisis and fear and despair. And about a severe snowstorm that was sweeping across the country.

Winterberg drank his tea and listened.

'My father said that death always came to Reichenberg with bad weather, yes, yes, with a sudden shift in the weather… so he always read the weather reports, yes, yes, he even wrote about the weather often for *Die Einäscherung*, he said a funerary director in Reichenberg had to be a good observer of the weather, a funerary director and also a gynaecologist, because everything is connected to the weather in Reichenberg, yes, yes, when there's good weather people are born in Reichenberg, when there's bad weather people die, as he always said… in the summer his Feuerhalle was always less busy than in November or December, yes, yes, precisely, when the fog lays over the city like a thick blanket, yes, yes, Reichenberg can be buried in fog for entire days, for entire weeks, no, for entire months… and so my father called the November corpses and the December corpses the fog corpses.'

Winterberg drank his tea, looked out of the window at the flurry of snow, and told me about the summer corpses.

About the autumn corpses.

About the winter corpses.

About the spring corpses.

'Most people in Reichenberg died in February and March, yes, yes, it was cold, but the ovens of the Feuerhalle never got cold on cold days, yes, yes, in those months the ovens were always glowing, and because they were glowing for so long, it turned to spring, as my father told me when I was still a small boy… in summer it was quiet, but when a sudden shift in the weather was predicted, my father knew it was about to get busy, yes, yes, in the cold room of his Feuerhalle he had space for thirty-five corpses, and on days with bad weather, there was often no room left, yes, yes…'

Winterberg told me about the January corpses. About the February corpses. About the March corpses. About the April corpses. About the May corpses. About the June corpses. About the July corpses. About the August corpses. About the September corpses. About the October corpses. About the November corpses. And then he went on to tell me about the December corpses.

'A cremation lasts about one and a half hours, yes, yes, at just under a thousand degrees, it shouldn't be hotter, yes, yes, the bones should be lovely and white, said my father, yes, yes, the bones should be as lovely and white as the snow out there, dear Herr Kraus, because only then do they crumble to a fine dust, only then can the soul break free, yes, yes, like an eagle taking flight and soaring away.'

Winterberg looked out at the snow and drank his tea.

'My corpse will probably take a bit less time than that, your corpse, dear Herr Kraus, probably a bit more, yes, yes, it would also depend on which of the two ovens we end up in, my father said that Oven Number 1 cremated the corpses a few minutes faster than Oven Number 2, Oven Number 1 was also always a few degrees hotter, regardless of whether you heated with coal or later with gas, no one knew why, not my father, not Rudolf Bitzan, not the stoker Ponocný, it was always a mystery… yes, yes, you'd probably take a few minutes longer, because you love your beer so much, dear Herr Kraus, beer corpses always take a bit longer, said my father, due to the fat, due to the mass, he said… but never fear, dear Herr Kraus, you too will be reconciled with your fate by the fire of the Feuerhalle after an hour and a half, if you don't manage to reconcile with your fate on your own before then, yes, yes, and then every corpse, even the plumpest beer corpses, fits in a three-litre urn… don't worry, dear Herr Kraus, it's not yet your turn, you still have a bit of time, you're not a December corpse… and tomorrow, tomorrow you really don't need to come.'

'I told you, I'm coming.'

'Thank you, Herr Kraus… shouldn't we really be on a first-name basis?'

'I'm Jan.'

'Wenzel… Wenzel Winterberg… after Saint Wenceslas of Bohemia, after our Bohemian patron saint, who brings and binds us together just as much as the water corpse of Nepomuk or dumplings or beer or the Moldau, regardless whether we speak Czech or German, yes, yes, dear Herr Kraus, my father saw through history, as you can see, Saint Wenceslas tried to reconcile the Bohemians with the Germans and tried not to wage war, just like my father tried to do with his Feuerhalle, with his eagle over Reichenberg, because he loved his homeland just as much as Saint Wenceslas did, Saint Wenceslas was killed by his brother Boleslas on the 28th of September, 929 or 935, just like my father was killed with a beer mug by one of Henlein's goons, yes, yes, by a daft labourer from a cement factory, on the 15th of March, 1939… yes, yes, precisely, Wenceslas was a lovely September corpse and my father was a lovely March corpse… when a fratricide stands at the beginning of a country, the beginning of a state, it can't turn out well, yes, yes, there's no escape, it's not as easily overcome as the Alps or the Bohemian Forest by the railway, it's not Königgrätz but this fratricide that is the true beginning of all our catastrophes, yes, yes, dear Herr Kraus. No, no, I've long since lost my fear of death, you can overcome the fear of death as well as death itself, yes, yes, the death is the largest range of all to overcome, the most important breakthrough, I'm already looking forward to the journey afterwards, I only hope that I'm not sharing a compartment with a bunch of fools who don't see through history.'

It was snowing and the radio was playing music. And Winterberg said, listen to that, the prelude to Richard Wagner's *Parsifal*.

'My father wanted me to be called Wenzel Winterberg so that when I wrote my initials, WW, the letters would look like the mountains that surround Reichenberg, yes, yes, that protect the city, just like the mountains protect the entire Bohemian valley, just like the two guardians of death protect his Feuerhalle… and in the middle, between the WW, is the most beautiful mountain that towers above the rest… no, it's not the Jeschken, as many would think, it's the Monstranzberg with its Feuerhalle. So I always know where I come from, my father said. And where I need to go… WW.'

FROM BERLIN TO PEENEMÜNDE

In the morning, it was snowing even more heavily.

The winter storm was forcing its way over Central Europe.

Over us.

Over me and Winterberg.

We bought train tickets to Peenemünde. We left the station and it was snowing and the train was late, just like all the trains on this day were late. Winterberg looked out of the window at the snowy countryside. He was silent for a long time, and only began to ramble somewhere around Prenzlau.

'It's not the Battle of Königgrätz that runs through my heart, not the assassination in Sarajevo, not Austerlitz, not all the other battles… those aren't my grave, dear Jan. My grave lies on the island of Usedom. And her grave, too… I promised her I would follow her… to Brünn and to Vienna and to Budapest and to Sarajevo and then beyond, but I didn't do it, I was too cowardly… I betrayed Lenka, dear Jan, I killed her, I'm the murderer I'm looking for, I distanced myself from her… yes, yes, I was relieved that she was gone, dear Jan, she was a burden to me, they laughed at me because of her, my friends, and even my mother, you just can't go out with a woman like that, you know what I mean, a Jew, it's not good, it's not right, I don't like it, I won't have a woman like that in my house, I don't want to be ashamed of you, what will people say? Yes, yes, that's how it was back then in Reichenberg… when Hitler arrived in the market square, the entire square was packed, I was there too, everyone cheered, Hitler left and then all hell broke loose, yes, yes, they chased the Czechs through the streets, they chased the Jews through the streets, they chased the communists through the streets, they chased the social democrats through the streets, they chased all the traitors through the streets, and my mother was right there with them, yes, yes… that night, Lenka's father hanged himself in his shop, yes, yes, that's how it was back then in the wonderful city of Reichenberg, it makes me want to vomit… I kept meaning to ask you, Jan… Kraus, Kraus is also a Jewish name, isn't it?'

'I have no idea.'

'Yes, I think so… I went to school with a Kraus… unfortunately he didn't manage to flee.'

'I've never thought about it. I don't have anyone to ask anymore, so… it doesn't matter to me, anyway.'

'Yes, that's true… it doesn't matter, of course… Lenka didn't know for a long time… until one day in school, two Henlein goons came up to her and said to her, hey, Lenka, tell us, you're not a real German, did you know that? You can't be here with us… piss off, you whore… she was maybe thirteen… yes, yes, that's how it was back then in Reichenberg… and I, a fool, was one of them, I know, it's all mad…'

'But that's all over now, that was ages ago.'

'Quite, quite… it's not over… it's like it was yesterday.'

The snow storm was getting stronger. We could now see the clouds of white through which our train was racing.

'I betrayed Lenka, yes, yes, I was even relieved when she left… I promised her that I would follow her, but I already knew then, at the train station in Reichenberg, in the underpass, that I wasn't going to follow her, and then I loved her and missed her all the more, yes, yes, all my wives resemble Lenka, all of them… and yet they weren't Lenka… too late, too late, I know what you're going to say, it's all mad, I'm mad, I know… thank you for coming.'

'But why are we going to Usedom?'

'Yes… why… that's where I saw her for the last time.'

'It's really not easy to understand.'

'You'll understand soon.'

We changed trains in Züssow amid the snow and the wind. The station was empty and so was the railcar to Usedom. Winterberg sat facing opposite the direction of travel and looked out of the window, but there was almost nothing to see, and then he looked down at his hands and then looked around the train. He kept looking around as if someone else were here travelling with us.

Following him.

Haunting him.

'Madness. It's all mad … it's all so far away. And yet it's all there.'

Then he looked again out of the window at the snow and storm, and I knew that our journey wasn't just going to be his, but also my personal Königgrätz.

He's mad.

I'm mad.

Mentally deranged.

He's going to land in the mental ward.

I'm going to land in the mental ward.

Or in prison.

And yet I was going with him.

Winterberg was the first and only sailor I'd ever brought back from the crossing. And I knew that now I would be punished for it, it's just not supposed to work like that. Our ships, like the trains, have a certain departure schedule. They take the sailors in only one direction. They always return empty, with a tired captain at the helm. With a captain who needs a drink. It was clear to me that I would be punished for capsizing our ship.

I looked over at Winterberg, who had fallen asleep. Outside I saw an old, grey house with a tattered German flag and a new-looking Imperial flag on a mast and with a couple of horses that stood on the field and watched the train go by. And I looked again at the old, small, fragile man with the thick horn-rimmed glasses that he was constantly cleaning, because perhaps he believed it would help him not just to see better in the distance, but also to see better through history. I looked at the old, tired, small man, who was as old as the Republic of Czechoslovakia. Like the Feuerhalle in Reichenberg.

I looked at Winterberg and thought about how often I'd considered leaving him somewhere.

With his Baedeker. With his magnifying glass. With his glasses. With his winter coat. With his history. With *Cornus sanguinea*. With his pistol. With his rope. With his historical fits. With all his madness. With Lenka. With all his dead wives. With the Englishman. With his *"beautiful land-scape of battlefields, cemeteries and ruins"*. With all the water corpses and noose corpses and defenestration corpses. With his Feuerhalles. With his Central Cemeteries. With his railways. With his train stations. With his tracks through the Alps. With his war. With his fog. With his battles. With his Königgrätz.

I should have done it, but I didn't.

. . .

The train stopped in Wolgast and waited for the railcar approaching from the opposite direction. It was snowing harder and harder, and I could see less and less.

Winterberg pointed at his ticket.

Peenemünde.

'We're almost there… I was here in the war as a soldier, as a locomotive driver actually, suddenly no one cared that my eyes were too weak to be a locomotive driver.'

The train left the station and Winterberg rambled.

'This bridge wasn't here back then, you used to have to travel via Swinemünde. I've never taken this route.'

He told me about the war and about the restricted area and the military's experimental research institute and the new secret weapons. He told me about the rockets that flew high over the island. About the rockets that exploded. He told me about the combustion chamber of the rocket motor, which they called the core, and which reminded him of the two ovens in the Reichenberg Feuerhalle, which Ponocný called the two cores. He told me about the officers and scientists and SS men and their wives and their children. He told me about swimming in the sea. He told me about the professor in the white tunic who developed the rockets. He told me about his lovely secretary. He told me how he often sat in the *Schwedenkrug* after his shift. He told me about the heavy Swedish cannonballs embedded in the walls, which had been found in Peenemünde after the Thirty Years' War. He told me how he began to draw and paint out of boredom. He told me how he painted Lenka and thought about the film *The Woman in the Moon* that he'd seen with Lenka in the Kino Urania in Reichenberg. He told me how much Lenka had loved the film. He told me how an officer saw the picture of Lenka one evening and asked him if he could have it. He told me that he was hesitant. He told me that Lenka was half-naked in the picture. He told me he didn't tell anyone who the woman was. He told me how the officer pasted his drawing of Lenka on the side of a test rocket on October 3, 1942. He told me how the Nazi rocket with the Bohemian Jew Lenka from Reichenberg flew into the sky as the first rocket in human history. He told me how the Nazis and the professor cheered and celebrated the entire night in the *Schwedenkrug*. He told me that the rocket with the woman in the moon, who was his Lenka, flew to the moon. He told me he didn't care when the others said that it wasn't true. He told me about the next rockets. He told me that there was blood clinging to the rockets. He told me that many more people died in the development of the rockets than in the strikes. He told me about the Czech forced labourers and the prisoners of war and the prisoners in the concentration camps. He told me about the bombings. He told me about the Englishman, who bombed Peenemünde and turned it into *"the beautiful landscape of battlefields, cemeteries and ruins"*. He told me about fire corpses and bomb corpses. About screaming and chaos and anger and panic and fear. About the many dead prisoners. About the unexploded bombs on the beach. About the graves in the sand. About the lime they had to spread over the corpses. That it looked as though they were sprinkling the bodies with snow. He told me how he was transferred as a locomotive driver. He told me about the trains carrying rockets to Holland. He told me about death in Antwerp. He told me about the end of the war. About the capitulation. About being a prisoner of war. He told me how he had learned English there. He told me how after three years he came to Berlin. He told me about the not very beautiful landscape of battlefields, cemeteries and ruins in the destroyed city. He told me about the empty looks and grey faces. He told me about hardship and despair and suicide. He told me about how he became a tram driver again. He told me about the loneliness of many women who were waiting for their husbands and who slept with him. He told me he thought the entire time about Lenka. He told me how he wanted to forget her. He told me how he forbade himself from thinking about her. He told me how he burned all his drawings of her. He told me how he couldn't forget her. He told me how he knew that he would have to follow her eventually to reconcile himself with his fate. He told me how he became sick with history. With historical fits. He told me how he lost himself in the fog of history.

We changed trains again in Zinnowitz. Winterberg was tired and looked at the snowy train tracks.

'I had to help unload a train here once. With prisoners. Many were dead.'

We continued on and were the only ones who got off the train in Peenemünde.

It was snowing and the locomotive driver was standing with the conductor in the doorway. They were smoking and watching us. The wind was strong and cold and drove the dark, heavy snow clouds above us.

'Are you sure you're not coming back?' asked the conductor.

'Yes, yes,' said Winterberg.

'This is the last train today,' said the locomotive driver.

'But in the schedule, it says…' I began.

'The schedule is the schedule and winter is winter. That's the Polish storm, it's no joke.'

'The Polish what?'

'The Polish storm. Never brings anything good, my mum always said, and she has to know, she was born out there in the east somewhere. So, are you coming or not? This is the last train today. And for tomorrow. You won't be able to leave.'

'Yes, yes,' said Winterberg.

'Maybe we really should go back.'

'All right, then go, I'm staying here.'

'What's wrong with him?' asked the locomotive driver. 'Has he still got all the china in the cupboard?'

'No,' I said.

'Well then, have fun skiing,' said the conductor, climbing back into the train.

The long, slender railcar gave a whistle and disappeared behind the curve.

It was quiet. I could only hear the wind. The Polish wind. And I could only see the snow.

'Someone in Regensburg once said something similar to me, the bad Bohemian wind … everything bad comes out of the east.'

'What?'

'Nothing. Where are we going?'

THE STORM

We walked along the narrow, icy road.

Past the dilapidated barracks.

Past empty houses.

Past black, fallen trees.

We left deep footprints in the snow behind us. Then Winterberg saw a small chapel.

We stood in the cemetery and looked at a snowy, moss-covered monument.

'This is where I became sick with history, yes, yes, it was right here, ever since then I've been so derailed by history.'

He told me how he would always have a half-hour break after arriving with the train in Peenemünde. So he would come here and look at this monument in the cemetery.

'"Fear not, O little flock! Gustav Adolf landed here in midsummer 1630. German admirers of the hero and friends of his people erected this stone in 1930,"' I read.

'This is where it all became clear to me.'

He told me about Gustav Adolf, who landed in Peenemünde in 1630 with a thousand Swedish soldiers. He told me about the Swedish redoubt in Peenemünde. He told me how the Swedes repeatedly attacked and plundered Reichenberg during the Thirty Years' War. He told me how the Swedes always came from Zittau down the street which was then called Wallensteinstraße and holds the same name to this day, the street in which he would later grow up. He told me how Gustav Adolf met Wallenstein in November 1632 at Lützen. He told me how Gustav Adolf became lost in the November fog, was shot in the arm, and fell from his horse and died. He told me how Wallenstein nearly also died at Lützen when his horse was shot. He told me how the

November corpse of Gustav Adolf was loaded onto a ship in Wolgast. He told me how the ship sailed past Peenemünde and the Swedish redoubt on the slow journey back to Sweden. Past the place where Gustav Adolf had landed two years earlier. He told me that two years later, Wallenstein too was dead. He told me that Peenemünde remained Swedish for almost a hundred years. He told me their neighbour in Reichenberg was called Schwejda, and he believed that one of their ancestors had been a Swede who remained in Bohemia because he'd fallen in love. He told me that Herr Schwejda drank like a Dane, as they say in Bohemia, like a Swede, as they say in Denmark. Like a Finn, as they say in Sweden. Like a Russian, as they say in Finland. He told me that schnapps corpses weren't a pretty sight.

'Yes, yes, there you have it, dear Jan, this is where I became sick with history, this is where I suffered the first historical fit, yes, yes, and then it only got worse... then I began to read books about history, and then it always made me think about my ancestors who had fallen at Königgrätz, yes, yes, Karl Strohbach and Julius Ewald, one from Tangermünde, the other from Ottensheim bei Linz, one grew up on the Elbe, the other on the Danube, both dead on the same foggy day, yes, yes, on the third of July, 1866, yes, yes, two July corpses... and when I learned that fact, I felt how Königgrätz ran through my heart, my heart began to ache, and I suffer from that heartache to this day, yes, yes, the vivisection of a living body, and then I began to dream about Königgrätz. About all the battles, but especially about Königgrätz... and now I know why I was punished like this, yes, yes, it's all because of Lenka.'

It was snowing and the wind was howling and it was difficult to see. We kept walking.

We saw the massive factory building and stood at the gate. The gate was locked.

'Back then there was a lot happening here, yes, yes, the new weapons for the final victory, yes, yes, the weapons of vengeance.'

We walked along the fence and saw that one of the large trees had fallen over the fence, and used it to enter the complex.

And suddenly we saw it.

A black-white rocket in the snow. It protruded into the sky, which was impossible to see, which had melted into the ground.

So lean.

So tall.

So beautiful.

So mute.

'That's her. My Lenka.'

Winterberg walked toward the rocket and wanted to embrace it.

'My Lenka…'

On the casing of the rocket, there really was a drawing. His drawing. The woman in the moon.

In stockings.

In high heels.

Lenka. Lenka Morgenstern from Reichenberg.

'This is a museum. It's only a copy.'

'That's not a copy, that's her, my Lenka… Lenka… Lenka… I've found you…'

He dropped his bag and ran off. I grabbed it and ran after him. But the storm was growing stronger and the snow heavier and thicker, and soon I couldn't see anything anymore. Just a high white wall all around me.

Winterberg was gone.

It was snowing.

The wind howled and blew through the trees.

The entire forest was howling and moaning.

The entire island.

And my head was also howling.

I searched for him.

But he was gone.

I shouted for him.

But he was gone.

I looked around.

But he was gone.

I didn't see him.

I could only see snow.

I was sweating and my heart was racing and soon I wouldn't be able to go on in the snowstorm.

I stopped moving.

And suddenly I heard something. It was a massive boom. And then I saw a bright light that rose slowly to the sky. I looked up at the light, shining through the thick flurry of snow.

Then it was still and white.

'Winterberg!'

I looked for him.

I thought, he has to be around here somewhere. I stumbled in the snow, fell over and stood back up and fell again and kept walking and screaming his name, which was swallowed up by the storm. I screamed until I couldn't scream anymore.

I came out of the forest and was standing on a massive surface of concrete. It was snowing and snowing.

I opened his bag and took out the pistol.

I pulled back the safety, cocked the gun and shot into the air.

'Wenzel!'

I shot again into the air.

'Winterberg!'

All I heard was the storm.

'Winterberg! Wenzel!'

It was snowing and I was cold.

'Winterberg!'

And then I saw a shadow through the snowstorm.

Winterberg heard me after all. I thought, he's coming back.

I called out for him. 'Wenzel! Here, here! Wait there… I'm coming!'

I ran to him.

But the snow was high and I stumbled and fell and stood up again and kept running towards him.

'Wenzel!'

It wasn't Winterberg.

It was a deer that came to me out of the snow.

A white deer in white snow in a white storm.

The small deer took a few steps towards me, stopped, sniffed in the cold wind, then came closer. I reached out my hand and the deer sniffed again. And suddenly I saw another deer, and then another, and another.

All around me were deer, a whole herd of deer, who were just as lost in the snowstorm as I was.

The storm raged around us and I looked at the deer and the deer looked at me. The snow was falling thicker and thicker and the wind was getting stronger and stronger and blew the snow into our eyes and I thought about the deer that we'd seen so often.

The deer in the Svíb Forest.

The deer in the Vienna Central Cemetery.

The dead deer between the tracks somewhere halfway between České Budějovice and Linz.

And then the deer disappeared.

I lit a cigarette and then saw nothing more.

Just a white emptiness.

A white loneliness.

BERLIN

We were sitting in the kitchen.

In the courtyard it was grey and black.

After the storm, it warmed up quickly.

The snow melted away within a few days.

The days are warm now.

Much too warm for the end of December.

I tell her our story.

She listens to me.

Looks at me.

She doesn't say a word.

I hold her hand.

And then I don't say another word either.

We sit in silence.

I open up a bottle of beer for us.

I pour the beer in a glass.

I'm thirsty. Craving it.

I do it too quickly.

The foam spills over the rim of the glass onto the table.

'You can stay here.'

'Thank you, but I can't.'

'Why not?'

'I have to go.'

'Where?'

'To Königgrätz, to the battlefields… to Chlum.'

'But why?'

'I have to settle some business there. Meet someone.'

I see how the foam slowly but relentlessly spills over like an avalanche in the mountains that can't be held back.

And suddenly I see in the foam the battlefield of Königgrätz.

I see an avalanche of soldiers that also can't be held back.

I see the pale face of Winterberg, his deep-set green eyes behind his thick, brown horn-rimmed glasses, his thin lips, his small round head.

I see Winterberg dancing from grave to grave through the Svíb Forest.

Through the central cemetery in Vienna.

Through the battlefield of Austerlitz.

Through his life.

Through *"the beautiful landscape of battlefields, cemeteries and ruins"*.

I see him sitting in an empty train to Sarajevo.

And I know that this time he'll make it.

He's not sitting there alone.

He's sitting there with Lenka.

Lenka Morgenstern.

It slowly starts to get dark.

. . .

The foam from the beer spreads further over the table, and I see how new bubbles are constantly being born.

How they grow.

How they touch one another.

How they explode.

How they sink.

And how they are reborn.

INDEX OF PLACE NAMES

TRANSLATOR'S NOTES

In *Winterberg's Last Journey*, Kraus and Winterberg travel through and discuss many different places in Central Europe which are, by their very nature, located at the intersection of multiple cultures, languages, and histories. As a result, many of these locations are known under multiple different names depending on the language (German or Czech) and era. The characters use these names differently in ways that reflect their way of thinking, the context of their conversation, or the historical era to which they are referring. The following tables provide a reference for the various names that refer to locations in the book.

CZECH REPUBLIC

Much of *Winterberg's Last Journey* takes place in the Czech Republic and especially in the region of Bohemia, where both of the main characters grew up, albeit during very different periods of the country's history. Winterberg, an ethnic German, was born in northern Bohemia during its last days as a province of the Austro-Hungarian Empire and grew up in the Sudetenland region of interwar Czechoslovakia; accordingly, when Winterberg refers to locations in the Czech Republic, he usually (although not always) uses the historical German place names that he would have grown up with. In contrast, Kraus, an ethnic Czech who grew up in southern Bohemia during the post-war communist era, is more inclined to use the contemporary Czech names for the same places, although he often makes use of the German names as well, especially in conversation with Winterberg. The characters' individual use of these terms has been mostly preserved in the English translation; the table below lists place names referred to in the text in both languages, sorted by the German name. A separate table is included underneath for specific locations within the city of Liberec.

German	Czech
Alt-Paka	Stará Paka
Aussig	Ústi nad Labem
Austerlitz (battlefield)	Slavkov u Brna
Bechin	Bechyně
Beneschau	Benešov
Bistritz (river)	Bystřička
Bodenbach	Podmokly (now: part of Děčín)
Böhmerwald ('Bohemian Forest')	Šumava
Böhmisch Leipa ('Bohemian Leipa')	Česká Lípa
Brünn	Brno
Budweis	České Budějovice
Brüx	Most
Datschitz	Dačice
Eger (city)	Cheb
Eger (river)	Ohře
Eisenbrod	Železný Brod
Elbe (river)	Labe
Franzensbad	Františkovy Lázně
Friedland	Frýdlant
Gablonz an der Neiße	Jablonec nad Nisou
Glatzergebirge ('Glatzer Mountains')	Králický Sněžník
Grottau	Hrádek nad Nisou
Grünthal	Zelený Důl (now: part of Brandov)
Hermanitz	Heřmanice nad Labem
Iser (river)	Jizera (Polish: 'Izera')
Isergebirge ('Iser/Jizera Mountains')	Jizerské hory
Isertal	Údolí Jizery ('Jizera Valley')
Josephstadt	Josefov Fortress (in Jaroměř)
Jitschin (also 'Gitschin')	Jičín
Jungbunzlau (also 'Jung-Bunzlau')	Mladá Boleslav
Kaiserburg	Chebský hrad ('Cheb Castle')
Karlsbad (also 'Carlsbad')	Karlovy Vary
Karlstein (castle)	Karlštejn
Kladen	Kladno
Kleinskal	Malá Skála

German	Czech
Kolin	Kolín
Komotau	Chomutov
Konopischt (castle)	Konopiště
Königgrätz	Hradec Králové
Königinhof an der Elbe	Dvůr Králové nad Labem
Kubohütten	Kubova Huť
Leitmeritz	Litoměřice
Liebenau	Hodkovice nad Mohelkou
Lischnei	Líšný
Lobositz	Lovosice
Lomnitz an der Popelka	Lomnice nad Popelkou
Lundenburg	Břeclav
Marienbad	Mariánské Lázně
Mies (city)	Stříbro
Mies (river)	Mže
Moldau (river)	Vltava
Münchengrätz	Mnichovo Hradiště
Neiße (river; also 'Neisse')	Nisa
Nikolsburg	Mikulov
Nimburg	Nymburk
Oderberg	Bohumín
Olmütz	Olomouc
Ostrau	Ostrava
Pardubitz	Pardubice
Podiebrad	Poděbrady
Pollauer Berge (low mountain range)	Pavlovské vrchy
Prachatitz	Prachatice
Prag (Prague)	Praha
Pilsen	Plzeň
Radbusa (river)	Radbuza
Reichenau bei Gablonz	Rychnov u Jablonce
Reichenberg	Liberec
Riesengebirge ('Giant Mountains')	Krkonoše
Saaz	Žatec
Sadowa	Sadová

German	Czech
Sankt (St.) Joachimsthal	Jáchymov
Semil	Semily
Schwarzawa (river)	Svratka
Schwarzenberg	Černá Hora
Skalitz	Skalice
Sobotka	Sobotka
Spielberg (hill and castle in Brno)	Špilberk
Strakonitz	Strakonice
Stresetitz	Střezetice
Tabor	Tábor
Tannwald	Tanvald
Tetschen	Děčín
Theresienstadt	Terezín
Trautenau	Trutnov
Turnau	Turnov
Walditz	Valdice
Wallern	Volary
Winterberg	Vimperk
Woleschka Valley	Oleška Valley
Wolinka	Volyňka
Zwittawa (river)	Svitava

LOCATIONS IN THE CITY OF LIBEREC (REICHENBERG)

The city of Liberec (or as Winterberg calls it: Reichenberg) in northern Bohemia plays an outsize role in *Winterberg's Last Journey*. It's the city where Winterberg was born, where he met his first love Lenka Morgenstern, and where he saw her for the last time; it's also the city where Winterberg's father operated the infamous *Feuerhalle*. Modern-day Liberec is the first stop on Winterberg's eponymous 'Last Journey', and the pre-war Reichenberg serves as a point of orientation for Winterberg throughout the text, being the focal point of his personal history and the place that he constantly returns to in his mind.

Despite the war and near-complete shift in population after 1945, the characters' experiences in the first five chapters of the book illustrate the enormous historical continuity present in modern-day Liberec. Winterberg's childhood home is still standing; the characters stay in the same hotel where

Winterberg's parents held their wedding reception; they crash a funeral party in the same *Ratskeller* restaurant where Winterberg's father was killed. In fact, every one of the landmarks that Winterberg reads out from his 1913 Baedeker is still standing today, albeit under a new name (often a direct translation of the former German name); even many of the noted hotels, restaurants, cafes and museums remain in service exactly as Winterberg describes them. The following table lists the German-language locations of Reichenberg mentioned by Winterberg along with their present Czech equivalents.

German	Czech
Altstädter Platz (main square)	Náměstí Dr. E. Beneše
Bahnhofstraße	1. máje
Berghotel (hotel)	Hotel Ještěd
Bismarkplatz (also 'Neustädter Platz'; public square)	Sokolske náměstí
Breite Straße (also 'Breite Gasse')	Široká
Cafe Post (cafe)	Kavárna Pošta
Feuerhalle	Krematorium
Gebirgsstraße (also 'Gablonzer Straße')	Jablonecká
Goldener Löwe ('Golden Lion'; hotel)	Zlatý Lev
Gutenbergstraße	Gutenbergova
Harzdorfer Talsperre ('Harzdorf Reservoir')	Vodní nádrž Harcov
Heimatstal (restaurant, tram station)	Hospoda domov
Hohenhabsburg (also 'Liebiegwarte'; viewpoint)	Liberecká výšina
Hotel Schienhof (hotel)	Hotel Praha
Jeschken (mountain)	Ještěd
Kaiser-Joseph-Park (also 'Stadtpark' or 'Volksgarten'; public park)	Lidové sady
Kaiser-Joseph-Straße (also 'Bayer-straße'; street)	Masarykova
Kreuzkirche ('Church of the Holy Cross')	Kostel Nalezení svatého Kříže
Monstranzberg (hill)	Monstranční vrch
Mozartstraße	Mozartova
Nordböhmisches Gewerbemuseum ('North Bohemia Museum of Industry')	Severočeské muzeum

German	Czech
Prager Straße (also 'Schücker Straße')	Pražská
Rathaus ('City Hall')	Liberecká radnice
Ratskeller (also 'Rathauskeller'; tavern)	Radniční sklípek
Röchlitz (neighbourhood)	Rochlice
Rosenthal (neighbourhood)	Růžodol
Schützenstraße	5. května
Stadttheater ('City Theatre')	Divadlo Františka Xavera Šaldy
Tuchplatz (public square)	Soukenné náměstí
Wallensteinstraße	Valdštejnská
Wiener Straße	Moskevská
Zentralhotel (hotel)	Městské info centrum (Tourist Info Centre)

OTHER LOCATIONS IN CENTRAL EUROPE

As a character obsessed with history, Winterberg occasionally uses the historical Austro-Hungarian German names for other locations in Central Europe, even though many of these names have fallen almost entirely out of use among contemporary German speakers. Some of these historical names (such as Agram for Zagreb) are out of date to the point that they are unrecognisable for the majority of modern (especially younger or non-Austrian) German readers, who would struggle to identify the places they refer to. Winterberg's anachronistic use of these names has generally been preserved in the English translation; the table below lists their modern equivalents.

German	Modern Name
Abbazia *(Italian)*	Opatija, Croatia
Agram	Zagreb, Croatia
Blumenau	Lamač, Slovakia
Bozen	Bolzano, Italy (South Tyrol)
Castua *(Italian)*	Kastav, Croatia
Danzig	Gdańsk, Poland
Dubitza	Kozarska Dubica, Bosnia and Herzegovina
Fiume *(Italian/Hungarian)*	Rijeka, Croatia
Gran	Esztergom, Hungary

German	Modern Name
Hermannstadt	Sibiu, Romania
Hohe Feste	Visegrád, Hungary
Kaschau	Košice, Slovakia
Klausenburg	Cluj-Napoca, Romania
Konstanza	Constanţa, Romania
Königsberg	Kaliningrad, Russia
Kronstadt	Braşov, Romania
Laibach	Ljubljana, Slovenia
Lemberg	Lviv, Ukraine
Liegnitz	Legnica, Poland
Lovrana (*Italian*)	Lovran, Croatia
Maggiore (mountain range; Italian)	Učka, Croatia
Meran	Merano, Italy (South Tyrol)
Ofen	Buda, Hungary (western bank of Budapest)
Plattensee	Lake Balaton, Hungary
Pola	Pula, Croatia
Pragerhof	Pragersko, Slovenia
Preßburg (also 'Pressburg')	Bratislava, Slovakia
Raab	Győr, Hungary
Quarnero (gulf; *Italian*)	Gulf of Kvarner, Croatia
Ruttka	Vrútky, Slovakia
Swinemünde	Świnoujście, Poland
Siebenbürgen	Transylvania, Romania
Sillein	Žilina, Slovakia
Steinbrück	Zidani Most, Slovenia
Volosca (*Italian*)	Volosko, Croatia
Waitzen	Vác, Hungary
Zenta	Senta, Serbia

FORTHCOMING TITLES

Jantar is an independent publisher based in London that has been praised widely for its choice of texts, artwork, editorial rigour and use of very rare and sometimes unique fonts in all its books. Jantar's guiding principle is to select, publish and make accessible previously inaccessible works of Central European Literary Fiction through translations into English... texts 'trapped in amber'.

Since its foundation in 2011, Jantar's list consisted, mostly, of works of Literary Fiction. In 2023, we begin to broaden our mission to include works of Science Fiction from Central Europe, a region rich in authors and stories in this genre.

Being Jantar, we begin our new SF list with the first recognised works in the genre written in Czech and Slovak. *Newton's Brain* by Jakub Arbes and published in a new translation by David Short, was first published in 1877, 18 years before *The Time Machine* by H.G. Wells. It first appeared in English translation in 1892. Arbes was much admired by Emile Zola.

Our second SF title was written in an uncodified version of 'Old Slovak' and published in 1856. *The Science of the Stars* by Gustav Reuss is arguably the first title to feature a balloon travelling to the moon. It is certainly the first to appear in any version of the Slovak language.

Later in 2024, we launch the much-anticipated new translation of *The Grandmother* by Božena Němcová. Together with Erben's *Kytice* (Jantar 2014) and Mácha's *May* (Jantar 2025), *The Grandmother* is one of the three founding works of modern Czech Literature. This new and complete translation will show, for the first time to English-language readers, the subversive, feminist, anti-theological and anti-Habsburg elements in this classic text. It will be published in a regular prose version and another illustrated by Míla Fürstová.

These titles and all our other titles can be purchased
postage-free world-wide from our website:
www.JantarPublishing.com

Barcode is one of many collections of short stories published by Jantar in English. In 2022, we published **Dead** and **Mothers and Truckers** by Balla and Ivana Dobrakovová respectively. Another, very popular, collection of short stories was published in 2018 called **And My Head Exploded**. Featuring 10 shorts stories, the book features the work and authors from the Bohemian fin-de-siècle era never previously translated into English.

In 2017, we published **Fox Season** by Agnieszka Dale, a collection of dazzling stories set in a London bracing itself for Brexit. It is now making its first appearance on university literature courses. The stories were described by Zoë Apostolides in the Financial Times as 'fascinating and refreshingly honest stares at life in a foreign place, whatever that definition might be.'

City of Torment by Daniela Hodrová, published in 2021 attracted very positive reviews in *The Los Angeles Review of Books*, *The Irish Times* and *New European Review*. The book begins, 'Alice Davidovič would have never thought the window of her childhood room hung so low above the Olšany cemetery that a body could travel the distance in less than two seconds.'

Birds of Verhovina by Ádám Bodor features a cast of weirdos and miscreants left to make their own way in the Carpathian Mountains. It was described by Diánna Vonnák in *The Times Literary Supplement* as 'one of those places you might visit but might never leave; it is reality on its way to becoming allegory.'

Carbide by Andriy Lyubka was published at the end of 2020 when we all thought the worst that could happen was to be locked-down by a global pandemic. Set in what now appears the very quaint Ukraine prior to its attempted evisceration by Russia, Lyubka describes another Carpathian periphery world populated by criminals, corrupt local officials and a delusional history teacher. Carbide was described by Kate Tsurkan in *The Los Angeles Review of Books* as 'a fast-paced tragicomedy which establishes the young author as Ukraine's modern-day Voltaire.'